LONEWOLF'S WOMAN

"Blade!" she whispered, her hand flying to her throat. "I didn't expect you to be..." Clad only in her thin white nightgown, she shivered and crossed her arms over her breasts. "Can't y-you sleep either?"

His sultry gaze moved over Elise from throat to toes. A bead of sweat formed on his neck and rolled downward. Emboldened by the darkness, Elise followed the droplet's odyssey with her fingertip. Trailing a hand down his chest to his low-riding waistband, she hooked her fingers there and tugged hard.

With a deep, fevered moan, he wrapped his arms around her and pulled her against him until she could feel the hammering of his heart. His mouth fastened on hers...

LONEWOLF'S WOMAN

DEBORAH CAMP

AVON BOOKS ◆ NEW YORK

AVON BOOKS
A division of
The Hearst Corporation
1350 Avenue of the Americas
New York, New York 10019

Copyright © 1995 by Deborah E. Camp
Published by arrangement with the author
Library of Congress Catalog Card Number: 94-96274
ISBN: 0-380-77757-6

First Avon Books Printing: March 1995

AVON TRADEMARK REG. U.S. PAT. OFF. AND IN OTHER COUNTRIES, MARCA REGISTRADA, HECHO EN U.S.A.

Printed in the U.S.A.

RA   10   9   8   7   6   5   4   3   2   1

In loving memory of James Conrad Camp,
a green-eyed, stubborn Irishman,
who was cherished by his family.

I miss you, Daddy.

I was living peaceably and satisfied when people began to speak bad of me.

—GERONIMO

We are peaceful; we are not aggressive. In this lies our strength.

—INDIAN ELDER

Chapter 1

JULIA LINCOLN LONEWOLF
SCHOOLMISTRESS
WIFE OF BLADE LONEWOLF
SHE LOVED CHILDREN
1851–1887

Blade Lonewolf stared at the inscription on the slab of granite set beneath a pin oak tree. A new, white picket fence surrounded the grave site. He looked across the land to the log-hewn house he had shared with Julia. Since his wife's death, he'd found no comfort there and had constructed a skin lodge next to it where he spent his nights. Someday he would have to deal with cleaning out that house and getting rid of all the little things that made him think of his life with Julia, but not now. Not today.

Moving away from the burial site, he went to the water trough where the mules had drunk their fill and methodically hitched them to the wagon. As he checked the harnesses, he caught sight of his reflection in the murky water. A savage looked back at him.

He stared at his image in amazement, noting the

fierce light in his eyes and the stern set of his mouth and jaw.

Straightening from his watery inspection, he ran a hand down his sweat-stained leather shirt. He couldn't go into town looking like a wild Indian. He'd send the townsfolk running for cover like scared chickens!

Grabbing his black braid of hair in one hand and his hunting knife in the other, he started sawing. He grimaced at the tug on his scalp, but continued the task until he'd shorn off his Indian braid. He scoffed at his efforts. Why, he could no more become a city gentleman than he could soar with the eagles!

Whiskers darkened the lower half of his face, a curse from his white forebears, and he used the knife to scrape them off, nicking his skin once or twice before he was done. He dabbed at the blood with his handkerchief and washed thoroughly with soap and cold water, eyeing the log cabin as an animal might eye a cage. Squaring his shoulders, he headed for it with all the enthusiasm of a pig to slaughter.

Entering the dark house, he strode to the bedroom to change his clothes. He focused only on the task, careful not to look at the room, the furniture; trying not to smell the mint and clove that Julia had sprinkled around the room. Underneath those pleasant scents he could smell death. Julia had died in that bed, ending a time in his life that had not lived up to his expectations.

A sense of failure lay heavy in his heart as he traded his leather pants and shirt for black trousers and the dark blue shirt Julia had made for him to wear when he went to her church. When he emerged from the house, he saw he had a visitor.

The short, wiry woman rubbed her eyes vigorously, as if not believing what stood before her.

"Hail to you, Apache," Airy Peppers said, swinging a leg over her little brown donkey and dropping to the ground. She wore a calico blouse and a split skirt, the hem of which brushed the tops of her dirt-caked boots. Her merry blue eyes widened and she tipped back her sunbonnet to openly appraise him. "You ain't half bad to look at with your face shaved and washed. Hey, I ain't seen them clothes in a long spell."

"I don't want to scare her off once she sees me," Blade explained. "Thought I ought to look as civilized as possible."

Airy propped her hands on her bony hips. "Civilized, huh? You could dress a tiger in a suit, but he could still take a bite of you." She laughed. "You smile when you meet her, and you'll win her over. Just like you won over Julia Lincoln."

"Is that what won her over?" He scratched at his freshly shaved chin. "I've been wondering."

"That, and that purty face of your'n." She displayed a toothy grin. " 'Course, it helps that you're built like a lumberjack."

He ran a hand down his face to hide his grin, then waved a hand at her, dismissing her lofty praise. Airy gripped his sleeve.

"You sure you want to do this? You don't have to go through with it if you don't want to. That little gal will find another home somewhere if you decide she ain't right for you."

"I promised Julia."

"But Julia ain't here no more, Blade. You've been living in that tepee, doing what you want when you want, keeping your own company. You sure you won't mind someone here underfoot? It ain't like having a new pup, you know."

"I know." He glanced at the sky. "It's getting late. I've got to go." He strode purposefully toward the wagon with Airy right beside him. "It will be good to have company again. It's been too quiet around here lately. Besides, I made a promise to Julia, and I mean to keep it."

"You ain't thought this through. I was talking to Cousin Dixie yesterday, and she said you told her you ain't set foot in that house since Julia died. That true?"

"You saw me come out of it just now, didn't you?"

"Hey, Apache, you expect that little gal to live in that tepee lodge with you?"

"She will sleep in the house."

"And you? Where you going to sleep?"

"I have to go now." Vexed by her questions, he climbed into the wagon and guided the mules toward town. "Don't worry, nosy woman. I'll make a home for her just like I did for Julia." He clucked the mules into a fast walk, escaping Airy's worried frown but not his own nagging doubts.

If only Julia had lived . . . if only he could have made her happy . . . if only they could have made children together . . . then he wouldn't be riding into town to claim a stranger as his own.

She noticed him right off.

He was hard to miss, being so tall and imposing and standing apart from the others on the platform. His ebony hair, blunt-cut as if by a knife, lay against his shirt collar, and his civilized clothes did little to temper his Indian features. An Indian! She'd never actually seen one in person!

Everything about him was large and imposing—his hands, his shoulders, his very presence. He held his hat in his hands, restlessly walking his fingers around the brim, as he scanned the area with dark, probing eyes. He had heavy brows and his skin was faintly lined by long hours in the sun. He put his hat back on, rocking it into a comfortable position, then propped his hands on his lean hips. People near him moved away, giving him plenty of room.

The shrill train whistle sent a jolt through her, and Elise St. John tore her attention from the savage beauty of his face to examine the other people milling around the train station. She wondered which ones would shape her future. Above their heads, a sign swung from rusty chains: CROSSROADS, MISSOURI.

How fitting, Elise thought, for she and her siblings were at a crossroads. This was their new home, a home far different from the one they'd known in Baltimore, Maryland. She gathered in a deep breath and smelled no hint of the sea, only horseflesh and manure.

Crossroads seemed to be stuck in the mid-1800s instead of keeping pace in 1888. No streetlights or streetcars or street vendors. Even the fashions were dated. She spied no bows or skirt draperies, no vibrant colors, no rich fabrics. Even the ladies' hats were tragically plain.

Elise touched her own burgundy-and-black velvet creation, feeling out of place in this collection of drab sunbonnets and straw hats. Her fingertips brushed against the lacy bodice of her garnet dress as she examined the simple shirtwaists worn by the other women. For the first time since she'd sold her fancier gowns to pay for her train ticket, she was glad. Obviously, she'd need no finery here.

The gowns were gone, but she still had memories of the elaborate balls and soirees attended by Baltimore's most dashing bachelors. Last season she'd received no less than a dozen marriage proposals—all of which had been retracted after her parents' death and the dissolution of her ties with the wealthy Wellby family.

Elise fought off the self-pity that threatened to overtake her. Let them wallow in their fortune, she thought, referring to her mother's side of the family. All their wealth would bring her grandparents no happiness in this life or in the one after.

Two cars down, the escorts from the Children's Rescue Society stepped off the train, both looking officious as they faced the anxious onlookers. Elise moved instinctively into the shadows. She'd been told not to follow her brother and sister to their new homes, and she was afraid the escorts would make trouble for her should she be found out. Keeping a low profile, she'd remained in the regular passenger cars, away from the ones used by the orphans.

"I am Mr. Charles from the Children's Rescue Society," the little, bespeckled man announced in a high-pitched voice. He pulled at his stringy mustache and cleared his throat. "Those who are here for children, please come forward and have your paperwork ready to present. Parents only! The rest of you stand back."

Mr. Charles weighed no more than one hundred pounds, but his bossy, squinty-eyed manner caused the townspeople to hurry to obey. Six people shuffled forward, while the others retreated.

It had been the same at every stop, Elise observed. One by one, the orphans had been given away like parcels instead of people. The whole process sickened her, and she wished she could magically whisk her sister and brother back to their home by the shore.

Elise noticed a clutch of women whispering behind their hands and studying the Indian surreptitiously. She glanced at him again, intrigued by his city shirt and trousers, in contrast to his teak-colored skin, jutting cheekbones and deeply set eyes. He looked at the train cars with an edgy alertness, as if he were ready to spring into action. What was he doing here? Who or what was he meeting on this train? He wasn't going to rob it, was he?

Fear stabbed her, then eased up when she noticed that he carried no weapon. So what business did he have here?

With a grand flourish, Mrs. Gadstone unfolded the paper from which she would read off numbers to match children with the adults holding the corresponding numerals.

Elise's heart constricted painfully when her brother, Adam, hopped down the train steps, then turned to lift their younger sister, Penny, from the car to the platform.

They're so young, so innocent! Elise thought, chewing on her lower lip to keep from crying out to them. How could her grandparents stand by and allow this to happen to their own flesh and blood!

Her thirteen-year-old brother tried to look brave, but Elise noticed the tight set of his mouth and knew he was on the verge of tears. His dark red hair, so like her own, shone in the sunlight. Freckles generously dusted his nose and cheeks. He was of average height for his age, but thin. He'd lost weight since their parents had died and the joy had been snuffed out of their lives.

Eight-year-old Penny's hair was fire-engine red and she bore the same crop of freckles. Her curly hair had been gathered into a topknot and tied with a blue ribbon that matched her gingham dress. She essayed a gap-toothed grin when she spied Elise and waved a dimpled hand.

Suddenly one of the other orphans—a boy of ten or eleven—bolted from the boxcar and dashed through the crowd amid squeals and shouts. Elise snapped her attention back to Adam, saw the flash of rebellion in his eyes and shook her head firmly. *Don't even think about it,* she thought as she mouthed, "No," to him and shook her head again. He wouldn't get far and would only make a bad impression on the people who were here to adopt him. Penny pointed a finger and tugged on Adam's sleeve.

"Look, Adam! A weel Injun!"

The lone Indian had snagged the maverick boy by the shirt collar. The lad squirmed, trying his best to break away, but the Indian held him fast. He lifted one large brown hand and with infinite tenderness stroked the boy's blond hair. The boy looked up into the bronze-colored face and, instead of squealing in terror, stopped struggling altogether as fascination overcame his panic.

Elise heard snatches of conversations around her, the words underlined with excitement and censure.

"Lonewolf . . . Oh, my word, that's Lonewolf . . . I heard he'd gone back to the reservation . . . What's he doing here? . . . Wild as a March hare, I hear."

"I say there!" Mr. Charles raised a warning finger at the Indian. Elise noticed that the finger trembled and that Mr. Charles's voice had climbed to a near shriek. "Unhand that child!"

Lonewolf. Elise turned the name over in her mind, finding it odd yet fittingly romantic. She supposed she should be scared, but he appeared to be civilized. She certainly hoped so! A man of his brute strength could do some damage among the timid, colorless people of Crossroads, Missouri!

Elise gleaned curiosity and fascination in the faces around her, but not fear. He certainly had stirred up some interest. She smiled, watching as he straightened the orphan's clothing and patted his shoulder reassuringly.

He captured one of the boy's hands and led him toward Mr. Charles. For all his size, his movements were fluid and lanky. He moved like an animal, at home in his body and confident of his place in the world. He walked slowly so that the lad could keep up with him. Handing the boy over to Mrs. Gadstone, Lonewolf afforded the youngster a quick, warm smile that was genuinely returned.

"Freddie, get back on the train," Mr. Charles said, giving the boy a push. "You get off at Joplin . . . and not before!"

Freddie dashed into the boxcar again, to the nervous laughter and whispers of the other orphans. Elise saw something akin to compassion flicker in Lonewolf's eyes as he stared at the train. She looked, too, and her throat clogged with pity at the sight of small faces pressed against the train windows.

She turned back around and her heart skipped a beat when she found that Lonewolf was looking at her. His dark-eyed gaze wandered over her stylish clothes, her plucky hat. One brow lifted as his eyes moved up to find hers. Elise felt as if her breath had deserted her. When he finally redirected his attention to the children lined up behind Mr. Charles, Elise gathered in a gulp of air. What had he been thinking while looking at her? she wondered. She was no stranger to masculine attention, but she couldn't read the messages in Lonewolf's eyes.

"Number twenty-seven!" Mrs. Gadstone called out, waving a yellow strip of paper. "Who has number twenty-seven?"

Elise slammed her eyes shut as her heart seemed to turn to stone in her chest. Number twenty-seven ... oh, how could she stand this ... how was she expected to bear it? When she opened her eyes, tears blurred her vision.

"Here, right here!" An older gentleman came forward, buggy whip in hand. A slender young woman trailed him.

Mr. Charles checked the number on the paper the man presented, then nodded. "Very good, sir. Let's see now ... which is it?"

"Adam," Mrs. Gadstone said, and Elise whispered the name with her. The Society escort snagged Adam by the forearm and hauled him forward. "He's number twenty-seven. See?" She indicated the number pinned to the back of Adam's white shirt.

Elise's chest tightened and her heart almost stopped beating. She forced herself to smile when she caught Adam's eye, and blew him a kiss. Then the older man clamped a hand on Adam's shoulder, staking his claim. It took everything in Elise not to snatch her brother away and run—but to where? Even Baltimore was no longer home to them.

"Come along, boy," the man said in a boisterous

voice. He was dressed in a black suit and wore a string tie. His snowy white hair lay in waves on his head and curled under at his shoulders. In contrast, his brows and mustache were as black as coal. He turned Adam around and around for a quick inspection, then grunted his approval. "Looks like I got the pick of the litter, doesn't it, Harriet?"

The dour-faced young woman hardly acknowledged Adam. "He looks fit."

Elise pressed her lips together to keep from sobbing aloud. She'd prayed that Adam's new parents would extend loving arms and warm kisses. This old man acted as if he'd bought himself a mule! Maybe he'd just come to fetch Adam and there was a loving family waiting back at the homestead. This might be his new grandfather, and the woman called Harriet might be his new older sister. She prayed for this scenario.

"Don't forget to sign the adoption papers and leave a set for us. Just hand them to me or Mrs. Gadstone," Mr. Charles instructed.

"That's all there is to it?" the man asked, taking Adam by the arm.

"Yes, sir. Congratulations." Mr. Charles patted Adam on the back. "You be a good boy. You're lucky to have a new home. Remember that."

Elise edged around a post to watch the man and woman lead her brother away. Adam glanced back several times, each longing look tearing chunks out of Elise's heart.

"Where's he going?" Penny asked, her voice rising with anxiety. "Adam! Adam! Take me, too!"

Mrs. Gadstone tried to quiet Penny by offering her a sucker, but Penny continued to whimper and cry out for her brother, her high-pitched voice sending shudders of agony through Elise. Unable to stop herself, Elise reached out a hand to Adam, her fingers trembling, tears spilling onto her cheeks. But she stood rooted to the spot when another number rang out.

"Twenty-eight," Mrs. Gadstone announced.

Penny! Oh, sweet Jesus! Not little Penny! Elise covered her mouth with her fingers, trapping a sob that quivered in her throat. Oh, the pain! She'd never known such agony, not since that terrible day when Papa and Mama had died. This was worse, though. This was the last of her family, and they were being parceled off like rations. She must stop them! If she had to kidnap her own kin, then so be it!

But the brave plan crumbled. She had no way to feed her brother and sister, no roof to spread over their heads, no money to buy clothes for them. She'd be lucky to make her own way without having to resort to selling herself in an upstairs room of some liquor palace.

"Number twenty-eight! I believe . . . yes, it's this little girl here."

Penny sniffed, wiped her eyes and stuck the sucker in her mouth, oblivious of what awful fate might lie ahead of her. Her innocence wrenched at Elise's heart and brought a new wash of tears to her eyes.

"Who has number twenty-eight?" Mr. Charles asked. "Speak up, please!"

Yes, yes, speak up! Elise thought. Get this over with. Don't prolong this torture. Her fingers and toes grew cold and she wondered if she might be slowly dying.

As if in a dream, Elise watched the tall Indian called Lonewolf stride forward, a sheet of parchment clutched in his hand. No, it couldn't be! Not him! She cringed, thinking of her little sister being raised by a savage. He must have been sent by someone . . . maybe he was a manservant to a rich farm family!

Mr. Charles glanced disdainfully at him. Elise clutched at the garnet material covering her heart even as the Indian parted his lips to speak.

Dear God, not him!

His voice emerged deep and booming, like thunder on the plains. "She belongs to me."

For an instant, blackness swam before Elise's eyes. Only her stubborn will kept her upright, although the train platform seemed to rock beneath her feet.

"You?" Mr. Charles aimed the tip of his sharp nose at the Indian. "Who sent you here?"

"No one sent me. This child is mine."

Elise stumbled forward to grasp a support post. She held onto it, her fingernails digging into the wood. Suddenly she wished that she and her siblings had died right along with their mother and father. Death would be better than this living hell. Being separated, sent to the ends of the earth, raised by cold old men and red-skinned savages— it was barbaric!

Lonewolf extended the paper he held. "It says so here. I am to have number twenty-eight. A girl child of eight years."

Elise could see the fancy crest of the Society at the top of the parchment as Mr. Charles snatched it from Lonewolf to study it for himself before giving it back. Meanwhile, Penny inched closer to the Indian and slipped two fingers across one of his wide palms. Elise gritted her teeth and edged forward. She'd grab Penny and run, she thought.

Maybe they'd stop her; maybe she'd get away. She had to try . . .

The Indian looked at Penny and tender emotion warmed his brown eyes. Elise paused, her fear eased by the big man's gentleness.

"Are you a weel Injun?" Penny asked.

"Yes." Lonewolf's smile was wide and heart-winning. "I'm part Apache."

Apache! Elise edged closer, determined to make a grab for Penny. She couldn't leave her poor, innocent sister in the hands of an Apache warrior! She'd read about them. How could the Society allow this man to take an innocent child?

Mr. Charles craned his neck to look around Lonewolf. "I don't see your wife, sir. Didn't she come along to welcome this little angel into your family?"

"My wife is dead."

No wife. The words swam in Elise's head. Her sweet sister living alone with this Indian! She opened her mouth to protest, but Mr. Charles stole the words from her.

"I'm sorry. You can't have this child." The pinch-faced escort snagged the bow at the waist of Penny's dress and pulled her backward and behind him, shielding her from Lonewolf.

"But I have the papers. I paid the money." Lonewolf waved the parchment in Mr. Charles's face. "She's mine."

"No, sir. These children are to go to husbands and wives, not to bachelors and old maids. The contract you signed states this in no uncertain terms." Mr. Charles peered at him through his thick glasses. "You can read, can't you? English, that is."

Lonewolf's withering scowl stifled some of Mr.

Charles's testiness, but the escort kept Penny anchored behind him.

"Shall I place her back on the train, Mr. Charles?" Mrs. Gadstone asked.

"Yes, unless . . ." Mr. Charles glanced around at the dozen or so people still milling around. "Anyone want to take this child? You can pay the money today and I'll draw up the correct papers. Anyone? She's a pretty thing."

Elise held her breath, her gaze flitting from one bland face to the next. No one came forward. No one cared about a little girl from Baltimore. But if no one adopted Penny in Crossroads, then where would she be taken to? Maybe to the next whistle-stop. That wouldn't be so bad. Elise could still visit Penny and Adam, as long as the distance wasn't too great.

"Very well, back on the train she goes." Mr. Charles flinched from the anger radiating from the Apache half-breed. "I'm sorry for your loss . . ."

Lonewolf glared at the small man. It was obvious he was barely holding himself in check. "I *will* take the child. I promised my wife I'd give her a good home."

"Yes, yes, but that's quite impossible now, isn't it?" Mr. Charles glanced behind him at Penny, who had begun to struggle and weep.

Elise placed a finger to her lips, motioning for Penny to calm down. The redheaded child sniffed pitifully, but stopped slapping at Mrs. Gadstone's hands.

Poor angel doesn't understand that this is a blessing, Elise thought, relieved that her sister wouldn't be placed in the care of the imposing Indian. There was still hope for Penny to have a solid, loving home where Elise could visit her and keep the family ties strong. She'd be near Adam, too. They'd all be together as much as possible.

"You must understand, sir, that your wife was the only reason we allowed this adoption to go through. She was white, yes? Well, there you have it." Mr. Charles spread his hands in an appeal. "You wouldn't have been allowed to adopt if it hadn't been for your white wife. We don't allow breeds to have the children. Now that your wife is gone, the contract is void."

"But I have paid," Lonewolf insisted.

"The contract states that the money will not be returned if the contract is breached. *You've* breached it, don't you see? You have no white wife. Your money is forfeited."

Penny wailed when Mrs. Gadstone tried to force her back to the train again. Her tear-stained eyes sought Elise, and Elise made calming motions. If only she could get her little sister to understand that everything was fine . . .

"Don't fret, child," Mr. Charles said, smoothing Penny's coppery hair. "You'll be placed on the train and we'll take you back to New York, where arrangements will be made for an adoption elsewhere."

Elsewhere? Elise turned stone cold as the import of what the escort had said dawned on her. Penny would be adopted by someone living God only knew where. Not near the next whistle-stop, probably not even in Missouri! How could she keep the family together that way? Panic bounced through her head, scattering her logic, separating her common sense from her wildest impulses.

Penny's eyes swam with tears and her trembling sob slashed at Elise as if with the bite of a whip. Through the pain and panic, an idea bloomed; an idea so preposterous, Elise knew she must act on it without further contemplation or she'd lose her nerve altogether.

Feeling as if she were living a nightmare, she moved forward, her body numb, her mind whirling like a windmill in a hurricane. She sensed Mr. Charles's regard as she stopped beside the Indian. Slipping a hand into the crook of his arm, she looked up at Lonewolf's brooding features and actually managed a smile.

"What's the problem, darling?" she asked in a voice that gave not one hint of the turmoil inside her. "Didn't you tell this man that you have a new wife? Didn't you tell him about me?"

Chapter 2

S he didn't look like a whore to him, so he figured the woman had lost her mind.

Gussied up in a fancy town dress of dark blood
red and wearing a hat right out of a mail-order
catalog, she bore the mark of the upper crust. Laying a hand over hers, he tried to disengage himself
from her grasp, but her fingers tightened on his
arm and went digging for bone. For a little thing,
she had one hell of a grip.

"What's this? Who are you?" Mr. Charles asked,
echoing the questions spinning in Blade's head.

"Why, I'm Mrs. Lonewolf," the lady in red said
with such certainty that she almost convinced
Blade of it. "And I'm going to be this little girl's
mother." With that, she scooped up the orphan and
bussed her freckled cheek. "Penny, isn't it? I'm
Elise St.—Lonewolf." She beamed at Blade, then
back at Mr. Charles. "We're newlyweds."

"Newlyweds?" Mr. Charles repeated, his tone
dripping with doubt. "Why didn't you tell me
about this new wife of yours, sir?"

Blade had never seen a face so perfect. She was
so pretty, he blinked, not believing his own eyes.
He shook his head, snapping out of the spell the

auburn-haired witch had cast over him. "She's not my—"

"No, she's not yet," the woman interrupted, "but she will be ours soon." She hugged the child, and the youngster responded happily by dropping her sticky, half-eaten sucker and wrapping her dimpled arms around the woman's neck. "You have a white wife—me—so the adoption can go through without a hitch. Isn't that wonderful?" She narrowed her eyes, urgency shining in them. Blade knew she was trying to tell him to go along with her crazy talk, but he had no intention of falling in with her. He had enough troubles.

He cleared his throat and started to turn away from the woman, but she edged closer to his side. "Mr. Charles, this orphan is promised to me, but I don't know what this lady—"

"Why, if it isn't Mr. and Mrs. Blade Lonewolf!"

The warm, incongruous greeting cut through Blade's explanation and he found himself staring, slack-jawed, at Dixie Shoemaker. The plump matron, who ran Crossroads's boardinghouse and claimed Airy Peppers as her first cousin, placed herself between Blade and the lady lunatic. Blade resisted the urge to strangle her.

"What are y'all doing in town?" she asked Blade, then gasped with delight. "Oh, is this the orphan you and your new missus are adopting? She's precious! Why, she sort of looks like you, Mrs. Lonewolf. Don't you see a slight resemblance, Blade?" Dixie turned her round face toward him and pummeled him with her flinty-eyed glare. "Take a good, hard look. *Now.*"

Feeling like a mule that had been clubbed to get its attention, Blade swung around to the young woman in red again. Yes, there was some resemblance between her and the child she held so possessively . . . so what? The girl kissed the woman's cheek and sniffed loudly, her tears drying, her sobs diminished. She seemed at peace in the woman's arms. An idea fell into his mind like a stone into a lake, sending out ripples of apprehension. Was this child *hers?* His heart melted a little toward her.

"Is this your wife or not?" Mr. Charles demanded.

"Why, of course she's his wife," Dixie answered with a short laugh. "Tell him, Blade, so you can adopt this little girl and take her home."

Dixie's stern tone wasn't lost on him, and the solution the other woman offered was tempting. He looked at Penny. He'd promised to make a home for the orphan he and Julia had paid for before Julia had taken fatally ill. The stranger raised her brows, giving him an arched look. She sure had grit, he thought, and if the child was hers, he wouldn't be the one to separate them.

"She's my wife," he heard himself say while a voice deep inside his head called him a softhearted jackass.

"Not so fast," Mr. Charles said, removing his eyeglasses and polishing the lenses on his lapels. "I must see some proof."

"Proof? What proof?" both women chorused.

"A marriage license," Mr. Charles said, smiling slyly. "Show me a marriage license and I'll let you take the girl. Otherwise . . ." He shrugged and replaced his eyeglasses slowly.

"A license . . ." The lady in red shared a forlorn frown with the child.

Foolhardiness nudged Blade and loosened his tongue. He spoke even before he was aware of his actions. "We will fetch the license."

"You will?" Mr. Charles asked.

"We will?" his fake wife asked.

"Oh, dear me," Dixie murmured, her lips twisting with worry.

"Yes," Blade answered firmly. "We didn't bring it. It's back at home, but I'll have it here before the train leaves."

"We're leaving in an hour," Mr. Charles said with a sniff of displeasure.

"Why do we have to prove anything to you?" the woman demanded of Mr. Charles as she continued to hold the orphan girl tightly and stroke her hair. "You didn't question anyone else. You just handed over the children as if they were feed sacks!"

"Something isn't right here." Mr. Charles laid a finger against his long, thin nose. "I smell something rotten."

The young woman tipped up her chin in a saucy gesture that made Blade want to grin. "It's probably your breath. I smell it, too."

Sassy little fox! Blade regarded her with a hefty measure of respect, while Mr. Charles sputtered in speechless affront. Plucking the child from the woman's arms, Blade handed her over to Dixie Shoemaker.

"You watch over her until we return," he ordered, then captured one of the younger woman's hands. "Come on. We have no time to spare." He speared Mr. Charles with a glare. "We will be back with the license."

Mr. Charles, his face still red from the woman's insult, pulled his timepiece from his vest pocket and examined it. "Be forewarned: I won't wait a moment longer than I have to. We'll be leaving at eleven sharp."

Blade leveled a forefinger at the small man and lowered his voice to a near growl. "You wait." Then he strode toward the heart of town, tugging the woman in his wake.

As they turned a corner, she stumbled and gave a yank on his hand.

"Hey, hey, Daddy Longlegs, hold up! I can't run a race in these skirts and petticoats!" She clamped her free hand around his wrist and dug in her heels to retard his progress.

He stopped in front of the bank to allow her to catch her breath and give him a moment to figure out if she was crazy, desperate or a little of both.

"Where are we going anyway? You live nearby?" She backhanded a stray lock of her auburn hair. "If you're thinking of fetching your old marriage license, you can forget it. Mr. Charles will notice right off that the date is wrong. We told him we are newlyweds, and unless you and your wife married a few months ago, then we're—"

"Why did you talk such foolishness to him?" Blade cut in, resting his hands on his hips and glaring down at her. She was a good foot shorter than he was, but she held herself erect and proud, getting the most out of each comely inch. "Why did you tell him you were my wife?"

"Because . . . well, because." She pressed her lips together in a stubborn line of refusal.

"Why?" he demanded, bending at the waist until they were eye to eye. He figured the child was the woman's illegitimate daughter, taken from her as payment for the sins of a fallen woman. The ordeal had left her touched in the head. When she didn't answer him immediately, he wrapped his long fingers around one of her small wrists and shook her.

"Ouch! Okay, okay! You don't have to break my

bones! I'll tell you the truth." She studied the toes of her high-button shoes for a few moments. "Penny's my sister," she said, barely above a whisper.

"Your sister." Her answer stunned him. He ran his gaze over the sheen of her hair, which was the color of polished cherry wood, and the faint dusting of freckles across her nose. Dimples poked at her cheeks, and her face was a perfect oval. His gaze continued its path down her creamy throat to the gentle swell of her breasts and hips. A beauty. He would have liked nothing better than to trace the shape of her body with his hands.

"That's right," she said, breaking into his lascivious thoughts. "What's more, my brother was also on that train. He was adopted by an older gentleman with white hair and a black mustache. A grandfatherly type. A younger woman was with him, probably his daughter, and—"

"Judge Mott," Blade supplied, his tongue feeling heavy in his mouth as his senses continued to riot.

"Is that his name?" She blinked her large blue eyes at him. "He's a judge, is he?"

"He's supposed to be. Retired." He wrenched his attention away from the flutter of a pulse beating in her throat. "Why are you sneaking around?"

"I'm not supposed to follow them. The Society warned me not to, but I couldn't let my brother and sister go without me! They are all I have left." She clutched at his forearm as she leaned close to him, her body pressing into his. "Please, listen to me. If we can convince Mr. Charles that we're married, then he'll let you have Penny. Otherwise, they'll send her somewhere else . . . far away from Adam and me. I want us to stay close. Can you understand, Mr. Lonewolf?"

He was agonizingly aware of her breast flattened

against his upper arm. Grappling for his self-control, he forced his thoughts away from her body's fit against his, only to admire the pouting set of her mouth. His loins burned.

"You might have started something you'll wish you didn't have to finish," he told her, his voice deeper, his words coming slow off his tongue.

A tide of pink rolled across her cheeks and she retreated a step. "I have no choice. Do you think we can fool Mr. Charles? Do you know of someone who can give us a marriage license?"

"Yes, I know of someone." Cupping one of her elbows in his hand, he goaded her into a brisk walk. "A preacher right here at the Rugged Cross Church."

"Ch-church?" Her voice broke. "You mean... you mean, a *real* church and a *real* preacher?"

He stopped at the steps leading up to the church's double doors and captured her wrists to keep her from bolting. "A real church, a real preacher and a real marriage. I made a promise to my wife to make a home for that child, and I mean to keep it, even if it means marrying a stranger."

Pulling herself up, she managed to look dignified and in complete control. "I, too, made a promise. I promised my brother and sister that we would remain close. Does this Judge Mott live near here?"

"He's my closest neighbor."

Her smile started in her eyes with pinpoints of light, then burst brilliantly upon her lips. "Splendid! This is turning out better than I'd dreamed." Looking at the doors and the cross etched on them, she gathered in a breath and squared her narrow shoulders. "Shall we hasten to marry, Mr. Lonewolf? We don't want that train to leave with Penny on it, do we?"

"No. Call me Blade."

She bestowed a brief smile on him. "And I am Elise. Elise St. John." With some hesitation, she extended her gloved hand. "A pleasure to meet you . . . Blade."

He shook her hand, feeling the smallness of it and how his swallowed hers. Her gloves were black and of fine kid leather. Store-bought. Instead of letting go, he guided her hand to the crook of his arm and escorted her inside the silent church. Nothing stirred, so Blade cleared his throat noisily.

"Who's that?" someone asked from the front of the chapel. Shadows shifted and a bald head shone briefly before Blade could make out the figure of the darkly clothed pastor, the very same pastor who had officiated the ceremony between him and Julia.

"It's Blade Lonewolf, Reverend Casper. I'm wondering if you have a minute. I need to get married."

The pastor chuckled as he came forward into a spear of multicolored sunlight that streamed through a stained-glass window. "Is that so? Married, eh? It's April, but you're too late for an April Fool's joke." The bald-headed man's steps faltered as he spied the woman standing at Blade's side. "Oh, and who is . . ." His jaw went slack. "You're not fooling me, Blade Lonewolf?"

"No, sir, I'm not. Me and this young lady would like to be wed. Now. Please."

"Why, I don't . . . where did you . . . how long . . ." The pastor looked from Blade to Elise and back again.

"Good morning, Reverend Casper," Elise said in a voice as cool and refreshing as a mountain stream. She offered her hand. "I'm Elise St. John, and I wish to marry this man. We'd be so pleased if you would do the honors for us."

"I . . . well . . . yes. Hello." Reverend Casper shook hands, but his smile was nothing more than a nervous twitch. "This is so unexpected. When did you meet this young lady, Blade? I haven't seen much of you since Julia's death, but I've heard you'd been keeping to yourself out there on your place."

Blade nodded. "I'm marrying this woman today and we're adopting the child me and Julia sent for. You remember?"

The pastor raised a finger. "Ah, yes! The orphan train rolled into town this morning, didn't it?" He pinched the bridge of his nose between his thumb and forefinger. "And you two are getting married. Just like that? Marriage is a holy bond. Nothing to be taken lightly or decided on the spur of the moment."

"We're quite sure we're meant to be together," Elise said, edging closer to Blade. "Please, won't you marry us? We're anxious to begin our lives as husband and wife."

Blade couldn't help staring at her. She was quite the little liar, he thought, amazed at her ability. Of course, she could just as easily turn those lies against him, too. His admiration dwindled, replaced by mistrust. There was nothing worse than a dishonest woman, and it appeared that he was on the verge of marrying one.

"Is this really what you want?" Reverend Casper asked Blade. "You're not looking to fill Julia's apron, are you? One wife can't be replaced like you'd change one plow mule for another."

"It's what I want," Blade assured him. "She's not Julia. I know that." Palming a silver dollar from his pocket, Blade pressed it into the preacher's hand. "I would consider it a great favor if you'd marry us."

The pastor shrugged and demonstrated a neat half turn toward the pulpit. "Very well. Let me get my Bible." He glanced back at them. "Well, come along if you want to be married by me."

Dutifully, Blade walked with Elise toward the pulpit and the huge wooden cross hanging on the wall behind it. Memories of his other marriage surged through his mind. After Julia had died, he had promised himself never to marry again. He wasn't cut out for it. Having a woman companion was fine, but he found nothing holy in matrimony. But here he was, standing beside a stranger who would soon be his wife. His second wife.

Studying her from the corner of his eye, he almost chuckled. Some wedding dress, he thought, viewing the saucy spirit beside him adorned in garnet. He smirked. A scarlet woman. As if reading his thoughts, she ran a hand across her skirt and flashed him an apologetic smile.

"If I'd known what I'd be doing this morning, I wouldn't have selected this dress. I hope you aren't embarrassed."

"Not me," he assured her. "It's *your* wedding gown."

"Yes . . ." She chewed fretfully on her lower lip. "So it is." Heaving a sigh, she shrugged. "Oh, well. It's not what every girl dreams of, but our intentions are noble. Shhh, here comes the pastor!"

"All right now." Reverend Casper sat at a small desk near the entrance to his personal office. "Name of the groom—Blade Lonewolf." Carefully, he wrote the name on the legal document. "Name of the bride—how is that spelled, dear?"

"E-L-I-S-E," she answered. "St. John."

The reverend scratched in her name. "Very well. Date of the marriage." He pinched the bridge of his nose again. "What's the date? April the—"

Blade started to supply the answer—the six-teenth—but Elise beat him to it.

"The twelfth," she announced, then shook her head sternly at Blade when he opened his mouth to correct her.

Again he was stunned by her cunning, quick mind. Always a step ahead of the game, he thought. Always using that pretty head for some-thing more than a hat rack. The twelfth would look better to Mr. Charles. Blade vowed to stay on alert around her, or she'd have him hog-tied and purse-whipped in no time.

"The twelfth," the preacher repeated, writing in the date on the license. "That's that. After the cer-emony, you two can put your marks on this, and it will be done." He came to stand before them and flipped open his Bible. "All right then. Let us begin. We gather here this morning, O Lord, to join this man and woman in holy matrimony . . ."

Elise didn't feel married.

Sitting beside Blade on the padded wagon seat, she shifted Penny to a more comfortable position in her lap and wondered if Blade felt any different. She smiled at the sleeping child; at Penny's slack mouth, long lashes, tumbled hair that curled damply at her temples and forehead.

All for you, Elise thought as a bittersweetness seeped into her. I've married a stranger and I'm headed to a place I've never seen—all for you and Adam.

The man next to her held the reins loosely, letting

the two black mules follow their instincts home. He'd removed his hat and a frisky breeze combed through his thick black hair. He smelled of leather and pine, of wind and wheat, of sunshine and shadow.

After the ceremony, when the preacher had told him to kiss his bride, Blade had removed her gloves and lifted her hands to his lips for a fleeting caress. Elise recalled her flash of disappointment followed by an unexpected thrill when his mouth had warmed the patch of skin on the back of her hand. Had she felt the tip of his tongue, or had it been merely her fanciful imagination?

She hadn't imagined the dark flame in his eyes when he'd looked at her through the canopy of his lowered brows, or how he'd held her gaze as he'd released her hand and straightened to tower over her. In that blazing moment she'd realized that they were truly married, that she had married a half-breed. Oh, her grandparents would certainly take to their beds if word reached them! Or maybe not. Her Wellby kin had turned her and her siblings out and obviously didn't care one jot what happened to them.

And what of this man? Did he care what happened to Penny, or did he care only about a vow he'd made to a dead woman?

"How long ago did you lose your wife?"

"I didn't lose her. She died." His glare was quick, cutting. "Five months ago."

"Oh, that's not very long." Elise ran a hand over Penny's hair. "You're still grieving, I guess." When he made no comment, she chanced a look at him and found him scowling at the backsides of the mules. "You're Apache?"

"Partly. Where are you from?"

"Baltimore, Maryland. Have you heard of it?"

His frown deepened. "Of course. I'm not uneducated. I'm school-learned." He glanced at her again. "Just like you."

"Is that so? How interesting. Were you instructed as a child by missionaries?"

"No, I went to a schoolhouse, same as everyone else."

"You lived as a white, then?"

"Since I was twelve, yes. Before that I lived with my father's people—the Apache. I started to school when my mother and I moved to St. Joseph, Missouri." One corner of his mouth lifted in a smirk. "Have you heard of it?"

She smiled at his gentle barb. "Yes, I have. I, too, am school-learned." The jousting eased the tension from her body and she rolled her shoulders to release more of it. "Is it much farther to your farm?"

"We're on it now."

"We are?" Her interest piqued, she surveyed the flat farmland. In the dim distance she spied a house through a windbreak of willows and birch trees. "Is that your home?"

He nodded. "Don't expect much."

"I'm sure it's quite lovely."

He delivered a chiding glance that made Elise want to make a face at him. She managed to maintain her dignity by ignoring him.

"How did you lose—how did your wife die?"

"Slowly."

Elise puffed out a breath of exasperation. "You know what I mean. What did she die of? An injury? An illness?"

"The doctor couldn't say. Julia was weak and her body was attacked by much sickness. She wasted away."

"How terrible. You had no children?"

"We do now." His gaze drifted to the sleeping child in her lap, and the lines and planes of his face softened. His eyes fairly glowed with tenderness; a sincere smile spread over his lips.

Elise's anxiety lessened. Maybe this man was heaven-sent. He might be brusque and of mixed blood, but he surely had a good heart.

Instinctively, she placed a hand on his forearm. She could feel the heat of his skin through the shirt-sleeve. "I appreciate what you've done. You're a good man."

Uneasiness frosted his eyes and tensed his muscles. He drew away from her, hunching his shoulders. Elise regarded him with a stab of regret. What had she done to make him recoil from her?

"What's wrong, Blade?" she asked. "Is it the marriage? I understand. Really I do." She leaned forward, trying to make him look at her. "I'm nervous, too. I don't know what's expected or . . . well, what I'm saying is that I have no expectations. Let's take it one day at a time—"

"You don't have to stay," he interrupted in that deep, rumbling voice that seemed to emanate from his toes. "I'll take care of Penny. You can leave whenever you want." He gave a quick, slashing shrug. "I don't see any reason to pretend we're something we're not."

"And what are we pretending?" Elise demanded, alarmed by his cool dismissal.

"That we're husband and wife."

"According to the law and in the eyes of God, we *are* married!"

His smile moved from one corner of his wide mouth to the other. "We're married, but we're not husband and wife. You're a bride and I'm a groom, and that's the way we stay until we lie together."

Jerking her face away, she felt her skin burn with embarrassment. The wagon jostled to a stop before a modest log cabin. A conical-shaped skin lodge stood beside it, and Elise wondered if Blade Lonewolf made his bed in there.

"It's better if you move on as soon as you can. You've no business here."

"No!" Draping Penny across her chest and shoulder, Elise eased herself down from the wagon, not waiting for Blade's assistance. "I'm staying," she told him, then pushed past him into the house.

"You can't." He stood on the threshold, filling the doorway, blocking the sunlight. "I don't want a wife."

"Too late." She rallied her courage sufficiently to fashion a fractious smile. "You've got one."

Chapter 3

Elise whirled away from his imposing form and went toward two closed doors. She opened the one on the left first, to spy a iron grillwork bed, neatly spread with a patchwork quilt. Throwing open the door to her right, she examined the narrower bunk beds built against the walls of the smaller room, the thin mattresses covered by off-white muslin sheets. She went inside and deposited Penny on one of the bunks.

"Just what the hell are you doing?" Blade asked from behind her.

"We'll take this room," she announced, unpinning her hat from her upswept hair. "I assume the other one is yours, or do you sleep outside in that tepee?"

"I told you that it would be best if you lived elsewhere. Maybe you can get a job in town." He set their two satchels on the floor, but he stood just outside the door, arms crossed, legs braced apart. Formidable. Stubborn.

Elise arched a brow. Well, she could be stubborn, too. Glancing back at her sister, who still slept, she placed a finger to her lips and tiptoed from the room. Once she had closed the door behind her, she turned to face him again. He hadn't moved, hadn't changed one nuance of his expression.

"What are you afraid of, Blade Lonewolf? Of me?" She spread a hand below her throat. "I won't be making any demands on you. Why, you can go about your business and I'll go about mine. True, I haven't much experience at keeping a home for a family, but I'm bright and I'll learn the necessary skills in no time."

She moved away from him to examine the crude cooking stove and the four shelves above it that held a sparse assortment of canned and bagged goods. She thought longingly of the huge pantry in her family home. There had always been more than enough of everything, and she'd never considered where it all came from and who paid for it. Cook had prepared the food and Justus had helped serve it. That was all she'd known, all she'd cared to know. Life had been simple and . . . well, deceptively safe. She'd been aware of her grandparents' displeasure with her mother's choice of a husband, but she'd had no idea of how deep their bitterness ran. Not until the day after her mother and father had died and her grandparents had refused to allow their son-in-law to be buried next to his wife had Elise seen the first dark glimmer of her grandparents' true nature. Only their daughter would be allowed in the family plots, they'd said. *He* could be buried in a pauper's grave.

"You know anything about cooking?" Blade asked, breaking into her reverie.

Elise shrugged and moved to examine the items on the shelves more closely. Some of them she hadn't heard of—what in heaven's name was Poke?—while others were standard, such as flour and molasses.

"I've watched people cook and clean, and I've often thought that I could fare well if pressed into service. My finishing-school teacher said I was quite artistic. I suppose I inherited that from my father. While he toiled as a . . ." Elise looked around for Blade, but he was gone. She was talking to herself. "Well, I never!"

She walked to the doorway and looked outside in time to see him enter the inky shadows of a hulking barn. What an odd person, she thought. He certainly hadn't been schooled in manners. What was he doing now? Trepidation crept up her spine. Was he saddling a horse for her to ride on into town?

Elise retreated, then shut and barred the door. She wouldn't leave Penny alone with him, and that was that! She sat in one of the four chairs placed around a scarred table near the hideous cookstove. The house was dark, the curtains drawn against the sun and the walls practically bare of . . . Curtains? Elise went to the window next to the stove. The curtains were yellow gingham with ruffles sewn along the bottoms. She turned an edge over and examined the stitches. They were irregular but neat. Hand-sewn. Julia's touch? "Julia," she said in a whisper. It was a pretty name, feminine and melodic. Much like the name Elise. Were there other similarities between her and the first Mrs. Lonewolf?

Elise pivoted to face the room again and search for any other signs of Julia. She found them in a doily and in a bud vase, in an ivory hand mirror tucked behind a shaving stand and in a book of poetry being used as a lid for a jar of honey. She knew she'd find other feminine touches in the bedroom with the iron bedstead, but she didn't go looking. She'd be trespassing in there.

"What am I doing?" she muttered, sitting heavily in one of the kitchen chairs again. "I've got more important things to think about."

Her husband, for one. Husband! She smothered a shiver by hugging herself tightly. What a kettle of fish she'd landed herself in!

"Elise?"

Nearly jumping out of her skin, she looked in the direction of the sleepy voice and motioned her sister closer. "So you're awake. That was a nice nap, hmmm? Come sit with me, Penny."

Penny held up her arms to let Elise lift her onto her lap; then she looked around curiously. "Who lives he-ow?"

Elise smiled in response to her sister's speech problem. *R*'s didn't roll off her tongue. "We live here now. Know what? We're going to work on pronouncing your *r*'s. I had trouble with them when I was your age, too, and Mama taught me how to say them."

"I miss Mama."

"Me, too." Elise fought back tears as she had done for the past six weeks since her parents' death. She'd allowed herself to cry once at the funeral. Since then, she'd been too busy, too frantic, to cry.

"Is this the Injun's home?"

"Penny, don't say it like that. It's *Indian*. Yes, this is the *Indian's* home, and now it's our home."

"Adam's, too?"

"Adam is staying nearby. We'll visit each other. That'll be fun, won't it?"

"How come he can't stay with us?"

"Because he went to live with that other family

for a while." She smoothed Penny's hair back from her forehead. "This is a nice place, don't you think? We'll be happy here."

"I guess. Where's my Inju—Indian?"

Elise nodded her approval. "His name is Blade Lonewolf and he's out doing his chores, I suppose." She kissed the top of Penny's head. "He's part of our family now."

Penny drew back to look into her sister's face. "He is? How come?"

"I . . . he . . ." Elise shook her head, finding the explanation nearly impossible. "He adopted you, and I married him."

"Why'd you do that?"

"So that we could be a family." Elise held her breath, wondering how Penny would take this news. Penny rubbed her eyes vigorously, and Elise thought for a moment that she was on the verge of breaking into sobs, but when she removed her hands, her eyes were dry.

"I'm hungwee."

Elise released her breath in a sigh. "I bet you are hungry. You haven't eaten anything since early this morning."

"Will you tell the cook I'd like some eggs and biscuits?"

"The cook . . ." Elise chewed on her lower lip. Cooking was now her responsibility. Maybe that would be a way to make Blade want to keep her around. She set Penny on her feet and stood. "Let me have a look around and see what I can stir up."

"You? You gonna cook?"

"Yes, Penny, I am," Elise said with confidence ringing in her voice. "It can't be all that difficult. I can't promise eggs and biscuits, but I'll serve up something edible, I assure you."

She looked in vain for a cookbook, but only managed to locate a bowl of eggs and half a loaf of bread on the verge of growing mold. Standing back, she stared at the cold cookstove, trying to figure out how to build a fire in it. About a dozen sticks of wood were stacked beside it, plus a few lumps of coal. Which one should she use, and what could she use to strike a flame?

The light changed in the room and Elise glanced around, thinking that Blade had returned. Suddenly a head poked through the curtains covering the kitchen window, and Elise swallowed a cry of alarm. She stared at the woman's big grin and reddish-blond, flyaway hair.

"Hey, there, missy! You look too old to be adopted." Her blue eyes spied Penny, hiding behind Elise's skirts. "Hold up. You're the one he went into town fer, ain't ya?" She looked at Elise again. "Was it buy two for the price of one?"

Elise managed a quick smile. "In a manner of speaking, yes. I'm Elise St.—er, St. John." She shrugged, momentarily confused by her own identity. She was married, but her husband didn't want her. Should she take the name of a man who wanted to be rid of her? "Oh, and this is my sister, Penny," she added, remembering her manners.

"Glad to meet up with ya. I'm Airy Peppers. Where's Blade?"

"Outside somewhere. The barn maybe. Should I call him for you, Mrs. Peppers?"

"Nah, and you can call me Airy."

"Thank you. I was just . . . just going to make tea. Would you care for a cup?" The social pleasantries of her former life returned to her as easily as last season's dance steps, but she could tell by Airy Peppers's baffled expression that her invitation was out of place.

"Tea, huh? Why, sure." She bobbed her head to one side. "Unlatch that door and let me in."

Elise opened the door to the woman, who strode in as if she was quite familiar with the house and its occupants.

"Are you a neighbor?"

"That's right. I live 'bout two miles from here as the crow flies. Through them backwoods." She gestured north, where trees grew closer together behind the cabin, then grinned at Penny. "Hi, thar, purty girl. You sure have brought a ray of sunshine into this gloomy old place."

Airy's boots sounded like gunshots as she crossed the plank floor to the stove. She eyed it, then touched a finger to the top. "Tea, huh? How you gonna brew tea on a stove that's as cold as my great-grandpappy's pecker?" She glanced over her shoulder with a grimace. "Pardon. I fergot about them young ears. Anyways, don't you think you ought to fire 'er up?"

"You must be the cook!" Penny rushed to the woman and tugged on her split skirt. "I would like eggs and biscuits, please."

"Penny, she isn't the cook," Elise said, mortified. "She's our guest. *We* must cook for *her*."

Airy planted her hands on her bony hips and stared at Elise as if she were the town oddity. "You cook, do you? Just what were you in mind of cooking, besides tea, missy?"

"Uh . . . eggs and biscuits. Would you care for some?" Elise prayed she would refuse.

"Sure, why not?" Airy sat in one of the kitchen chairs and waved toward the stove. "Get cracking.

I'll just watch. Maybe you've got a biscuit recipe different from mine. I'm always interested in learning something new."

"Very well." Elise tried to smile as she approached the stove. She looked at the fuel stacked beside it and reached for a lump of coal. "I suppose I'll use this to start the fire." She handled it carefully, using only her thumb and forefinger. With her other hand, she opened the fire door and tossed the coal inside. "There."

"You gonna cook in that get-up?"

Elise looked down at her dress and knew she must appear ridiculous to this woman. With a sigh, she surrendered her pitiful show of self-sufficiency. "You know how to start a fire in this stove, don't you? Would you mind helping me? Penny's hungry and I'm at a loss . . . my clothes . . . I haven't even unpacked. He just brought us here and left! He told me to leave, too, but I'm not going anywhere without my sister. Besides, we're married and I'm honor-bound now to stay and make the best of—"

"Whoa up thar!" Airy pushed to her feet and thrust her face near Elise's. She poked a finger in one ear and jiggled it. "Did I hear you say something about a marriage?"

"Yes." Elise forced herself to calm down. "I married Blade Lonewolf this morning at the Rugged Cross Church."

"Holy smokes!" Airy's blue eyes stretched to their limits. "Why did you go and do that for?"

"To stay close to my sister. They weren't going to let him adopt Penny unless he had a white wife. If they put Penny back on the train, she'd be taken off somewhere, away from me and Adam—"

"Who's that?"

"Our brother. He was adopted by a judge."

"Judge Mott?"

"Yes, that's right."

"Oh." Airy looked away. "Well, that's some story. I can't believe Blade would . . . and he told you to hit the road, did he?"

"Yes, but I won't. I'm going to cook and clean for him. I'll earn my keep." She glared at the stove, which was quickly becoming her enemy. "If you'd show me how to light that thing, I'd be most grateful."

"Honey, when was the last time you cooked up a meal?"

Elise smiled, feeling inept. "Never, but I want to try. I *must* try."

"You got any plain dresses? I'd hate to see you ruin that one."

"Yes, I have some suitable for working in."

"You go change and I'll gather up some fuel for this here stove." Airy made a face at the sticks of wood beside it. "Shoot, that ain't enough to get this here stove lukewarm. Go on, and then I'll show you how to work this contraption. Once we get 'er going, I'll share my biscuit recipe with you and we'll fry up some eggs while we're at it. Go on now. Me and little Penny will go fetch some wood."

"You're very kind," Elise said, hurrying to the smaller bedroom to change. "Have you known Mr. Lonewolf long?"

"Long enough to know that he ain't called lone wolf for nothin'," she said, then herded Penny out of the cabin.

Elise stared after them and tears burned the backs of her eyes.

"*I won't cry*, she thought with firm resolve, but

a single tear defied her to wet a path down her cheek.

Blade stared at the steaming platters of fried eggs and potatoes, golden biscuits, and the big bowl of milk gravy. He lifted his gaze slowly to Elise. "*You* cooked this," he said, then tried again. "You cooked *this*."

Elise hid her hands behind her back and crossed her fingers. "Yes, that's right. Aren't you hungry?"

He removed his sweat-stained hat and hung it on a peg. "I thought I saw Airy's mule outside earlier."

Elise watched as he ran a hand roughly through his blue-black hair, making it fall across his forehead and the tops of his ears. Even across the room, she could smell him—earthy, tangy, spicy. She sniffed, liking the aroma of a hardworking man.

"Well?" He lifted one of his thick brows.

Elise gave a start and forced her thoughts away from his stirring presence. "Airy . . . oh, yes. Your neighbor. Yes, she stopped by and I told her I was your new wife. She was quite surprised."

He smirked. "*I'm* surprised that she believed you. She expected me to return with a child, not a wife."

Elise shrugged with indifference. "Won't you wash up? Dinner's getting cold."

"Let's eat," Penny demanded.

"Wait one more minute," Elise said, gesturing to her to quit fidgeting in the chair. "Sit up straight and act like a lady, Penelope Joanne."

Blade ambled over to the washstand. He poured a couple of inches of water from the bucket into the shallow porcelain bowl, then rolled up his shirtsleeves. Elise admired his muscled arms and long-fingered hands. He worked the ball of lye soap into a lather and applied suds to his hands and arms, clear up to the elbows. Streaks of gray, soapy water ran down his arms to his wrists. After rinsing off, he reached for a towel hanging from a metal ring. Orange-tinted sunlight played over his clean arms.

Elise squinted, not believing her eyes for a few moments. What were those darker streaks? Had he missed a few dirty places? No . . . no, those were— Elise sucked in her breath, and he spun around. She pointed a shaky finger at him.

"I . . . I am sorry. I noticed your . . . those markings on your arms. They're permanent?"

He examined his forearms and the faint blue lines running up them, interspersed by dots and arrowhead-shaped marks. "Yes, but they're so faded, I hardly know they're there anymore. I've had them since I reached manhood." He held his arms out straight for Elise and Penny to inspect. "Marks of a warrior," he said rather proudly, then swung a leg over the back of the nearest chair and sat in it. "Let's eat."

"How'd they do that to you?" Penny asked.

"Penny, I don't think we need to hear that at the supper table," Elise said.

Penny shrugged. "Okay." She made a grab for the gravy.

"Not so fast, young lady," Elise admonished. "You've forgotten something, haven't you?"

Penny wrinkled her nose. "You do it."

"Very well." Elise looked across the table at Blade and tried not to stare at the tattoos on his arms. "Unless you'd like to lead us."

"Lead you where?" His eyes twinkled, giving her a glimpse of his devilish nature. "I thought we were going to eat."

Penny smothered a giggle behind her hands, and Elise offered an indulgent smile.

"Lead us in grace," Elise said patiently. "You're the head of this household, so I thought you might want the honor."

He leaned back in the chair and crossed his arms against his chest. The markings weren't so terrible, she thought. He was right. They were hardly noticeable, but they branded him "different"—different from her in nearly every way. Could she and this man ever be comfortable with each other? His expression was too complex for her to read.

"You go ahead." His voice was deep and rasping.

Elise conceded with a lift of her brows, then bowed her head. "Dear Lord, thank you for this lovely meal after an eventful day. Please bless this family and bless Adam's new family. We are your faithful servants and your dutiful children. Amen."

"Amen!" Penny said with more enthusiasm than was necessary; then she grabbed the gravy bowl again. "I want a biscuit."

"'Please,'" Elise instructed. "Remember your manners. Would you care for some eggs, Blade?"

He nodded and took the platter from her. "You didn't have to put yourself out. I can cook for the girl."

"The *girl* is called Penny, and I didn't put myself out."

That, at least, was the truth, she thought with an inner cringe. Airy had prepared the dinner, showing her how to build a fire in the stove, how to make biscuits, where the utensils were stored, and so many other things that Elise's head had begun to spin.

While frying the eggs, Airy had cooked up the

scheme of letting Blade think that Elise had prepared the meal, and she'd promised to return tomorrow to teach her how to cook other types of food. Elise felt guilty, but she shared Airy's belief that she had to make herself useful if she wanted to live on Blade Lonewolf's homestead.

"Mighty tasty," Blade said after sampling the food. "I didn't figure you for much of a cook."

"My menu selections are limited, but that can be remedied. I plan to—experiment with recipes." She glanced at Penny, hoping her sister would be able to keep their secret. Penny had agreed to the pretense, but Elise knew her for a poor liar.

"Guess you thought I'd want to keep you if you proved yourself a good cook."

Elise studied him. The twinkles were still there in his eyes, but she got the impression he was serious. "I hadn't thought about that, since I see no reason why I should have to prove anything to you. We're married. I have every right to remain here."

His attention was diverted to Penny for an instant. Penny smacked her lips, obviously enjoying the meal, and he smiled at her. But his smile dimmed when he looked back at Elise.

"I can't understand why you won't go into town and make your own way."

Elise stiffened her spine, hurt by his words. "Because we are married."

He reached for another biscuit, split it open and poured gravy over it. "You mock marriage."

"I do not!"

"You forget that I was married, truly married. What we did today was get a piece of paper for a little man who knew a couple of liars when he saw them. You're being fool-headed if you think you'll be happy here."

"As long as Penny stays here, I'll stay here. *That* will make me happy."

He shook his head. "You are stubborn. Stubborn as a jackass."

"So are you," she shot back.

Penny giggled again, looking from one to the other. "You two look funny, all squinty-eyed."

"Hush, Penny, and eat," Elise said.

Blade smiled at Penny again and shrugged his suspenders off his shoulders. He let them hang at his sides. Rocking his head from side to side as if to relieve bunched muscles, he unfastened three shirt buttons. He scratched at the center of his tanned chest, between bulging muscles where a few curling hairs nestled.

Elise couldn't help but stare, wondering how comfortable he planned on getting. She was relieved when he settled back to his meal.

"If you didn't want to be separated from your sister, why did you let her be adopted?" Blade asked.

"Because I had no choice." Her mouth was as dry as cotton. Nerves, she thought, feeling them thrum inside her like plucked violin strings. The man set her nerves to tingling. She took a long drink of water before continuing. "I couldn't provide for my siblings and we had no relatives who would take us in. Adam and Penny were placed in my grandparents' care, and they turned them over to the Children's Rescue Society without even telling me. When I found out about it, the papers had been signed and I was told that the only way I could stop the proceedings was to prove I could make a living for them." She pushed aside her plate, her appetite gone. "I could do nothing in the short time they allowed me."

"What happened to your mother and father?"

"They were killed in a carriage accident. It was raining and the road was muddy, washed out in places. They crashed into a shallow ravine. The carriage struck a tree and my mother and father were . . . they died before anyone could find them." Her voice had grown husky and she cleared her throat. It was difficult to talk about the accident and deal with the awful scenes that flashed through her mind. Had they suffered? How long had they lived before death took them? She prayed that their lives had ended instantly, but she would never be sure.

"Are *your* parents still alive?" she asked, wanting to think about something else besides the carriage that had been reduced to splintered wood.

"No. They have been dead many years."

Elise's gaze slipped to his arms again, and the strange web of lines. Were other parts of his body decorated in this fashion? She blinked, refocusing her eyes, and found that he was watching her, smiling at her.

"What is it?" she said defensively.

"I have a few markings on my chest and back too. Want to see?" He started to undo more buttons.

"No!" She felt her face flame.

"I do," Penny said, rising to sit on her knees in the chair and get a better look at him.

"No, you don't!" Elise forced her voice lower. "Penny, go get ready for bed."

"What bed?"

"Where you were napping. Your nightie is folded on the bunk. Now go on. I'll join you as soon as I finish cleaning these dishes." She stacked

Penny's plate on top of her own, keenly aware of Blade rising from his chair and moving toward her. She jumped slightly when his brown hands captured her shoulders. A tingle raced up her arms and around her heart.

"See to the child. I'll wash the dishes."

"I'm afraid we haven't settled anything. We should talk and come to an understanding."

He guided her to one side so that he could collect the dishes off the table. "I understand that your notion of marriage is different from mine."

Elise gave Penny a push toward the bedroom and leaned down to be closer to her ear. "Go on now," she whispered, then straightened and turned back to Blade once she was sure Penny had obeyed her. He was placing the dishes in a large, shallow pan.

"You don't have to do the dishes. They're my responsibility." Elise took a step closer to him. "You could use a woman around here, you know. I'm sure you miss your wife."

"Yes, but what has that got to do with you?" His golden brown eyes glimmered. "Are you offering yourself? You'll share my blanket tonight?"

Elise pulled back in alarm. Was he serious? Blast his devilish eyes! "No! I . . . we hardly know each other. Can't you see how—how wrong that would be?"

"We're married, as you keep reminding me."

"Yes, but we can't just . . . you wouldn't want to bed a complete stranger!"

His grin lifted only one side of his mouth. "Wouldn't be the first time."

"Well, it would be for me," she stated, frowning mightily at him.

"Would it be your first time with a stranger or your first time with anyone?"

His question brought a tide of color to her cheeks. She could feel it, hot and telling. "Both."

He nodded. "I thought so." He turned his back on her and poured water from a bucket over the dishes. "I don't care to break in any more high-spirited young fillies. Too much trouble. See to your sister."

Elise moved quietly toward the bedroom. "You're letting me stay, then?"

"I'll sleep on it."

She started to ask him where he planned to sleep on it, inside or outside, but then thought better of it. It was enough for now to know that he wouldn't be trying to sleep with her.

Slipping inside the bedroom, she closed the door and wished it had a lock of some sort. She turned up the wick on the lantern and tucked the covers around Penny.

"Did you say your prayers tonight?"

Penny nodded, twisting onto her side. "Do we have to stay in this house? Can't we go back to Baltimoah?"

Elise bent over her to kiss her forehead. "There isn't anything left for us in Baltimore, Penny. We're going to be happy here. You'll see."

"I keep thinking maybe Mama and Papa might not be dead. Maybe they got lost and those people in the accident that night belong to some other family."

"They're gone, honey." Elise ran her thumb over Penny's warm, freckled cheek. "But you've still got me and Adam."

"Wonder if Adam's sleeping all alone. You think he's got his own bed?"

"Maybe. We'll visit him in a few days and see for ourselves. Good night, little one."

"Good night."

Elise sat on the other bunk and listened to the clatter of dishes in the next room. The mattress beneath her was hard. She felt it and realized it was stuffed with straw instead of feathers. With a long sigh, she went to stand by the window and looked up at a fat, sad-faced moon.

It seemed as if the whole world was lonesome tonight.

Chapter 4

Hooking the basket handle on her arm, Elise stepped outside with Penny. In the morning light, the farm looked fresh and green and big. Trees were abundant near the cabin but had been cleared out in the fields, with only an occasional lonely oak or elm to give refuge from the relentless sun.

"I don't see Alonewolf, do you?" Penny asked.

Elise smiled and touched a finger to the tip of Penny's freckled nose. "It's Lonewolf, Pen, not A-lonewolf. I think we should call him Blade."

"Okay."

"I can see him. Look, straight out that way past the barn. See that speck? That's him, I believe."

"Are we going to walk all that way?"

"Oh, it's not so far." Elise descended the three porch steps with Penny at her side. "And it's a beautiful day."

"Will we see Adam?"

A cloud seemed to descend as Penny directed Elise's thoughts to their stray lamb. "Maybe, but probably not."

"When can we see him?"

"We'll try to visit tomorrow. I'll speak to Blade

about it. For now, we should get used to our new home."

Elise stopped and turned back to the house. Wood-hewn, it was smaller than it felt inside. A rock chimney climbed up one side; a naked trellis climbed up another. The porch would be inviting with a couple of rocking chairs on it, Elise thought. She eyed a low tree branch and decided it cried out for a rope swing.

"This place has promise," she said, mostly to herself.

"It's nothing like the one in Baltimoah," Penny noted. "It's little."

"Well, we don't need a bunch of rooms to clean. This is large enough for just us."

They walked on, their joined hands swinging between them. As they passed the barn, Elise nodded at it. "We'll investigate in there later. I'll bet there are horses and mules and all kinds of interesting things inside."

"Let's look now!"

"No, we must get this breakfast to Blade first." Elise hoisted the basket she carried. The contents weren't fancy—hard-boiled eggs, leftover biscuits and a jug of water—but it was the best she could do without Airy's guidance. She couldn't yet find the courage to cook without Airy standing beside her. Perhaps after a few days she'd become more self-confident. In the meantime, she didn't want to burn the cabin down while trying to fry eggs.

Thankfully, Blade had fired up the stove that morning before Elise or Penny had awakened. When Elise had roused from her sleep, Blade had already left for the fields. She didn't know if he'd fixed himself breakfast, but she decided that even if he had, he could use more nourishment after toiling in the fields.

"What's planted out he-ow?" Penny asked, skipping ahead of Elise to the first rows of humped earth.

"I'm not sure," Elise admitted. "We'll have to ask Blade. Penny, let's work on your pronunciation. Growl for me. Say 'grrrrr.' "

Penny grinned. "Grrrrrr."

"That's good. Now say 'grrr-oh.' "

"Grrrr-woe."

Elise shook her head. "Try again."

"Grrrr-oh."

"That's right! *Grow*. You practice that every so often, and try 'grrr-een' while you're at it."

"You think I talk funny, Elise?"

"You talk a little like a baby, and you're not a baby anymore. You're a young lady, so you should sound like one."

"I'd love to be a lady." Penny pirouetted and flipped her long hair up on her head. She batted her carrot-colored lashes outrageously.

Laughing, Elise regarded her young sister with new awareness. Penny had lost her baby fat and most of her baby mannerisms. Perhaps their parents' death had robbed her of the last days of her innocence. Of course, at the age of eight, Penny was ready to shed the first stage of life and embrace the next, but Elise couldn't deny a stab of regret.

Brushing aside the melancholy feeling, she pointed upward at a set of whirling blades. "Look at the windmill, Penny. Can you hear it singing?"

Penny cocked one ear. "It's squeaking."

Elise laughed. "Well, it's all in what you want to hear, I suppose. I like to think that it's singing to me."

"Why does it spin?"

"It brings us water from belowground. That's how it's done in the country."

"Let's wace."

"I can't run with this basket. You go on. Run to that forked tree up there beside the path."

"Okay. Weddy . . . set . . . go!" Penny darted ahead, yellow skirts and red hair flying.

Elise picked up her pace while familiarizing herself with the layout of the farm. She'd noticed a chicken coop east of the cabin. A corral, feed lot, hog pen and goat pen spread out behind the weathered, unpainted barn. She'd counted ten cows, five hogs and a couple dozen goats. A fat, dappled gray horse paced in the corral. Up ahead, she could see two mules tethered to a shade tree, while two more labored with Blade farther on.

A farm wife. That was what she was now. Farm wife. Elise tried it on, finding the fit strange, even uncomfortable. She knew nothing about farming, nothing about livestock or much of anything other than attracting suitors and being a lady of leisure.

The courtesies and social graces she'd been taught would be of no use in Crossroads, Missouri. What she needed was instruction in sewing, cooking and cleaning. Her knowledge of a working farm was minimal. While she'd heard of slopping the hogs, she had no idea how it was done. And, yes, she knew that cows gave milk, but how did one manipulate an udder to squeeze out the milk? Hens laid eggs, but would the fowl attack her if she attempted to take the eggs? If she'd only known what her future held, she would have paid closer attention to the house help and how things worked, instead of spending her time learning how to handle a household staff and how to waltz like a dream.

"Out of breath?" Elise asked as she approached Penny.

"No. I found a snail." Penny held out her hand, palm up, to show off the slimy treasure.

"Ooo, Penny! That's not a snail; that's a slug! Drop that nasty thing!" Elise hunched her shoulders against the revulsion rising in her. "Don't wipe your—" Too late, she thought as Penny rubbed her hands on her yellow skirt. "Never mind." She shaded her eyes with one hand and located Blade again. He'd stopped the mules and was looking in her direction. She waved. He didn't wave back. Elise held up the basket, but he turned to his mules and farm implements.

"He is the rudest human being!" she exclaimed.

"Blade?"

"Yes."

"He doesn't like us ve-wy much."

"He doesn't know us. Once we get acquainted, he'll be different."

"We should go live with Adam."

"This is our home, Penny," Elise insisted. "We must try hard to make Blade glad he brought us here."

"I'll pick a bouquet for him," Penny said, bending to pluck a dandelion.

Elise smiled, touched by her sister's gesture. "That's nice, Pen. I'm sure he'll like that." *And if he doesn't, I'll make him sorry!* she mentally added.

They were only a few feet from him when he yanked on the reins to stop the mules in their traces. He glanced at Elise, a frown creasing his wide forehead.

"I don't have time to stop and chat."

Elise drilled him with a hard glare. "We aren't here to chat. I brought you some food and drink. I didn't know if you'd eaten this morning."

"And I brought you these," Penny said, holding out a fistful of dandelions and primroses.

Magically, the frown disappeared and a tender smile graced his wide mouth. His eyes crinkled at the corners. Elise saw that the skin in those crinkles was a paler color for want of the sun. When he wasn't smiling or squinting, the pale lines fanned out against his dark bronze skin. A streak of dirt arced across his left cheekbone. He pulled off his work gloves, and Elise noticed that the stitches on them were coming undone.

Amazingly, she pictured herself mending them, and this amused her. Mending gloves! Why, she barely knew how to thread a needle! Still, if he asked her, she'd give it a try. She wanted desperately to gain his respect.

He wore a sky-blue shirt and dark work pants that were full in the legs but hugged his backside. His heavy black boots had seen better days, as had his faded red suspenders. His straw-hat brim looked as if it had been chewed in several places. He took the flowers from Penny, his strong fingers gentle as they pressed against the fragile stems.

"Much thanks," he said, his voice huskier than usual. He removed his hat and tucked the blooms under the leather band. "I'll just put them here."

"That looks nice," Penny said. "We have eggs and biscuits. Want some?"

"I guess I can stop for a few minutes. Let's go sit under that tree." He looked pointedly at the basket, and Elise handed it to him. "I made do with beef jerky and milk this morning."

"I would have thrown something together for

you if you'd awakened me," Elise said, although she hated to think what kind of mess she would have made in the kitchen.

"I don't wake people up. That's what I have a rooster for."

A rooster . . . Elise dimly recalled a raucous crowing earlier. She had placed the feather pillow over her head to drown out the noise. Back in Baltimore, her mother had kissed them all awake each morning. Her loss gaped inside Elise like an open wound, and she shut her mind to the memories, however sweet. If she allowed herself to dwell on the many things she missed about her parents, she'd dissolve in a puddle of tears and Blade Lonewolf would send her packing for sure! She sensed he was a man who kept himself on a tight rein.

Elise removed the tablecloth from the basket and spread it under the tree. Blade set the basket to one side of the cloth, then sat with his back braced against the tree trunk, one leg bent, the other stretched out in front of him. Elise and Penny sat near him, and Elise unpacked the basket.

"I hope you like hard-boiled eggs."

He reached for one. "I like them okay." He peeled off the shell and ate half the egg with one bite.

"Good." Elise watched in amazement as he finished off the egg with one more huge bite. "And here's some bread, and a jug of water. I bet you're thirsty." She glanced toward the mules. "Should we water the animals, too?"

"I watered them earlier. They're fine."

"What are you planting out here?"

He looked at her with a measure of surprise. "Nothing. It's too early to plant."

"Then what are you doing?"

"Plowing. I'm harrowing under the winter wheat and getting the ground ready for planting." He peeled the brown shell off another egg, glancing at her through his thick, inky lashes. "You know about as much about farming as a hog does about hip pockets on work pants."

Elise gave him a scathing glare. "I never suggested that I was familiar with farming. Penny, would you like a boiled egg?"

"No, thank you." Penny looked toward the mules, then placed a hand on Blade's bent knee. "Can I pet the ponies?"

Blade looked around. "The ponies? Oh, you mean the mules?"

"Uh-huh. Will they bite?"

"If they bite you, I'll bite them back. Go ahead. You can pet them all you want."

Penny laughed and scampered toward the big-eared mules. The soft sunlight played over their shiny hides, picking out red hairs among the dark brown and black.

"How much land do you own?"

"Sixty acres, but I use twenty of it for grazing."

"You have livestock?"

"I have a few cows and a couple of horses."

"I saw one horse in that corral by the barn."

He nodded. "The gray? That's Janie. She's ready to foal, so I'm keeping an eye on her."

"That's why she looked so heavy! I thought you'd overfed her."

He shifted his eyes sideways to deliver a dubious glance. The simple gesture made Elise feel like the class dunce. "The sire is out to pasture," he said.

"And what is his name?"

"Bob."

"Just Bob?" Elise asked, tickled by the no-nonsense name. "Not Prancer or Black Magic? Just Bob?"

He shrugged, finishing off the last of the egg. "Bob's good enough for him. He seems to like it."

Blade drank deeply from the jug of water, and Elise watched his Adam's apple slide up and down his strong brown throat. A drop of sweat rolled down his face and splashed onto his shoulder, making a darker blue dot on his light blue shirt. He pulled a handkerchief from his back pocket and wiped his face. His scent drifted to her again— earthy, warm and, well, male.

She closed her eyes, privately amused at her thoughts. How did she know what maleness smelled like? Why, she'd been kissed on the mouth only four times in her whole life, and two of those times had been most disappointing. The other two had been pleasant—one of them had even released a little thrill in her. Of course, she'd heard from the other debutantes that Darby Rourke of the Nelson Rourkes was quite a ladies' man, and he'd proved to be the most experienced of her beaux. Darby was the kind of gentleman who forgot his manners if a lady didn't keep reminding him of them.

Suddenly she felt the power of Blade's stare. She lowered her lashes and peeked at him. He studied her intently.

"What were you thinking about just then?" he asked.

"Home," she admitted, but didn't elaborate. "Why?"

"You looked kind of dreamy. I thought . . . oh, never mind." He leaned his head back and stared at the sky. "You could go back to Baltimore. I'll see to it that your sister is raised right."

"You don't understand. Where Penny and Adam are, *that's* my home. All I have in Baltimore are memories."

"And family. You have family there."

"None that matter." She watched as he peeled another egg. She wished she had more food to offer him, and hated her feelings of inadequacy. "Blade, do you think we could visit Adam tomorrow?"

"Tomorrow? I'll be busy tomorrow." He put the whole egg in his mouth, much to Elise's astonishment.

"When, then? When can we visit?"

He took his time chewing and swallowing. "In a few days," he said finally. "Give him a chance to settle in."

A few days? Did that mean there was hope? She sent up a quick prayer. "So you've decided I can stay? Without a fight, I mean."

He gave a short laugh. "Wouldn't be much of a fight." Directing his attention away from her, he stared moodily at the horizon. "You may stay for as long as you want—which won't be long, I reckon."

"Are you so hard to live with?"

He glanced at the tablecloth and the basket. "I'm no picnic and my life here is no party."

"Perhaps I can make life easier for you."

"How?"

"Oh, by cooking your meals and—"

"When you learn how," he interrupted.

"Last night's supper wasn't so terrible, was it? You cleaned your plate."

He met her gaze. His wide mouth dipped at the corners. "You're still holding to the story that you cooked those vittles?"

Everything in her went still for a few seconds;

then her heart kicked and sent blood flooding to her face and neck. "Wh-what do you mean . . . story?"

"I mean you're lying through your teeth—as usual."

"As usual!"

He sprang to his feet and took a final long pull from the water jug, emptying it. "Airy Peppers cooked that meal, and she's probably heading over here right about now to cook tonight's meal." He corked the crock jug and dropped it onto the tablecloth. Reaching into the basket, he withdrew three hard biscuits and shoved them into his pant pockets. "Lying to me isn't going to make my life any easier."

Elise wrestled with guilt and decided to plead for understanding. "I'm sorry. I don't like to lie, but I—"

"For someone who doesn't like it, you sure do it a lot." He started to walk off and leave her with her stinging feelings and mounting frustration.

"Stop right there, Blade Lonewolf!"

Blade turned back to Elise, one black brow raised in inquiry. "What is it? I've got work to do."

From the corner of her eye she saw Penny glance toward them with a worried frown. "Penny, go pick a bouquet of flowers for our supper table tonight," Elise said, never taking her gaze off Blade. When Penny wandered over to a cluster of butter-colored wildflowers, Elise moved a few steps closer to Blade. "Any lies I have told I'm sorry for, but you don't go out of your way to be helpful. I've been trying to be pleasant and generous, and all I've gotten from you are frowns and threats."

"Threats? What threats?"

"You've told me that you want me to leave here

and find work in town!" she reminded him hotly.

"That's not a threat. That's a suggestion, and a damned good one, if you ask me."

"Nobody asked, and I happen to think it's a stupid suggestion. My place is here."

He rubbed his hands together slowly, as if testing the calluses. The flowers tucked under his hatband seemed out of place, and Elise captured her lower lip between her teeth to keep from grinning.

"You can stay. Nobody will be making you leave."

Relief flooded through her. She reached out in a gesture of pure instinct and laid a hand on his warm arm.

"Thank you," she said, sincerity ringing in her voice. "Thank you so much. I couldn't bear being separated from Penny. She . . . we've been through so much lately . . ." Tears pricked her eyes and wet her lashes as long-denied emotions welled up inside her. "I've been so distraught, so frantic, trying to keep Penny and Adam close to me that I—well, I haven't even had time to mourn Mama and Papa's passing. Sometimes I forget that they're gone, and then I remember and I . . . oh . . . it's been quite . . . that is, they're dead. I know that. I'll never see them again, never again hear Mama's laugh or Papa's loud snoring at night. I swear, he could lift the roof off—"

The overwhelming pain and explosive grief hit her like a cannonball in the chest. She clutched at Blade's arm as her knees trembled and tears spilled onto her cheeks. Her throat thickened, allowing only a groan to escape her.

And then he opened his arms and Elise collapsed against him, sobs overtaking her as the finality of death swept over her like a black ocean wave. She buried her face against his chest and knotted her hands into fists, crumpling his shirt between her fingers. Moments might have passed; minutes might have expired; time might have stood still. She didn't know, didn't care. The dreadful days that had followed her parents' fatal accident shook her very soul, and she could only hold onto the rock that was Blade Lonewolf. She breathed in, catching the aroma of sun and sweat.

His hands moved across her back and then one cupped the back of her head. Blunt-tipped fingers pushed through her hair. A weakness spread from her heart to her knees. She knew she should stand on her own two feet again, but she liked the feel of his hands on her and the solid comfort of his body against hers. For a few moments she held her breath and wished that time would stop.

"Elise, what is it?" Penny asked, setting time in motion again.

"She is sad about your mama and papa dying," Blade explained, before Elise could fathom an answer. "She'll be done crying in a few moments. You go ahead and pick that bouquet. That will make her smile again."

His explanation, so simple and so true, went straight to Elise's heart. She raised her head to look up into his face and bask in his gentle smile.

"I'm sorry," she whispered. "I don't know what . . . I haven't cried like that since the night I heard of their deaths."

He placed a hand alongside her face and his thumb stroked beneath her eye, wiping aside her tears. "Saying good-bye is hard."

"Yes, so very hard." *He knows. He knows about this pain, this horrific loss. His parents. His wife. So much loss in his life.* She glanced toward Penny and offered a shaky smile when her sister held up a clutch of dandelions. "Those are pretty, honey."

Reluctantly, Elise opened her fists, releasing Blade's shirt. She tried to iron the wrinkles from it with the flat of her hand, and in doing so discovered the interesting contours of his chest muscles. His smile was no longer gentle. Now his mouth curved in a knowing grin and his eyes darkened to cinnamon.

The intimacy of what they'd just shared caught up with her, and Elise felt her face and throat grow even warmer. She brushed her hands across his chest once more, something wanton within her demanding one last contact, and then edged away from him. As his arms released her, she knew a moment when she wanted them back around her, holding her, shielding her from a world that had been cruel of late.

"I'm not given to hysterics," she said with an embarrassed laugh as she wiped away the vestiges of her tears. "You were kind to allow me to dampen your shirt." Now that her composure had slipped back into place, she felt awkward, so she scooped up the basket and tablecloth. "Come along, Penny. We've taken up enough of Blade's time." She directed a mischievous smile his way. "Besides, Airy Peppers will be at the house soon."

Blade backhanded his mouth, smothering a lusty chuckle.

"See you at supper," she called cheerfully to him as she took Penny by the hand.

"I'm partial to Airy's beans and corn bread," he drawled as he moved with long, easy strides to his patient mules. "She stirs up a tasty bread pudding, too."

"Sounds like a wonderful meal to me." Elise

stood there for another moment, watching the grace of his stride, the proud width of his shoulders, the cocky angle of his head. He wasn't such a bad sort, after all. And he was quite attractive.

Her palm tingled as she recalled the rigid muscles of his chest. Heat engulfed her and she whirled away in a wild tangle of skirts.

"Come on, Pen! I'll race you back to the house!"

And she ran, letting the air cool her hot skin and blow out the flickering flame of forbidden desire.

Chapter 5

It was a good thing Homer and Sam knew the fields instinctively, because for the first hour after Elise's visit, Blade was in a fog and offered them no guidance.

He kept remembering how she looked—as if she were flying across the field, her hair fluttering against her back like autumn leaves, her skirts flashing up to provide tempting glimpses of her slim ankles and shapely calves.

His mind drifted to how she'd felt in his arms, so small and fragile. Her heartbeats had tapped against his chest and her body had trembled with her heart-wrenching sobs. She'd smelled of spring—honeysuckle and tea roses—and her hair had been warm and soft against his cheek, in his hand.

Holding her in his arms had not aroused him, but his heart had opened to her . . . just a little. He wasn't given to overt displays and he wasn't the type to make friends easily, so he'd surprised himself when he'd reached out to her, cleaved to her, comforted her. She had a way about her. Like a newborn kitten, she was hard to resist.

"Whoa, Homer and Sam." He pulled on the reins

and the mules stopped. Homer swung his head around to look at Blade. They'd come to a halt in the middle of a row. Blade gazed out at the fields to check their progress and focus again on the task of plowing under the winter wheat.

He removed his hat and ran a handkerchief over his face. "I know, I know," he said to Homer. "We're not supposed to stop here, but I'm getting my bearings."

That gal sure had rattled his brain. He hadn't dwelt on another woman since Julia's death. It was a relief to think of someone else for a change.

Replacing his hat, he knotted the leather lines again and looped them around his waist. Gathering them in his gloved hands, he clucked his tongue and the mules set off again, straining against the leathers to drag the plow over the field and bust through the earth.

He tried to pay attention to the rows, occasionally tugging on the lines or uttering a command to correct the mules' progress, but his thoughts returned to Elise. It was difficult for him to think of her as his wife. In fact, he rejected the notion so strenuously that he hadn't allowed himself to contemplate their unconventional union. After all, he hardly knew the woman. Not that he wouldn't enjoy getting to know her. He'd like nothing better than to kiss those pouty lips, to hear her moan with passion as he stretched out on top of her, to take her breasts in his hands and her nipples in his mouth . . .

He jerked his mind away from the picture of such delights. Sweat rolled into his eyes. He was overheated, and not from the sun.

There were huge gaps in what he did know about his new wife—frustrating gaps. She was from Baltimore, but what sort of life had she led there? Why had no relative come forth to keep the siblings together?

Among the Apache, there were no orphans. On the contrary, relatives campaigned for children who had lost their parents. Elders of the tribe often had to make the difficult choice of which relatives could take in the child or children.

But Elise's relatives had turned their backs— why? Did their attitude have something to do with Elise or with her parents? Questions about her whirled in Blade's head like spokes on a wheel. Why hadn't she stayed in Baltimore and wed someone there? Why had she insisted on remaining under his roof? What circumstances had forced her to marry a stranger? Since it seemed that she was bound and determined to stay, he figured he might as well discover what he could about her.

A vision of her laughing blue eyes and the dimples that winked at the corners of her mouth obliterated all else for a few moments. He didn't realize that he was smiling or that the mules had stopped again until Sam snorted and yanked on the lines.

"What is it?" Blade asked, shaking his head to emerge from his pleasant stupor. He lifted the lines over his head and moved toward the team. Homer blew noisily through his flared nostrils. Sam stamped a foot. Neither tried to go forward.

Must be a hole, Blade thought, stepping carefully over the ground until he located the depression. Gopher hole. He took his place behind the plow and looped the tied lines over his head and shoulders again to hang at his waist.

"Gee, Homer, Sam," he coaxed, and the mules high-stepped gingerly to the right, around the hole and past it. "That's good, boys. Haw. Haw, Homer." The mules moved left, straightening the rows.

Homer curled back his lips and snorted, then shook all over. Sam tossed his head, jerking the lines.

"Okay, okay, settle down. I'll pay better attention," Blade promised, grinning a little at his mules' contrary behavior. If everything didn't go just so, they revolted. Mules were like women that way. Hard to please, but necessary to good living.

Sam strained the leathers again and skinned back his ears. Homer issued a coughing neigh. Blade gripped the lines with focused determination and put all thoughts of blue eyes and beribboned petticoats aside.

"Would you mind placing this rocker on the porch for me? You can bring it back in later."

"On the porch?" Blade scratched his head at Elise's request. "What's wrong with it staying right where it is?"

"Oh, nothing. I just wanted to sit on the porch for a while, now that Penny's settled in bed for the night. It's rather warm in here, and the air smells lovely this time of the evening. Would you mind? You could join me, if you wish. I'd appreciate the company."

He grabbed the arms of the rocker and lifted it from its place in front of the hearth, then carried it out to the porch. She talked funny, he thought. She used words like "rather" and "quite."

"Where were you reared?" he asked as he set the rocker where she indicated.

"In Baltimore. All of us were born there. Mama, too. Oh, wait. Papa was from the Virginia hill country. He had come to Baltimore as a young man

looking for work when he met Mama at church."
She fluffed out her skirts before easing herself into
the rocker. A heart-shaped brooch glistened at her
throat. She touched it and rubbed the ruby surrounded by seed pearls. Sighing with contentment,
she looked up at him. "This is pleasant. Will you
join me?"

He shrugged and sat on the top porch step. Leaning back against a post, he waited for her to speak,
hoping she'd talk more about her life in Baltimore.
But she seemed mesmerized by the deep purple
horizon where stars were being born.

"Didn't you have a man back there?" he asked.

She gave a start, clearly nonplussed. "A m-man?
You mean a beau? No, not anyone in particular. If
I had been spoken for, I wouldn't have traveled
here, would I?"

He smoothed a palm over his bent knee where
the fabric of his pants had worn thin and needed
patching. "Thought your man might have given
you that ruby pin."

"No. This was my mother's. She gave it to me."

He regarded Elise again—his new bride. Starlight painted her face with an ethereal glow. "How
come you didn't have a man interested in you?
You're easy on the eyes."

She arched a brow. "Why, thank you for that
stingy compliment, Mr. Lonewolf. As a matter of
fact, I had several marriage proposals before—"
She snatched her attention from him and directed
it back to the night sky.

"Before what?" he prodded, although that went
against his rules. His Apache teachings ingrained
in him patience and a respect for others' secrets.
"And where are your people? Why did they allow
this?"

"Allow what?"

"This!" He motioned around him, at himself. "This marriage, this journey of yours to a faraway place. Why did they allow your sister and brother to be placed on that train?"

A sigh whispered past her lips. "You ask a lot of questions, but I can certainly understand how peculiar it all must seem to you. My people, as you call them, are cowards, trembling at the feet of my grandparents, who are as empty of feelings as corn husks."

He studied her more intently, waiting for her to reveal the source of the bitterness coloring her voice. She twined and untwined her fingers in her lap and rocked with a more agitated pace.

"You see, they never approved of my mother's choice in a husband. They felt that she'd married beneath her station. Mama was an only child, doted on and spoiled. She was supposed to marry into one of the old, respected families of Baltimore society, but she fell in love with a courtly young cobbler from Virginia, from a family of coal miners."

A firefly glowed in front of her, distracting her. She issued a soft gasp and reached out to catch it. Curling her fingers carefully around the insect, she held out her hand so that he could see the glow between her fingers.

"Isn't it magical?" she whispered, her eyes shining as softly as the light in her hand. "It carries its own lantern."

So do you, he thought, admiring the shimmer of her eyes and the radiant animation on her face. She opened her fingers, and the insect lifted from her palm and floated into the gathering darkness. A rooster crowed twice, and she swiveled her head in its direction.

"That's Red," Blade told her. "He's probably showing off to his hens, just to remind them who rules the roost."

"Males," she teased. "They're born to strut and make noise." She ran a hand over her skirt, then pleated it with her fingers. "I saw Bob today." Her eyes sparkled. "He's a pinto, right?"

Blade nodded. "That's right. Black and white with a little brown on him. He roams free most the time."

"How do you catch him when you want to ride him?"

"I whistle for him."

Her blue eyes widened. "That works? You whistle and he comes running?"

He smiled. "Sure. He likes me."

"Oh, of course." She looked at the pleats she had made in her skirt. Her thoughts diminished her inner light and she drew a breath that quivered when she expelled it. "I'm trying to think how to explain my situation to you . . . Well, you see, my grandparents provided our family with an allowance. They were always a bit cold and distant, but I never dreamed how void they were of compassion until Mama died. They acted as if she were the only one of their family and that the rest of us were nothing to them. They refused to allow Papa to be buried next to her. I spent what money was left to me, burying Papa as close to Mama's plot as I could manage. Oh, it was so cruel and so unnecessary."

Anger built within Blade, slow and steady. He had to look away from the pain evident on her face. His admiration for her grew. She was brave, he allowed. For one so young and sheltered, she showed grit. "They are your only kin?"

"No. I have a smattering of aunts, uncles, cousins, all on Mama's side. We never knew Papa's family. His parents are dead and he only had one brother, who never married. I believe he died in a mining accident several years ago. Anyway, none of Mama's relatives would go against Grandmama and Grandpapa Wellby's wishes, fearing they, too, would be financially ruined."

"It's good you left that place and those people." He bounced a fist on his knee to relieve some of his ire. "Someday they'll regret their actions."

"Oh, I do hope so," she said fervently. "They can keep their money and their big mansion and servants and all their jewels and china and crystal!" She stroked the ruby brooch, and he wondered if it was the only jewelry she still owned.

He thought about what she had said as the purple light failed and dark blue blanketed the sky, broken by sheets of stars. He felt a stab of misgiving about the life she'd described. She was so unlike him. She'd never fit in here.

"Your life in Baltimore was among the privileged," he said after a while. "You had servants and fine things."

"Yes, that's right." She shrugged. "The money my grandparents sent my mother each month was sufficient to allow Papa to pursue his passion." She glanced at Blade. "Poetry."

If she'd said, "Spitting in the wind," it would have made as much sense to him. He examined a white scar across his third knuckle to keep from catching her eye until he could ward off the mocking laughter clamoring in his throat.

"What kind of job is poetry for a man?" He knew

that his question was inappropriate the moment it was out. Her glare scalded him. "He earned a living with it?" he asked, trying again to pose a suitable query.

"No, but Papa's poetry gained plaudits from high sources. He had one poem published in *Scribbler's Quarterly*."

"And he was paid money?"

She pressed her lips together in that firm line he was beginning to recognize as a sign of irritation. "No, but he received a copy of the quarterly without charge. I told you he didn't have to worry about making money as long as the Grandparents Wellby continued their allowance."

"No wonder they didn't cotton to him," Blade mumbled into his chest.

"What? What did you say?" she demanded, clutching the chair arms and leaning forward to dare him. "You said something derogatory about my father. Now what was it?"

He grimaced, wishing he'd kept his thoughts to himself. "I only said that I could understand how your grandparents might be disappointed in him—him not working and all."

"He did work! He toiled in the arts." She sat back in the rocker, her jaw jutted out, her eyes blazing blue fire. "We were proud of him, and his poetry was lovely. He was well thought of among our circle of friends. In fact, he was often asked to recite his poems at dinner parties and other special occasions."

"That's nice," Blade said, confused. Perhaps this sort of thing was acceptable in Baltimore, but in Crossroads, making poetry wasn't the same thing as making a living.

She whipped her head around to glare at him.

"So you condone my grandparents' behavior toward my father and his children, do you?"

"Condone . . ." He shook his head, unfamiliar with the word.

"You think it's perfectly all right?" she elaborated.

"No. I was only saying that your grandparents might have thought he should support his family and not allow them to do it. A man is often measured by his pride."

Elise opened her mouth to speak, seemed to think better of it and faced front again, her arms folded tightly against her body.

"I don't mean to offend," Blade ventured. "Your mother's husband was a good father, and being loved and respected by his children is worth a lot."

As her expression softened, so did his heart. Her smile was faint, but her body relaxed. She unfolded her arms and nestled her hands in her lap. Blade released a long breath, relieved to be back in her good graces.

"Yes, he was well loved by all of us." Her voice sounded musical to him, like plucked harp strings, sweet and angelic. "And he loved us with all his heart. Why, there was nothing he wouldn't do for us. Nothing." She swallowed hard, and Blade knew she was near tears.

"You decided to come here instead of staying in Baltimore," he said, guiding her away from memories of her father. "Why didn't you accept one of the marriage proposals?"

"Oh, those," she said, her tone harsh. "Those proposals and the men who posed them disappeared after my parents died and it became known that the Wellbys had disowned us. I was no longer considered good marriage material. Society scorned us. We were outcasts."

Outcasts. He nodded with empathy. He'd felt like the odd man out most of his life. He'd left the Apache while still a boy, but had found no comfortable place for himself among his white relatives. By the time he'd decided he'd like to go back to the Apache, it was too late. His people had been rousted from their land and herded to a reservation. The life Blade had known with his tribe was gone—gone forever.

Only out in his fields, out on the land given to him by his white mother's people, did he feel rooted, centered.

"We had a lovely house in Baltimore." Elise tipped her head back and began to rock, slowly, peacefully, as memories wafted through her; memories that made her expression dreamy. "I had my own room, next to Penny's. Adam was down the hall, closer to Mama and Papa's big room. The two upstairs maids were not much older than I, but the downstairs maid and butler were ancient! Cook was a jolly old thing with a shiny black face and corkscrew hair. She called us lambs. 'Skedaddle out of my kitchen, little lambs,' she'd say."

Elise's voice drifted to a whisper and she closed her eyes. Blade found himself transfixed, struck by the perfection of her profile and the lush curl of her lashes. There wasn't anything imperfect about her: not her mouth, her nose, her chin, her hair or her creamy complexion.

His gaze traveled from the enchantment of her face to the temptation of her body. Her breasts, round and high, were of average size for a body as petite as hers, and her waist was narrow. He remembered how his hands had spanned it, the tips of his fingers touching. He found himself looking at her breasts again, wondering ... were her nipples pink or light brown?

Something warm burst open in his stomach and flooded into his groin, giving life and strength to that part of him that had lain dormant for too long. He shifted his backside against the hard planks of the porch and let the sensation reign for a few more moments. It felt good and it felt right. He was a man in his prime. His marriage to Julia and her death had not changed that.

He forced his gaze away from Elise, feeling slightly ashamed but good all the same. What man wouldn't experience a quickening when looking upon a woman as fine as Elise? The painted ladies at the Rusty Keg Saloon in town couldn't hold a candle to her.

People would be talking. They'd be wondering why another nice-looking white woman was living out here with the half-breed Lonewolf. Damn, he couldn't help but wonder the same thing himself!

"Do you want to bed down now?"

He jerked all over and heard the bones pop in his spine. His manhood pressed against his fly. She looked at him curiously, and he knew he wore the expression of a man caught with his pants around his ankles. What had she asked him? She hadn't said *that*—he was dreaming, wool-gathering, putting words in her mouth.

"Do you?" she asked again.

"Do I what?"

"Want to go to bed?"

He couldn't speak, couldn't think.

"You don't have to sleep in that tepee, you know."

"I don't?" He shook his head, denying his own

ears. Surely a woman like her wouldn't offer to let him spill his seed into her without wanting something in return . . . or without screaming her lungs out.

"Of course you don't. This is your house, and there is an extra bedroom in there where nobody sleeps. You used to sleep there, I take it, so you can sleep there again."

Reality crashed down on him, and the first decent erection he'd experienced in months sagged.

"Did you sleep in the tepee before we arrived?"

"Yes." He throbbed. He ached. Cold sweat dotted his forehead.

"But why?"

"I like it." In fact, he had begun to hate it. The lodge had become too cramped, too lonely.

"I see."

"You see what?" he challenged, his voice sharp after her unwitting refusal to bed him.

"I see that you don't feel comfortable in the house, either because of us or because of your wife."

He shrugged, unwilling to share the most personal parts of his life with her.

"I've often wondered what's become of our house in Baltimore. It was sold, of course, and I can't help but think how it must have changed with strangers in it. I don't believe I'd be comfortable in it now. It would be too awful to go from room to room and face the memories."

"That was Julia's room," he said, not meaning to speak aloud. Wishing he had kept a tight rein on his tongue, he averted his face and stared hard at the glittering horizon.

"Yes, it was her room, but it was your room, too. Your room together," Elise said, her voice whispery with understanding and sympathy. "As you told me, saying good-bye is hard. I suppose, in a way, it's better that Mama and Papa were taken together. They loved each other so very much. They were inseparable. Was it like that with your wife?"

Pushing to his feet, he stretched and twisted from side to side to unkink his muscles, pointedly ignoring her question. She wouldn't like his answer, he told himself.

"I'm sorry if I'm being too nosy." She rocked, the toes of her lace-up shoes setting her in motion. "We've both suffered great losses and I just thought we might—"

"Did Airy show you how to cook breakfast?" he asked — no, demanded. He winced. Damn it all, he hadn't meant to bite her head off!

She blinked, stopped rocking, and her back came away from the rocker's support. "I . . . well, yes. I believe I can prepare something edible. If you'll be good enough to awaken me in the morning, I'll try my hand at it."

"I'm not your upstairs maid." Frustration gnawed at the edges of his self-restraint. "If you can't get up by yourself, then never mind. I've been doing for myself a long time. I don't need anything from you." He gave her his back, his words ringing in his ears. An aching spread through his loins, branding him a liar. Why couldn't he stop thinking about how her body had curved into his, so pliant, so perfect?

"Well, fine."

He heard the chair creak behind him as she rocked, faster and faster.

"Forgive me my sad lacking in life," she added.

"How have I survived all this time without being awakened by fowl?"

"I'm going to bed," he announced, since there was no use trying to talk when his gut was in a knot and his loins burned with a persistent fire. Should be used to it by now, he thought. Sure wasn't the first time he'd been consumed with a burning need, only to be hit with the cold splash of denial. Guess a man couldn't ever get used to such a fate. It went against nature. After Julia's death, he'd vowed never to mix with another fragile flower, and here he was, tending an orchid when he was a man better suited to dandelions.

"We're going to have to find a way to get along, you know," she called after him as he headed for his tepee. "It's not good for Penny to be brought up amid hostility. I want to be your friend!"

He ducked inside the tepee and sprawled onto his pallet. Flinging an arm across his eyes, he cursed his fate, his inability to control his own urges, and her sky-blue eyes and rich auburn hair.

Friend. He groaned and rolled onto his side. He didn't want to be her damned friend.

Chapter 6

❦

She won't last a month here, Blade thought as he trudged behind the plow the next day. Why, even her name didn't belong in Crossroads. Elise St. John. So highfalutin. So out of place. Like his.

Blade put that similarity out of his mind. He didn't need to be counting the things they had in common. He should focus on the hundreds of things they didn't share.

A woman used to upstairs and downstairs maids, butlers and cooks had no business on a farm in Missouri. She'd never done a day's work in her life. All she knew about were dances and high society, tea cakes and poetry.

"Poetry," he said, spitting out the word.

Up ahead, Belle and Tom, his two other plow mules, faltered to a stop and skinned back their ears. Blade clucked his tongue to get them going again.

While he'd like to meet Elise's grandparents and teach them a thing or two about charity, he could understand that they might have been disappointed in a son-in-law who'd been content to lounge on his backside and rhyme words while they put bread on his table. But how could they lock out their grandchildren? They must have hearts of lead to be able to disown a sprite like Penny. He didn't know much about the boy. In fact, he couldn't recall what Adam looked like, having seen him only at the train station. Adam hadn't received favor by being adopted by the judge. Judge Mott wasn't an easy man to please.

As if his thoughts had acted as a summons, Blade caught sight of the judge's fancy red buggy jostling along the road that shot through the middle of Blade's land to the house. The older man pulled the buggy to a stop and waited for Blade to reach the end of the rows near the road.

Blade guided the team into a turn and set them on other straight furrows before he tugged on the lines.

"Good morning to you, Lonewolf," the judge said, tipping his black, flat-crowned hat. "I see you're making progress. That double plow cuts your time by half."

Blade cocked one hip and removed his handkerchief from his back pocket. He mopped sweat off his face and neck. "I'll be ready to plant when it's time. You need something?" He didn't waste pleasantries, since the judge never came around unless he had a reason.

Judge Mott grinned and his black eyebrows jumped higher on his forehead. "Heard you took yourself a wife. Some say you plucked her right off the orphan train along with that little girl you and Julia ordered up."

"I married again." Blade shoved his hat back to push the shadow off his face. He wanted the judge to see that he was serious and wouldn't take kindly to any smart-alecky remarks. "She's the sister of the little one. That boy you adopted is their brother."

The black eyebrows lowered menacingly. "So it's true. He told me his sisters were living around here somewhere. Hope that doesn't cause problems for us." He popped his buggy whip again and again, making it sing. The powerful black gelding hitched to the buggy quivered like an animal familiar with the vicious kiss of the whip.

Blade's gut knotted as it always did when he had to talk to his neighbor about delicate matters, and he cursed the day he'd become indebted to Judge Lloyd Mott. He'd shaken hands with the devil when he'd borrowed money from the judge and put up his land as collateral.

"So your wife is white. Just like Julia." Judge Mott chuckled and the whip sang out, slicing the air. "You attract white women like a magnet, Lonewolf. Did you have to buy her like you bought her sister, or did she come along just to keep close to her kin?"

"I didn't buy her, and I didn't buy her sister. I paid for the train ticket and for the care the Society had given her, same as you did."

"That's right, except I had the money to do it." The judge's gaze slipped to Blade like oil across water. "Does your bride satisfy you?" He looked down the road toward the log cabin. "I'd like to meet her. In fact, I've brought a welcoming gift." He held up two jars. "Harriet's pickled pigs' feet."

Blade's throat flexed and it was all he could do not to make a disagreeable face. "She's not here. She's at Airy's."

It was a lie. A bold-faced lie. But everything in him resisted a meeting of the judge and Elise, especially if he couldn't be there to protect her. Not that the older man would do anything vile. Judge Mott had a way of saying one thing while his expression said something entirely different, usually something odious.

"What's she doing there?" Mott set the jars down in the buggy again.

"Woman things, I guess."

"Better keep her on a short leash for a while. I wouldn't let Harriet spend any time with Airy Peppers. It's not proper for her and her cousin to be making moonshine in the woods. If I was the law around here now, I'd smash that still and put those two old birds out of business."

"They aren't the only ones making whiskey around here."

"They're the only *women* making it," the judge asserted, squinting one black, fathomless eye. "Brewing whiskey isn't seemly for women. If men allow women to indulge in such activities, our society will become depraved. Mark my words, Lonewolf: It's a man's obligation to keep women in line. Since Eve, they've been as conniving and cunning as the devil. It's in their blood." The buggy whip danced in his hand and sang its wicked tune.

The lecture reminded Blade that the judge had been known as Malicious Mott on the bench, but he'd served only two years before being pressured to retire. Airy claimed he had been asked to step down because someone discovered that he had no legal background but had earned the honorary title during the Civil War, when a Confederate general had bestowed it upon him. The judge was a Rebel through and through, and hadn't conceded along with his compatriots. Blade could see, in his treatment of others, that the judge believed some people were meant to rule over others.

"Here, you take these jars and tell your new wife I'll come around and meet her another time."

Blade took the jars of pigs' feet. "Much obliged. I'll tell her." He set them in the soft soil, away from the road. He knew Elise would want him to ask about her brother.

"I know you want to get back to work, so I'll be going." Judge Mott took the reins.

"How's the boy?" Blade asked.

"The boy? You mean my orphan?"

"Yes. His sisters have been asking."

"You tell them not to worry any about Rusty. That's what I call him. He gets three square meals a day and a bed of his own."

The judge turned the red buggy around, stirring up a cloud of dust that coated Blade's mouth and stung his eyes. Blade grabbed the gelding's halter and jerked him to a prancing stop.

"What's on your mind, Lonewolf?" Mott asked, regarding Blade with a superior air.

Blade released the halter. "They want to visit him."

"Maybe later. We'll see."

"They miss him, and I bet he misses them. I thought I'd bring them around some evening. We won't stay long."

Judge Mott leaned closer, an unfriendly smile stretching his lips beneath a narrow black mustache. His jet eyes and matching brows were in sharp contrast to his pasty skin and snow-white hair. "Maybe you didn't hear me, Lonewolf," he said, slowing his words so that his Southern accent was more pronounced. "I said I didn't think visiting would be wise. The boy belongs to me now, and I don't want him whining for his sissies."

Blade checked his rising anger and moved back

from the buggy. He said nothing, not trusting himself to speak, but he held the judge's gaze for long, speaking moments. Finally, the judge snapped the whip and the gelding bolted into a trot. The garish red buggy rolled away as Blade gathered in one calming breath after another.

He shook inside with impotent anger. Clenching his fists, he let off steam with visions of pounding the older man's smirking face. He hated having his feet held to the fire, and Mott was doing that every chance he got.

What was the old devil hiding? Why not let the boy see his sisters?

Blade stared at the misshapen pigs' feet in the pickling jars and wondered what was going on at his neighbor's place. He didn't think Judge Mott would harm the boy. He figured Mott would put Adam to work. Another slave, and damn the Yankees.

He'd meant to put off any visit to the judge's to give the boy a few weeks to get used to a new life, but the judge's peculiar manner changed Blade's mind. He'd take Elise and Penny there tomorrow. Mott wouldn't like it, but Blade decided it was more important to check on Adam than to please his neighbor.

Besides, sooner or later, Mott would have to meet Elise, and Blade wanted to be there to make the introductions. Julia had liked Judge Mott and had insisted they go to him when they needed money, but Blade had never trusted him. Even though the man had loaned him the money, his feeling about Mott hadn't changed. He'd leave the judge alone with Elise about as quick as he'd leave a coyote alone with his best laying hen.

*　　*　　*

Elise sat motionless, waiting for the first spoonful of stew to disappear into Blade's mouth. He savored the tender meat and vegetables. She'd probably been laboring over the stove all afternoon.

"Well?" she said when she could stand the silence no longer. "What do you think?"

"I think Airy prepared this."

"No, I swear to you. I did it all by myself—well, Airy told me to add more freshly ground pepper and green onions. But other than that, I did it. You can be honest. I won't break into tears if you think it can be improved upon."

"Only one thing would make this better."

"What?" Elise strained forward, aiming her attention at his stew bowl. "Salt?"

"No. A bigger spoon."

She blinked in confusion. "A bigger . . . ?"

He waved the soup spoon. "If I had a bigger one, I could scoop more of it into my mouth."

A smile broke over her face and she released a spate of pleased laughter. "You like it? Really?" At his nod, she laughed again. "Well, bless my britches! I finally did something that meets with your approval!"

He hesitated before shoving another spoonful into his mouth. Had he been so critical of her? He felt the nip of shame, and knew that she told the truth. But why couldn't she see that this arrangement could never work? A man and a woman living together under the same roof with no touching, no mating—it wasn't right. It wasn't fair to either of them.

"And the corn bread." She shoved a plate of it closer to his elbow. "Eat some of it . . . please."

"What about me?" Penny asked. "Don't I get some?"

"Of course. Help yourself." Elise propped her elbows on the table and rested her chin in her palms to watch him, as if obtaining his kind words had become her mission in life.

Blade enjoyed her attention and relished her desire to earn compliments from him. He nodded and gave her a wink of encouragement, and she beamed. Lord God, she was pretty! She wore an emerald dress of some kind of shiny material he'd never seen before. Ivory lace decorated the cuffs, neckline and bodice. The ruby brooch winked back at him from its place at the base of her throat. She dressed better than any woman in the county, he figured. And these were what she called her "day dresses." He couldn't imagine what Baltimore women wore at night. Must be swaddled in laces and ruffles from head to toe, he thought, then took a huge bite of the corn bread. It was delicious. She learned fast.

"I believe you have a penchant for cooking," he said around the mouthful of butter-flavored bread.

"So do I," she agreed, tipping her chin at a preening angle. "I still have much to learn, but look what I've done already! Why, less than a week ago I hadn't the faintest idea what ingredients were required to make a pan of corn bread. I didn't even know if it was baked or fried."

"I don't think we ate it back home, did we?" Penny asked.

"We had it a few times. Cook preferred flour instead of meal breads." Elise eyed the stove. "I'm going to try my hand at baking loaves of bread tomorrow."

"There is an art to it," Blade cautioned. "It's in the kneading and the resting."

"Ah, yes. I remember how Cook labored over a

ball of dough for hours. Perhaps I'll wait for Airy to instruct me on bread baking."

"That might be wise. Takes a lot of flour, and it would be wasteful if the bread didn't turn out, seeing as how a sack of flour is so costly." He held up the wedge of corn bread. "But there will be no waste to this. I intend to eat every crumb. What I don't finish tonight I'll have for breakfast."

"For breakfast? I can make a better breakfast than that for you. I did all right this morning, didn't I?"

"Yes, you did fine, but I like crumbled corn bread in a bowl of milk. Makes a good breakfast." He enjoyed the food for a few minutes while she watched him down every bite. "How did you manage to haul yourself out of bed this morning?"

"It wasn't too difficult." She glanced at Penny, then smiled. "I only had to drag my bed to the window so that the morning sun would hit me squarely in the face. I opened the window to hear Red's crowing better." She faced him again. "I was surprised to find that you were already up and out of the tepee."

He shook his head at her elaborate wake-up plan. "I do chores before breakfast. I'm usually milking by the time Red starts greeting the dawn."

"I could help you with your morning chores," she offered. "What else do you do, other than milking?"

"I feed the livestock and chickens. I gather eggs—"

"Gather eggs," she interrupted with enthusiasm. "I could do that! Do they bite?"

"What, the eggs? Nah, they're harmless." Blade grinned at the way she wrinkled her nose and pursed her heart-shaped mouth. "Chickens don't bite. They peck."

"They wouldn't peck us, would they?" Penny asked.

"If they try, you just shove them to one side. A setting hen might try to flog you."

"Oh, my!" Elise's blue eyes grew round with alarm. "What's that?"

Blade chuckled low in his throat at her reaction, then saw that Penny wore the same expression of distress. "It's not so bad. The old hen runs at you and tries to slap you with her wings. Sometimes she tries to spur you, but all you have to do is wave a broom at her or throw a stone and she'll back off."

"You don't want them to have babies?" Penny asked.

"Some of them, yes, but I can't let every hen sit on every egg she takes a mind to, or I'd be overrun with chickens."

"So do you think Penny and I could gather the eggs?"

He thought about it for a few moments before he conceded. "I suppose. You'd need to collect them early, before the sun heats the air."

"We can do that," Penny said.

"What about milking?" Elise said with less enthusiasm. "I don't suppose I could do that. The cows are used to you."

Blade started to agree with her, although her reasoning was askew, but then he thought of how hilarious it would be to watch her try to milk his Jersey cows.

"I suppose I could teach you to milk."

She said nothing, but peeked at him from beneath her lashes, her silence more potent than any argument she could have made. She wanted him to let her off the hook.

"First you need to try your hand at churning butter. Penny can help you with that, too." He sat back, enjoying the interplay. "Then there is laundry to do. That'll take a couple of days. In a few weeks you and Penny can help me put in the garden. How are you at canning? Ever done it? Well, there's always a first time." He snapped his fingers. "That reminds me. I have a gift for you."

"Oh? What kind of gift?"

He went to fetch the jars where he'd left them on the front porch. Returning, he stuck them close to her face so that she could get a good look at the gelatinous goop. "Pickled pigs' feet. One of the neighbors brought them by."

"Ooo! *I'm* not eating them!" Penny said, hiding her eyes.

Elise drew back in revulsion. "Good gracious, why in the world would anyone want to pickle *those*?"

"Ever eaten one?" Blade teased. "They're salty, but as tender as a baby's backside."

Elise turned her face aside. "I can't bear to even look at them. Take them away, please." She shivered and swallowed hard. "I can assure you I won't be eating them or canning them. If you want such a disgusting thing, you can fix them for yourself."

"Have Airy show you how to boil up some cow's tongue," Blade continued relentlessly, setting the jars on the washstand. "You've got to steam it good or it's as tough as leather. Got to get the blood out of it. You know, the Apache women eat buffalo tongue raw. The heart and liver, too."

"Elise, tell him we won't eat such things," Penny

pleaded, yanking on her sister's sleeve.

Elise narrowed her eyes suspiciously. "He's poking fun at us, Penny. Blade has no intention of eating tongue, just as I have no intention of cooking one!" She shook a finger at him as he sat across the table from her again. "Shame on you, Blade Lonewolf."

He grinned, sharing the moment of congeniality with her. "Pigs' feet aren't so bad. You ought to try one just so you can say you did."

"I might, if I get drunk enough."

He laughed—really laughed, deep and bursting from his throat.

Elise stared at him, amazed; then she laughed with him until her eyes brimmed with mirth. His breath caught in his throat at her loveliness, and warmth coiled in his loins. God, he wanted her!

"It's good to laugh together, isn't it?" she asked, wiping the glistening tears from her eyes. "Feels wonderful."

He regarded her for a long, breathless moment. "I haven't had much to laugh about lately."

She averted her gaze, her smile fading like a sunset. "Neither have I." Then she drew a short breath and expelled it. "But life goes on, and we grasp at what's important, at what's left."

"There isn't much out here for a woman like you."

"What does that mean, a woman like me?"

"A woman used to the finer things in life," he explained, although he thought it unnecessary. "Not much around here to laugh about. No dances, no socials, no—"

"Those things can be easily changed," she interrupted. "In fact, I bet there *are* dances and socials, but you never paid any attention to them." Her gaze fell on the jars of pigs' feet and she looked away quickly. "Which neighbor sent those things?"

"Harriet Mott."

"Harriet Mott . . ." She shook her head. "Have I met her?"

"The judge's wife."

"Oh!" Her eyes lit up like fireworks.

"May I be excused?" Penny asked, pushing aside her empty stew bowl. "I want to play with my dolly."

"Yes, go on, Pen." Elise waited for Penny to scamper into the other room before she faced Blade again across the table. "Did you ask her about Adam?"

"I didn't see her. I spoke to the judge. He rode out to where I was plowing."

"Well, did you ask him about Adam?"

Her eager expression tugged at his heart. He knew she'd been worrying about her brother and had exercised extreme patience in not demanding that she be taken to him.

"Nothing's wrong with him, is there?"

"No, nothing." He waved aside her concern. "I'll take you and Penny to see him tomorrow morning after breakfast."

"Thank heavens!" She stacked her hands on top of the brooch and her face glowed with gratitude. "I so want to see him. Why, he must think we've deserted him. Adam tries hard to be brave, but he's just a scared little boy. Oh, he'd never admit that, but I know him. I'm so afraid he'll . . ." Her voice trailed off and she captured her full lower lip between her teeth. Rising, she grabbed the coffeepot from off the stove and refilled Blade's chipped white cup.

"You're afraid he'll what?" Blade asked, looking

up into her face as she stood beside him. The scent of rose water drifted from her skin, and he thought how easy it would be to slip his arm around her waist and press his face between her breasts.

"I'm afraid he'll become so unhappy that he'll run away and try to go back to Baltimore," she confessed, her eyes glittering like sapphires.

"He'll want to stay close to you," Blade reassured her.

She moved away to place the pot back on the stove. Instead of sitting down again, she went to the front window and looked out at the moon-splashed land. "Is that your wife's grave out there?"

"Yes."

"Would you mind if I planted some flowers around it? Maybe some jonquils or tea roses?"

Her beauty, inside and out, astounded him. He ached to tell her so, but he was afraid he'd sound stupid. He didn't know how to talk to a woman like her—a woman raised around poetry and social graces.

Elise was as bright as a daffodil and as talkative as a magpie. Her personality bubbled. In a way, she was easy to talk to, he realized, because she wasn't shy or awkward.

She turned sideways to face him. "Would that be all right with you, Blade?"

He blinked, remembering her question. "Yes. She would have liked that."

"Good."

What a smile she had! His heart lifted and he felt himself smile back.

"Thank you, Blade."

"For what?"

"For agreeing to take me and Penny to see

Adam. I was beginning to think you were going to try to keep us from him."

"Why would I do that?" He pushed his chair back from the table and stretched out his legs, crossing them at the ankles.

She tapped a finger against her lower lip in thoughtful regard. "Do you like the judge?"

Blade ran a hand down his face to camouflage any grimace that might cross it; then he clasped his hands behind his head. "What you should understand is that Judge Mott is an important person in Crossroads."

"Why? What's he done?"

"He knew important people during the War Between the States. He's got money, too, and land. He leases out a few houses in town."

"Does he still serve on the bench or is he retired?"

"Retired. He's a gentleman farmer now."

"Gentleman farmer. Is there a distinction there?"

Blade grinned. "Gentlemen farmers let others tend their fields while they watch."

"Oh, I see." She glided back to the table and began stacking the soiled dishes.

Her hands were small-boned and without scars or wrinkles. Smooth, he thought. They'd feel like lotion on a man's skin.

"But you didn't answer my question, Blade. Do you like the judge?"

"I did answer your question," he corrected her. "You just didn't listen." He stood and opened the stove door. While he added a few more sticks of wood to the fire, he sensed her frowning countenance. "What you didn't hear is that whether or not I like the judge doesn't matter one whit." He straightened slowly to face her. "While we're at his place, you let me do the talking."

"Why? What's wrong with the judge? Is he fearsome?"

"He's powerful and he's got an eye for the ladies." He couldn't resist chucking her lightly under the chin. "Try not to chatter like a squirrel around him. He might take it wrong and think you're looking to be unfaithful to your new husband." He grinned at her shocked expression.

"He doesn't sound like a gentleman to me!"

Blade plucked his hat off the peg by the door. "I'm going to check on the stock."

"Blade?"

He turned back to her. Her eyes were wide with worry.

"Adam's all right, isn't he? Judge Mott wouldn't hurt him or anything?"

"You can see for yourself tomorrow." He closed the door on any other sticky questions she might ask him. He didn't want to add to her fears and he didn't want to lie to her. He only hoped that tomorrow's visit wouldn't make matters worse—for all of them.

Chapter 7

~~~~~~◇◇◇~~~~~~

"Oh, my!" Spying Judge Mott's plantation house, Elise snapped to attention next to Blade on the wagon seat.

"What do you see?" Penny asked, scrambling up behind them and placing a hand on their shoulders to steady herself.

"The house," Elise said. "Will you look at that place! It's very grand, isn't it?" She turned to Blade, who looked fine in a clean white shirt, black vest and black trousers. The sun blinked off his highly polished black boots. "Did he have it built?"

"No, it was already there, but it was damaged some during the war and he fixed it up. Airy Peppers's cousin was born and raised there."

"You're talking about Dixie Shoemaker?"

"That's right. You remember her from the train station?"

"Yes, and Airy talks about her a lot. So that was her family home? Did they lose it during the war?"

"Her family died off during the war. All that she had left was Airy, Airy's folks, three or four brothers and sisters, all living in the Carolinas. Dixie married an older man and they tried to keep the family place, but he died and Dixie couldn't do it by herself. She was behind on taxes, and Judge Mott paid them up and took over the place. Dixie runs the boardinghouse in town now."

"I don't suppose she or Airy much likes Judge Mott."

"Has Airy said something to you about him?"

"No." Elise pondered his rapping tone. "Why, is there something I should be told about?"

He pulled his "town" hat—black with a red band—down lower on his forehead. "Remember about keeping quiet."

"Yes, yes." She yanked at her black gloves. "I'll mind my tongue, and so will Penny. I swear, you act as if this man is a coyote and we're a bunch of helpless lambs."

Judge Mott was sitting in a savanna chair on the edge of a field where men toiled with plows and mules. An umbrella stuck in a stand shaded him from the sun. He wore black from head to foot, and his longish white hair was gathered into a short queue that peeked out from under his hat.

Hearing the wagon, he looked over his shoulder, then returned his attention to the field. Elise could sense his instant, blazing displeasure at having company. She'd seen him clutch the chair arms and his eyes narrow. Beside her, Blade had also tensed, encouraging Elise to closely observe the behavior of the two men. No matter what Blade said—or wouldn't say—it was obvious he didn't like the judge one bit.

Blade stopped the wagon near the older man's folding chair, alighted, then helped Elise and Penny down to the gravel road. He motioned for them to stand back while he approached the silent Judge Mott.

" 'Morning," Blade offered, stopping beside the

gleaming cherry-wood chair. "Thought you'd like to meet my new family."

The judge's dark eyes lifted up to confront Blade. "I didn't expect visitors, Lonewolf, so I can't offer any hospitality. Of course, surprise guests don't deserve much, to my way of thinking."

Elise's spine stiffened. She heard him say something else, his voice dropping to a whisper, and she moved forward in time to catch the last few words.

". . . don't want any interference from them!"

She cleared her throat noisily and reached back to grip Penny's hand. Both men twisted around to her. The judge finally rose to his feet and touched the brim of his hat. He offered her a mendacious smile.

He was older than Blade, but not as elderly as Elise had first thought. His white hair, she supposed, had been that color for most of his life. It was odd that his eyebrows and mustache had not also turned white, but remained coal black.

She took him to be about fifty years old; a fit fifty, as he sported strong hands, erect posture and a trim physique. His skin was the color of paste, his lips too thin, his eyes set too close. He'd tied a charcoal-colored handkerchief around his neck, and it was spotted with perspiration.

"Mrs. Lonewolf, I take it?"

Not used to that name yet, Elise forgot what she was going to say to him and merely extended a gloved hand, which the judge immediately accepted. Bending at the waist, he pressed his lips to the black satin before letting go.

"Lonewolf, you are a lucky, lucky man," he said, never taking his eyes off Elise. "First Julia and now her. How do you do it? Why, my mouth simply waters when I imagine having something so delectable in my life."

"This is Penny," Blade said, resting a hand on the child's head.

Elise released a long, quiet breath as the judge switched his attention to Penny. She wiped her gloved hand on her skirt, giving in to an impulse she couldn't resist. Feeling soiled and wanting to spare Penny, she pinched a pleat in her sister's russet pinafore and tugged her backward, then slipped a protective arm around the girl.

"Charmed. If I'd known you were coming, I would have told my cook to bake some fudge for you."

"We didn't want you to go to any trouble," Blade said. "I brought them to see where their brother lives."

"And to see our brother, of course," Elise added, gaining glares of irritation from both Blade and Judge Mott.

Penny pressed a forefinger to her lips. "Shhh," she hissed at Elise. "We told him we'd be quiet," she whispered.

Mott hooked his thumbs beneath his gray suspenders and ran them up and down as his gaze did the same over Elise's face and body. "The boy's not here."

"Where is he?" Elise asked, refusing to be hushed and wishing she could yell at him to stop inspecting her as if she were on the auction block.

"Harriet took him into town." The judge leaned toward her and winked. "Harriet's my missus. She's not much older than you."

An ebony-skinned man approached, hat in hand, his face shiny with sweat.

"Mistah Judge?"

"Yes, what is it, Hamm?"

"You want I should wash the buggy now, Mistah Judge?"

"Didn't I say I wanted it washed this morning? Go and do it and don't bother me. I'm speaking to these people."

"Yes, suh." The man hurried away.

"They're like children," the judge complained. "Can't do anything without asking a hundred questions." He rubbed a finger over his thin mustache. "Take my new ward; why, he doesn't know anything about farming. I never saw a male child so dense in all my born days." He seemed to enjoy Elise's look of outrage. "I was telling Harriet only this morning that the boy was dumber than any woman on God's green earth. He doesn't know a hoe from a whore, that one."

Elise opened her mouth to give the judge a tongue-lashing, but Blade's even tone cut her off.

"What's going on in town?"

"Not a thing that I know of," the judge said, dancing around Blade's real inquiry.

"You said the boy was in town," Blade expounded with a droll quirk of his lips.

"That's right. Harriet's having him fitted for some clothing. He didn't have any proper work pants or shirts. Needs a hat, too." Mott propped a hand on the back of the savanna chair and addressed Elise. "We work for our supper around these parts, Mrs. Lonewolf. Your brother will learn valuable lessons with me." He sighed heavily. "I only wish he knew something about farm work. I don't have the time or the patience to teach him every little . . ." He stopped and his gaze shifted to Blade. "Maybe you can help me out there, Lonewolf."

Blade stood with his hands shoved in his pockets, his stance casual, but Elise sensed his alertness, as if he were ready to defend or defeat.

"You seem to have taken an interest in the boy, so I'll bring him around early tomorrow and leave him with you. You can teach him how to plow. I told him to watch my workers, but he hasn't caught on."

Elise could tell that Blade was on the verge of declining. A frown pinched the skin between his eyes and he pursed his mouth as if he'd tasted something sour. She knew he was forming a polite refusal, so she jumped in ahead of him.

"Please do, Judge Mott." Elise ignored Blade's thunderous glare. "Blade will be happy to teach him, and I'll be happy to see my brother again."

"Now, now, Mrs. Lonewolf, let's get something straight. I'm expecting the boy to learn how to work, so I don't want you coddling him. He's had too much of that already. That's why he's not worth spit."

"I beg your pardon, sir!" Elise guided Penny behind her, shielding her from the argument she was about to commence. "My brother is—"

"Bring him around after breakfast," Blade interrupted, angling his body so that he partially blocked Elise from the judge's view. "I'll do what I can."

"That's what I like to hear. I scratch your back, you scratch mine." Mott chuckled, then sat in the savanna chair under the umbrella. "I'll tell Rusty y'all came by."

"Who is Rusty?" Elise asked.

"That's what I named him."

Elise's mouth dropped open. "N-named him! He has a name, sir. Adam Jamison St. John."

"He'll go by Rusty around here," the judge said, his tone ringing with finality. "Elmer!" he yelled across the field. "Straighten up your row or I'll box your ears!" He grabbed up a paper fan and created a sultry breeze in front of his face. "Damn darkies," he muttered. "Gotta watch them every minute."

Blade's fingers bit into Elise's elbow and he forced her to turn around, then herded her and Penny to the wagon.

"Rusty, indeed," Elise huffed as Blade pushed her up into the wagon. She fluffed her skirts, her anger building as she directed a scathing glance at the back of the judge's head. "And he called his workers darkies as if they are slaves! Someone should inform him that *the war is over and the Rebels lost!*" She said the last more loudly, and even though the judge didn't turn around, she knew by the way he stopped fanning for a moment that he had heard her.

Blade swung up beside her, grabbed the reins and jerked the team into a tight circle. He issued a shrill whistle to urge the mules forward.

"I suppose you're irritated with me," Elise said, reaching for the parasol at her feet.

"Irritated, hell! I'm so mad I ought to paint my face for war!" He swung around to her, muscles working in his jawline and a vein throbbing in his left temple. "What did I ask you to do? I asked one damned thing of you, and you promised me you'd do it. What? Tell me!"

She popped open the parasol, creating a pool of shade. "Stop yelling. I promised to curb my tongue, but you tricked me, so it's not my fault that I had to break my word."

"Tricked you? How did I do that?"

"You didn't tell me that Judge Mott was an ill-

mannered ogre. No one could keep quiet around
that man." She cast her gaze in his direction. "No
one except you, it seems. How you can stand by
and allow him to insult you and us is beyond me.
I don't mind telling you that I'm disappointed in
you, Blade Lonewolf. I thought you were a chiv-
alrous man, but it seems I was wrong."

"Rein in your runaway mouth and listen to me,
damn it all."

"Mind your manners, please. A gentleman
wouldn't speak such vulgarities in front of a lady
and a child. You should be ashamed."

"I never told you I was a gentleman, so get off
your high horse, Miss Mouth," he bit out. "The
judge is my neighbor—an important neighbor—so
I don't want him riled. I have to get along with
him, and that's why I asked you to put a leash on
your opinions. I should never have brought you to
his place."

"Stop yelling!" Penny covered her ears. "I hate
yelling."

Elise forced herself to calm down. After a few
minutes, she trusted her voice to emerge civilized.
"It's a pity Adam wasn't there."

"He *was* there."

She looked at Blade's stern, glowering countenance. "But the judge said—"

"He lied. Hamm said he was going to wash the
buggy, remember?" He glanced at her to catch her
nod. "Well, Harriet wouldn't go into town unless
she went in that red buggy. Adam was around
there somewhere. Maybe in the house."

"Why did the judge lie to us? Why didn't you
challenge him?"

"Because we were on *his* place and we were unexpected and unwanted visitors. I wasn't going to

start a feud. Besides, he's bringing the boy around tomorrow, so you can see him then. From now on, you'll let me handle the judge and keep your nose out of it. Remember that you're living here on my charity."

Elise bit her lower lip so hard, she was certain she'd bruised it. His charity! One thing the judge had said was right on target: Blade Lonewolf was lucky to have her. Now she had only to convince him of that.

The red buggy stopped alongside the field and Adam jumped out.

"Here he is, Lonewolf," the judge called. "Much obliged. I'll send Hamm for him in a few hours. Now you do what this man tells you, Rusty, or he'll scalp you for sure!" Cackling at his joke, Mott reined the black horse in a tight semicircle and headed back down the road.

Blade grasped the lines and tugged. "Whoa up, team." The mules slowed and stopped.

Adam stood at the edge of the field and kicked at clods of dirt. He wore a new straw hat with a wide brim, overalls that draped his body and a dark brown shirt. His feet looked overly large in brown work boots.

"Come on over here," Blade said. "I can't teach you anything but how to yell if you stay that far away."

Obeying, Adam high-stepped across the field to Blade, never looking up, but his shoulders were squared and his gait was deliberate. Blade held out his hand. "Blade Lonewolf. Glad to meet you, Adam."

Adam's blue eyes slipped upward slowly, followed by his hand. He shook hands with Blade firmly, like a man. "Thanks for not calling me Rusty."

"I'll call you what you want to be called. I figured you'd rather go by Adam. Your sisters will be out here in a few minutes. I asked them not to bother us until dinnertime, but I don't reckon they'll be able to wait that long."

Adam grinned, just a little. "The judge told me last night that they lived here. Knowing 'Lise, she's been hiding somewhere, waiting for the buggy to leave."

Evidently he knew his sister well, because no sooner had he got the words out than a shrill cry floated to them. Blade looked toward the sound and saw Elise and Penny running hell-bent across the field, arms outspread, faces beaming with joy.

Adam moved like a young deer, sprinting across the rows of earth to be enveloped by his sisters' loving arms. Emotion gathered in Blade's throat to form a knot. He had to swallow three times before he could breathe again. Yanking his handkerchief from his back pocket, he turned aside and blew his nose, embarrassed to be caught with his feelings exposed.

"Oh, Adam, you've lost weight!" Elise held her brother at arm's length to examine him. "And look at your hands! They're scratched up and callused! What has that monster been doing to you? You can tell me. Don't be afraid of him."

"I'm not afraid of him!" Adam said, a bit too forcefully for Blade to believe him. "I hate his bloody guts, but I'm not afraid of him."

"Has he hurt you?"

"No, he just . . . he treats me like I'm one of those mules. And that wife of his!" Adam made a horrible face. "She's the one who's scared of him. She jumps like she's been knifed every time he says her name. *Everybody* there does. He acts like a king and we're all his subjects."

"Oh, poor, poor dear." Elise clutched him to her and looked over the top of his red head. "Did you hear that, Blade? Judge Mott is mistreating him!"

"He said that the judge hasn't hurt him," Blade replied.

"He's lost weight."

"He's wearing clothes that are too big for him. They feed you over at the judge's, don't they, Adam?"

"Yeah." Adam sighed heavily. "Hog slop. That's what they eat over there. Boiled this and pickled that. And at every meal they serve something wretched like chitlins or grits." He pretended to spit something vile on the ground.

"How terrible. No wonder you look pale." Elise ruffled his hair. "I'll send food home with you. Lots of it."

"No, you won't. He can eat dinner with us, but you're not going to insult the judge by sending food over to his place." Blade motioned for Adam. "Now we've got work to do, and it's way too early for dinner, so you two clucking hens had better get on back to the house."

Elise's face fell. "But we have so much to catch up on, and I want to—"

"At dinner. We'll meet you over at that tree." Blade pointed to a spreading oak. " 'Round about one. Cook up a bunch of something because we'll be hungry as bears after hibernating. Now go on."

"But I—"

"It's okay, 'Lise." Adam bussed her cheek. "We'll talk during dinner. I was brought here to learn how to plow, so I'd better get on with it." He leaned over to give Penny a hug. "I'll see you both in a little while."

"I'll fix something delicious for dinner." Elise pushed back the straw hat to get a good look at his face. She cupped his chin in her hand and angled his head one way and then another. "Have you been ill?"

"Are *you* going to cook?" he asked in a teasing tone.

"Yes, I am. I've been taking lessons."

"Is that so?"

"Yes, and I've gotten pretty good at it. Just ask Blade." She looked at Blade. "Tell Adam how well I'm doing with the meals."

"He can find out for himself—later." Blade motioned for Adam again. "Come over here, younger brother. I'll have you plowing a straight row in no time."

As Adam approached, Blade's glance took in Elise's beatific smile and then latched onto it. She wasn't smiling at Adam; she was smiling at him! And her eyes—they were glowing with pleasure so contagious that he caught it himself. What had he done to deserve such a crowning look from her? He guessed she was grateful that her younger brother was within kissing range, and that her gratitude embraced him as well. He smiled back at her.

"You walk alongside for now and watch me, Adam. After a few rows, I'll let you drive the team."

When he glanced in Elise's direction again, she was already walking back toward the house with Penny.

"Do these mules have names?" Adam asked.

"Yes, the blacker one is Homer and the other one is Sam. See how they pricked their ears? They heard me. Mules are smart. Smarter than horses."

"You think so?"

"I know so. When it comes to farming, you can't do any better than a mule. Horses are good travelers, but mules are good farmers."

"The judge's mules hate me."

"I don't think so. You just have to know how to talk to them. I'll teach you."

"I hope so, because the old man is losing his patience. He expects me to start pulling my weight or else." Adam kicked at the disked soil. "I hate him. I'm not going to be a farmer, no matter what he says or does."

Blade craned forward, snaring Adam's attention. He was a good-looking boy with auburn hair and blue eyes like Elise's. His profile was chiseled, his jaw square. Blade could easily imagine him in short pants and knee socks and a fancy suit coat and tie, the kind of clothing wealthy children wore in finishing schools back east. A faint sprinkling of freckles gave the only color to his otherwise white skin. Elise was right. He looked sickly, but Blade guessed his illness had more to do with his spirit than with his health.

"You don't know me and there's no reason why you should listen to my advice—other than out of respect for your elders. But I'm going to offer a few wise words because I know the judge better than you do." Blade pointed a finger at Adam in warning. "Don't cross him. He's bigger and meaner than you. He's a bully and he's used to getting his way."

"So I should go along like some stupid cow?" Adam spread out his arms in a burst of aggravation. "I'm not a dumb animal and I don't want to be a farmer! I want to be a sea captain."

"Look out there, Adam." Blade nodded straight

ahead at the flat earth. "You spy any oceans or seas out there? We're not anywhere near a coast."

"I'm going back to Baltimore . . . someday."

"Until that day, you'll captain a plow. Don't shut your mind to any kind of learning. You never know what will come in handy." Blade jiggled the lines. "See these?"

"Reins."

"Yes, but these are long, so they're lines. I tie them and loop them around my waist like a belt. The mules know what to do, but sometimes they drift off course, so you've got to adjust the rudder." Blade sent the boy a wink and got a grin in return. "Instead of port and starboard, we call them haw and gee."

"What about prow and stern?"

"Uh . . ." Blade looked ahead at the mules. "Ears and ass?"

Adam doubled over laughing, and Blade laughed with him.

Halfway to the house, Elise heard male laughter skipping on the breeze. She paused and looked over her shoulder, but she was too far away to see Blade and Adam.

"Was that them?" Penny asked.

"Yes." Elise smiled. "I'm glad they're getting along so well."

"Adam looks skinny."

"We'll fatten him up and put color in his cheeks again," Elise vowed. "That pig roast we put on should be done by the time we get back to the house. I'll make slaw like Airy taught me, and we'll have pork sandwiches. What a feast!"

"We going to take it all out to the fields?"

"Yes. I'm going to sneak a couple of sandwiches

to Adam to take back to the judge's place. I don't care what Blade says."

"Blade's mean!"

"No, he isn't, Pen." She slipped an arm around her sister's shoulders. "And I know you don't believe he is either. You just said it to make me feel better. Blade's a good man." She remembered how he'd called Adam "younger brother." That had meant so much to her, that casual acceptance of her beloved brother. And Blade was helping Adam now, showing him how to please Judge Mott so that his life would be easier.

"Blade's a good man," she repeated, recalling the special smile he'd given her before he'd busied himself with his plow and team. Her heart had fluttered as it was doing now, behaving like a startled bird.

And it *was* startling, she thought. Finding a man like Blade Lonewolf so attractive that he could make her heart race just by smiling at her was startling indeed!

Chapter 8

~~~~~ OO ~~~~~

Elise stood on the porch and stared at the tepee, where Blade had taken refuge immediately after supper. She'd wanted to talk to him about Adam, but he'd indulged Penny in conversation throughout the evening meal. After supper, he'd scooted out the door and into his tepee while Elise had had her back turned.

Crossing her arms, she considered calling him out. He'd probably say he was asleep and that he'd talk to her in the morning. But in the morning he'd probably grab a biscuit as he dashed out. She was beginning to know him—too well. He wasn't telling her something about the judge, and she wouldn't sleep a wink until she could ease her mind.

Calling out to him wouldn't do. This required drastic measures. She tipped her head to one side, pondering her plan. She'd been wondering about that tepee . . .

Her decision made, she went down the porch steps and moved briskly to the conical structure. The flap didn't appear to be secured in any fashion.

"Blade?" She counted to five. "Blade, I'm coming inside." She heard a frantic shuffling and a muttered oath. After giving him another handful of seconds, she swept aside the flap and peeked in. "Are you decent?"

"No! What's wrong? What do you want? I'm sleeping."

"Sleeping? Heavens, I just tucked Penny in and you're already sleeping? That's not like you at all."

"You've only been here a matter of days. What do you know about my habits? I'm tired."

Her eyes adjusted to the dim, flickering light sent out by a single candle melting in a shallow tin that used to hold chewing tobacco. The interior smelled of suede and smoke. Blade lay on his side, his wide chest bared to the waist, a colorful Indian blanket draped across his hips and legs. His black hair fell in a natural side part, the tips brushing his bare shoulders.

She'd seen him shirtless that morning. Rising earlier than usual, she'd entered the kitchen to catch him at the washstand, his upper torso gleaming and damp. She'd tried not to stare at the pale tattoos on his chest—lines and dots matching those on his arms. Fascinating! He'd hurried through the rest of his toiletries and into a clean shirt. Elise had realized that he must do this every morning before she awakened and after he'd finished his predawn chores. She wondered how she could school herself to arise before Red's wake-up call, because she had enjoyed the spectacle, especially since her presence had made him nervous, edgy . . . as he was now.

She tried not to stare at him, but the sight of his smooth, muscled chest drew her gaze like a honeybee to a blossom. She advanced on hands and knees.

"You wanted something?" he asked sharply, running a hand through his hair. "You're old enough to know better than to walk in on a man in bed."

"I didn't walk, I crawled, and that's not what I call a bed." She eyed the thin pallet that was barely wide enough for his body. Elise hadn't expected the tepee to be so small. She sat down with difficulty and arranged her skirts in a fan around her. When the hem trailed over his hand where it lay on the pallet, he pushed the fabric back roughly and glared at her.

"What are you doing?" His tone bristled with irritation.

Elise dismissed his rude welcome and twisted around to examine the drawings on the skin walls of animals and men with bows and arrows.

"I said I was sleeping," he repeated.

"Yes, I heard you the first time," she said, sighing. "But you aren't anymore." She delivered a bright smile and touched her fingertips to an illustration of a buffalo. "Are you the artist?"

"Yes."

"Is this what you do in here? Paint on the walls?"

"It's decoration. You hang paintings on the walls; I do my own."

"So what is this? A buffalo hunt?" she asked, examining the figures of red, black, brown and white.

"Yes. And this is the white man's army raiding our camp." He brushed his fingertips across a painting on the other side of him. "This is my uncle." He touched a fallen figure with a spear sticking out of his chest. "He was seventeen when they killed him."

"Were you there when he died?"

"Yes. I saw it." His golden eyes focused on her.

"I painted this to honor him—to remember him."

"Blade, do you hate white people?"

One corner of his mouth quirked. "Of course not. I don't often understand them, but I don't hate them. You think I would marry two white women if I hated the white race?"

"I don't imagine anyone would blame you if you did hold a grudge against us."

"War is not good for anyone."

She glanced around, striving to lighten the atmosphere. "This tepee is quite something, but it's barely big enough for you to stretch out. I thought tepees were home to whole families."

"As the family grows, the tepees are enlarged. This is the type a scout takes when he's on a hunt." He crossed his legs under the blanket and scratched at the patch of hair in the center of his chest. "You awakened me for a lesson in skin lodges? This couldn't wait until morning?"

"I want to talk to you about Adam."

He shifted onto his other side, presenting his back to her. His skin tone was even, and she realized that he must work in the sun shirtless.

"That, too, can wait until morning," he drawled.

"No, because you'll slip away like a puff of smoke in the morning and not give me the opportunity to speak to you." She curved a hand over his shoulder. The simple touch of her skin upon his was powerful—so powerful that she snatched her hand back as a quivering made itself known throughout her limbs. She buried her hands in her skirt.

He looked over his shoulder at her, his eyes half closed, his lashes casting long shadows on his cheeks. "Do you look upon me as a block of wood?" he growled at her. "You shouldn't be here.

Go back into the house, where you belong."

A block of wood? Was he saying that . . . Did he find her attractive? Even irresistible? She bowed her head to hide a smile.

Elise cleared her throat. "How did Adam do today? Did he learn fast? Do you think he's big enough to push that plow? He's only a child."

"He doesn't push the plow; the mules pull it," Blade said, sounding sleepy and bored. "A little work won't hurt him."

"But isn't the judge expecting him to do a man's job?"

Blade flopped over onto his other side, his face revealed to her. Cradling his head on his folded arm, he stared relentlessly at her.

"Wh-what are you looking at?" she asked, running her fingers over her curling hair.

"A deaf woman." He settled his head more comfortably. Tension quivered in the air like the threat of thunder. His eyes glittered in the candle's glow.

Elise wanted to touch his shoulder again, but she didn't. She squeezed her hands together in her lap and tried to think of something else to ask him—something safe. Then she looked at him again and her thoughts scattered like autumn leaves.

His underarms were nearly hairless. Her gaze drifted to his wide torso and the strands of inky hair curling around his dark brown nipples and the springy strands sprouting in the center of his chest where the bulging muscles formed a valley. A visceral response curled in her stomach and rifled an edginess through her.

"I'm not going to get rid of you, am I?"

Elise jerked her gaze away from the drawings on his chest and arms to the ones on the tepee walls. She fluffed her skirt with shaking hands. Her heart boomed in her ears and she felt hot, feverish. "I only wanted to talk. Where's the harm in that?" She traced the petals of a flower printed in the fabric of her skirt. "Why did you adopt Penny? You didn't have to take her. You could have placed her back on the train and let someone else adopt her. Why did you insist on going through with it?"

His fingers chased a lock of midnight hair off his forehead. He crossed his arms. She sensed his careful study of her, but continued tracing the flowers on her skirt. She found direct eye contact with him too much to bear, like staring at the sun.

"It had been arranged."

"Yes, but that's no reason," she said, her forefinger dancing idly around a rosebud.

"I promised Julia," he said, his voice sharp with impatience. "We paid for the child. I thought Julia would get well, but she didn't. I didn't want to break my promise to her."

"Blade, are you telling me everything about Judge Mott? You're not afraid of him, are you?"

His silence alarmed her more than his growling and shouting. Elise looked up to confront the fury in his almond-colored eyes. She held her breath, realizing too late that she'd bruised his pride.

"I am afraid of no man," he said, each word carrying honor. "I choose to live in peace."

"At what price?" She marveled at her courage to pursue the subject, given his bristling demeanor.

"I will make no war with Lloyd Mott over a boy who thinks he's too good to till the soil."

Biting back angry words, she elected to keep a civil tongue. "I suppose you think I'm overstepping my bounds. I imagine you aren't used to women forcing issues or arguing with men." She tried to select just the right words as she meticulously outlined a leaf on her skirt. "I wasn't raised to walk ten paces behind men or to allow them to do my thinking for me."

His brown hand covered hers and her heart stuttered. She glanced up through her lashes. His eyes gleamed. Such strange eyes, she thought. Light brown, almost sand colored, with golden streaks that radiated from the darker brown centers. Feral eyes, such as those belonging to a wild animal.

"You only think you know me and where I come from," he said, his voice a low purr that lifted the fine hairs on her nape. "Apache life revolves around its females."

With his hand enveloping hers, it was difficult for her to think. When his thumb swept across her inner wrist where a pulse danced, all thoughts ceased. She looked at him and could not look away. His gaze held hers, commanded hers. His lips moved and she missed his first few words. Her heartbeats drummed incessantly.

". . . and the bridegroom lives with his wife's people," he said, his voice finally penetrating. "We trace our history through our females. They are valued and never expected to walk behind a man or be his slave."

"Then why did you want me to be quiet around Judge Mott? Why did you get so angry when I spoke my mind in front of him?"

"Because the judge is not Apache. He isn't interested in a woman's opinion." Blade removed his hand from hers and sat back.

Elise swung her legs beneath her again and started to crawl out, but another thought seized her. "Did Julia ever stay in here with you?"

He ran a hand down his face. "No. The tepee

wasn't here when she was alive. I set it up after she died."

"So am I your first female visitor in here?"

"Yes." Golden light undulated across his shoulders and sparkled in his eyes. "It's been a long time since I've been with a woman. A *long* time."

Her breath caught in her throat and her good sense told her to change the subject—quick! "What does an Apache man do once he selects a woman to wed?"

His lazy grin chided her. "If the woman and her family are in agreement, then the man erects a home in his wife's family's cluster."

"So did this land belong to Julia?"

"No. Julia's family lives in California. This land belonged to my mother and was given to me."

Elise sat back on her knees. "Your mother gave you this place?"

"Yes. After my father died, my mother took me back to her family in St. Joseph. Her people owned this land also, and it was given to me when I reached eighteen years."

"Did your mother move here with you?"

He shook his head and his hair fell across his forehead. "She remained in St. Joseph and died there when I was twenty-three."

"She was white?"

"Yes, and her family never completely forgave her for marrying an Apache and living with his people." Blade's hooded gaze moved over her. "People will think you're dirty now, living out here with me."

She frowned, holding his gaze, mesmerized by it. "I don't care."

"But you will. You were a woman of society, but

now you're only a half-breed's wife. People might shun you."

"People already have, and it had nothing to do with you."

A drop of perspiration rolled down his chest and was caught in the dark, curling hairs. Elise knew an irrational moment when she wanted to lean forward and collect that diamond drop with the tip of her tongue.

"My mother was the only survivor of a Cheyenne raiding party," he said, crossing his arms against his chest and unknowingly depriving her of her wish. "When my father found her, she was wandering alone, her feet bloody from walking miles, her body burned by the sun. She had nearly lost her mind. My father saved her and fell in love with her."

"How romantic," Elise breathed, dazzled by the story and the storyteller.

"He loved her so much that he took her as his second wife."

"Oh, so he'd been married before?"

Blade angled closer to her. "He was married *then*."

His meaning escaped her for a few moments until she read something mischievous in his eyes and drew in a quick breath. "You mean . . . your father had two wives at once!"

"That's right. It is done sometimes among the Apache. A man usually keeps with one woman, but my father's first wife knew he wouldn't be happy without my mother. She allowed him to take a second wife."

"And your mother . . . she went along with this arrangement?"

"She told me that she would rather have died

than live without my father. Like you, she saw romance in odd places. Later, the romance wore away. She stayed because of me, but she longed for her own people. She always felt like the second wife—which, of course, she was. She had hoped he would treasure her more."

Elise smiled sadly. "She fell out of love?"

He leaned closer still until Elise thought they might bump noses.

"Love had very little to do with it. My father lusted for my mother and was crazy to have her. But the match was not a good one—once they were alone, skin to skin."

Elise frowned. "I don't think I understand. Are you saying that your father was interested only in the chase?"

"I'm saying that some people aren't meant to mix. My father was . . . rough, brusque, and my mother was raised around gentlemen. My father took what he wanted when he wanted it. My mother resented that. She wanted to be petted and courted, even after marriage." He sighed and dropped his voice to a whisper. "I believe that the best relationships are between people with the same upbringing, the same religion, the same heritage."

"Now you sound like all those narrow-minded people who call you names."

"Maybe they're right. Look at me. I don't belong anywhere."

She looked. She saw a man of stunning vitality. She saw rippling muscle and sinew. She saw bronze, smooth skin. She saw silky blue-black hair. She saw a generous mouth that sorely tempted her.

Elise shook herself out of her daze. "You belong here. This is your land, your home."

His eyes grew darker. "Ah, but do *you?*"

Elise's pulse boomed in her ears. His face was close to hers, his breath mingling with hers. Her eyelids grew heavy. She swayed toward him.

He lifted a hand to her face and rubbed her lower lip with his thumb, back and forth, moving her lip across her teeth as he watched with smoky eyes. Elise's breath came in short gasps and her dress seemed to fit too tightly across her breasts and ribs.

"You'd better go," he said softly, his hand trailing over her throat, his fingertips slipping down the slope of her left breast. "Go while I am in the mood to let you leave. In another minute I might forget that I am a gentleman. Like my father, I might take what I want and your feelings be damned."

She looked at him, saw that he meant every word and refused to listen to the voice in the back of her mind urging her to stay and allow him every indiscretion.

Outside again in the night air, she stood and dashed to the safety of the porch. She stared at the tepee, trying to understand the moods of the man within it and the feelings he stirred in her. He had spoken of lust, and Elise was certain she'd just experienced it. Lust. Wasn't that a sin?

She went inside the log cabin and paced like a caged animal. Without realizing it at first, she found herself standing on the threshold of the other bedroom—Julia's room, as Blade had called it. The door was open—had she opened it?—and the interior was dark and full of mystery, like Blade's eyes a minute ago.

Elise crossed the threshold and smelled mint and some other odor—clove, perhaps? Drawn to a photograph on top of the bureau, she picked it up and went to the window to examine it by moonlight. So this was Julia, she thought, surprised by the woman's appearance.

Julia sat on a stool in front of a quilt, hung as a backdrop. Hands folded primly in her lap, she had her head bent in a diffident posture. Her smile was kind. Her hair looked dark, perhaps dark brown, and was stretched into a tight, tidy bun at her nape. Her dress was also a dark color with a high collar.

Elise brought the photograph closer and saw the lines at the corners of Julia's eyes and around her mouth.

"Why, she looks older than Blade," Elise whispered. She placed the photograph on the bureau again, wondering how she could bring up the subject of Julia's age without offending Blade.

Gliding her fingertips across the quilted coverlet, she sized up the bed and tried to imagine Blade in it. He seemed better suited to his tepee, actually, although it peeved her that he slept out there instead of inside with her and Penny. Her toe bumped against a trunk positioned at the foot of the bed. She stepped back to study it and the padlock. The lock hung crookedly. Bending closer, Elise found it was unlocked. She straightened and tried to talk herself out of snooping. She failed.

The lid lifted, held onto the trunk by wobbly leather straps. Elise propped the lid back against the bed as the aroma of cedar surrounded her. She dropped to her knees and rested a hand on the top garment—a white dress with ivory buttons. Julia's wedding dress? Lifting it, Elise peeked underneath to find a plush Indian blanket of tan and black and bright rust. Tucked at one end of it were papers tied with a shoelace, and a photograph album.

Elise looked inside the album, finding faded photos of what must have been Julia's family back in California. There were no photos of Blade. What had his life been like as her husband? Had he been deliriously happy? Somehow, Elise didn't think so. Something had gone wrong.

Feeling guilty for having poked around in what was none of her business, Elise closed the trunk lid. She left the room and sat at the kitchen table, her heart and head full. It was natural for her to long to know Blade better, she reasoned. After all, she was married to him, and if she expected to raise Penny and live under Blade's roof, she must be prepared for the inevitable. While she was naive in some areas of human emotion, she was not so innocent as to be unaware of the male's need to mate. Blade Lonewolf was no different from any other man in that respect.

Eventually, he would want to exert his rights as her husband. His needs would overpower him and . . . and what? What would it be like, her journey from maidenhood to womanhood?

She stared at a shaft of moonlight falling through the window and remembered his confession—he hadn't been with a woman in a long time. A delicious shiver raced up her spine and a smile curved her lips. Oh, she was becoming such a little tart!

Laughing under her breath at her predicament, she lay her head down on her arms and let her thoughts drift like a cork on water. They carried her back into the tepee with Blade, and she dreamed of all the things that might have happened if she had chosen to stay.

Chapter 9

Carrying another basket of wet laundry to the lines strung between poles near the house, Elise stared across the flat farmland. She blinked and dropped the basket at her feet. Was the sun playing tricks on her, or was that . . . She shaded her eyes with one hand to get a better look at Blade riding bareback across the field. He was headed for the barn astride Bob, his Indian pinto pony.

With his shirt tied around his middle, his chest and arms gleaming in the sunlight, Blade was a living, breathing fantasy. He gripped the pony with strong legs and gathered handfuls of mane, using it to guide the halterless horse. Blue-black hair flowed over Blade's head like dark ocean waves. He used his hat as a soft whip to get more speed out of Bob. Where was he going in such an all-fired hurry?

Elise had never seen anyone ride without a saddle or bridle, and she realized she was holding her breath, afraid he might fall from his mount at any moment. The pony slowed to a trot as he approached the barn and disappeared from Elise's view.

"Drat," she whispered, staring at the barn and

hoping to see the horse and rider again. Disappointed when they didn't reappear, she looked at the laundry basket and chided herself. "Calm down, girl," she said under her breath, then gave a short laugh. "If you don't watch out, you'll be infatuated with your husband!"

She was tempted to go check on Blade and discover what had brought him from his fields before midday, but then she decided he would call if he needed her. The sun was strong, and a stiff breeze flapped the shirts and dresses Elise secured to the lines with wooden pins.

Her muscles burned, so she paused to massage the small of her back and let her mind wander from the task. Anytime she gave her thoughts free rein, they raced to Blade, as they did now. Images of the tepee's interior floated past her mind's eye—the drawings, the candle's glow painting the width of Blade's bare chest, shoulders and face.

Closing her eyes, she could see him before her. Such a ruggedly handsome face with its high cheekbones, bold nose and sensuous mouth. From the first time she'd seen him, his looks had attracted her, in spite of all the stories she'd heard about the savagery of Indians. Something about him had made her believe that he was different, that the stories weren't true at all. She recalled how gentle he'd been to the boy who had tried to escape the orphan train. She'd seen a glimpse of his heart then and had decided that he wasn't a savage.

Opening her eyes, she stared sightlessly at the fields. Last night in the tepee stayed with her. She recalled inconsequential things—the sparse hair under his arms, the scar between his first and second ribs on the left side, a light brown birthmark below his navel. He'd spoken to her of lust and he'd planted its seeds within her. She couldn't think about Blade anymore without feeling flushed.

Now she had the sight of him riding bareback to add to her memories. If only Bob's black mane and tail had been decorated with feathers and bits of silver! And Blade should have worn only a breech-clout and moccasins. He should have carried a long spear instead of his hat!

Lonewolf, the great Indian brave! she thought with a smile. Had he ever *really* looked like the picture in her mind? Was this how his father had looked to his mother? If so, then it was no mystery why she'd decided to stay with him instead of returning to civilization.

Her situation wasn't so different from mine, Elise thought. His mother had had no immediate family to return to, and Blade's father had rescued her and offered her a home. Blade had rescued Elise, after a fashion, and he'd turned his home over to her, a white woman. Was that how he thought of her? Did he ever think of how it would be to kiss his new wife?

Snatching up a muslin bedsheet, Elise fumbled to find the corners. Did he ever fantasize about her? she wondered. Did he ever awaken from dreams so vivid and carnal that his body was drenched with sweat and his heart felt as if it had exploded in his chest and his breath left his throat raw and scorched?

A pesky breeze galloped in from the north and flattened the wet sheet against the front of her. Blinded, Elise tried to pull the clinging fabric from her face. The sheet seemed to have a mind of its own, tenaciously grabbing her face and hands. Her fingers brushed against something solid. No, *some-*

one. She moved back in alarm as the sheet was stripped away.

"Oh!" She found herself staring at Blade. He let go of the sheet and it fluttered like a sail. He had put his shirt back on, but he was still hatless and gloveless.

"What are you doing at the house?"

"Checking on Janie. She didn't eat much this morning."

Elise looked toward the barn and the corral, where Blade kept Janie. "Penny wants to name the baby horse when it gets here. I told her I'd ask— well, heavens!" she exclaimed as the wind picked at the bedsheet again and plastered it to her side.

Laughing, she fought it off with Blade's help. The fight loosened her hair, which she'd braided and pinned in a circle at the crown of her head. She felt the braid slide and swing like a pendulum against her back. Curling wisps clung to the corners of her eyes and mouth, and she pulled at the strands, still laughing under her breath.

"This laundry is getting the best of me," she confessed. "I'm glad you showed up to help me fight the b-battle." Her voice broke on the last word as the expression on his face registered, striking a corresponding chord deep inside her.

She hadn't seen that particular expression on Blade's face before, but she'd recognized it easily enough on other men. Her mind began to whirl and wobble like a loose wagon wheel. How long had he been watching her . . . what had happened to make him want to kiss her?

"I . . . Blade?" She waited for him to move first and realized that he wasn't the only one who wanted to be kissed. He swallowed hard, and she sensed he was fighting himself. His eyes darkened with desire.

He struck like lightning, his mouth moving over hers, hard and fast and brilliantly. His arms circled her and brought her up against his chest and stomach. He kissed her, not as if it were their first kiss but their last. Intense, powerful, masterful and so full of shattering emotion that Elise felt her knees give way. Curving one hand at the back of his neck, she buried her fingers in his wind-tangled, sun-warmed hair. She sagged in his arms, supported by his strength, her lips melting, parting, admitting the shock of his tongue.

His tongue! In her mouth, taking, ravaging, trying to mate with hers!

Elise gave a mighty push and stumbled backward out of his embrace. She stood apart from him, her lips burning from his kiss, her breath sawing in her throat, her chest heaving against the leaping of her heart.

The wind scampered across the land, snapping the sheets, billowing out empty sleeves and pant legs, cooling the fever of passion.

Blade slowly ran the back of his hand across his mouth in a gesture that wasn't a wiping off but a rubbing in. His gaze played over her like a flame.

"We . . . that is, I can't allow such liberties." Elise winced at her prim words after her wanton behavior. "A kiss, yes, but you . . . well, it went beyond that." What was she saying? Was she making any sense?

A rakish grin inched up one corner of his thieving mouth. "What, you've never had a man's tongue in your mouth before? I thought you'd been courted all over Baltimore."

"I have, but by gentlemen."

He laughed without humor. "By *gentlemen*, hey?" Essaying a courtly bow, he mocked her. "Gentleboys, you mean." He aimed a forefinger at her. "If you don't like the way I kiss, then don't be visiting my lodge and swinging your hips like a barn door in a windstorm!" With that, he strode toward the corral.

Elise stared after him, his parting words leaving her speechless. When had she swung her hips at him? Was he implying that she was *asking* for his attentions? Why, the nerve! She never in her life—

Liar.

The single condemnation cut through her automatic denial that she was anything but a well-bred lady.

She'd asked for his kiss and she couldn't blame him for obliging her. Certainly it wasn't his fault that she had discovered too late that she'd grabbed a Missouri twister by the tail.

Was kissing with one's tongue something done by Apache or all Indian tribes? She'd ask Airy, who seemed to know a little about everything.

Peering around the flapping laundry on the lines, Elise watched as Blade's long legs carried him into the shadowy interior of the barn. She ran her tongue over her lips, which tingled from the onslaught of his kiss. She thought of Darby Rourke, the ladies' man back in Baltimore. Even Darby couldn't stack up to Blade Lonewolf when it came to kissing. And Darby wasn't a boy! He just wasn't quite so . . . so brazen.

Bending to the basket again, she removed another piece of laundry. As she finished her task, her mind kept returning to one singularly bothersome detail. When Blade's tongue had courted hers, she had responded in kind! If this was some kind of Indian way of kissing, then how had she known how to do it?

The jingle of harnesses sailed on the breeze, and Elise stepped around a billowing sheet to spy Airy Peppers's mule-drawn wagon. Great day! Airy had brought her cousin Dixie, too! Elise waved happily, forgetting the laundry as she walked toward them.

Dixie Shoemaker doubled over in laughter and Airy Peppers slapped the tabletop again and again in a fit of hilarity.

Elise regarded them with annoyance. "It's not *that* funny. I'm seeking your advice, not your guffaws."

"Oh, dearie me." Dixie wiped the tears from her eyes. "You think it's an Indian custom?"

"I don't know what to think. The men in Baltimore don't do it, so I'm at a loss."

"Honey child, the men in Baltimore didn't do it to you, but they do it," Airy assured her. "You put the brake on and stopped them before they could try a deeper kiss. *That's* why you never experienced it before now."

"But it's not done just among Indians," Dixie added with another laugh. "And that alone doesn't make Blade a savage or a brute. He was only doing what comes naturally."

"But *is* it natural?" Elise asked, leaning closer to the two visitors and lowering her voice. She glanced in Penny's direction and was glad that her sister was still lost in her own world with her two doll babies. "I almost responded to him, but something tells me I shouldn't and that I shouldn't allow him to do such things to me. Isn't it akin to a soiled dove's behavior?"

"Well, if it is, then we're *all* scarlet women," Airy proclaimed.

Elise looked from Airy to Dixie. "You mean you've both . . . you've both . . ." She raised her eyebrows to finish the question.

"What?" Airy asked teasingly. "Have we both what? Been kissed? Yes, we confess."

"Airy, you know what she's asking," Dixie chided, patting Elise's hand. "Yes, dear, we've both been kissed in that way. It's nothing to be ashamed of as long as you only allow special men the privilege."

Airy screwed up one eye. "What in tarnation are you talkin' about, Dixie Lynn? Don't go feedin' this gal more slop." She rested an elbow on the table and swayed closer to Elise. "If you like a fella, then you let him know it by kissing him long and hard." Sitting back, she gave a nod. "That's all there is to it. Nothing wrong or naughty, nothing soiled or sinful. What happens between a man and a woman ain't nobody's business but theirs anyways."

"You don't have to worry about Blade," Dixie assured Elise. "He's respectful of ladies."

"Bah!" Airy batted a hand at her cousin. "He's a man, and a man takes what he can get and is thankful for it."

"But Julia always said that Blade was a perfect gentleman and that's what set him apart from everyone else."

"That's what she *said*," Airy noted with a sly wink. "But I never believed it for one minute. What sets that stud apart from the others is his swagger and that smoldering in his eyes when he spies a woman he'd like to bed."

"Airy, hush your mouth! You're talking about this young lady's husband," Dixie whispered urgently. "Julia's head wasn't turned by those things."

"Sure it was," Airy said. "She just couldn't admit it. She saw in Blade good breeding stock and she wanted herself a brood. The men courting her were either too old or too stupid or too married for her to take seriously. Blade Lonewolf was prime stock."

"Oh, Airy, how you go on," Dixie admonished with a shake of her head that sent her gray-and-white curls in motion. "Don't listen to her, Elise. She's always thought of men and women the same as she does her heifers and bulls."

"And don't you act as if you ain't heard the stories told about how Blade Lonewolf is so well packaged that the painted gals at the Rusty Keg offer themselves to him at no charge."

Elise's eyes widened. She had to admit that she'd admired Blade's "package" many times, but to think that saloon girls were doing the same thing unnerved her. And they offered themselves to him! Did he take them up on those offers? She shook her head, not wanting to investigate that question too closely.

"I did hear that," Dixie confessed. "But I didn't believe it."

Airy gave a slow wink. "Believe it. He's not only got the tool, he knows how to use it. That's what those saloon girls say anyway."

"What was Julia like?" Elise asked. "I saw her photograph and she looked . . . well, older than I."

"Oh, she was," Dixie agreed.

"Older than Blade, too," Airy said. "By about ten years."

"I thought so," Elise admitted. "Was she pretty? I couldn't tell by the photograph. She looked kind."

"She was a good teacher," Dixie said. "Pretty? Well, yes, I suppose she had her moments. She had a gentle way about her."

"I saw that her gravemarker says she loved children," Elise noted.

"Yes. Blade had that made special for her," Airy said. "He felt bad about how things happened between them."

"What do you mean?"

Airy exchanged a speaking glance with her cousin. "Uh, nothing. Is there anything else we can help you with? He's not still sleeping out in that tepee, is he?"

"Yes, he is."

Airy rolled her blue eyes. "Bless my britches, the man is hard to figure. He's been as lonely as a wolf facing a full moon, but he beds down in that tepee when he's got company right here in this cabin. Don't make no kinda sense to me."

"I've told him he should sleep in here, but he calls that other room 'Julia's room,' and he seems loath to set foot in it."

"That so?" Airy stared at the closed bedroom door, her face clothed in contemplation.

Dixie cleared her throat noisily and pushed her chair back from the table. "We need to be trotting home. I want to hit town before dark."

"If you don't want to talk about Blade and Julia's marriage, will you talk about Judge Mott?" Elise asked.

"That old bird," Airy said with venom. "What about him?"

"You know he has adopted my brother, Adam."

Airy nodded and Dixie looked vexed.

"Blade says we shouldn't rile the judge. What do you know about him?"

"I know that he's as low as a snake," Airy said. "But Blade knows what he's talking about. The judge can act on people like a plague."

"There's no love lost between us," Dixie admitted with a smile. "People around here tolerate him, but I don't know of anybody who really likes him. He thinks he's better than most everyone else, and that rubs everybody the wrong way."

"What about his wife?" Elise asked.

"Harriet has had a hard life from what I've heard," Dixie said. "When the judge asked for her hand, her folks pretty much sold her to him. They're poor hill folk and the judge traded them a few cows, a sack of seeds and a bundle of money for Harriet. Poor gal thought she was going to live like a queen, but she got a rude surprise. Mott treats her no better than a field hand."

"I always thought the judge was sweet on Julia," Airy said, rising to help herself to the coffeepot. "Remember how he'd come around and they'd sit and talk for an hour or more? Used to make Blade so mad he saw double."

"Airy Peppers, what a thing to say! Why, Julia and Lloyd Mott weren't sweet on each other!"

Airy set the coffeepot back on the stove lid with a *whack*. "I didn't say that. I said *he* was sweet on *her*."

"Airy, watch your mouth," Dixie ordered. "You're talking about things you can't possibly know anything about." She arched a brow. "You could have poured us some coffee while you were at it."

Elise jumped up before Airy could move. "I'll pour. You're my guests." She refilled Dixie's cup and then her own. "I'm so glad you two visited. I was hoping to see you today."

"Did we ease your mind any?" Dixie asked, her face pinched with concern.

"Yes." Elise sighed as she returned to her chair. "But there is still so much I don't understand about Blade, and he's not that easy to talk with. He's a man of few words."

"That's the Apache in him." Airy blew at the steam rising from her cup. "Them Apache is close-mouthed."

Dixie frowned. "You sound as if you've been around them your whole life, when I know as sure as I'm sitting here that Blade Lonewolf is the first one you ever met!"

"I talked to a trapper who knew whole tribes of them and he told me that they count words like bankers count coins!" Airy set her cup down and glared at her cousin, daring her to contradict her.

Elise sipped her coffee, lost in thought for a few moments. "I noticed at the train station that people talked about Blade as if he were an oddity. No one came to his defense except Dixie."

"That's true." Dixie twisted a curl of her hair around her forefinger. "Most folks don't know what to think of him because they don't take the trouble to get to know him."

Airy drained her coffee cup. "He ain't never done nobody any harm. He's a good man."

Suddenly the door bounced open and Blade stepped inside. "Hate to break up this hen party," he noted, his brown eyes taking in the scene before him, "but we've got more company."

"We do?" Elise asked. "Is it Adam?"

"No." Blade glanced outside. "It's James and Mary."

"The Walkingbirds?" Dixie smiled broadly.

"It's been ages since I've seen them!"

"Who?" Elise asked.

"My cousins," Blade told her. "From the reservation."

Chapter 10

Standing before her bedroom window, Elise watched Blade and his cousin erect another tepee between Blade's and the cabin.

"Walkingbird," she whispered. "James and Mary Walkingbird."

Elise had been introduced to the guests, neither of whom had shown any surprise about their cousin having taken another white wife. Dixie and Blade expressed their pleasure at seeing the Apache couple again. The Walkingbirds had been trading blankets and furs and were heading home with their leather pouches full of coins. However, they'd stopped off to help Blade get the cotton crop planted.

Mary Walkingbird stood to one side with Penny while the men stretched the skins over the conical framework of the tepee. Short and stocky, Mary had long black hair that hung in twin braids down her back. She had a round face and a pug nose. Dressed in a leather shift, knee-high moccasins and a beaded jacket, she smiled at something Blade said, and dimples appeared in her cheeks.

Her husband, a few inches shorter than Blade, had a barrel-shaped chest, long torso and short

138

legs. His dark hair hung down his back, but the top had been shorn to only a couple of inches. The short hair stuck up like a rooster's comb. He wore leather pants, a gray shirt and a black vest. His black moccasins stopped midway between his ankles and knees. He motioned toward the house, and Elise stepped back into the shadows.

Blade frowned and shook his head. He said something that made James extend his hands in an appeal. Blade shrugged, then swung around and started for the cabin.

Elise whirled away from the window and hurried into the main room. She sat in the rocker and grabbed up a book, trying to appear engrossed in it when Blade entered.

"They won't be any trouble."

Elise looked up from the book. "How long will they be staying with us?"

He shrugged. "Hard to say."

"They plan to sleep outside with you?" She tried not to allow her feelings to color her voice. Lord, how she hated that tepee of his!

"Yes. They're erecting their own lodge."

She shrugged. "They could have Julia's room."

"They're used to a lodge. You don't have to be afraid of them."

Elise closed her book. "And who says I'm afraid of them?"

"Weren't you afraid of me when you first saw me?"

"No." She met his gaze levelly. "Were you afraid of me?"

His mouth formed a perfect smile. "Terrified."

She couldn't help but grin with him. "Liar."

The gentle jesting soothed her. She stood up, intent on closing the distance between them as her blood heated, fired by his smoldering eyes and the memory of his kiss. He took a stride toward her, but then the door opened behind him and Mary stepped inside.

Elise tore her gaze from Blade and smiled stiffly at her guest. "Hello. May I help you with something?"

Mary closed the door behind her. "I thought you might like me to help you get supper on the table."

"Supper." Elise gasped. "Good heavens, supper! Where's my mind today? I haven't even begun ... no matter, I'll throw something together."

"Can I help?" Mary asked again.

"Yes, if you don't mind."

"I'll be outside with Penny and James," Blade said, slipping out the door.

Elise glanced around, wondering where to begin. "Would you like an apron, Mary?"

"No. What are you cooking?"

"I don't know. The day has been so full of surprises that I haven't had a moment to think ..." She examined the shelves and tried to remember what they had in the smokehouse. "We have cured ham out back ..."

Mary came to stand near her, perusing the shelves. "Ah, pigs' feet!" She snatched the jars off the shelf. "We like these."

Elise tried not to curl her lip in disgust. "You do?"

"Yes, very much."

"Then you can prepare those. I'm not sure how they're cooked."

Mary unscrewed the lid of one jar. "They're already cooked. You just put them on a plate."

"Oh." Elise stepped back as the aroma of pickled pork escaped from the jar. "I think I'll fry up some ham steaks, too, and we'll boil potatoes and onions. I believe we have a jar of Julia's crowder peas left ... yes, here they are. Just one more jar, so we might as well eat them." As she turned to set them on the table, she noticed that Mary was examining her as if she were a puzzle. "Is something wrong?"

Mary shook her head. "You said her name like you knew her."

"Did I?" Elise moved toward the back door. "I didn't." She opened the door. "I'll just go to the smokehouse for the ham steaks. I won't be a minute."

When Elise returned, Mary was peeling potatoes and had set a pot of water on the stove to boil. The pigs' feet adorned a plate in the center of the table. Elise kept her eyes away from them, afraid she'd lose her appetite entirely.

"So you've been on a trading expedition," she said, trying to coax conversation from her guest.

Mary nodded. "We went to St. Joe and St. Louis."

"That's quite a journey."

"Not so far."

"And you were successful?"

"We traded or sold everything we brought. Could have sold more if we'd had them. It's enough."

"That's good." Elise regarded the woman out of the corner of her eye. "You know, Mary, I couldn't help but notice that you and James showed no surprise when Blade introduced me as his wife."

"It's his business."

"Well, yes, but you weren't the least bit taken aback?"

"We figured he'd have a woman around sooner or later. He likes women."

"So you expected him to remarry quickly."

"Not marry."

Elise digested this news while Mary smiled teasingly. "Oh, I see. Did he explain that I'm Penny's sister?"

"We didn't ask."

She decided to abandon this tack. "Have you known Blade since childhood?"

"James has. I met him when I married James."

"How long have you been married?"

"Ten years."

"Ten years!" Elise stared at her, thinking she'd heard wrong. "But you can't be more than twenty years old!"

"Twenty-two."

"You married when you were twelve? Where were your parents?"

Mary looked curiously at her. "They arranged the marriage. It was a good trade."

"Trade?" Elise dropped the ham steaks into the hot skillet. "How old was James?"

"Fourteen."

"I know girls who have married at fourteen or sixteen, but twelve! That seems too young. If Blade had remained with the Apache, I suppose he would have married much younger, too."

"If his mother allowed it. She was white."

"Yes, I know."

Mary placed the potatoes and a peeled onion into the boiling pot.

"Do you have any children?" Elise asked. She dumped the crowder peas into another skillet to heat them on the stove.

"Four."

"Four children." Elise shook her head, feeling left behind in a cloud of dust. "Boys, girls?"

"Three boys and a girl. We left them on the reservation with my family." She placed a hand on her stomach. "I will have another baby when the leaves fall."

"Another one? Congratulations."

"You'll have a baby soon. You look more healthy than Julia. If you need a midwife, I will come."

"Thank you, I'll remember that. Was Julia ill most of the time?"

"She never carried past three months."

Elise laid down the fork she was using to turn the ham slices. "Are you saying that Julia lost a baby?"

"One. Maybe two." Mary shrugged. "She wanted children and Blade tried to give them to her. But the Spirits wouldn't allow it."

The front door opened and James came inside with Penny.

"Blade's checking on Janie," Penny said before Elise could ask. " 'Lise, Mr. Walkingbird smokes a pipe just like Papa did."

"That's nice. We'll have supper on the table soon, Pen. You'd better wash up."

"Pigs' feet," Mary said, pointing to the platter and getting a big grin from her husband.

"Ewwww!" Penny made a face and dashed outside.

Mary smiled. "You don't like pigs' feet either?"

"I must confess that I've never eaten any, but I don't like the looks of them." Elise set the platter of fried ham steaks on the table. "You and James can eat all of them."

James glanced at Julia's closed bedroom door, then around at the main room. "Everything looks the same."

Elise examined her surroundings in light of

James's comment. He was right. Everything was the same. Julia's touch was all around them. It was as if she were still in residence and Elise was only a visitor.

"I didn't want to upset the cart too soon," she explained to James and Mary. "But I'm thinking I might move the supper table closer to the window so that we can look outside while we eat."

Mary nodded. "That would be good. James, you move it now."

"Now?" Elise repeated.

"Why not?"

Elise studied Mary's bright eyes and encouraging smile. "You're right. There's no time like the present."

That night Elise awoke, her heart in her throat, her eyes wide with alarm. Something had awakened her . . . but what? Pushing her hair off her forehead, she reached for her dressing gown and slipped into it. She slid her feet along the cold floor in search of her slippers; then she heard a faint cry.

"Penny?" She squinted against the darkness and was able to make out the small lump in the bed. "Pen, are you awake?"

The muffled cry came again, and then Penny thrashed violently and a high-pitched scream violated the stillness of the night. She shot up straight in bed and screamed again.

"Pen!" Elise flew across the narrow space and grabbed her sister by the shoulders. "Penny, wake up!" She shook her until Penny blinked and shuddered. Her face was ghostly white in the darkness. Her lower lip trembled and her eyes watered.

"Elise?"

"Yes, sweetie." Elise combed Penny's long hair

with her fingers. "You had a bad dream. Do you remember?"

Penny nodded as tears spilled onto her freckled cheeks. "Uh-huh. Mama and Papa . . . they're sobbing . . . they hurt! Blood on them . . . they're holding out their arms to me and calling to me! Why can't I touch them?"

Elise embraced her, rocking back and forth. "It's okay now. Hold onto me."

A soft knock sounded on the door.

"Yes?" Elise called.

"It's Blade. Is everything all right in there?"

"It's Penny. She—" Before Elise could say more, Blade had opened the bedroom door. He held a lantern, and the light bathed his face and naked chest and shoulders with gold. "Is she ill?" He strode into the room, the lantern filling it with bouncing light. "Should I go for the doctor?"

"She had a bad dream. She does that sometimes, ever since Mama and Papa died." Elise used the hem of her dressing gown to wipe away Penny's tears.

"They were calling to me," Penny said brokenly. "They were bloody and sobbing."

"Oh, honey, I wish you didn't have these bad, old dreams. I wish there were something I could do." Elise looked up at Blade.

He set the lantern on the table and reached for Penny. Surprised, Elise let go and he swept Penny into his arms. He dipped his head to look her straight in the eye.

"Your parents are not hurting, Penny," he said solemnly. "They are in the spirit world, where there is no pain or unhappiness. You don't have to worry about them. They are safe and well. If they could return here, they would not."

"They wouldn't?" Penny asked, her eyes rounding. "Not even to see me again?"

"Not even for that, because they know you have a fine home again and are taken care of and loved. Where they are, it is paradise."

"Is it Heaven?"

"Yes, that is what some call it. It is a place where no one wants to leave. Someday we will all live there forever. Someday we will all be together again. Until then, you should not be afraid for your parents. They left this world hand in hand, the way it was intended. They had done all that was required of them here, but you and your brother and sister have not yet fulfilled your purpose."

Guilelessly, Penny trailed a fingertip down Blade's lean cheek to the corner of his mouth. "I like your lips. I think I'll give you a kiss." And she did.

Blade laughed and rubbed noses with her. "I like everything about you, little Penny."

Oh, to be a child, Elise thought miserably. To be able to simply kiss him, to tell him what a beautiful mouth he had and to trace the shape of it as Penny was doing. Elise tore her gaze from the tender display, chiding herself for feeling envious of her little sister. She tidied the bedclothes and plumped the pillow. Blade slid Penny under the covers, and Elise tucked her back in.

Standing beside the bed, Blade leaned over to pat Penny's shoulder. His chest pressed against Elise's shoulder and she closed her eyes, momentarily shaken by the picture they must make. A family. Papa standing beside the bed and Mama sitting on the side of it as they said goodnight to their child.

Looking up, Elise fell into his eyes. A yearning careened through her, bouncing against her heart, ricocheting in her stomach and spreading fire along her inner thighs. She stared at his mouth, transfixed, and wanted desperately to trace the outline of it with her fingertip, to kiss him softly, then lavishly.

He straightened away from her and she saw that he was disconcerted. Retreating, he grabbed the lantern and made for the door.

"No more bad dreams, Penny," he murmured, losing some of his natural grace as he backed into the wall. He ducked out of the room, taking the light with him.

Elise frowned into the darkness. What had she done to make him practically trip over himself to get away from her?

"Will you sleep in my bed?" Penny asked. "Just 'til I fall asleep?"

Elise removed her dressing gown and pulled back the bedcovers. Her white nightgown matched Penny's, Christmas gifts from their parents two years ago.

"Don't mind if I do," she said, snuggling next to Penny. "I could use a hug. How about you?"

Penny flung an arm over Elise and squeezed. "Elise, will I have to go to school again?"

"Yes."

"When? Will Adam be there?"

Elise smiled at Penny's new usage of the *r* sound. She'd been practicing daily. "I'll talk to Blade about it, but I think it would be good if you started school soon. Next week, perhaps. I suppose Adam will be there. I can't imagine why he wouldn't be in school."

"Then I can see him ev-wee day."

"Everrry day," Elise corrected her. Then she grasped Penny's comment. "That's right. We can see him every day at school!" She hugged Penny closer. "Won't that be wonderful? Oh, Pen, I think you should begin school tomorrow. Why wait?"

The school was set on the southern edge of Crossroads and consisted of three rooms. Children of all ages played on rope swings and scampered across the grassless yard. A few women stood at the front gate, catching up on the news after having dropped off their children.

The new teacher, Mrs. Doris Wheeler, rang the bell and the children raced one another up the steps. Elise moved out of their way and headed for the wagon parked near the entrance. Blade waited for her there. She accepted his hand and he helped her up to sit beside him.

"Mrs. Wheeler says there is a school wagon that can come out our way to pick up Penny for school and bring her home. It costs a dollar a month."

He nodded. "That's something to consider. Was the teacher nice?"

"Yes, and Penny is glad to be back in school." Elise adjusted her blue skirt over her petticoats. "Adam hasn't been to school yet, Blade."

He unwound the reins and released the brake. Clucking at the mules, he guided the wagon onto the road.

"You *do* think the judge will bring Adam to school, don't you?" Elise persisted.

"I suppose."

"The teacher said that sometimes boys Adam's age quit school and work in the fields."

"That's true enough, especially around here."

"But Adam *must* continue his schooling. If he's not in school by next week, I'll speak to the judge about it."

"Elise, you're not his mother."

"No, but I'm his sister and—"

"And the judge is his guardian now. He'll decide whether Adam attends the school."

"You can talk, talk, talk, Blade Lonewolf," she said, sitting ramrod-straight and firming her jaw with resolve, "but I *will* speak to that man about Adam's schooling if I must. If Judge Mott thinks I'm interfering, that's too bad."

Blade scowled and muttered something under his breath.

"Did you notice those women back there staring at us?"

"You're white and I'm a half-breed. People will stare. I told you that."

"I don't think they would stare if you weren't so unfriendly."

He whipped his face around to glare at her. "Unfriendly? I don't stare at them as if they have two heads and horns."

"No, but you don't smile and greet them either."

He frowned. "That's not my nature. Besides, in the eyes of those white women and not a few Indian women, I am lower than a snake's belly."

The wagon rumbled over the rough road, heading out of town and toward fence rows and mooing cows in pastures.

"I happen to be a white woman," she said archly, "and I don't think you're dirty or beneath me."

"Oh, yes?" he sneered.

"Yes," she insisted.

"Then you would lie with me?"

"Lie . . ." She faced front, stunned speechless by his request.

"That's what I thought."

His smug tone incensed her.

"I would not sleep with any man I didn't love," she stated emphatically. "But if I did, then I would have enough sense to do it for money at the Rusty Keg Saloon. You're familiar with those painted women, I hear."

He narrowed his eyes. "Who told you this?"

"It doesn't matter. What needs to be said is that I just don't understand you. You're a good man, so why not allow people to see that more often?"

"I'm friendly to people who are friendly to me. I learned long ago not to hold out my hand first unless I want it chopped off."

"Blade!" She stared at him, shocked. "What a horrible thing to say. Why would you assume that everyone is out to do you harm?"

"Why?" His dark eyes swept over her. "You have led a life—up until recently—that was safe and happy. In my early years, I watched my people go off to war and never come back. I saw the white armies force us off our land. Later, when I lived with my mother's people, I was treated with scorn by other children. They laughed at me, made fun of the way I talked, the way I wore my hair, the color of my skin. And you ask me why I think I won't be accepted by every man, woman and child I meet?"

"Oh, Blade." She shook her head, appalled at the glimpse of his life he'd given her. "I wish I could take away your pain."

He stared ahead, not saying anything for a few minutes. "You can do something for me, Elise."

"What?" she asked, eager to help.

"Let me handle the judge."

"Will you ask him about Adam's schooling?"

He nodded. "I will."

Elise released a long breath. "That's all I ask. For now."

He chuckled and shook his head at her. "For now, huh? I don't like the sound of that."

She laughed with him. "Am I such a trial, Blade?"

The humor in his eyes faded, replaced by something far more fetching—desire. Slowly, he lifted a hand. Elise's heart bucked. What was he going to do?

With infinite care, he plucked something off her hat and showed it to her.

"A butterfly!" she breathed.

Its white-and-yellow wings were held motionless by Blade's fingers. He released them, and the butterfly rose and floated on the breeze.

"It must have thought you were a sweet blossom. Easy mistake to make."

Elise smiled at him and felt her cheeks color at his softly spoken compliment.

Blade cleared his throat and took up the reins again. He slapped them against the mules' rumps and the wagon lurched forward. "Step spritely, boys. I've got cotton to plant!"

Chapter 11

⌒~⊙◯⊙~⌒

Bob topped a rise and Judge Mott's house appeared. Sitting astride his flashy pinto, Blade clucked the agile animal into a trot. He'd left his fields in the middle of the day and told James that he'd be back soon. Having been raised in the Apache way, James had asked no questions.

In all his years Blade had never met a woman as stubborn as Elise. She was deaf and blind to common sense. Why couldn't she simply do as he asked? Mainly, he'd told her to let him handle the judge, but she had forced this confrontation when Blade knew damn well he was sporting with the devil. Judge Mott could ruin him, but what did Elise care? All that concerned her was her own kin and what she thought they deserved out of life. To hell with everyone else!

A softer, kinder inner voice tempered his foul mood as he neared the judge's house. He was being unfair to Elise. She was trying to make a home for herself and Penny with him. She'd learned to cook and clean and do laundry. She'd taken over the tending of the small animals. She'd even started moving the furniture around and placing vases of fresh flowers in the rooms. He hadn't liked it at

first, but Mary had told him that it was necessary.
Every bird wants to feather her own nest.

He hopped off Bob and tied the horse to the
hitching post in front of the house. As he climbed
the porch steps, the front door opened and Harriet
Mott stepped out. She wore a sheer white dress and
was barefoot. Blade could see the silhouette of her
legs and hips through the thin material. Her nipples poked at the bodice. He focused his attention
on her wan face. She smiled and curled a strand of
her mousy brown hair around her forefinger.

"How-do, there, Blade Lonewolf," she said,
twisting from side to side as if she were itchy all
over. "What brings you here in the middle of the
day?"

"Is the judge around?"

"Why don't you come inside for a glass of mint
tea? I got some raisin cookies, too." She regarded
him through her lashes. "You look parched."

"Is the judge in there?" Blade repeated, blatantly
ignoring her offer. What he didn't need was the
judge thinking he was nosing around Harriet. "I
have to talk to him."

"Don't you want to talk to me first?" She giggled, displaying discolored teeth. "I bet you'd have
more fun talking to me." Her gaze slipped down
and came to rest on the juncture of his legs.
" 'Course, we don't have to *talk*."

"I'll go look around for him." He started to turn
away.

"He's out behind the privy. They're digging a
new hole," Harriet said, her voice no longer hon-
eyed. "I guess you've got all you can handle with
that red-haired wife of yours, huh? She polishes
your sword regular, does she?"

Blade sent her a cold, calculating look. "She

knows how to please a man and *she's* a lady." His aim was true. Harriet stumbled backward, her expression vicious. He left her staring after him and went around to the back of the house and beyond a stand of young trees.

Five or six men were working behind the outhouse with shovels in hand. The judge sat nearby in his savanna chair, an umbrella shading him from the sun. Sensing Blade's approach, he leaned forward to see past a tree. When he recognized Blade, he waved him over.

"What brings you here in the middle of a workday, Lonewolf? Got a problem, I guess."

"Not really. I wanted to talk to you about Adam."

Judge Mott crossed one leg over the other. His gray pants were immaculate and knife-pleated. His boiled white shirt was loose with big sleeves. He wore no tie, but sported a straw hat that he had cocked at an angle.

"Don't know anybody by that name."

Blade tamped down his impatience. "The boy. I came to you about him."

"Rusty, you mean? Has he done something I should know about?"

"No. I was wondering why he's not in school yet."

"Were you, now?" Judge Mott ran a fingertip over his narrow black mustache. "And how is that any of your business, Lonewolf?"

"You don't want my wife interfering, is that right?"

"That's right." His black eyes slid sideways to find Blade. "I'm Rusty's boss now."

"If you don't want her around here, then it would be best if you placed him in school. Otherwise, she'll be coming over here to change your mind, or she'll try to school him herself."

Mott chuckled and slapped one knee. "Lonewolf, will you listen to yourself? Can't you control your own wife, man? You tell her to keep her butt at home or she'll be sorry. That's how it's done, Lonewolf. Don't let her dictate to you. Be a man!"

Blade didn't give him time to blink. In a mere handful of seconds, he had uprooted the umbrella and tossed it aside, giving himself easy access to the judge. Taking the older man by the shirtfront, Blade twisted the cloth until it tightened around Mott's neck and brought him up out of the chair to face Blade, man to man.

"Now, Judge, I didn't want to fight you over this. It's not important enough, but when you question my manhood . . ."

Lloyd Mott's eyes narrowed to slits of smoking rage, but he didn't struggle or speak.

"Place the boy in school, or I'll come by every morning and take him there myself. His sister says he's bright and should get some more learning, and I agree." Blade could feel Mott's workers staring at him, waiting to see what unfolded and whose side they would have to take. He released the judge slowly and stepped away from him. "The townspeople respect you, Judge Mott. They'd think it peculiar if you didn't send that boy to school."

"He needs to farm."

"Then put him in school half a day like the other farmers do with their older boys. At crop-picking time, they close the school for a month so the children can help with the harvest."

The judge's removal from the chair had unbalanced his hat. He set it at its correct angle again and smoothed out wrinkles from the front of his shirt. "And if I let Rusty go to school half a day, you'll keep his meddling sister away from here?"

Blade nodded.

The judge smiled with forced congeniality. "Why not, then? It'll set a good example for other gentlemen farmers who might think to remove their older boys from the school. We must support the school, mustn't we? I suppose the youngest one is already attending."

"She started this week."

Judge Mott motioned for the workers to continue. "No one is talking to you," he said crossly. "Get on with it! I want that hole dug and the outhouse moved over it before sundown, you hear? If the job's not finished, y'all can finish it by moonlight." He glanced toward the umbrella, which lay in the grass. "Lonewolf, before you leave, plant that umbrella again—right where it was before." Then he sat in the savanna chair and waited to be obeyed.

Blade smiled ruefully and picked up the umbrella. He stabbed it into the ground, barely missing the man's foot, and felt satisfied when Mott flinched.

"There you go, Judge," he rasped. "I sure wouldn't want your lily-white skin to blister or turn brown. Hell, somebody might mistake you for a breed or a darkie!"

The judge's eyes were black, fathomless, chilling. "Good day, Lonewolf."

Blade smirked at the older man and stared him down, making him look away first. Then he set off at an unhurried pace.

"Get on back to your side of the fence while you can still claim it," the judge called after him—now that his back was turned.

Blade's gut twisted. He kept going, hating the judge for holding that threat over him like a hangman with his hand on the trapdoor lever. Someday . . . someday the judge would have to harvest the poisoned crop he now sowed, Blade thought, but that didn't ease his ire. He clenched his jaw so tightly that he had a pounding headache by the time he reached home.

Hearing the rhythmic scrape of metal across metal, Elise followed the sound behind the barn, where she found Blade. He held a whetstone between his knees and passed a shovel's blade across it again and again, sharpening the instrument.

"Blade?"

He looked up and his eyes narrowed. "Something wrong?"

She smiled. "No. I just wanted to talk. We haven't talked since your cousins arrived."

"We talk all the time."

"Not alone."

He propped the shovel against the side of the barn. "What do you have to say to me that you can't say in front of others?"

Dropping the whetstone to the ground at his feet, he removed his hat and passed a shirtsleeve across his forehead. Elise propped a shoulder against the barn and shook her head. He looked far too appealing with his shirt hanging open, unbuttoned, exposing his muscled torso. "I have nothing to hide, Blade. I only wanted to talk to you, and to thank you. Adam is in school now. I guess you spoke to the judge."

He nodded. "You've seen your brother?"

"Yes, I saw him this morning. He was very curious about you. He asked me all kinds of questions."

"Such as?" Blade picked up a rake and ran the pad of his thumb over one of the tines.

"Such as, have you taken any scalps?"

His gaze flashed to hers. "Your brother thinks I'm dangerous, is that it? He's worried about your welfare."

"No. You're the first Indian he's ever met and he doesn't know what to make of you."

Blade leaned the rake back against the barn. "You can tell him that I have never taken a scalp. Your people are the ones who started that story. Apaches don't believe in such savage acts."

"They don't?" she asked, amazed.

"They don't," he repeated more sternly. "The Apache have never been interested in war."

"Everything I've ever heard about the Apache paints them as violent people. Why, look at Geronimo!"

"Geronimo wanted to live free and not be forced onto a reservation. I would fight for that. Wouldn't you?"

"Yes, of course, but the stories one hears—"

"All one-sided, I'm sure. I was a boy while the wars raged. I saw my relatives ride off—both men and women—and come back dead or half dead. Sometimes they never returned. We did not make war. We were forced to fight."

"But the Apaches have such a fierce reputation!"

"Because we would not lie down like dogs and be whipped!" His voice had risen and he dropped his head for a moment to gather his self-control. When he looked up again, the angry flush was gone from his face. "I knew the Apache as good people. When they had to fight, they were fearsome warriors, but being warriors wasn't their highest purpose in life."

She reached out and touched the markings on his chest, surprising him. He reared back a little, his eyes widening. His skin felt as if a fire ran underneath it. She traced a pale, straight line across the center of his chest, her fingertips delving into the strands of slick hairs there. She was surprised at her own boldness, but glad for it. The feel of his skin—so hot, so satiny—made her weak-kneed.

"Did this hurt?" Elise asked, giving in to her curiosity about him.

He gave her a crooked grin. "I smoked loco weed and drank whiskey before my elders commenced these markings. I don't remember much about it."

"Did you ever go to war with them?" She dropped her hand, scolding herself for being so wanton. What must he think of her?

"I left the Apache only days after the ceremony that declared me a man, a warrior. My father died and my mother took me away."

"How did your father die?"

"He was killed during a Papago raid. My mother saw them kill my father and take his scalp."

Elise gasped and placed a hand to her mouth. "Oh, no!"

"It brought back all the bad memories of when her family was slaughtered. She grew afraid of all Indians, even the Apache. But she wasn't happy in the white man's world either. She was never happy again."

"Your poor mother." Elise sagged back against the barn wall. "She must have been glad she at least had you."

"But I left her, too." His smile was strangely sad

and tugged at Elise's heart. "She wanted me to leave, though. She knew I would find peace here on this land."

"And have you?" Elise glanced in the direction of town. "Crossroads certainly hasn't thrown out the welcome mat. I was shopping today for material at Keizer's Dry Goods store with Mary. The Keizers called her a redskin and told her to leave or they'd shoot her!"

Blade's jaw firmed. "What happened?"

"I gave them a piece of my mind and refused to spend one cent in their old store."

He folded his arms and regarded her, a grin lurking at the corners of his mouth. "And just where are you going to buy material for Penny's school clothes if not at Keizer's?"

"I stopped by Dixie's boardinghouse. She gave me some old bed linens. I'll make Penny's clothing out of those."

"You'll what?" He frowned and straightened, towering over her, throwing his shadow over her. "I won't have that child going to school dressed in old pillowcases."

"You won't be able to tell they were linens. Dixie is going to dye them pretty colors. I can use some dress patterns she has on hand. Dixie is quite talented at such things, you know. She'll help me." Elise mirrored his frown. "You don't think I should have traded with the Keizers, do you? Not after they insulted your cousin!"

He pointed a finger at her. "I think you had better curb your temper and your tongue, or you will find yourself in more battles than Geromino."

She lifted one shoulder in a halfhearted shrug. "I would rather wear rags than buy dress material from the Keizers."

He shook his head, but smiled. "I'm sure Mary appreciated your show of spirit. Now, I should get back to work."

"Wait." She snagged him by the arm. "Please. I—I have something for you."

He lifted a brow. "You do?"

She pulled a new pair of leather gloves from her apron pocket. "Since I didn't have to spend money on material, I bought these for you from a traveling merchant. I was posting a letter to a friend of mine back in Baltimore, and he was hawking his wares outside the telegraph office." She held out the gloves, urging him to take her offering. "I remembered how yours were coming apart at the seams."

"Gloves."

"Work gloves," she amended. "The merchant assured me they are of the finest quality and should last for years."

He took them from her and turned them over for a careful examination. Finally, he put his long-fingered hands into them. When he lifted his eyes to hers again, his had warmed with appreciation.

"Much obliged. Thanks for thinking of me."

"Well, of course I'd think of you! You're my husband." She admired the gloves hugging his hands. "You work so hard and I . . . well, I . . ." She felt his intent examination of her features, and her skin heated as if a flame danced across her face, her neck—everywhere his gaze touched. He nudged her chin upward with his thumb until her eyes met his. He lowered his head to brush her lips with his. His breath singed her tender skin. Elise stood on tiptoe, offering her mouth, herself. With a strangled groan, he caught her shoulders and his mouth came down hard on hers.

Somehow her hands found his bare skin. Her fingers moved over the bulging muscles of his chest, skimmed his nipples, discovered the tautness of his stomach. His teeth bumped against hers and then his tongue slipped inside, stroking and mating with hers. He tasted sweeter than sin. Elise clung to him, hoping the kiss would never end.

"Cousin! Blade? You got those tools sharpened yet?"

Dimly, Elise heard James and the tread of moccasins on soft earth. Blade cursed under his breath and leaned back from Elise. He grimaced with regret.

"When are they leaving?" Elise asked, knowing she was rude to do so.

Blade grinned and started to say something, but James chose that moment to round the corner and approach them. Blade let go of Elise.

"She bought me a new pair of gloves and I was thanking her properly."

Elise felt her cheeks redden with embarrassment. She drew in a long breath before turning to face James, who was grinning like a drunken sailor.

"I didn't mean to interrupt," he said, giving Blade a sly wink.

"That's okay," Blade rejoined; then, to Elise's utter astonishment, he swatted her backside as he walked past her. "Better get supper on, woman. My belly's so empty, it's rubbing my backbone."

He and James ducked around the corner before Elise could recover sufficiently enough to form a protest. She touched her hip where his handprint could still be felt, but then she remembered his fevered kiss and her irritation melted away.

Oh, dear. She might have underestimated Blade Lonewolf. He might be more dangerously charming than even Darby Rourke back in Baltimore! In fact, he could probably give Darby lessons in the art of seduction.

After all, when she'd been with Darby, she had defended her virtue with gusto, but when she was with Blade, her virtue seemed a trivial thing.

Oh, dear.

Chapter 12

After feeding the mules and checking on Janie, Blade sat on the milking stool and examined the harnesses and lines for signs of wear. A gray tabby cat rubbed against his pant leg and purred loudly. Violet shadows pooled at his feet and dust motes danced in the hazy sunlight.

He examined his new gloves and thought of when Elise had given them to him two days ago. Smiling, he recalled how she'd asked when his cousins would be leaving. He'd been wondering the same thing. Planting was almost done. Guilt bit at him. Usually he longed for visits from his family, but it was different now . . . now that Elise was in his life.

"Blade?"

Glancing up from the leathers, he nodded at James, a silhouette in the doorway.

"You'd better look at this," James said, switching to the Apache language.

Blade stood and hung the riggings on protruding nails in the barn wall, grateful for the intrusion. Although he wanted Elise, he couldn't allow himself to imagine that she would be happy with him. His mother hadn't been happy with his father and

Julia hadn't been happy with him. He needed no further examples.

He followed James outside and around to the back, his curiosity piqued. James stepped aside and Blade stared in disbelief at the pile of splintered and broken farm tools. Shovels, rakes, saws, axes and hatchets lay in a jumbled stack, their handles deliberately broken and busted.

"What do you make of this?" James asked in his native tongue.

Anger, hot and quick, flared in Blade. He kicked at the heap and one name smoked in his mind. "Looks like someone is out to do me harm."

"You know who?"

"Yes." Blade knelt and examined the destruction more carefully. "Must have happened last night. I haven't been around here since yesterday."

"You think it's Judge Mott?"

Blade glanced up, struck by his cousin's intuition. "Wouldn't be surprised." He picked up some of the metal parts he'd save to make new tools. "I threatened him, and he probably got his back up over it."

"Threatened him about what?" James retrieved the broken handles.

"About Adam. Elise wanted the boy in school, but the judge had decided to keep him out."

"You will have more trouble along these lines," James said. "This is only the beginning. You could avoid your neighbor until you took this wife. Now you will be forced to confront him, or your wife will make even more trouble for you. Does she know about your agreement with the judge?"

"No."

"You haven't told her of this?" James asked, surprise lifting his voice.

"I told you, she's not really a wife. I owe her no explanations. The agreement I have with the judge is private and something I don't share with just everyone."

"It doesn't matter that you don't share a marriage bed with Elise," James said. "She is family now."

"I don't think she'll hang around here long."

James carried an armload of the broken handles to a wheelbarrow a few steps away and dumped them in. He brushed dirt off his hands. "Why do you think she will leave?"

"She won't be happy here."

"She won't leave her sister and brother."

"She can find work in town."

James crouched beside Blade and placed a hand on his shoulder. "It might be better if you looked at things as they are instead of how you think they will be. She is here now and not making plans to go anywhere."

Blade rose to his feet. "I don't know what goes through her mind or her heart."

James shrugged. "Ask her. She seems to be a woman who likes to talk."

Blade smirked. "That's true enough."

"Having a wife to take care of your new daughter is good. Her cooking is not so bad, and she's a pretty white woman."

"All that's true," Blade conceded. "But I didn't want another white woman. I wanted a woman like Mary."

"Apache."

Blade nodded.

"You could have stayed with the tribe and married one, but you went with your mother to live with the white eyes. You think an Apache wife is easier to please?"

Blade chuckled. "No woman is easy to please, but I might understand an Apache woman better."

"My cousin, I must be honest with you." James gathered the last few pieces of wood. "Women of all colors can bring joy or sorrow. You married this woman—"

"To adopt the child," Blade reminded him.

"Whatever the reason, you married her and you have a duty to her." James squeezed Blade's shoulder. "Instead of waiting for her to grow unhappy and leave you, perhaps you should use this time to understand her."

Blade glared at the wheelbarrow full of broken tools. "She already brings trouble to me. She preys on my mind."

James issued a sharp bark of laughter. "What you need is exactly what a wife can give, my cousin, and the color of her skin doesn't matter. Who knows? Maybe *you* prey on *her* mind."

Blade frowned. "She's an innocent. If I tried to find pleasure with her, she'd fight like a wildcat."

"I don't think so. That's not what I see in her eyes when she looks at you. I think she might purr like . . . like that pussycat." He nodded at the tabby that had followed Blade outside and was pressing its lithe body against his bent knee.

Blade stroked the cat's small head. Images of his time with Julia came back to him and he mentally winced. "If we bedded together, she would only feel beholden to stay, no matter how unhappy she might be."

"When did you begin to dwell on the darker side of life?" James asked with exasperation. He gathered the splintered pieces of wood and threw them into the wheelbarrow. "She is sunshine, while you are darkness. It would be good if she pierced you with a ray or two of light. Otherwise, you won't be fit for any woman—especially not a woman like my Mary." He strode away, his footsteps muffled, his movements jerky with frustration.

Blade pushed aside the cat and went to stand by the wheelbarrow. He figured the judge had sent a couple of his hired hands to do this damage. Just a reminder that he wouldn't take any backtalk from Blade without retaliation.

Pushing the wheelbarrow, Blade guided it into the barn and left it there. Tonight, after supper, he'd come out and start to repair the tools. It would take him several days to make and attach new handles. Damn the old coward.

Blade went to the house. The aroma of fried chicken drifted through the front door and his stomach responded with hunger. Penny sat at one end of the porch with her dolls. She smiled at him.

"Smells like supper's on," he said.

"It's chicken and gravy," Penny told him.

"My favorite." He paused to run a hand over the top of her head. Fondness for the child wove through him like a bright ribbon. He always made time for her in the evening, sometimes telling her stories, sometimes having her tell him one. He couldn't imagine life without her sunny smile and gleeful chattering. "You're speaking better and better."

"I practice, and my teacher helps, too."

He entered the aromatic cabin. Mary and Elise were at the stove, talking and laughing as they dished up chicken and potatoes and gravy. A big pan of baked biscuits and a jug of milk were already on the table.

"Blade, wash up," Elise said, flashing him a smile. "Supper's almost ready. I was talking to Mary about the letter I received today from a friend."

"You got mail?"

"Yes. I stopped by the post office this morning when we took Penny to school. I'd written my friend, Donetta, several letters and she finally answered. She also sent me an article that appeared in the Baltimore newspaper, about the orphan train and how Adam and Penny were placed on it." Her blue eyes sparkled with mischief. "Donetta said my grandmother was mortified by the article."

She took out a newspaper clipping from her apron pocket and waved it like a flag. "It was in the society section, and the writer—Donetta's cousin, as it turns out—questioned how the Wellbys could allow their only grandchildren to be taken to the wilds of America and given to complete strangers." She laughed and tucked the article back into her pocket. "Isn't that grand?"

Blade removed his gloves, rolled up his shirtsleeves and slipped his suspenders off his shoulders. The fact that she was keeping in touch with her friend in Baltimore sent mixed feelings through him.

"Maybe they'll send for you." He glanced back at her.

"Who? The Wellbys?" Elise laughed. "That's doubtful, and I wouldn't go back to them anyway."

"You say that now, but if it really happened, you'd go back—back to your old life." He poured water into the shallow wash pan and lathered up the soap ball. "Even if you couldn't take your sister and brother with you."

Elise set a large platter of fried chicken on the

table and delivered a snapping glare to him. "If you believe that, Blade Lonewolf, then you don't know me at all."

As he washed the grime from his arms, hands, neck and face, he thought of how her statement harmonized with James's advice. He didn't know her. He assumed much about this woman he'd married, and that wasn't fair or prudent.

Clad in a blue dress, Elise wore her hair in a long tail tied with a white ribbon. Her colorful patchwork apron cinched her waist, accentuating her slim figure. Blade dried his arms and hands as he watched her pour milk into tin cups. He remembered the feel of her skin and how her eyes had grown luminous right before he'd kissed her.

"You don't have to wait for us to be seated, Blade," Elise said. "I have to find Penny and get her washed up for supper."

"She's out on the porch."

"Penny, come inside," Elise called, poking her head out the door. "Hurry and wash your hands. Supper's ready. Now, where's James?"

"I'll get him." Mary went to fetch her husband.

Blade sat at the head of the table, struck by the feeling of family. The wholesome food, the cheery cabin. Cheery cabin?

Things were different, he thought, looking around at the rearranged furniture. The chairs were closer to the fireplace and on either side of the round, woven rug. The table was near the window, and a pretty tablecloth—he vaguely recognized it as belonging to Julia—draped the table. Pots of flowers and ferns sprouted at every corner and on every shelf. Silver-framed photos of Penny, Adam, Elise and two other people—their parents?—stood on the mantel above the fireplace. He sniffed. He couldn't smell Julia anymore. Now he smelled Elise.

"Am I done?" Penny held out her clean hands for Elise to inspect.

She tweaked Penny's cheek. "You're done. And here's James, so we can sit down to supper now." She took the chair on Blade's right. "Is it my turn to say grace?"

Penny nodded, clasped her hands and bowed her head. James and Mary closed their eyes. Blade followed suit.

"Dear Lord, thank you for our family and friends. Blade is almost finished planting his crop, so please bless the seeds and help them grow. Amen."

Her sweet, thoughtful prayer nudged his heart. He lifted his gaze to hers and a moment of understanding and gratitude passed between them.

"Adam loves the school. I saw him again today." Elise handed Blade the platter of crisp, fried chicken.

"I'm glad." He selected a drumstick.

She placed another drumstick on his plate. Blade saw her secret smile and his heart expanded. Did she know how pretty she looked in that blue dress? Did she have any notion how her dimpled smile shot hot blood to his loins?

"You want me to work on carving out new handles for your tools?" James asked. "I'm good at carving."

"I remember." Blade watched with amusement as Elise piled potatoes onto his plate. He liked getting special treatment from her. "I thought we'd both work on them in the evening. It will take several days to replace all of them."

"What happened?" Mary asked. "Did you leave the tools out and the wood rotted?"

"No." James looked to Blade for an explanation.

Blade grimaced, wishing James hadn't mentioned the tools. The supper had begun pleasantly, but he suspected it wouldn't stay that way now. "We found them in back of the barn. They were all busted."

Elise regarded him carefully. "You mean someone deliberately destroyed your tools?"

"Looks that way."

She sat back as if the news had winded her. "What is wrong with the people around here? I never saw such a bunch of back-stabbing cowards in all my life!" She flung a hand toward Mary. "First the Keizers at the dry goods store and now this! I was hoping this town would be a good place to raise Adam and Penny, but I have serious doubts. How will they turn out, growing up around all this hate?"

"I like my school," Penny said around a mouthful of potatoes.

"That's good, Pen. Don't talk until your mouth is empty, please." Elise sighed and sat back in her chair, abandoning the food on her own plate.

"Calm down and eat. You've fixed a good meal. Let's enjoy it." Blade bit into a drumstick and smiled, hoping the compliment would soothe her temper.

"I think something should be done about people like the Keizers," she went on. "And I think you should ask around and find out who destroyed your tools, and then do something about it."

Blade put down his fork and met her gaze levelly. "What do you think I should do, scalp them? Burn them out? Declare war?"

James snickered behind his hand and Mary ducked her head to hide her smile.

"Don't be flippant," Elise scolded. "I should think you'd go to the sheriff or the marshal or whomever and report it."

"Then what?" Blade asked patiently.

"And then the law officer will take care of it."

"Uh-huh." He gave her a look saved for fools and returned to his meal.

Elise examined the unruffled expressions around her and wanted to scream. "So that's it. Someone breaks up all your tools, Mary is told to get out of the dry goods store and that's it. I should think at least one of you would be the tiniest bit vexed."

"I'll handle it my own way," Blade stated firmly. "Yelling and fighting aren't always the best ways to make your point. I have learned to choose my fights carefully. This is not a hill I wish to die on."

She eyed him pensively, sending a wariness through him. Now what?

"Did the white children in your school accept you when you and your mother moved back to Missouri?"

Her intuition unnerved him. How did she know where his most sensitive memories were hiding?

"No, not really." He looked at her, deciding to give her the truth. "Children can be cruel."

"Did you want to go back to the Apache?"

"Yes, but I couldn't leave my mother." He shrugged. "The schooling I was given has served me well."

"Did it? I wonder." She regarded him intensely. "Did the people around here accept your marriage to Julia?"

He swallowed with difficulty and glanced around the table. Mary and James pretended to be deaf. Penny listened attentively. Why did Elise keep bringing up Julia? He fought the urge to ignore her by changing the subject, but he could tell by the glint in her eyes that she was bound and determined to wrench an answer from him.

"Yes, they accepted the marriage. Julia was respected in town. They wanted her to stay on as the teacher." *There. Now eat.*

"And after she died, did they continue to accept you?"

He shrugged and caught James's eye, but his cousin didn't ride to the rescue. James knew he didn't like to talk about his marriage, but maybe James thought he should talk about his first wife with his new wife.

"I didn't notice. I haven't been in town much since Julia died."

"Can you buy things at the dry goods store?"

"Yes, I suppose."

"He's married to another white woman," Mary pointed out.

Blade frowned at Mary, and she ducked her head.

Elise looked from Mary back to Blade. "And, between wives, would they accept your money? Did they trade with you before your marriage to Julia?"

"Some did, some didn't." He glanced sharply at her from the corner of his eye. "I didn't marry Julia for that."

"Of course not," Elise hastened to agree. "I'm only trying to understand how these people think. I'm surprised they didn't turn their backs on Julia. I suppose she must have been a wonderful teacher or they would have done just that."

"She loved the schoolchildren and they loved

her," he said, wishing to end the talk of his first wife.

"What about you?" Penny piped up. "Did she love you?"

Blade's gut clenched. Penny waited for an answer, an answer Blade didn't want to voice. He felt Elise staring at him. Could she read the truth on his face? He chewed the inside of his cheek, then reached for the bowl of gravy.

"The gravy is good," James said with a nervous grin. "And I don't usually care for milk gravy much. I like meat gravy. But this is good."

"Thank you." Elise swung her attention back to Blade, waiting.

"Adam told me the other day that the judge won't plant for another week," Blade said.

"So we'll have a head start," James said, jumping on the new topic.

"Penny, you want some bread?" Mary offered the platter of corn bread, and Penny dropped a square of it onto her own plate.

Blade sensed the uneasiness around the table and was glad when Elise allowed the awkward moment to pass unchallenged. She ate her food but kept glancing at him, her expression inquisitive. The talk centered on the weather and planting times, safe topics far removed from Julia and marriage and love.

Someday he might discuss those things with Elise, he thought, but not in front of others. Besides, he couldn't answer Penny's question with a simple answer. Julia's love had never been constant. Like a flame, it had flickered, flared briefly and then died . . . on their wedding night.

Chapter 13

Alighting from the wagon, Elise smiled up at Mary, who held the reins. "I won't be a minute," she promised, then hurried into the post office to send a reply to Donetta.

" 'Morning, ma'am." The postmaster peered at her over the top of his half-moon glasses. "Got a letter, I see."

"Yes. Post it to Baltimore, Maryland, please." Elise handed it to him. She'd written Donetta to thank her for her correspondence and to assure her that she, Adam and Penny were faring as well as could be expected.

She would have liked to see Donetta's face when she read the part about Elise's marriage to the man who had adopted Penny. Knowing Donetta, Elise didn't doubt that the news would spread like wildfire through Baltimore society. Wonder what the Grandparents Wellby will think of that, she asked herself, then smiled, imagining their discomfort at being talked about in hushed, shocked tones.

She paid the postmaster and returned to the wagon where Mary waited. The street was busy, since it was Saturday. Wagons and buggies were parked two-deep and the hitching rails were full.

Children chased one another as their mothers and fathers shopped and caught up on the town gossip.

"It's planting time and farmers are needing more supplies," Mary noted. "And it's a pretty day, so everyone wants to get away from the fields for a while."

Elise nodded and gripped the wagon's hand-holds. She was about to pull herself up to the seat when a familiar profile caught her attention. Adam!

Standing outside the feed store, he carried a big sack of grain on his back. A hulking black man toted three huge sacks across his massive shoulders. He and Adam heaved the grain into a wagon bed and started back to the store.

"Adam!" Elise called as she sidestepped horses and vehicles to cross the street to him. She waved, capturing his attention, and a smile broke across his face.

Nearing him, Elise noticed something different, something wrong . . . His smile was crooked, tight. Sunlight touched the right side of his face, and Elise gasped when she saw the bruises and abrasions there.

"What happened to you?" she demanded, resting one hand on his shoulders, while she gingerly explored his injuries with the other.

He winced and yanked back his head. "Oww!"

"Tell me how this happened. You poor thing, the whole side of your face is bruised! And these cuts and scratches are deep. *When* did it happen? I saw you yesterday morning at school and—"

"A little accident, dear lady." Judge Mott walked toward her, using an ebony cane with a lion's head handle carved from ivory. "There's no need to fuss over the boy. He's fit as a fiddle."

"How did this happen?" Elise asked in a firm tone.

"A mule got spooked and dragged the boy and the plow across the field before anyone could stop the fool animal." He patted Adam's shoulder. "Scared him more than it hurt him, didn't it, Rusty?"

"His name is Adam," Elise stated.

"These accidents happen all the time on a farm," Judge Mott continued as if Elise hadn't spoken. "Builds character and makes a man more careful."

"What spooked the mule?" Elise asked, already suspecting that the judge had created this "accident." A cruel streak ran through the man. His black eyes and brows looked sinister against his pale skin, contrasting with his white hair. He certainly had an aspect of villainy about him.

"Maybe the animal saw a snake. It's hard to say. You don't have to worry yourself over this boy anymore. He's my charge now."

Elise placed her arm around Adam's shoulders and gathered him close to her side. "Judge Mott, you must understand that I will always be concerned for Adam's welfare. He is my brother, no matter who adopts him."

The judge lowered his black eyebrows and his glance flickered over to Adam. "Tell her that a mule dragged you, boy, so she'll go on about her business. What do you think spooked that old mule? A snake, you reckon?"

Adam's throat flexed as if he were swallowing words. "Yes, an old snake in the grass," he said, his lips so tight they barely moved.

The judge gave a wag of his head. "Go on, boy. Finish your job."

Adam stared defiantly at him for a few moments

before he disengaged himself from Elise and went inside the store for another sack of grain.

"I hope you cleaned those scratches and medicated them."

The judge chuckled. "I can see that muleheadedness runs in your family. Looks to me like you'd have all you could handle living with Lonewolf. The gals at the Rusty Keg say he's quite . . . well, demanding." His thin lips twitched. "Guess they'll have to do without his business now that he's got you."

The man's chicanery chafed her nerve endings. "Sir, where were you brought up?"

"Why, I was born and raised in St. Louis." He struck a pose, the cane planted firmly, one hip cocked. His white suit and shirt were immaculate, his black shoes shiny, his string tie perfectly knotted, his black hat tilted at an arrogant angle. He was a big man in a Lilliputian town.

"Really? From your manners, I thought you might have been raised in a barn." She tipped up her chin to give him a long glare down the bridge of her nose. "Good day, sir."

She thought her comment would have brought a thundercloud to his face, but instead, he grinned broadly. Removing his hat, he bent at the waist with a sweeping flourish.

"Good day, dear lady! I look forward to our next meeting. I hope it isn't so brief. I have a feeling I will enjoy crossing swords with you. But be forewarned. I'm an accomplished swordsman and will never be bested by something as insignificant as a woman."

Giving him an arch look, she marched past him, straight into the store to waylay Adam.

"I'll bring medication for those scratches Monday morning at school. Until then, keep them clean."

He nodded. "Elise, he—"

"Get on out here, Rusty," the judge called. "Don't keep me waiting."

Adam tensed and something akin to hatred flared in his blue eyes. "I've got to go. See you."

Elise let him pass. She watched from inside the feed store as Adam slung the heavy sack into the wagon, then sprang into the bed himself. The wagon rolled away. Elise stepped outside and waved. Adam didn't respond. He sat motionless, staring with eyes that could have belonged to an old man.

"Where is she?" Blade demanded of Mary. He stood in the living room, having come inside for a drink to find only Mary and Penny, but no Elise.

"Who?" Mary asked, too innocently.

"You know who." He propped his hands at his waist and looked around the room in exasperation. "Where did she get to? The smokehouse? The cellar?"

"She went for a walk."

"A walk." He looked from Mary to Penny. "Penny, where did your sister go?"

Penny glanced fearfully at Mary.

"Answer me," Blade said softly but firmly.

"To see Adam," Penny said in a small voice. "Just to see Adam. That's all. She'll be back before supper."

"To see Adam?" Blade ran his hands up and down his face as frustration whirled in him like a tornado. "Why didn't someone stop her? Mary, you should have stopped her! She shouldn't go there by herself."

Mary laid down her knitting, which she'd been showing Penny how to do. "She is grown and I'm not her keeper."

"But you know I don't want her over there!"

"What's all the shouting about?" James asked, coming inside the house.

"Your wife let Elise traipse over to the judge's without telling me about it."

"I told him I'm not her keeper," Mary repeated for James. "She is a grown-up."

"That's right," James agreed. "We are guests, not shepherds."

"But you know I don't want her over there— especially by herself." He rounded on Mary, his fury taking over his good sense. "And you should have at least told me that she was going there!"

James stepped neatly between his wife and Blade. "You will not speak to Mary that way, cousin. You forget yourself. You are yelling at your own misery. My wife has nothing to do with this."

"I . . . I'm sorry." Blade saw Penny's worried expression and forced a smile on his face. "Penny, did you collect the eggs this morning?"

"No. I was late for church and had to hurry."

"Better go get them now. I saw some new baby chicks earlier. Guess they hatched this morning."

"Goody!" She grabbed a pail and raced out the front door, braids flying.

Blade went to the water bucket and drank a dipperful of the cool liquid. When he turned around, he found Mary and James studying him carefully. "What's wrong now?" he nearly barked.

"You need to get yourself a woman." James folded his arms against his chest and exchanged a slow nod with Mary.

"I have a woman and she's out there," he said,

pointing a finger at the door. "Out there, sneaking around my back!" He heard his near bellow but was helpless to stop himself from overreacting. Aggravation boiled in his mind and he felt as restless as a penned-in stallion.

"You maybe should find release with your wife instead of yelling and stomping around here like a mad grizzly," James suggested, a grin lurking in his eyes.

"I will find release as soon as she gets herself back home where she belongs, and I can tell her that I won't have her sneaking—"

"He's not talking about that, hardheaded man." Mary giggled. "He's talking about releasing yourself with her in your tepee or in that spare room nobody uses anymore."

Blade moved uneasily toward the front door and stared out, hoping to see Elise on the road. "I'm in mourning." He jumped slightly when James landed a hand on his shoulder.

"Your Julia has been dead many months now, my cousin. Your marriage died with her, but not your manhood. You have gone into town once or twice to sport with the saloon women, but that isn't the same as loving on your own woman—a woman who hasn't slept with every other man in town." He leaned closer and his lips nearly brushed Blade's ear. "It is time you took your wife into your bed, my cousin. Otherwise, you might bust."

Blade jerked away, angry at himself and the truth his cousin spoke. Then he saw her—a dot on the horizon. "There she is, damn her!" He bolted out the door and his long strides ate up the distance.

As he grew nearer, he saw her pause as if startled to see him; then she continued her pace. He advanced and she offered up a hesitant smile.

"I've been visiting Adam. Is something wrong?"

"Don't play innocent with me," he charged, his hands clenched at his sides as he towered over her. "You and Mary make quite a scheming pair, but I'm no fool!"

"Whatever are you shouting about?" she asked.

Good question, a calmer voice responded within him, but his boiling emotions overruled it. "You are not to leave this place without telling me first! You know better than to go to the judge's without me!"

"Begging your pardon, but who made you king? I'm not your devoted subject, Blade. I am your wife. I am also a free woman and I shall do as I please." She laid a hand against his shoulder and gave him a push as she walked past him.

He grabbed her arm and flung her around to him again. His body thrummed with need and it was all he could do not to crush her to him and kiss her until she was breathless.

"I am your husband, woman! You will do as I say." He hated how he sounded—loud and brutish—so he let her go and walked straight across the field with no clear destination in mind.

"And just where are you going?" she shouted after him.

He didn't answer, since he had none. All he wanted was to get away from her before he did something he'd regret. Like sweep her up into his arms, take her to the barn, fling her into the hay and make love to her until he knew her body as well as he knew his own. Only then would he be satisfied. And then this smoking, black, heavy ball of need in him would be gone. Finally gone.

* * *

Elise walked gingerly into the barn, where she'd seen Blade earlier. Moving on cat's feet, she peeked into the horse stalls and was surprised to find him sprawled on the hay.

"Blade?"

He sat up, eyes widening, then narrowing. "What do you want?"

"To apologize."

He cursed under his breath and lay back down.

"Please, let me explain, Blade." She stepped into the stall. "I needed to see Adam, and I didn't want to fight with you about it." She waited for him to respond, but he only stared moodily at the beams overhead. "I was worried about Adam, and it's a good thing I did talk to him. He's threatening to run away."

"Run away to where?"

"Anywhere. He hates the judge and the judge's wife. I've never seen him so . . . so angry before. It scares me."

Blade lifted his gaze to find hers. His softened. "Don't be scared. It's natural for a boy his age to be angry, to be bucking at all the restraints placed on him."

"It's more than that."

"Yes, he has never had to work and he is finding he doesn't like it."

"No, that's not entirely true." She sat beside Blade on the hay. "He was plowing when I found him. He told me that he likes to work in the field because he can get away from the judge there. Nobody nags at him when he's working."

Blade smiled faintly. "Sounds like me."

"Yes, it does in a way. You like being out in those fields, too. Away from me."

He propped himself on his elbows. "No, that's not why I like working the fields. I like it because I can think and plan and dream. Nobody is around to tell me that my dreams are foolish, that my plans will fall to ashes at my feet."

"People have said that to you?"

"All my life—all, except my mother."

"Your father didn't believe in your dreams?"

"No." He picked up a piece of straw and stuck it between his lips. "My father had other sons besides me."

"Oh. From his other wife?"

Blade nodded. "He never knew what to make of me. After all, the white people were making war and my father was married to a white woman and had a half-white son. When he would talk about the hated white eyes, he would glance at me with shame in his eyes."

"But he loved your mother! Why couldn't he love you?"

"My mother was a prize." He smiled. "I don't think he meant to fall in love with her. He just couldn't leave her to die, so he brought her back to camp. She was a beautiful woman, and so different from any other he'd met." Blade snatched the piece of hay from his mouth and tossed it aside. "But I was hers, never his."

"Blade, it pains me to hear about your upbringing. I had so much love in my life, and you had so little!" Elise placed a hand on his arm. "When your mother died, did you go back for her funeral?"

"I went back before she died. She was ill and sent word. I arrived on a Thursday and she died on Friday. I think she held on just to say good-bye to me."

"It appears that white women have taught you the most about love."

He jerked his gaze to hers as if her statement startled him; then a wry smile touched his mouth. "But not all the lessons have been pleasant."

She fell silent, not knowing how to respond to him. Finally, she patted his arm in a soothing gesture. She felt him tense under her hand and she pulled away. His eyes flashed a warning which her heart responded to by beating furiously. Elise drew in a shaky breath.

"Are you still angry at me for going to see Adam?"

He frowned. "No, but I don't want you going over there again without telling me first. Did the judge see you?"

"I don't think so."

Mary's laughter floated to her, followed by Penny's. Their voices grew closer. Elise sighed, wishing for more private time with Blade. It seemed she never got to talk to him for more than ten minutes without interruption. She had nothing pressing to say to him. She just wanted the time to get to know the man she'd married. Was that asking too much?

Blade dipped his head to catch her gaze. "Why are you frowning?"

"Was I?" She smiled. "I . . ." She shook her head, unable to find a polite way to tell him that she wished his cousins would pack up their tepee and hit the road. "It's nothing." She started to rise, but he caught her wrist, his fingers warm and strong.

"Where are you going? Why don't you stay and talk a while?"

Her heart sputtered, then raced. He wanted to be alone with her! "Why, I'd like that, but I—"

" 'Lise!" Penny barreled around the corner and

into the stall. "Come quick! The pigs got out and are heading for the pasture!"

"Oh, for heaven's sake!" Elise sprang up and hoisted her skirts above her ankles, making ready for a mad sprint. "There's never a moment's peace around here anymore!" She exchanged a look of regret with Blade before she ran out of the barn, followed by Penny.

Chapter 14

❧⁓⊙⊙⁓

The night lay upon him like a heavy blanket of heat. Blade stared up at the tepee's apex where it opened to reveal a patch of stars. He told himself to relax and asked for sleep to come, but his flesh drummed with a thousand pulses and his mind stirred with images of lips and thighs and cornflower-blue eyes.

Coupling with Elise would be disastrous. He understood her well enough to know that she would feel truly connected to him if they shared such intimacies, and even if she were unhappy with him afterward, she'd stay with him out of duty. Like Julia. But he could not live like that again with a woman. The next woman who shared his bed would do so joyfully and equally, not out of duty or to get a child.

Maybe he should ride into town. The gals at the Rusty Key were always flirting with him. Before he'd married Julia, he'd visited the upper rooms a few times. Although it hadn't been the best sex he'd ever had in his life, it had been sex. Something was better than nothing.

He covered his eyes with one arm as he rejected that idea. The woman he wanted wasn't at the

Rusty Key. He yearned for Elise with a passion more keen than any he'd ever known. It would be so nice to capture one more kiss from her full pink lips.

Images of her floated behind his eyes, and his loins burned anew. Lately, everything she did made him want to tell her that she'd come to mean so much to him—too much. The past two days he'd ached with no relief in sight. Kissing her only made it worse. He wanted to crush her beneath him and be lost inside her. He wanted to unpin her hair and bury his face in it, then work his way down to—

Soft murmurs interrupted his reverie. Turning his head, he listened. They came again—one voice deep, the other sweetly feminine. Blade closed his eyes in resignation. Mary and James. Their tepee was next to his, and this wasn't the first time he'd heard them. But not tonight, he pleaded with clenched teeth. Please, not tonight!

Mary giggled. James groaned. Silence. A rustling of bedclothes. Mary moaned. James said something that made her moan again.

Blade clamped his hands over his ears, but it was too late. He knew what they were doing in that tepee next to his, and the hunger inside him beat its drum again. Blade pushed off the bedclothes and emerged from his tepee into the cool night air. He breathed deeply and reached back inside for his pants. He had to get away, he thought, before he went mad.

What was that?

Elise sat up in bed and looked around the room. Penny slept peacefully. Moonlight streamed through the open window; a breeze fluttered the curtains. Nothing was amiss, but something had awakened her. Maybe a dream.

Soft moans . . . heavy breathing . . . panting . . . the sounds flew through the window to Elise and brought hot color to her face. She froze, listening and knowing that Mary and James were making those sounds. She was used to them, having heard them several times since the couple had pitched their tepee just around the corner from her bedroom window.

At first she'd thought that one or both were in pain or having a nightmare, but then she knew, as any woman or man knows, even if the person hasn't made those noises yet. The sexual creature within every human recognized the music of mating.

Not tonight, she thought, holding the pillow over her head to muffle the noises. She'd had a devil of a time calming down enough to sleep, and now she was wide awake again.

Envy poked at her and she realized how much she wanted a man of her own. Watching Mary and James exchange glances and secret smiles made Elise wish for that kind of intimacy.

Didn't it bother Blade at all? she wondered. Didn't he yearn for a relationship? Of late, it was all she could do *not* to pine for Blade's attentions. She breathed in deeply, almost feeling his touch in her mind and melting under it.

Elise lifted the pillow in time to hear Mary's sharp cry of satisfaction.

Enough! She bounded from the bed and escaped from the room. She closed the door softly behind her so as not to awaken Penny. What she needed was a long, cool drink, she decided, turning blindly to feel her way across the main room.

She gasped as her gaze collided not with an empty room, but with a tall, wide presence filling her vision.

"Blade!" she whispered, her hand flying to her throat in a startled gesture. "I didn't expect you to be . . ." Her words fell apart like ashes in the wind. His sultry gaze moved over her from throat to toes. She had neglected to put on her robe and stood before him clad only in her thin white nightgown.

"Can't y-you sleep?" she whispered, barely able to force the words out. He made no response other than to rake her thoroughly with his smoldering eyes.

Her nipples perked up, begging for attention, and they were swiftly rewarded as his dark eyes found and admired them. Elise shivered and crossed her arms over her breasts. She started around him just as he started around her in the same direction. They bumped against each other and his arm came around her, pulling her up against him until she could feel the hammering of his heart.

She looked up into his face, a face so handsome she could hardly believe her good luck. His hair looked like black waves of silk, and she longed to rub her face in it and drink in the intoxicating scent of him. A bead of sweat formed on his neck and rolled downward. Emboldened by the semidarkness and the sexual glint in his eyes, Elise followed the droplet's odyssey with her fingertip, down his neck, across his shoulder, over the bulge of his chest wall and directly to one of his flat, dark brown, diamond hard nipples. She flicked it with her fingernail.

Blade panted heavily. Veins stood out in his neck. Elise trailed a hand down his chest to his low-riding waistband. Obeying a series of commands issued from a primitive part of her, she hooked her fingers there and tugged hard.

With a deep, fevered moan, he wrapped his arms around her and pulled her against him. His mouth fastened on hers, and she parted her lips. His tongue swept inside to tease and tantalize. Determined to experience his kiss fully, Elise wound her arms around his sturdy neck and positioned her mouth more completely beneath his.

His tongue was delicious inside her mouth—slick and satiny and oh, so agile. He nibbled on her lips and she felt him smile as one of his big hands moved over her hips to cup and lightly squeeze.

Never had she been handled in such a way! Oh, Lord, what she'd been missing!

Raining kisses over her face, he murmured words that had never been spoken in her company—sexual words that made the blood pound more furiously in her veins. He stroked her back and buttocks, molding her body to his. She felt him grow hard with desire.

"I want you," he whispered. "All I can think about is you—the shape of your hands, the color of your eyes, the way your mouth flowers under mine."

His lips dipped lower, down her throat and across her collarbone. Lower. His hands supported her breasts and lifted them. He met her gaze and his eyes were smoky with desire. One corner of his mouth quirked and then he took her left breast into his mouth, wetting the fabric of her gown. He suckled hard, and shooting stars of pleasure arced through her. Then his tongue smoothed over her flaming nipple, and sensations, new and overwhelming, covered her like fiery sparks.

Shocked and scared of her own body's reactions, Elise tore herself from him and put a chair between them. He stood facing her, legs apart, arms slightly out from his sides, hands open and ready to gather her to him again. Elise shook her head.

"Don't deny me now, woman."

Woman. He couldn't even call her by her name! She wished to smite him with her damning glare. "Say my name," she ordered fiercely.

He tipped his head at a curious angle. "What?"

"Say it. My name."

Understanding erased the frown lines from between his eyes. His lips parted. He moistened them with his magical tongue. "Elise Lonewolf." Rough velvet, his voice, and her name had never sounded so sinful.

"It's about time," she told him, gripping the back of the chair.

"You think you can play with me like a cat plays with a mouse? You think you can light me like a lamp and blow me out just like that? Is that what you did to the men in Baltimore?"

"The men in Baltimore never placed their mouths on my bosom!"

"Light in the brains, I guess."

"No, they just knew I wouldn't permit it."

He came forward with catlike steps. "We need to understand each other better, you and me."

Elise gripped the chair more tightly as he came to stand beside her, shoulder to shoulder.

"Elise?" His voice was a warm breeze against her face. She could do nothing but look up into a face that haunted her dreams and nearly every waking hour.

"Yes?"

"I am a man."

"Yes."

"And I will take what a woman offers."

"Yes."

"So . . ." He palmed her breast again, smiling when she jerked backward. "Don't offer it unless you want me to take it."

Her mouth was dry, but she made herself speak. "You can't just grab me, throw me down and have your way. I'm your wife, not a saloon tart!"

"Yes, you *are* my wife." His gaze remained on her breasts. Elise glanced down and felt her face flame. Her gown was damp over her nipple—damp from his mouth and tongue.

"You're right to expect certain things from me," she said, her voice sounding weak and shaky. Did he have to look at her with such hunger? How to explain to him that she wanted him but was afraid . . . afraid of not doing the right thing, of not pleasing him. "Being with you is . . . well, it's my duty as your wife, isn't it?"

In an instant the hunger in his eyes was replaced by the blaze of rage. *"Duty."* He almost spit the word in her face. "Don't talk to me of duty!" His voice emerged like thunder and his face grew red with fury. He smacked the wall behind her with the flat of his hand.

Elise blinked, startled by his quick temper. She heard Penny whimper.

"Elise? What's that? Elise!" Penny called.

"Go on," Blade growled. "Get back in there. Go!"

Elise retreated into the bedroom and closed the door on Blade's furious expression. Good Lord! What had she said?

"Elise, what's wrong?" Penny asked, sitting up in bed.

"If only I knew." Elise wrung her hands. "Go back to sleep. Everything's all right."

"Why was Blade yelling?"

"I don't know. Go back to sleep, Pen." Elise listened, but heard nothing on the other side of the door. After another few minutes, she peeked out into the main room. Blade was gone.

Back to his blasted tepee, she thought. She'd come to despise that thing. Lying back on her bed, she reviewed the past few minutes of her life. She felt hot and achy, and her breasts and lower limbs seemed heavy and full. Her pulses thrummed.

Why did he take umbrage with everything she said to him?

She glared at the moon floating in the dark blue sky and wished she could learn not to talk so much. Every time she talked to Blade, she pushed him farther away, when all she wanted was to be closer to him.

"What do you mean you're leaving?" Blade watched as James and Mary packed up their belongings with practiced efficiency. "I thought you were going to stay until the cotton was planted."

"You don't like much. You can do the rest." James handed Mary a bedroll to tie on their pack horse.

"Why are you leaving so suddenly?" Blade spread out his arms. "Why are you in such a hurry?"

"You don't want us to stay to help you plant," Mary said in her flat, no-nonsense way.

"What are you talking about? Of course I want you to stay." He glanced back at the cabin. "I was only kidding about you two being noisy at night. I'm glad your marriage is satisfying."

"You need time to yourself," Mary said, exchanging quick smiles with James. "We think it is better if we leave so that you and your new wife can be alone."

Blade settled his hands at his waist and glowered at them as they prepared to go. "Now stop this. You're staying until all the seeds are sown."

"You're jealous," Mary stated unflinchingly.

"I am not jealous," Blade argued hotly. "Jealous of what, anyway? You talk in riddles."

James placed a hand on his shoulder. "Cousin, I have tried to counsel you. I have tried to help you sort through your problems and your feelings, but I've failed. It's time we go so that you and your wife can talk. While we are here, you spend too much of your idle time with us and leave your wife and new child alone in the cabin." He squeezed Blade's shoulder. "That isn't good, cousin. You must make family ties if you want to keep them here with you."

Blade ran a hand through his hair, irritation rising in him like a black moon. "She won't be happy here," he murmured for James's ears only. "She lived in a big house with servants. She stays here only for her sister. She stays because of duty."

"For now," James said. "Things can change."

"She likes you," Mary added, moving closer to eavesdrop. "You like her, too. You think she's pretty. I've seen you looking at her."

"Yes, I've looked. I'm a man." He shrugged, dismissing the observation. "And when I touch her, she bolts like a filly."

"Once she's used to your touch, she won't." Mary glanced at her husband and smiled. "She is probably more afraid of what you make her feel than she is of you. I was that way with James at first."

"Yoo-hooo!" Elise stepped out onto the porch and waved to them. "Breakfast!"

Mary walked toward the porch. "We are leaving. Can we take some biscuits and meat with us to eat later?"

"Leaving?" Elise's expression was crestfallen as she came down the steps to Mary. "But you can't! What's wrong? Why are you leaving so quickly, and without warning?" She looked past Mary to Blade. "Did something happen?"

"No use begging them," Blade said, frowning. "They are determined to go, although I need James to help me finish planting."

"It's better if we are on our way." Mary smoothed her hands over her rounded stomach. "I miss my children and I must take care of the one growing in me. I want to be home before I become too large."

Blade shook his head. Excuses! Mary and James had come here fully intending to stay until after the cotton was planted, but now they had it in their heads that they were keeping him from Elise. He could tell by their shuttered expressions that he wouldn't be able to convince them otherwise. With a muttered oath, he picked up the bundle of poles that had supported their lodge and carried them to the pack horse.

"Don't waste your breath arguing with them," he told Elise. "Give them some biscuits and sliced smoked ham."

Mary nodded. "That will taste good later on the trail."

Elise looked from Mary to Blade and threw up her hands. "This is so sudden, I . . . Very well." She placed an arm around Mary's shoulders and mounted the steps with her to the porch. "I do wish you'd stay a while longer, but I understand your desire to be home again . . ."

Her voice drifted away as she and Mary entered the house. Ah, yes, she can certainly understand that, Blade thought bitterly. Home for her would always be Baltimore, but duty would keep her anchored on his farm.

"I spit on duty," he murmured.

"What, cousin?" James asked, peering curiously at him.

"Nothing." He embraced James in a farewell hug. "Sometimes I wish I could go with you to the reservation."

James leaned back, gripping Blade's upper arms, an understanding smile spreading across his lips. "You have seeds to sow here, Lonewolf. Many seeds."

Blade shook his head, catching his cousin's double meaning. Laughing, they packed the Walkingbirds' belongings and strapped them to the three sturdy ponies.

Chapter 15

Sitting at the table with Penny, Elise shared glasses of milk and oatmeal cookies with her while Penny rattled on about what had happened at school that day and how much she missed James and Mary.

"I miss them, too," Elise said, resting her chin in her hand with a sigh. "Today seemed to last forever. It's hours before dark, but I feel as if it should be dark already. I kept busy, but I also found myself wanting to talk to Mary."

"She's nice," Penny agreed. "And she knows so many things. Sewing and tanning and cooking. I bet she was homesick for her children, though."

"Yes. Do you ever get homesick anymore, Pen?"

Penny wiped off a milk mustache and grinned. "Not like I used to. If I had to leave now, I'd cry."

"You would?" Elise asked, surprised by her sister's turnabout. Just a few days ago Penny had been sad-faced and wanting to go back to Baltimore!

"I like my teacher and I like Blade. I like having you as my mother. I like the way I talk now." Her grin widened. "And I love my new kittens and chicks. They need me to help take care of them,

199

'Lise. I've got to feed them now and make sure they have fresh water. Oh, I never had such fun in Baltimore!''

Elise watched in amazement as Penny sprang up from her chair and skipped toward their bedroom to change out of her school clothes and into one of the simple dresses that had been fashioned from Dixie's old bedsheets. Mary had embroidered them and Elise had added roses made from ribbons. Penny loved them better than her store-bought clothes.

Envying her sister, Elise wished she could settle in so snugly. But something held her back, and that something was Blade Lonewolf. Until he opened his heart to her, she'd always feel as if she didn't quite fit in.

Being wanted physically by him wasn't enough. She wanted him to want her in every way. Couldn't he understand that? Why couldn't he see that all this was new to her and that she only needed him to go slower? But maybe she was wrong to expect that from him. She was used to men in waistcoats, men who were slaves to society's expectations. She wasn't used to a man like Blade who acted on his instincts, who didn't ask permission but simply let passion rule. To be honest, that was one of the many things she found exciting about him. It was her own tumultuous feelings that frightened her the most. She couldn't think when she was around him. Maybe that was good. Maybe that was how it was supposed to be between a man and a woman who were meant for each other.

Heavy footfalls sounded on the steps and porch; then Blade burst into the room, his eyes wide and full of energetic sparkle.

"Penny!" he called, before his frenetic gaze fell on Elise. "Where's Penny?"

"Changing cloth—"

"Here I am!" Penny ran out of the bedroom. She buttoned the last fastener at the collar of her dress, one that Dixie had dyed sky blue.

"Come with me." Blade beckoned her to follow, then motioned to Elise, too. "Both of you. Janie's foaling!"

"Yippeee!" Penny dashed past him.

"Is she all right?" Elise asked, hurrying after Penny and Blade.

"So far." He broke into a lope, and Elise ran after him into the barn and to the horse stalls at the back.

Janie lay on her side in a deep bed of fresh hay. Her dappled gray hide was wet and her sides ballooned like bellows. Penny stroked her black mane and murmured encouragement. At the other end, Blade examined the mare's progress.

"She's close," he said, glancing up at Elise, who stood near him. "You're not going to faint, are you?"

Annoyed by his poor opinion of her, Elise released an exasperated sigh. "I helped in the delivery of Penny, I'll have you know. Papa went for the doctor, but they didn't return in time. I followed Mama's instructions and had the cord cut and Penny washed and swaddled in blankets by the time Papa got there with the doctor." She lifted a brow at his look of astonishment. "I'm not as useless as you think."

He had the good grace to grimace before turning away from her. Janie whimpered, low and taxing. Blade rested a hand on her bulging stomach. Penny stroked the mare's mane.

"That's right, Penny. You stay there and hold her

head. Pet her and tell her she's doing just fine."
Blade slipped a hand inside the horse.

"Is it in position?" Elise asked, dropping to her
knees beside him.

"Yes. Everything seems okay." He removed his
hand and wiped it and his forearm on a rag. "I
suppose all we can do is wait."

Elise nodded and made herself more comfortable
by drawing her knees up to her chin and wrapping
her arms around her skirt-covered legs. Blade
stroked the mare's side occasionally and kept a
sharp eye on her progress.

"Penny and I were talking about how much we
missed your cousins today."

Blade nodded. "Me, too."

"I was thinking that perhaps I can help you plant
the rest of your crop." She studied the rafters above
her, but felt his perusal of her features.

"It's hot, hard work."

"I put in the vegetable garden by myself. I've
seen children working in the fields, so I'm certain
I could handle it. Penny could even help out on
Saturdays."

He bent to examine the mare again. "I'm almost
done with the planting anyway."

Elise stared at the back of his head and resisted
the urge to smack him. She'd been edgy and bitter
all day, and his rejection heightened her aggravation. "I just wanted to do my share, that's all."

He didn't face her, but she saw his body stiffen.
"You want to do something more? You can stop
jumping every time I touch you."

"I don't."

He glanced around at her. "Oh, no? You *do* remember last night, don't you?"

"Yes, but that wasn't just touching," she whispered to him, careful that Penny wouldn't hear. "That was groping. If you had gone slower, been more considerate, told me that you care for me and that—"

"It's all my fault, is it?" he demanded, his jaw firming.

"Should I fill up her water bucket?" Penny asked.

"What?" Blade glanced at the nearly empty bucket. "Yes, that's a good idea. Maybe Elise should go with you and help you carry it."

"I carry water all the time," Penny said, giving him an odd look before scampering out with the bucket in hand.

Elise glared at him, angry that he'd tried to get rid of her. "If you'd take the time to look at us occasionally, you'd see that Penny and I have become quite efficient around this farm. I chopped firewood last week. I hitched the mules to the wagon today and picked Penny up at school."

"I noticed."

She propped herself on stiffened arms and regarded him over the tops of her knees, torn between the urge to slap him and kiss him. "But never a word from you," she said, her voice quivering with an anger that had germinated in his rejection last night. "Not one word of praise. Not a smile or a nod of approval. Nothing. Were you this cold and ungiving with Julia? I suppose it's best she couldn't have children by you. Children need encouragement and open affection."

He swiveled on the balls of his feet, his brown eyes glittering dangerously. "Who told you that Julia couldn't have my children?"

She felt trapped, and knew she'd have to betray her source. "Uh . . . Mary. Was it a secret?"

"It's nobody's business, is what it is." A muscle ticked near one corner of his mouth. "You'd do well to remember that."

He started to give her his back again. Elise shot a hand out and grabbed his arm.

"Blade, we've got to talk. Last night when you—"

Janie gave a grunt and her body jackknifed, ripping Blade's attention from Elise. She rose to her knees, eager to be of help.

"What's happening?" Penny asked, lugging in the bucket of water.

Reaching out, Elise snagged it by the rope handle and helped Penny place it to one side as the horse thrashed again.

"Here it comes . . ." Blade positioned himself and bent to assist the new life. He grabbed the emerging hooves and pressed a hand on Janie's side. "Come on, girl. One more big push and we'll have this licked."

As if understanding his directions, Janie released a long, sighing moan. The filly spilled out in a slimy gush of fluid and afterbirth.

Blade grinned and Penny let out a squeal of delight.

"It's a girl, isn't it?" Elise asked breathlessly.

"Yes, a filly." Blade pushed the newborn toward Elise. "Take her for a minute while I see to Janie. Penny, bring that bucket of water over here."

"Yes, sir." Penny set the bucket close to Blade. "Is Janie going to die?"

"No, little one." He paused in his sponging of the horse to smile at Penny. "She is a new mother and she's tired. She'll be on her feet in a few minutes. We won't be able to keep her down."

"Is this her first baby?"

"No, her second. She had a colt two years ago."

"Where is he?"

"I sold him to a horse breeder in the next county." Blade washed off Janie as he talked. "I won't sell this filly, though. I'll keep her, and someday she, too, will be a mother."

"You like babies, don't you, Blade?"

He nodded, his smile full of tenderness. "Yes, very much."

Elise choked back tears of shame. Why had she said that his inability to father a child with Julia had been fortunate? It was so petty of her to hurt him just because she was hurting.

The filly struggled to her feet. Elise grabbed an old, ragged horse blanket and rubbed the filly with it, wiping off most of the fluid and the remains of the birth sack. The newborn's spindly legs trembled, but held her upright. She was iron gray with a few white spots. Her mane and tail were ebony. A black streak ran along her spine. Elise followed the dark ribbon with her fingertip.

"Lineback," Blade said, watching her. He stood and moved closer to the filly. "That's what that's called in a horse. She's a pretty color."

"She's a beauty." Elise looked up into his face. He smiled at her, and her heart expanded. "Oh, Blade, I'm sorry for . . . for everything." The words tumbled out of her. "Last night I was frightened of my feelings. It wasn't you, it was me. And just now, when I said that about—"

He shook his head. "Not now. Later." His gaze flickered to Penny.

Elise nodded, admitting he was right. What they needed to say to each other should be said in private.

"What will you name her?" Penny asked, flinging her arms around the wobbly filly.

"I'll let you name her," Blade said, gently pushing Penny back as Janie lumbered to her feet. "I told you she was all right."

Janie shook her head, flinging her wet mane. She stomped her hooves, then shook herself all over. Penny laughed at her antics.

"Looky, Janie." Penny pulled the filly over to the mare. "Here's your little baby. 'Lise, let's call her Gwenie after Mama."

"That's a good name," Elise said, "and in keeping with the others around here. We certainly can't have a Smoky or a Princess. Not around Bob and Janie."

Blade chuckled at her good-natured sarcasm. "Your mother was called Gwenie?"

"Only by my father. Her name was Gwendolyn. Some of her friends called her Gwen. Papa called her Gwenie." Elise started to rise from her knees. Suddenly Blade's hand was there. Smiling, she slid her fingers against his palm and let him help her up. He didn't let go of her hand. "I'm not sure how my mother would take to having a horse named after her," Elise noted with a light laugh.

"She wouldn't mind," Penny asserted. "Know what? I love Gwenie already." She gingerly stroked the filly's damp, pointed ears.

"Step out of the way, Pen," Elise instructed. "Let Janie examine her new baby and clean her up."

"Look! Gwenie's already trying to drink milk!" Penny's voice lifted with excitement as the filly nudged Janie's underbelly, sniffed, then lipped a distended nipple. Janie nickered, shifted and settled down to let her newborn nurse.

"They're just doing what comes natural." Blade

looked at Elise. There was a challenge in his statement, in his expressive eyes.

Elise held his gaze. He still clasped her hand, more tightly now. "Yes. At first it's rather startling, but then it all seems as right as rain."

His lips parted and he blinked. She realized she'd surprised him. Blushing, she also realized she'd surprised herself as well.

After supper the next evening, Blade sat sprawled in the rocker, one leg outstretched, the other bent at the knee. He'd spent the previous night in the barn with Janie and the new filly. Tonight he looked bone-weary. Elise closed the bedroom door softly, but he heard her and made a motion to stand.

"No, stay there," she entreated, holding up one hand.

"I should check on Janie and the filly."

She shook her head vigorously, so that her hair fanned her back and shoulders. His hair fell in disarray across his forehead, and his jaw was dark with stubble. He sighed and eased back into the chair.

"Penny's asleep?" he asked.

"Soundly," she answered.

The room grew crowded with tension. A light rain tapped on the windows and roof. A single candle burned on the table, giving out little light. Elise could barely make out Blade's features. She stared at him, wanting to be in his arms, but was unable to get a clear sense of how he was feeling. Giving a little sigh, she turned to move to the door, thinking that a breath of rain-washed air would be nice and might lessen the tightening in her chest.

He moved so quickly that she let out a startled gasp. His mouth covered hers and his arms bonded

her to him. Grateful that he'd finally made his
move, Elise plunged all ten fingers through his hair
and positioned her lips more completely against
his. His tongue entered and mated with hers in a
silken dance of desire.

"Is this what you wanted?" he breathed into her
mouth. "Is it?"

"Yes, you know it is," she whispered back to
him, combing his hair with her fingers. "It's what
we both want."

"You don't even know what you're asking for,"
he rasped, his hands moving down her body in a
scorching caress. "Remember last night? You were
smart to push me away."

"No, I was stupid. I was afraid."

"You should be afraid."

Suddenly he let go of her and retreated. The
hand he pulled through his hair trembled slightly.

Elise captured his other hand, linking her fingers
through his. "Let's go into the bedroom." She
stood in front of him, telling him with her eyes how
much she wanted him.

He ran a fingertip down her cheek, across her
lower lip. "Are you a devil tempting me or an angel saving me?" he whispered before touching his
mouth to hers. He nibbled lightly at the corners of
her soft lips, then outlined them with his warm
tongue. She arched against him and his hands
spanned her hips, pulling her closer until she felt
him straining against his trousers.

He went down on one knee before her and she
dropped to her knees, facing him. Taking his time,
he unbuttoned the front of her dress, his eyes
speaking eloquently to her. To show him that she
wouldn't change her mind tonight, she tugged his
shirt free from his trousers and lifted it up and over

his head. The sight of his bare, gleaming chest sent a frisson of weakness through her.

"I never knew a man could look so beautiful," she confessed. Muscle sculpted his arms and chest. She touched him with tentative fingertips. His skin felt like hot satin as she smoothed the flats of her hands over his chest and kissed the base of his throat. "You'll have to show me the way, Blade. I've never been down this path before."

He gathered handfuls of her auburn hair. "I don't want to hurt you."

"You won't," she assured him.

"Oh, but I will. That's what I'm trying to tell you."

"You'll be gentle," she said, her confidence in him unshakable, her lips sandwiching one of his brown nipples. "If we take it slow . . ." She kissed his other nipple, then lifted her mouth to his. His mouth opened over hers and seemed to pull at her. When he ended the kiss, he was breathing heavily. A pulse leapt in his throat.

"I hurt Julia."

The strain in his voice set her back from him to stare into eyes that were suddenly haunted. "What do you mean you hurt her?"

A frown creased his brow. "I hurt her, plain and simple."

"It was her first time with a man?"

"Of course."

"From what I've heard, it's often a bit painful the first time."

He released her hair and framed her face with gentle hands. "I hurt her every time after that, too." He trailed his fingertips down her throat. "White, well-bred women . . . they are more . . ."

"More what?" Elise asked, not liking where this

was heading. "White, well-bred women are more what?"

"Delicate," he said with a quirk of his lips. "They're more delicate and smaller. They need men who . . . who are better suited to them."

She brushed aside his hands. "Smaller than you, you mean."

He seemed reluctant to agree with that, but then he seized on it and nodded. "Yes, that's probably why white men often have mistresses. Their wives give them children, of course, but they take their pleasures with servants or with painted women." He must have sensed the anger rising in her, because he added quickly, "And they are discreet so as not to dishonor their wives."

She could hardly believe her ears! With colossal will, she managed to keep her voice level. "Is that the arrangement you had with Julia? Did you slip in the back door to visit the painted women at the Rusty Keg so you wouldn't dishonor her?"

He sat back on his rump and glared at her. "I wasn't talking about me. I honored my wife. I was never with another woman while Julia was alive. Never."

She believed him. How could she not when his jawline looked as rigid as rock and his eyes were clear and guilt-free?

"But she was narrow-hipped like you, and she was . . ." He paused, and Elise could feel him searching for the right word. "Tight," he finished. "My mother spoke of this once. She, too, had endured great discomfort when she was with my father. She warned me that I should be careful when I was with . . . well, with frail women."

"Frail? That's rubbish." Elise scowled at him, and he scowled back. "Let's talk about this, Blade."

She sat back and pulled her knees up. He sat cross-legged across from her and scowled at the floor.

"Talking won't do any good."

"It will do *me* good," she insisted. "As a matter of fact, I think we both need to clear the air. Julia was with child at least once—isn't that right?"

"Twice. She was with child twice." Even as he said it, the pain settled like a shadow on his face. "The doctor said she shouldn't try to bear children again. She wasn't built for it, and our times together were never good for her. I knew before the doctor told her. I knew she would never bear a child."

Elise eyed Blade curiously. "How did you know that?"

He seemed uncomfortable and was unable to look her in the face. "I knew because . . ." He shrugged, words failing him.

"You said she was too small. Too narrow, too? Didn't you think a baby could come into the world through her? Maybe because you were a . . . shall we say a tight fit?"

He nodded, then leaned back on his arms. "I don't want to talk about this anymore." He rolled his shoulders and angled his head from side to side to relieve tight muscles. "I know more about such things . . . more than you."

"Blade . . . are you rejecting me?"

His gaze snapped to her face, then lowered slowly to her breasts. She felt his resolve waver. Pushing the top of her dress off her shoulders, she tipped her head to one side.

"Blade, I asked you a question."

His eyes grew heavy-lidded and his breathing became choppy. Elise relaxed a little. He wanted her. She could see the hunger in his eyes. Confident again, she pulled at the ribbons on the front of her chemise, but only managed to knot them.

"Let me." He brushed her hands aside and unlaced her chemise with skillful, steady fingers. She noted that he seemed quite knowledgeable about women's undergarments and how to remove them swiftly.

He bared her breasts, and she could have sworn she saw flames leap in his eyes. His tongue laved the sensitive skin between them. Elise clutched at his hair and rode a series of tremors that raced through her.

He pushed her dress and petticoats down over her hips. "I can fight you no more," he confessed throatily. "I hope you don't regret this."

"I hope *you* don't."

"I won't, don't you worry. I've wanted you almost from the first moment I saw you."

Her breath caught in her throat. "You have?"

"Oh, yes. The dark fire of your hair . . ." He brushed a hand over it, gathered the ends and held them to his nose. "It begged for my hands to become tangled in it. And the perfect oval of your face asked to be traced by my fingers." His fingertips moved from her forehead around to her chin. He touched his tongue to her lips. Elise's tongue peeked out to caress his. He opened his mouth wide over hers, suckling, drawing her very spirit into him.

Her bones liquefied and she lay back on the floor. He moved above her, his face and body filling her vision. On arms straining with muscle, he lowered his upper body until he was resting lightly upon her. His mouth flirted around her ear, her cheek. He trailed a fingertip along one side of her face and across her moist lips.

"You're so beautiful, how can it be that you're my bride? What did I ever do to deserve such riches?"

Elise could hardly breathe. Her heart expanded, crowding her chest and throat with rapturous emotion. Was he truly saying these things to her, or was this a dream? If a dream, she wished to sleep forever, for she would never tire of his raspy voice, his wondrous words, his flirting tongue.

"At the clothesline that day . . . remember?"

"Oh, yes," she said, sighing. How could she forget?

"I have never wanted a woman so much in all my life. Your mouth tasted sweeter than honey." He kissed her, his tongue dipping into the honeypot. "When I look at you, I can't believe that you have been placed in my path. I think that you can't be happy here. You are too fine for this place, too fine for this man."

She smoothed her thumbs over his high, proud cheekbones. "I've been your blushing bride for too long. Make me your wife, Blade Lonewolf. Make me your woman."

Chapter 16

With the lamps extinguished and only flashes of lightning illuminating the room, Elise and Blade rose and finished undressing each other. A sweet fever built within Elise as she accepted Blade's whispers of appreciation and anticipation.

The sight of his nakedness awed her. She pressed the palms of her hands upon his chest, so taut, so powerfully muscled. The intricate tattoos were barely visible, and only when lightning sizzled brightness into the room. His wide torso tapered to his waist and hips. His stomach was flat, ridged with muscle. Elise stared at his manhood, stunned by its size, its color, its shape, everything about it. It thrust from a nest of dark hair, proud and erect. She wanted to touch it, but she didn't, unsure how he would react to such an advance on her part.

He took her in his arms, his mouth moving over hers, his body angling hers down until she lay on the floor beneath him. She stroked his back as his mouth continued to court hers with soft, plucking kisses. He tucked her more securely beneath his big body and kissed her until her lips felt swollen and slick.

His tongue tapped against her lips and she

214

opened her mouth wide for the magic he could create. She traded tongue caresses with him, stroking and sliding and making purring noises of pleasure deep in her throat. She couldn't get enough of him. Clutching at his shoulders, she ran her hands restlessly over his back and down his spine to his hips. Kneading his tight buttocks, she pulled him closer, wanting that connection her body craved. He stroked her from shoulder to thigh, his fingers spread wide, his tongue spearing her mouth, his hips beginning to rock forward and back.

He caught her behind one knee and brought her leg up to ride high on his hip. His hard member was impossible to ignore. Elise directed one hand down between their bodies and discovered hot, satiny skin. She made a fist around him. He stilled and his breath whistled down his throat as he flung back his head, eyes closed, mouth pulled in a grimace.

"I don't mean to hurt you," she said, her fingertips dancing lightly up and down his length.

"You're not hurting me," he said between gritted teeth.

"Then why are you grimacing?"

He lowered his head to her exposed breasts and flicked one stiff nipple with the curled tip of his tongue. Pleasure shot through her like an arrow and Elise arched her back and moaned.

"Why are you doing that?" he asked, kissing the pebbled center of her other breast. "Could it be that it feels so good that you think you might die?"

"Oh, yes," she breathed, her fingers tightening on his organ again. He was so big, so thick! Her thumb explored the moist tip. He emitted a ragged sound and kissed her hard and long. When Elise grew dizzy, she broke free of his mouth. "You take my breath away!"

"Then let me give it back." His sipping lips skimmed down her throat, seared the skin between her breasts and danced like a flame over her stomach.

Her quick series of gasps evolved into panting when he nuzzled the thick thatch of auburn curls. She parted her thighs. He tasted her, his tongue delving, exploring. She shivered and the room swam before her eyes.

"Oh, no, no," she begged, clutching his head. "You shouldn't do that."

"I want all of you," he murmured. "You taste like milk and honey, my sweet wife."

Sweet wife. She melted beneath him.

Was this the Indian way? she wondered, her thoughts hazy and malformed like wisps of smoke. Was this how the Apache men made love to their women? With their mouths and tongues on those most private of places?

The mysteries of their bodies overwhelmed her. She grew moist and heavy. Her body throbbed with a hundred pulses and a roaring commenced in her ears. Something shifted in her stomach, then spiraled through her body as he continued to nuzzle her, kiss her, caress her. Elise drove her fingers through his hair and held on tight as a powerful force thundered through her body. She shuddered violently, her throat flexing and releasing sounds of wonder, of passion, of carnal pleasure.

When she returned from that shattering apex, she blinked and saw that Blade had shifted to fit his hips between her thighs. He smiled at her and pushed a damp lock of her hair off her temple. Gently, slowly, he guided himself into her. His intrusion shocked her body, making it tighten. He waited.

"I . . . I'm sorry," she murmured, but he shook his head and pressed tender kisses to her lips.

"I am satisfied. Don't be sorry."

With horror, she realized he was preparing to leave her. She clutched his hips and pulled him toward her.

"I am *not* satisfied," she told him. "And I won't be until we are one."

"But, Elise, you are small and I—"

She gripped him and guided him to her. Locking her heels at the base of his spine, she proved her determination by thrusting her hips forward. He caught her buttocks in his hands and lifted her higher to receive him.

Bracing himself, he entered her slowly, experimentally. Elise's body accepted him, adjusted to him, gloved him. She knew a moment of knifing pain that brought sudden tears to her eyes, but passion reigned supreme. She sank her teeth into her lower lip and held onto Blade's shoulders, unsure of what to do, but wanting to do right by him. She'd never known anyone like him. From her tragedy had come this man, making up for much of the sadness she'd endured since her parents' deaths. And now he was smiling at her, his brown eyes warm with understanding and tenderness, his hands gentle and instructive.

He moved in and out of her and she cleaved to him, so caught up in the myriad of new sensations that she was barely able to initiate anything. She had time only to react by kissing him feverishly, by kneading his shoulders and upper arms and by wrapping her legs around his undulating hips as he took her on a journey to fulfillment.

He filled her completely. He commanded her wholly. Her earlier notions of lovemaking fell to ashes. Something shattered inside her, releasing waves of pleasure. She heard herself moaning. She felt her head thrashing as shudders convulsed her. Bright lights flashed behind her eyelids and she murmured Blade's name as if in a fever. She kissed his shoulder and gave a little whimper when he burst inside her in a shower of embers.

Collapsing in her arms, he breathed her name on a long, languid sigh. He held her against his warm body as rain tapped against the windowpanes and the thunder grew distant. Elise skimmed her fingertips down his spine and breathed in his musky scent.

She belonged to him now. Body and soul.

Elise had no idea when she fell asleep. Blade's soft, probing lips awakened her. She found herself still on the floor with Blade lying beside her. He held a long feather—an eagle's feather, she thought—and he used it to trace a pattern around her breasts, down around her navel, back up to her nipples. She grabbed his wrist to stop him.

"How long have I been asleep?"

"Minutes."

She raised her head to look across the room. It was no longer darkest night. The rain clouds had dispersed and the moon had emerged.

"More than minutes," she corrected him. "We didn't wake up Penny, did we?"

"No." He kissed her cheek. "And it's hours before dawn. How do you feel?" His gaze flashed to her lower body. "Can I do anything for you?"

She stroked his rough cheek with the back of her hand. "Yes, you can make love to me again."

His brows lifted. "Now?"

"Do you have something better to do?"

He laughed wickedly and cupped her between the legs. Her squeak of shock was muffled by his mouth and tongue. When the kiss finally ended, Elise glanced over his shoulder, suddenly worried about Penny finding them.

"Let's go to your bedroom, Blade," she suggested. "Just in case Penny gets up early or needs to visit the outhouse."

"I like it here."

"But Penny might—"

He denied her request by plucking kisses from her lips and caressing her nipples with the feather. Again her bones melted and all rational thought fled. She moved with him, returned his feverish kisses and accepted him once more into her body. Though it was a tight fit, it was a wondrous pleasure, for he filled all her emptiness and touched off fiery sparks deep, deep inside her. She loved the way his body surged against hers, the guttural sounds he emitted, the manipulation of his fingers on her breasts and mound, the slippery, sucking slide of him. He was a powerful beast moving over her, yet she felt in control until that shattering moment when both of them were controlled by passion alone.

She was keenly aware of his release into her body and she realized that what they were doing went beyond earthy pleasure. They could be making a baby.

A baby. She closed her eyes and held him fast. His breath spread against the side of her face, and his body was slick with perspiration. No doubt he would be a good father and she would be a loving mother, but would they be wise to have a child before she was certain of his happiness with her? Because she wasn't sure of anything about him. Even now she sensed him holding back. She had his body, but not his heart.

Over his shoulder, she spied the bedroom doors, side by side, both closed. One, it seemed, was permanently shut to her. Julia's room.

His refusal to bed her in that room rankled Elise. Why was he clinging to Julia's memory? Sometimes she felt that he was struggling with guilt when he thought of Julia. But why? What had he done to feel guilty about? And what kind of marriage had he had with Julia? The questions buzzed, but she doubted that Blade would be in the mood to answer them. She knew she should be happy that she'd convinced him to exercise his husbandly duties. At least she had dispelled his silly opinion of small-framed white women.

Now she had only to win his trust and his heart. She sighed heavily at the thought.

"What's wrong?" Blade raised his head to look at her. "Are you regretting becoming my wife?"

She smiled and curled a lock of his inky hair around her finger. "Of course not." She snuggled into his embrace, using his arm as a pillow.

She realized she'd been wrong in what she wanted. She didn't want to be only his wife. She wanted to be his one, true love.

Something, she suspected, Julia had never been.

Pouring Blade another cup of coffee the next morning, Elise blew playfully at the black hair curling over his collar. "You need a haircut."

She placed the coffeepot on the stove and started to resume her place at the table, but he caught her around the waist and hauled her into his lap. He kissed her lips, her throat, the underside of her jaw.

Elise looked past his shoulder to the front door, keeping an eye out for Penny, who was gathering eggs and feeding the chickens.

"Do you think Penny noticed there was something different about us this morning?" She combed his hair with her fingers, flicking a dark lock so that it fell rakishly across his forehead.

"What would she notice?" His voice was muffled against her skin. His tongue tickled over a fluttering pulse behind her ear.

"Well, that we . . . can't keep our eyes off each other."

He chuckled and looked at her. "Or our hands." Even as he said it, his fingers worked two buttons free on her dress. "Your breasts are the prettiest I've ever seen, my Elise. So white with those pink nipples. And they taste better than ice cream or honey or any sweet thing I can imagine."

Elise shivered, wanting his mouth on her, tugging at her breasts, torturing her nipples, which were already puckering beneath her chemise.

"I want to see your whole body bathed in sunlight," he whispered. "Then in moonlight. Then in sunlight again."

"Oh, Blade, I want you so." She pressed her mouth hungrily to his and felt her body melt, making itself a giving vessel for his.

"Someone's coming!" Penny called from the porch yard. "I think it's Miss Peppers!"

Blade muttered an expression foul enough to make Elise blush. She scrambled off his lap and buttoned her dress while he strode almost angrily to the door.

He turned back to her, his face grim, his eyes still shining with desire. With a weary sigh, he shrugged his suspenders up onto his shoulders. "Damn poor timing, but we can't be rude."

"Of course not," Elise agreed, though she was glad that he was irritated at the intrusion.

He waved and stepped out onto the porch. "Good morning, Airy. Come inside. There's still coffee in the pot."

Elise set a clean cup and saucer on the table and poured black coffee into the cup. Airy entered, pulling off her gloves and yanking at her sunbonnet ribbons.

"I tell you, I'm mad enough to eat the devil, horns and all." She slapped her gloves inside her bonnet and threw the whole mess into the rocker. "I know who did it, too. I know as sure as I'm standing here."

"Who?" Blade asked.

Airy glared at him as if he'd called her a bad name. "Don't you play stupid with me, Blade Lonewolf. You know who did it, too, and it's high time we both stopped going blind around him." She pressed upward on her tiptoes in a feeble attempt to be at eye level with Blade. "Some things are more important than land or other worldly possessions. Things like honor and doing what's right."

"Sit down, Airy, and have a cup of coffee," Elise urged. "And do tell us what you're so upset about."

Airy plunked herself down into a chair. "My still was smashed last night."

"Your moonshine still? Who did it?" Elise asked with a gasp.

Airy closed her eyes and swiveled her head around, so that when she opened her eyes again, she focused them squarely on Blade. "Tell her, big man. Tell her who did it."

Blade folded his arms against his chest and chewed on the inside of one cheek. Then, with a shake of his head and a grimace, he turned away from the two women. "Mott." The name carried clear as a bell.

"Judge Mott?" Elise repeated. "Why would he smash your still, Airy?"

"'Cause he doesn't like any woman to make money, that's why. He thinks alls we're good for is cooking, cleaning and having babies. He thinks we all need to get a man and let the man make the money. Why, he's been fuming about me and Dixie's still since last year. Last night he sent over a couple of his field hands to smash it up."

"You saw them?"

"I didn't have to see them," Airy said. "Some things you just know—like you know a good man from a bad man without him saying a word. Lloyd Mott is bad plumb through."

"Oh, dear, and Adam lives with him." Elise picked up a dishcloth and twisted it into a tight cord. "Blade, do you agree with Airy? Is Adam in danger living with that man? I never liked the looks of the judge. He's got those awful black eyes that reflect no light." She realized she was rattling. "Blade?"

He straddled a chair. "I'll help you rebuild the still, Airy. We'll make it better than it was before."

Airy landed the flat of her hand against the table. "You with me or agin me, Lonewolf? I'm here to tell you I'm declaring war on that old devil."

"War?" He smiled indulgently. "You think the judge will take cover when he hears about me and you joining up and forming a war party?"

Airy grinned. "Then you're with me, are you? By damn, I knew you'd land on the right side if somebody goosed you and made you jump."

He held up a cautionary hand. "I'm not interested in wars, Airy. Besides, I've got more to lose than a whiskey still."

What did he have to lose? Elise wondered, and hoped he or Airy would reveal the details without her having to ask.

"I know what you got invested," Airy allowed. "But will you surrender everything for this here land? Will you go around with your tail between your legs? Will you let the whole town see that you'd lick the judge's boots just to keep hold of this here—" Airy clamped her jaws together. "I see I've riled you."

Elise glanced at Blade and swallowed hard. Yes, he was riled. No doubt about it. The veins in his neck stood out and a dark tinge of red stained his neck and face. He'd bunched his hands into tight fists, dangerous fists.

"Blade, Airy, don't go on like this," Elise pleaded. "Airy, you've had a bad morning, finding your still destroyed and all. Blade, you understand that Airy didn't mean what she said. She's upset, that's all."

"She meant it," Blade said, his lips barely moving.

Airy shrugged. "I ain't going to lie. I meant every word."

"Airy!" Elise said, shocked. "You don't think so lowly of Blade. I know you don't!"

"I don't think lowly of him a'tall," Airy said. "I just think that if he don't stand up on his hind legs now, I'm going to have to change my opinion of him."

"Airy, I am very close to asking you to leave my home," Blade said, his voice deeply dangerous.

"Let's calm down, please." Elise set a cup in front of Blade and poured him some coffee. "Why do you think the judge smashed your still, Airy?"

"Because he as much as said he was going to at church a few Sundays ago. Came up to me after the service and told me I shouldn't be allowed inside the chapel, seeing as how I sold moonshine. I told him that Crack Metzer and Enis Holstrom should be barred as well, since they'd both been making whiskey a lot longer than me." She blew at the coffee before taking a sip. "Then he told me that Crack and Enis got families to feed and I was only feathering my nest for me, myself and I. He looked me square in the eye and said he wouldn't be surprised if'n my still were put outta business." She swallowed more hot coffee, her eyes watering as the scalding liquid went down.

"Well!" Elise looked from Airy to Blade. He stared moodily at Airy. "Sounds as if he did everything but leave his calling card, wouldn't you agree, Blade?"

Blade remained stoic and silent.

"I heard tell that he busted up all your tools, too." Airy leaned on one elbow and narrowed an eye at Blade. "What did you do to him to make him strike back at you?"

Elise waited, but it was obvious Blade wasn't about to answer. She did. "He asked the judge to send Adam to school. The judge didn't appreciate the advice."

Airy sat back in her chair and crossed one thin leg over the other. Her split skirt hiked up enough to display the tops of her scuffed boots. "I can see you're fuming with me, Blade Lonewolf, and I do regret that. I reckon I regret it as much as you regret making a deal with Mott. I told you not to shake hands with the man. I told you it would bring you nothing but grief."

Penny's laughter chimed in the distance and Blade's expression softened. He glanced out the door, then returned his damning gaze to Airy.

"It was a good trade. I have no regrets."

"Oh, what you got for that money bettered your life, it's true, but you're lying about having no regrets. Every time you look at that man, you regret having to treat him better than you would a mangy dog."

"Excuse me, but what deal are you talking about?" Elise broke in, her patience exhausted. When Airy stared at her in openmouthed shock, she braced herself and swung around to Blade. "Would you please tell me, Blade?"

"It's nothing for you to worry about."

"Good, then it won't hurt me when you tell me," she insisted.

Airy hooked an elbow around the back of her chair and sipped her coffee. "Why, shoot, Blade, I thought sure you would have told your wife about your deal with the judge. I didn't know it was a big secret."

"It's no secret, but it's not yours to pass around either."

"What?" Elise demanded. "I gather that you've promised some land to the judge. Or have you rented some to him?"

Blade drew in a chest-swelling breath. "The judge gave me some money and I put my land up as collateral. The note's due soon."

"And if he don't pay up, the judge gets his land," Airy added with a frown of concern.

"*All* of the land?" Elise asked, then gasped when Airy and Blade nodded. Numbly, she stood and crossed the room to the doorway. The land undulated before her, then blurred. The land. Their livelihood. The bedrock of their new family. She wiped aside the tears that had gathered in her eyes, and realized that the parcel of soil and grass and trees was more than property. Blade loved the land, and Elise and Penny had begun to think of it as their home. Would they lose it? A spear of bright hope cut through her gloominess and she pivoted to face Blade again.

"But you'll be able to pay the judge back, won't you?" she asked.

Blade stared morosely into his coffee cup. "I don't know. It doesn't look good."

Elise covered her heart in reaction to a stab of pain there. "Oh, Blade . . . n-not the land. He can't take your land."

"I mean to talk to him about giving me a little more time. I figure he'll be reasonable."

"Ha!" Airy slapped the table. "Yeah, he'll be as reasonable as a stepped-on rattler!" She aimed a finger at Blade and squinted as if leveling him in her sights. "He's licking his chops already and anticipatin' adding this sixty acres to his holdings. He might let you share crop, if you smile and say 'Pretty please.'"

Pieces began to fall in place as Elise stared at Blade. Suddenly she understood his reluctance to cross his neighbor and his request that she stay away from the judge's home. But there was one big piece missing from the puzzle.

"Blade, why did you need money? Why did you have to borrow from that man?" She spread out her hands and looked around at the meager cabin and furnishings. "What did you need so badly?"

His eyes seemed sunken in their sockets, and the skin around them appeared to be bruised. "A better life, like Airy said," he rasped, then cleared his throat. "And something I could not give my wife," he added, his voice hoarse, raw. "A child."

Chapter 17

Sympathy for him closed her throat. Elise looked from Blade to Airy, and the older woman pushed herself up from the chair.

"You did your part, Blade. The good Lord just didn't want it to happen that way. Guess He wanted Penny and Elise to share this home with you." She came around the table and placed a hand on his shoulder. "You're the worst I ever saw about blaming yourself for happenings that you had no say so in, one way or t'other."

Elise smoothed her damp palms down her rust colored skirt. *I should be comforting him*, she thought. *Not Airy.* Her reluctance and awkwardness served to illuminate her dubious place in his life. His love-making had thrilled her, answered her craving for him, but she remained in the dark about where she stood. By his side or in the background?

How did one reach a man with such pride? How could a woman truly know her man if he showed his heart in glimpses and guarded it zealously? And to be truthful, she was angry at him for not having confided in her before now. He might not have told her if Airy hadn't spilled the beans, leaving him no choice.

"I should be going," Airy announced. She patted Blade's shoulder again before retrieving her hat and gloves. "I got all stirred up and came over here in a huff. Probably said things I shouldn't have." She smiled at Elise. "Hope y'all don't hold it agin me. I get so mad sometimes ..." She shook her head and laughed.

"Don't be silly, Airy." Elise placed an arm around the woman's bony shoulders. "We don't blame you one bit for being mad, and we sure don't hold it against you."

"I'll help you rebuild the still."

Airy and Elise both turned back to Blade. He ran a blunt fingertip around the rim of his coffee cup, and a smile poked at one corner of his mouth.

"You don't have to," Airy said. "Me and Dixie built it before. We can agin."

"You need lumber?" He glanced up to see Airy's considering expression. "I got some to spare. I'll bring it around to your place."

"Much obliged." Airy grinned. "You forgive me, I guess."

He settled back in the chair, arms akimbo, legs apart. "I stopped listening to your prattle years ago."

Airy's eyes flashed with humor. "Guess that's why you do so many darn fool things. If'n you'd been listening to me, you'd be a rich man by now."

They all shared a laugh. Elise escorted Airy outside and waited until the older woman and her mule were well on their way before she went back in. She was surprised to find Blade emerging from the other bedroom, a packet in his hands. She recognized the collection of envelopes immediately from her snooping in the trunk.

"Now that you know, you should know it all."

He dropped the bundle on the table. "Come here and sit down." His voice was low, his tone resigned. He sat in one of the chairs and removed several sheets of paper from the top envelope. He pushed them toward Elise when she joined him.

"What's this?"

"The agreement the judge drew up. I signed it. It's all legal and binding."

Her hand trembled as she reached for it. "You didn't want me to see this ... to know about it."

Blade moved his empty cup aside and folded his arms on the table. "It wasn't any of your concern."

"Oh, no, not any of my concern at all," she said with biting sarcasm. "I just live here." She unfolded the document and began to read. When she reached the pair of signatures at the bottom, she swallowed hard. "You should have signed this in blood." The judge would control all of Blade's land if Blade didn't repay him. Folding the paper again, she handed it back to him. "Julia approved of this?"

"It was her idea."

Animosity churned in Elise and she sat sideways in the chair to avoid looking at Blade. This had been Julia's solution to her childless state, to put everything Blade owned on the auction block? Incredible!

"And this note is due next month. Why didn't you make it come due after the crop was in, when you'd logically have more money?"

"The judge wanted it this way, and I figured I could pay him back by then anyway."

"Can you?"

He shook his head. "We had monstrous rains last spring that flooded the fields. I had to replant. The cotton I finally raised wasn't of good quality, and

I didn't get top dollar. I barely made enough to pay for this year's planting."

"Oh, Blade. This is disastrous!" She rested her forehead in her hands as the dire possibilities circled in her brain.

"Doesn't have to be. I think I can talk the judge into extending the due date."

"You do?" She studied his face, looking for a crack in his optimism.

"There's a chance."

Not wanting to call him a liar, Elise decided to take another tack. "I don't quite understand, Blade." She stood and paced, restless with the futility boiling in her. "Julia was a teacher. She was surrounded by children all day. Why was it so important to her to have one, even at the expense of her home here?"

He shrugged. "She loved children."

"Yes. I've read that inscription on her gravestone. I love children, too, but . . . that!" She pointed at the document. "To sacrifice so much!"

"It wasn't just Julia's doing. She married to be not only a wife but a mother, too. Being a mother was very important to her. I couldn't stand to see the joy and hope dying inside her. I had to do something. When we heard about the orphan train, we knew it was our last chance, but we didn't have enough money to send to the Society."

"So you gambled everything . . . for Julia." Elise stared at the bare third finger of her left hand and felt bereft. He would never make such a sacrifice for her, she thought. He hadn't even purchased a wedding band for her or asked if she wanted children someday. But for Julia, he had been willing to move mountains, lasso the sun and sign over his life to a man he despised.

"It didn't seem like a gamble then. It was a solution. An answer to our prayers."

"But you must have realized how impossible it would be to defer to the likes of Judge Mott!"

A shadow seemed to pass over his face. "He and Julia got along well."

Elise stopped pacing as she tried to imagine this. "How could anyone get along well with that man?"

"They shared a love of books and such. I'm not a worldly man, but the judge is, and Julia needed someone to talk to about the finer things. He would come by every so often for supper. Afterward they would sit and talk. She enjoyed hearing his views."

Elise suppressed a shudder. "I wish I could understand, but so much of what I've heard about Julia baffles and confuses me."

"Such as?" Blade sorted through the other envelopes, then held up one. "Our marriage license."

"Which marriage?"

A ruddy color stained his neck and ears. "To Julia."

"Naturally." She chopped off the rest of what she'd like to say in retort. She would like to ask if he had ever thought to buy Julia a ring and if he had ever made love to her in the middle of the floor.

"You're not jealous, are you?"

Elise whipped around, not finding his suggestion the least bit funny. His smile spiked her anger.

"Jealous of a dead woman?" he goaded, his lopsided smile growing.

"No, I'm not! But I am angry that you waited until Airy let the cat out of the bag to tell me about this. You won't be the only one without a home if you can't pay that debt, you know."

His smile faded. "I know."

"But you don't think of me as family." She gave a derisive laugh. "You don't think of me at all!"

"That's a damn lie and you know it." He rose from the chair, hands bunched into dangerous fists, mouth tensed into a grim line. "I thought of you last night, didn't I?"

"Oh, yes. When you're hard and aching, you think of me. I guess I should be flattered."

"You're complaining? You're saying you didn't enjoy last night and this morning?"

Drawing on her courage and nerve, Elise confronted him. "Blade, did Julia make you happy? I ask only because I sense that you haven't been happy for a long time. Maybe even before Julia died."

"What difference does that make, whether I was happy?" He laughed scornfully at her. "You can't understand that happiness isn't the golden nugget for most of us. You were brought up to think that being happy is your birthright, but I was brought up differently. Putting food on the table, having a roof over your head, making a living for yourself, raising a family—these are the important things in life. If they bring moments of happiness, then those moments are unexpected gifts."

"You're wrong, Blade," she said, rejecting his version of life. "Happiness is not a birthright, but it is a noble pursuit, especially in a marriage. You can't convince me that you married Julia and didn't expect to be happy with her." Before he could answer, she stepped close to him. "You didn't put your land in jeopardy for any other reason than to make your wife happy. You could have lived without a child, but she couldn't—or wouldn't."

He stuffed his hands in his pant pockets and

moved away from her, out to the porch, where a pleasant breeze cut through the sun's heat. "I'd never seen her so radiant as the day we were told that one of the orphans would be ours. A girl of eight, they said in their letter to us, and she'd be arriving in only a few weeks! But then Julia took ill. At first I thought—we all thought—she had eaten something bad, but the pains in her stomach got worse. The doctor examined her time and again, but he couldn't do anything for her. He said a sickness had set in, probably after the last baby we lost."

Elise walked out onto the porch. Blade stared straight ahead, but she sensed that he was looking at his past. She didn't interrupt, believing he wanted to tell her about this painful time he had endured.

"She took medicine, but nothing helped. I even brought an Apache holy woman here and she did what she could, but she said the fever in Julia's body had taken a firm hold and she couldn't persuade it to let go."

"And you promised Julia that you'd make a home for Penny, no matter what?"

He nodded, his features solemn. "I had failed Julia in a way, but I swore I would honor her last request to give the child a home."

"How did you fail her, Blade?" Elise asked, sincerely confused.

"I wanted roots; someone to make this a home and not just a farm. I wanted a woman of my own, a wife to share my dreams and my triumphs and my challenges. Julia did all of that and more." A smile, fleeting and bittersweet, visited his face. "She wanted children. She wanted a husband and then a father to her brood. She wanted to stop teaching and devote herself to her own offspring. She wanted a man she could build a dream on. I failed her in all of this."

Elise clutched his arm. "You are not wholly to blame for that, Blade. Some women are made to bear children and some aren't." She gripped his arm harder when he moved to pull away. "And did it ever occur to you that no man would have pleasured Julia? From what I've heard, I think she was frigid." Elise blinked, stung by his snapping gaze. "I'm sorry, but that's my opinion."

"She was loving and giving and—"

"To children, yes, and to people in need and in all works of charity. But perhaps she had a puritan mind when it came to coupling, Blade. Did you ever talk to her about your problems in bed?"

"We didn't have to talk about it."

She let go of him and leaned back against the support post. "Julia didn't know spit about making love and she wouldn't talk about it," Elise surmised. "I know you well enough to believe that you would have asked her what you could do to alleviate her discomfort."

Agitation twitched his lips. "This is all dead and buried. Why talk about it now?" He went back inside for the packet of letters and replaced them in Julia's room. "I have work to do," he said, heading for the peg where he'd hung his hat.

He looked too good to let the fields have him, Elise thought with a grin. He smelled of soap from his morning wash and his jawline was as smooth as a baby's backside. She'd watched him shave while she'd finished cooking breakfast. She'd almost burned the sausage.

Elise plucked his hat off the peg before he could reach it. She held it behind her back. "What will we do if you can't pay back the judge and he won't extend the time for payment?''

Blade looked away, wincing as if stabbed by the thought. ''I won't lose it.''

''But you need to keep Mott from getting angry at you, right? That's why you don't want me to go to his place and interfere with Adam.''

''It's best. At least until after some decision is made about our deal. Now, give me my hat.''

She grinned. ''You want it? Take it.''

He tried to look vexed, but his eyes sparkled with mischief. ''I don't have time for games, Elise.'' His gaze strayed from her face to her body. ''You look pretty this morning.''

She knew he was thinking about last night. ''Do I look like a wife?''

''Do you feel like one?'' he parried.

Elise pondered the question. ''Not really, but time will remedy that. Someday I hope you feel like a husband. My husband.''

''I already do.'' He reached behind her and snatched his hat from her hands, but instead of placing it on his head, he sailed it sideways. It landed on the kitchen table. ''Come here, you.''

He hooked an arm around her waist and hauled her into his embrace. His mouth seared hers. Elise gave a little squeak, his ardor taking her by surprise, but she recovered quickly and a moan of pleasure escaped when she parted her lips. His tongue played lazily with hers. Elise held his face between her hands and kissed every beloved feature of it.

''You should never be jealous of Julia,'' he whispered against her skin, his arms tightening around her. ''I never found such pleasure with her as I found with you last night.''

His confession brought a lump to her throat. "I'll be thinking of you all day. Shall I bring you a noon-day meal?"

"I'll come inside today. I'll be working in the barn mostly."

"I'll ring the bell when it's ready."

"Too bad it's Sunday. We could be alone..." His warm lips smoothed down the side of her neck. His teeth caught at her skin. "I'm hungry for you, not for food."

"Blade!" She pushed his arms away from her, afraid that he might tempt her to make love to him again in the brightness of day. She shook her head and laughed. "You'd better go. I might forget I'm a lady and behave like a common tart."

He chuckled and gave her backside a playful pat before he retrieved his hat from the table. "If Penny weren't wandering around, I'd satisfy my hunger right here and now."

"Blade!" She tried to act shocked.

He smiled, not believing her wide-eyed expression for a moment. "I'll wait until tonight for another taste of you." He strode outside, leaving Elise red-faced and light-headed.

The church's Sunday night service was well attended. Blade had wanted to drop Elise and Penny off and pick them up later as he usually did, but Elise had insisted that he come in with them this time. He didn't mind Sunday morning services, he'd told her time and time again, but he didn't care for the more social gatherings on Sunday evenings.

The reason behind his acquiescence wasn't lost on Elise. Since the wall had tumbled between them, they hated to be separated. She supposed all lovers felt the same way, but surely, no other woman on earth felt exactly like her. After all, no other woman had Blade Lonewolf as her husband.

Glancing at him from the corner of her eye, she admired his stature and handsome profile. The choir director led the congregation in song, and Blade's clear bass was easy for Elise to pick out from the others around her. He wore a fresh white shirt, black trousers and boots; his vest was cut from soft chamois. His hair was combed straight back and gleamed in the candlelight. He smelled of cedar and pine.

The voices faded with the last note of the spiritual. Reverend Casper stepped up to the pulpit.

"That was lovely. Don't your hearts soar when singing the praises of our Lord?"

Murmurs lifted from the congregation. Penny fidgeted beside Elise. Reaching into her reticule, Elise produced a scrap of paper and a lead pencil. Penny accepted them with a big smile and began drawing a horse. Since Gwenie's birth, Penny spent every free minute in the stables or the corral. Not even the new chicks or kittens could entice her from the prancing, playful filly.

"Before we leave tonight, I'd like to remind you that our roof can't take another rainy spring." The pastor glanced up with worry. "We must put a new roof on our chapel this summer. To that end, the ladies are planning a bake sale next Friday right outside under the birch tree. We need pies, cakes, cookies and bread to sell, ladies. Please sign up to make as much as you can. My wife will be stationed outside the door to receive your pledges. Let us pray."

Elise bent her head, but heard little of the closing prayer. She replayed in her mind things she'd heard about Julia's importance to the community. Julia would have volunteered to make a whole table full of baked goods. The bake sale would be a good way for Elise to involve herself in the town and make inroads in changing people's opinion of Blade and other Indians.

Wanting to race for the door, where Mrs. Casper sat at a small table with a sign-up sheet before her, Elise restrained herself.

"You and Penny go ahead," she told Blade. "I'm going to pledge my share."

Blade took Penny by the hand. "We'll bring the wagon closer."

Elise nodded and took her place in line behind three other townswomen. She was dismayed to see Mrs. Keizer standing to one side of Mrs. Casper. Elise heard a familiar voice and glanced behind her. It was all she could do not to scowl when she saw Sally Carpenter, Gladys Keizer's friend in bigotry.

"Next?" Mrs. Casper said, and smiled at Elise. "What can you bring us Friday, dear?"

"Berry cobbler and oatmeal cookies," Elise replied, naming her two best desserts. "I could bring a couple of loaves of honey-wheat bread, too."

Before Mrs. Casper could respond, Mrs. Keizer reached past her and dragged Mrs. Carpenter closer.

"Now here is a woman who can bake cobblers," Mrs. Keizer said. "Put her down for three cobblers and four loaves of bread. I'll bake six dozen oatmeal cookies."

Mrs. Casper jotted down the pledges. "Oh, that's wonderful! Thank you Mrs. Carpenter. Your cobblers are legendary!"

Somehow Sally Carpenter moved to stand directly in front of Elise. Another woman edged toward the table, pressing Elise off to the side.

"And here's Lily Binder," Mrs. Keizer said, snagging the woman's sleeve and tugging her forward, also ahead of Elise. "She can bake apple pie that melts in your mouth! And her chocolate cake! Oh, my. Put her down for both."

The chattering women moved around Elise like a river around a fallen log. When a large woman with a horsey face nearly knocked Elise off her feet, Elise gave up and stumbled outside. Tears swam in her eyes and she swiped angrily at them. She looked back into the church, glaring at the women who had snubbed her.

Suddenly Dixie Shoemaker's sweet face came into view. Dixie maneuvered through the crowd to lay a hand on the sleeve of Elise's leaf green dress.

"You go ahead and bring cobblers and cookies and whatever else you want. It's for the Lord, not for those heartless old hens."

Elise smiled and hugged Dixie close for a moment. "I'm glad I have you and Airy. I'm sorry about your still," she added in a whisper, not sure such business should be discussed near the church.

Dixie adjusted her yellow bonnet, which matched her dress. "I don't know what gets into people's heads to make them think they've got a right to run everybody's life. It doesn't matter, though. We're building a new one that will turn out a brew so fine, we'll be able to charge double for it." She giggled girlishly. "Just you wait and see."

"Do they know about your . . . business?" Elise asked, nodding toward the women inside.

"Everybody knows, honey. Their husbands buy our brew all the time, and the wives act like they don't have a clue, but they know." Dixie winked. "Just like they know about their husbands visiting the Rusty Key's painted ladies."

"Why did they accept Julia, but not me?"

"Their children loved Julia, and Julia made their children love school. It's difficult to keep children in school around here. The fathers want them to help in the fields, not learn numbers and letters. The children, lots of times, would rather work than learn, but Julia made learning fun for them. Mothers generally understand that learning can mean their children won't have to pick cotton all their lives." Dixie started down the church steps, and Elise walked with her.

Through the gathering dusk Elise spied Blade climbing into the wagon and helping Penny to sit beside him. She stood beside the road with Dixie and waited for them.

"And you won't let those old hens keep you from bringing your wares to the sale?"

Blade stopped the wagon beside Elise. She looked back at the lamp-lit church. Mrs. Keizer and Mrs. Carpenter stood at the top of the steps, their gazes on her and their heads together in heated gossip.

"We're good cooks. We ought to get together and bake up something special—something no one can resist," she mused aloud to Dixie.

"That's the spirit!" Dixie said with a giggle.

"Speaking of spirits . . ." Blade winked as he reached out a hand to help Elise up into the wagon. "That whiskey cake you and Airy bake every Christmas for me ought to sell real well."

"Blade, you're a right smart feller," Dixie proclaimed with a happy laugh. "That's what we'll make. Whiskey cake. Why, they'll be swarming over them like flies!"

Blade aimed a finger at her. "Now you're talking. I'll be around to Airy's after supper with the lumber."

"Much obliged, Blade. I'll be there, too." Dixie fished a hard candy from her dress pocket and gave it to Penny. "There you go, sweetie pie."

"What do you say, Pen?" Elise prompted.

"Thank you, Mrs. Shoemaker," Penny responded.

"Why, you're mighty welcome." Dixie looked from Elise to Blade and a slyness tinged her smile. "You've got a good woman there beside you, Blade Lonewolf. Hope you know that." Then she turned and walked briskly away.

Blade clucked and the mules started off. "You know, Julia lived here since she was a girl."

Elise looked at him inquiringly. "Did she?"

He nodded. "I was thinking about horses."

Elise shook her head, baffled. "Horses? I thought you were thinking about Julia."

"No. Horses." He waved at a passing wagon, then guided the mules with a steady hand on the reins. "You introduce a pretty, young mare into a herd and the other mares hate her on sight. They nip at her and chase her around. If she catches the eye of a stallion, the mares will gang up on her and try to keep her away from him. They'll try their best to run her out of their territory."

Elise listened, wondering what he was trying to tell her.

"After a spell, though, that mare stops being a stranger. The sun sets enough times until the herd gets used to her. One day that mare is allowed to drink at the stream with the others. She grazes with the others and nobody tries to chase her off."

"That's very interesting, Blade, but I—"

"I heard those wicked-tongued women back there," he said, turning to face her.

"Y-you heard? But you were outside with Pen—"

"No. Penny saw some school friends and wanted to talk to them. I went back in and watched that old mare Mrs. Keizer chase you out of the pasture."

Elise refused to let him see how the women had hurt her. She adopted a breezy tone. "We'll have the last laugh. Those whiskey cakes will sell, no matter what Mrs. Keizer and those other women think of me."

"It's not you. It's me, Elise. They look down their noses at anyone of dark skin. I started to tell those women what I thought of them, but we were in a holy place."

Elise rested a hand on his shirtsleeve. "I'm glad you didn't make a scene. They aren't worth it."

"Someday they will include you. They will welcome you. If they hadn't known Julia before she married me, they would have shunned her, too."

"I'm not interested in friendships with them. I have good friends. Airy and Dixie, your cousins, Penny's teacher. I'll make more. Mrs. Keizer isn't someone I would want to have tea with anyway."

"I wish you could be proud to be my wife, but—"

"I *am* proud," she interrupted him, squeezing his arm. "Nothing those women say can ever change that, Blade Lonewolf."

He squared his shoulders and cast her a look that was almost bashful. "Dixie is right," he whispered, his voice suddenly hoarse. "I have a good woman sitting beside me."

Elise rested her cheek against his shoulder and closed her eyes, eyes that had filled with sentimental tears.

Chapter 18

Setting aside the butter churn, Elise placed a hand against the small of her back and twisted her upper body to relieve her knotted muscles. Since returning from church, she'd churned for nearly an hour while Penny and Blade had checked on the animals. Now Penny and Blade sat on the porch, and Elise could hear Penny's chattering and Blade's occasional word.

Since the filly had been born, Penny had grown more attached to Blade. The blessed event had made him even more special in her eyes, especially since he allowed her to spend all the time she wanted with Gwenie, and he called the filly "Penny's pony."

While getting ready for that evening's church services, Penny had confided to Elise, her eyes all aglow, that Blade had promised she would be the first to ride Gwenie.

" 'Lise, he says that since I named her, I can have her," Penny had said, excitement making her tremble. "She's mine! And Blade says he'll help me train and saddle-break her when it's time. He'll teach me to ride and everything!"

Elise smiled at the memory as she moved silently

246

to the door and peeked out. Blade sat on the top step, Penny on the bottom one. Starlight illuminated their faces. Penny, her legs drawn up and her arms circling them, related her most recent scrape with Domino, the barnyard's fussiest hen. Blade, a charming smile on his lips, listened and chuckled occasionally. He sat with his knees spread apart and his elbows propped on them, an empty coffee cup in his big hands.

Elise's nerves fluttered along with her heart. Ever since last night, she'd been hard pressed to keep her emotions at bay. Just looking at him made her pulses drum incessantly. Images of their private times together flitted through her mind, tempting her, making her want him madly.

He looked so good to her that it was sinful. His arms, bared by his turned-up sleeves, were deeply tanned and rippled with muscle. She remembered how safe she felt in his embrace, how small, how delicate, how totally feminine. The markings on his arms were beautiful to her eyes now because they reminded her that he was of two worlds, two cultures. Both had shaped him, but neither had completely claimed him. He was a loner, a maverick. He had carved out his own place and then he had made room for her and Penny in it. For that alone she could love him, but she loved him for far more. She loved him because he needed her, although he probably wouldn't admit it, and because he made her feel wanted, cherished, desired.

". . . and if I even come near her chicks, she runs at me, squawking and flapping her wings," Penny complained to Blade, breaking into Elise's reverie. "The other hens aren't mean like Domino. Why, she even tries to peck at old Red! He crows at her and gives her chase when he gets enough of her pecking and clucking. I don't know why Domino's so contwa . . . contrrary."

"You say your words good now."

"You think so?" Penny grinned up at him. "I try hard."

"Domino is a good mother," Blade said. "She doesn't trust anyone or anything around her chicks."

"Not even Red? He's her husband, isn't he?"

Blade gave a chuckle. "In a way, yes." He ruffled Penny's hair.

Elise pressed a hand to her heart, which seemed to swell with each sign of affection he showed. Did he love Penny?

Does he love me?

"Roosters, generally, aren't good fathers." He gazed out at the land. "Among animals, that is often the case. Once the offspring are born, the mother pretty much does all the caretaking. Sometimes the fathers hunt and bring home food, and sometimes they do nothing at all."

"My papa was a good father," Penny said. "And you're a good father, too. Maybe I'll call you Papa Blade."

Penny's suggestion arrested Elise's heartbeats for a few moments as her gaze flew to Blade. He looked startled, but then his eyes crinkled at the corners and he smoothed a hand over Penny's coppery hair.

"If you ever want to call me that, it would be fine with me. Such a name would honor me."

The pleased expression on Penny's face sent Elise back into the house. She moved blindly toward the stove, one hand at her throat, the other over her eyes as she dealt with the aftershocks of the exchange she had witnessed.

She hadn't expected to be nearly knocked off her

feet by Penny's devotion to Blade. Nor had she anticipated the rush of panic that had surged through her. True, she had been aware of Penny's growing affection for Blade since the night Gwenie had been born, but . . . *Papa Blade?*

Where did this place her real papa? That was what picked at Elise, this traitorous feeling. Should she encourage her little sister to think of Blade Lonewolf as her new father, or should she discourage it in deference to their deceased father?

Penny was only eight and she needed a flesh-and-blood father, Elise told herself. Keeping their father's memory alive was important, but not to the exclusion of any other man's paternal love.

Elise had needs as well. She needed a husband, in every sense of the word. Not just physically, but emotionally. She needed to know where she stood with Blade.

Uncovering her eyes, Elise looked toward the spare bedroom. She could call Blade her husband, but she wouldn't feel it until she was sure he loved her. Until he could sleep with her in that room, she wouldn't—*couldn't*—trust her feelings for him. She could think of no greater pain than to give all of herself to Blade, only to discover that he had given merely a portion of himself to her.

"Elise?"

The caress of his voice feathered a delightful shiver down her back. She turned, and Penny wrapped her arms around Elise's waist.

"She's yawning," Blade said. "But she says it's not time for bed."

"Well, she's wrong." Elise smacked Penny's rump playfully. "Get in there and undress, young lady, and be sure to wash off the dirt and grime before you put on a fresh nightgown and small-clothes."

"Okay. 'Night, Blade." Penny skipped to the bedroom she and Penny shared. *Used* to share, Elise corrected herself.

"Good night, Pen."

Blade's use of Penny's shortened name didn't go unnoticed. Elise looked across the room to where he filled the doorway. Starlight bathed his shoulders and limned his slim hips. She saw the flash of his white teeth.

"Smallclothes?"

Elise laughed lightly. "My mother called them that. It's an old-fashioned word."

"You have most interesting smallclothes." He treaded closer on silent feet.

"And you have few, I noticed. Sometimes none."

"Oh, you've noticed that, have you?"

"Yes." She turned, deftly sidestepping him, wanting to make him wait a little longer. "And what is so interesting about my unmentionables?"

His laughter sounded more like a rumbling purr. "Yet another odd word. What is interesting? Ribbons and laces. Whalebone and embroidery. Very fancy, but I don't think you need most of them. Your figure is perfect without those contraptions."

"Spoken like a gentleman who is trying to turn a lady's head." Pleasure purled through her.

"We *are* sleeping together tonight, aren't we?"

Her breath caught in her throat. Flames seemed to leap from her stomach into her chest. "Y-yes, if you want."

A feral grin captured his mouth. "Oh, I want."

"B-but I have to get Penny settled in first." Flustered by his straightforwardness, she started to go toward Penny's room, but Blade caught her around the waist. His lips caressed the side of her neck. His hands skimmed over her hips and splayed along her thighs.

Her knees weakened and she was alarmed at her own raging need to give herself over to him. With great effort, she stepped out of his embrace.

"Blade, I have to check on Penny and tuck her in."

"Very well, little mother. I'll be waiting for you out here."

Glancing back at him, Elise saw the intention in his brown eyes and in his suggestive smile. She looked at the door of Julia's bedroom before she went into the room next to it. She wanted him. Oh, how she wanted him! But if he thought he'd take her on the living room floor again or in that tepee tonight, then he was bound for disappointment!

As promised, Blade was waiting for her. He'd removed his shirt and shoes and slipped his suspenders off his shoulders, so that they dangled at his hips. His eyes glittered darkly as his hands moved to the buttons on his fly.

Elise shivered uncontrollably and kept reminding herself that this was the time to test his love for her—if he had any. She smoothed her sweaty palms over her nightdress and watched his expression change from desire to lust. Having unbraided her hair, she captured a lock of it and curled it around her finger as she seized the moment to admire his male arrogance. He knew he looked virile and handsome to her eyes. He knew, and he gloried in it. His stance told her so.

He stood before her, legs braced apart, eyes all aglitter. The smile poking at one corner of his mouth sent a spiral of longing through her, but she held her ground, knowing that once he enclosed her in his arms, she would be hopelessly, willingly, lost.

"All I've thought about today is you," he confessed, his voice deep, rough-edged. "But I couldn't tell if your mind was on me. I couldn't tell if you were waiting for this moment when we could be alone together."

"You couldn't?" She arched a brow. "I thought I was being obvious. Can you tell now?"

His gaze drifted from her face to her breasts, covered by the sheer white material. She felt her nipples pucker to diamond hardness.

"Ah, yes. Come here, Elise." He held out one hand, fingers outstretched.

She meant to deny him, but her body commanded her mind. Before she could think, she had erased the space between them. She drove her fingers through the cool silk of his hair and brought his mouth down to hers. He was as ravenous as she, his lips stroking hers, his hands splaying against her back and moving to capture her hips. She kissed his cheekbones, his chin, the pale lines at the corners of his eyes. He was smiling when she kissed his mouth again.

"Elise, Elise," he whispered as his lips explored a pulse at the base of her throat. He began gathering her nightgown in his hands.

His passion for her nearly obilterated her intention, but a moment of sanity prevailed. She trailed her hands down his arms and linked her fingers with his.

"Come with me," she said, tugging on his hands. "Tonight we're going to do this the proper way." She backed toward the bedroom doors. She sensed the moment when he realized her destination because he tensed and some of the luster left his eyes.

Elise reached behind her and opened the door to the spare room. "There's a comfortable bed waiting for us in there, Blade. We deserve a night of un-interrupted bliss, and I don't want to worry about Penny seeing something she shouldn't."

"Then let's go to my lodge. It's a warm night and the sleeping pad is soft." He trailed a finger down the side of her face. "Almost as soft as you. Ah, Elise, I want you so much that I stand here trem-bling. Come on." He curved an arm around her waist and braced his other behind her knees. He lifted her into his arms as if she were as weightless as a feather. "Remember the night you came into my lodge? It was all I could do not to take you right then and there."

"Why didn't you?" She draped her arms around his neck, wanting him so much that she was begin-ning to weaken in her resolve. If only he'd give her a sign . . . show her that he cared more for her than for his memories of his first wife. A wife who had never satisfied him.

"Why didn't I?" he repeated, smiling, his teeth flashing white against his deeply tanned skin. "You would have let me? I don't think so. You didn't want me then as you want me now." He nuzzled her temple where her hair curled damply. His breath was hot, his breathing rapid. She could feel his heart hammering in his chest. "And I was afraid I would hurt you—that you wouldn't like it."

"I surprised you, didn't I?"

He nodded, his nose rubbing the side of her face, his tongue inching out to trace the shell of her ear. "You're full of surprises." He started toward the front door.

Elise gathered handfuls of his inky hair "Wait. Why sleep on the ground when we can sleep on a feather bed?" She looked over his shoulder at the bedroom door. When he made no move toward it, she wiggled in his arms. "What's the matter, Blade? Aren't I good enough to bed in there?"

Torment entered his eyes and pulled down the corners of his mouth. "Of course! Don't talk foolish. What's wrong with my lodge?"

"That's the place where you sleep alone. You sleep with me now."

He let her slip down his body until her feet took her weight again. He turned away from her and ran a hand down his face in frustration. She could hear the rasp of his beard against his palm.

"Don't you . . . care about me, Blade? Can't you see that this is important to me?" She placed a comforting hand on his shoulder. "It should be important to you, too. My feelings should be important."

"They are."

"Then prove it."

He stood with one hip cocked, his shoulders not as squared as usual. Elise sensed his frustration and understood it. She wanted to fling herself into his arms and forget everything except the moment's passion, but passion would eventually fade and she'd be left with these nagging feelings of not being good enough.

"You are stubborn," he said finally.

"Me? Ha! You win *that* prize! It's only a room with a bed, Blade. And from what you told me, what you did in that bed wasn't all that grand."

"That's right. The bed is . . . it holds bad memories for me. I want us to make good memories. Can't you understand?"

Elise nodded. "That bed is your marriage bed

and you don't want to take another woman into it. Not even your wife." She sighed. "But how am I to live here with you when you post a No Trespassing sign on that door?"

He glared at the room—Julia's room—and determination firmed his jaw and narrowed his eyes. "You're right. Let's burn the damned thing."

Elise blinked. "Wh-what? You mean burn the room? We can't! We'll catch the whole house on fire!"

He strode past her. "No, the bed. Let's burn it. I'm sick of it. I'm sick of everything—the memories, the guilt, the pain, but especially that goddamned bed."

He grabbed each side of the feather mattress and with a mighty grunt lifted it off the frame. Elise snatched the quilt off it and dropped the patchwork spread to the floor. She followed Blade as he wrestled the unwieldy mattress out of the room and out the front door. The scent of clove accosted her, and she was glad to breathe in the night air.

Blade threw the mattress on the ground with a grunt and a flourish. Then he went back inside for the bed frame. The rope frame was easier to carry outside. Elise waited for him. He tossed it on top of the mattress, both a safe distance from the house.

Shifting her attention to Blade again, Elise noted his heaving chest, his gleaming skin, his mussed hair. He looked as if he'd fought a battle, but she knew the battle lay ahead of him. She went inside for the lantern. She hadn't imagined he would go to such measures to burn the last bridge between his past and his future, but she liked this plan. Maybe once the bed was gone, Blade could finally put his demons to rest and devote himself to building a new life with her.

When she returned, he took the lantern from her and stared gloomily at the bed and mattress. Finally, he splashed oil over the mattress, then stood opposite her and doused the bed between them. Plucking a match from the clip, he then set the lamp to one side and held out the matchstick, staring at it as if it were a magic charm . . . or an evil omen? She couldn't tell.

"Want me to light it?" she offered.

He shook his head, but made no move to make a flame with it. Instead, he stared at it, then at Elise, then at the mattress. Regret lay upon his face; regret so trenchant that Elise looked away, unable to bear it a moment longer. Was she being selfish, petty? Should she embrace him, tell him he needn't resort to such drama to please her? Should she simply take his hand and lead him to that wretched skin lodge and be glad for whatever piece of his heart he offered?

She drew in a hiccuping breath. "Blade, this isn't important to me. *You* are important to me. I probably shouldn't cause such a snit over it, but if I am to stay here, I will not be the second wife. Your mother put up with that, but I won't. I want to be your *only* wife. If you hold out any hope for us, then *light that match.*"

One side of his wide mouth lifted to form a rakish grin. She had to wait another eternal moment before the match scraped against his pant leg. The flame coughed, sputtered and caught, then was sent sailing into an arc. Elise didn't see it land. All she saw was the burst of flames accompanied by a muffled boom. Fire engulfed the feather mattress and rope bed, quickly reducing them to ashes and embers. Elise watched the transformation, sensing Blade's nearness as he circled the flames and moved toward her. The fire heated the atmosphere, making the air undulate, and cast a golden, inconstant light.

She looked at Blade. Naked desire flamed in his eyes. She opened her arms to him, every nerve in her body firing. He pulled her against him.

"All I want is you," he said, his mouth pressed against her neck. "I don't care where or how, but I do care about when. It's got to be now."

"Yes." She flung back her head and the stars spun above her. "Now."

He carried her inside, away from the crackling, spitting fire, and tread without hesitation to the bedroom he had once shared with Julia.

He set her on her feet, kicked the door closed and, before she could resist or rejoice, grabbed the hem of her nightgown and swept it up and over her head. With a flick of his wrist, the garment fluttered and settled like a cloud on the floor, near the quilt.

Elise shivered as cool air breathed over her exposed skin. She felt her cheeks flame with self-consciousness. Blade grasped her wrists and forced her arms away from her breasts and stomach, then brought her arms around him. His body was hot against her skin. Their skin seemed to seal together as if their very pores were ravenous.

She stroked his naked back and shoulders and he nuzzled her neck and tongued her earlobe. He grabbed her behind the knees and lifted her. She instinctivly wrapped her legs around him, which seemed to please him immensely.

"Ah, yes!" He held her tightly against him and speared her mouth with his silky tongue. He cupped her buttocks in his hands while his mouth made mad love to hers.

He took a few steps and pressed her back against the wall, using it to keep her in place while he palmed one of her breasts, lifted it and sandwiched its throbbing peak between his lips. She rested her head against the wall, eyes open but seeing nothing. All her awareness focused on the wizardry of his mouth as he took her breast inside and suckled her deeply, strongly.

A trembling snaked through her limbs and she felt herself grow moist. He shifted, planted his feet sturdily and entered her with one driving thrust.

She thought she might die of pure rapture at having him buried completely in her. He ground his hips, going in even deeper, pressing her spine against the wall. He flung back his head. Engorged veins stood out in his neck, and his lips stretched into a grimace of pleasure. Then he burst inside her. She felt him, every nuance, every quick, jolting release. Sweat beaded on her brow, burned her eyes, blurred her vision. She went limp, draping herself over him, rubbing her aching breasts against his chest.

He panted hot breath against her cheek and pressed hotter kisses to her lips as he whirled away from the wall and lowered her to the cool quilt.

"Tomorrow I'll prepare us a proper bed," he vowed, straightening to stand over her and admire her high, full breasts, her flat stomach, her flared hips, the damp triangle of russet between her thighs.

Elise glanced down at herself, wondering how much the darkness shielded. Starlight painted her skin a soft blue. Flipping her hair back over her shoulders, she looked up at him again. The intensity in his expression sent a weakness through her.

"You are a vision. A night dream." He still wore

his trousers, though they were unbuttoned and exposed his organ. He pushed them off and kicked them aside, suspenders and undergarments sailing with them. Naked, he came to her, all sinew and bronze skin and crisp, dark hair.

She curved a hand at the back of his neck and brought him with her as she lay on the soft quilt and bed pillows. She parted her thighs, making room, making it known that she wanted him, needed him.

Caressing his wide shoulders, she enveloped him with her limbs. He gathered her beneath him as he laved her breasts with his tongue. She moaned as her nipples tightened until they were almost painfully erect. A shudder coursed through her. Writhing in mindless desire, she slipped her hands down to encircle him, to ease him inside her. He was satin. He was steel. He groaned her name and plunged wholly into her. Her body stretched wide to accept him.

Elise pressed kisses to his chest and neck as he moved in and out of her. She dug her fingers into his shoulders when her own body quickened to a burst of desire that left her to ride the mighty waves of his passion. He jerked and emptied into her in four powerful thrusts. Elise chanted his name and tasted his salty skin, taking love bites from his shoulders.

Combing his fingers through her hair, he gathered fistfuls of it and tipped back her head to rain kisses down her throat.

"Do I pleasure you, wife?" He rubbed against her, setting off another tremor.

"Yes. Oh, yes," she murmured. "Do *I* pleasure *you*?" He was still semi-hard inside her. She tightened her inner muscles around him, earning a grimace of painful pleasure from him.

"Yessss," he hissed.

"I satisfy you?" she asked, partly teasing.

"You inspire me." He moved slowly, withdrawing, plunging, then repeating the motion until Elise was quivering and moaning his name.

Their desire culminated in soft cries of pleasure and soughing breaths that mingled and heated the air around them. Blade rested his head on her breasts and Elise idly twisted inky strands of his hair around her fingers as the night deepened and coyotes called for mates in the distance.

After a while, Blade stretched out on his back and guided Elise into his arms. She laid her head on his shoulder.

"I'll rig up something tomorrow," he murmured, sounding as if he were already half asleep. "Even if it's nothing but a pad stuffed with hay."

Elise smiled. He was talking about the bed. *Their* bed in *their* bedroom. She sniffed tentatively, but could smell no clove, no mint, only the musky perfume of their lovemaking.

She fell asleep, still smiling, and more in love with him than before.

Chapter 19

Walking across the big yard to the barn the next evening, Elise heard Blade and Penny before she spotted them. Their laughter floated on the warm breeze, enticing her to hurry inside the big structure. To her amazement, she found Blade holding Penny under her arms and turning in a circle. Penny grasped his elbows and laughed, delighted at being a human windmill.

"Faster . . . faster," she ordered, barely able to get out the words, she was giggling so hard.

Blade's feet moved quicker and he swung Penny until her small body was perpendicular to the hay-strewn ground. Blade reared back, his muscles straining, and his straw hat tilted and fell off. He paid it no heed. Only when he spied Elise did he slow and set Penny back on her feet.

"Hello, there," he said, his face growing ruddy because he'd been caught acting like a kid. "You want something?"

"No." Elise grinned, amused at his antics with her little sister. "I just wondered where you'd sneaked off to after supper."

"We're checking on the stock," Penny said, slip-

261

ping a hand into one of Blade's. His fingers curled around hers automatically.

Elise propped a fist on one jutted hip. "Is that what you call it?"

Penny giggled and looked up at Blade. "He was swinging me, that's all. We've already seen to the animals."

"How are Janie and Bob?"

"Full of oats," Penny answered, grinning.

Elise smiled, recognizing Blade's words coming out of Penny. Her younger sister's growing affection for Blade pleased her. Penny was a loving child, but her swift devotion to Blade was something to behold. A lump formed in Elise's throat and she thanked her lucky stars for guiding herself and Penny to Blade Lonewolf's homestead. When she thought of all the other fates that could have been theirs, she shuddered.

For the first time since coming to Crossroads, Elise saw fewer clouds on her horizon. Sheer happiness bubbled inside her. She longed for the dark of the night when Penny would be fast asleep and she would be in Blade Lonewolf's arms again.

"When you two get through roughhousing, you can come on back to the house. I've got hot fried pies on the kitchen table."

"No fooling?" Penny jumped for joy. "Cocoa-and-sugar ones?"

Elise nodded. "And apple and raisin."

"Let's go!" Penny tugged at Blade's hand.

"Hold up. I thought you were going to help me check over the harnesses for weak places."

"Oh, that's right. I did promise."

"You go ahead and finish your chores. The pies will be on the table when you're through." Elise exchanged a smile with Blade—the kind that wives give their husbands—then turned and walked slowly back to the house.

She didn't hurry. The twilight was soothing. Lightning bugs glowed and crickets chirped. She thought of the straw-stuffed mattress Blade had fashioned that morning. He'd taken Penny to school and returned with a bed frame he'd paid Dixie bottom dollar for. The new bed awaited them. Did a new, happy life await them as well?

Elise drew in a deep breath, enjoying the perfume of honeysuckle and jasmine. An unpleasant odor threaded through nature's sweet scents, and she snapped to attention. She scanned the area, knowing that someone was near—someone who hadn't seen bathwater in a spell.

Just when she was about to run back to the barn for Blade, she caught sight of a thin, bony-shouldered figure standing in the pooled shadows of the porch.

"Who is it?" she asked, her voice calm and even. Whoever it was, she sensed no danger in him. "Please, who . . ." The words skidded and slipped on her intake of breath. "Adam? Adam, is that you?"

Elise hitched up her skirts and hurried forth, taking the porch steps by two. It had been several days since she'd seen him; he'd skipped school, and Elise had been reluctant to seek him out because of her new understanding of Blade's circumstances. Guilt-ridden and heartsore, she stared at him, wondering if he'd come to ask her if she'd deserted him. Adam wiped his mouth and chin with the back of his hand.

"I went inside," he said. "I ate two of those pies on the table."

"You're welcome to them." Elise raked her fingers through his slick, dirty hair. "What in heaven's name ... why, you are absolutely filthy, Adam St. John! Come in here. I want to see you in the light. I cannot believe the dirt caked on you!"

She clutched his shoulders and pushed him ahead of her. When she had him near the lit lantern, she turned him around to face her. Her eyes widened at the sorry sight of him.

His clothes were stiff with dirt and his hands, face and neck were gray with it. Beyond that, Elise didn't like the expression on his face. He looked hard and bitter, older than his years. The boy she'd known was barely recognizable.

"Why are you running around like this? Doesn't the judge have a bath in his house?"

"Yeah, but I don't like to use it. It's in the kitchen and the judge's whore likes to sneak peeks when I'm naked."

Elise's fingertips flew to her lips in shock. "I never! The judge's wh ... who?"

"Harriet."

He said the woman's name on a sneer and his pitch rose to mock a female's voice. Elise recalled that he always said Harriet's name that way—as if he despised her.

"Harriet is his wife, as you well know, young man."

"She's nothing but a bought wh—"

Elise pressed her fingertips to his cracked lips. "No more of that name-calling in this house, Adam Jamison." She sniffed and wrinkled her nose. "You stink. Take those clothes off while I heat some water for your bath."

"Bath? I don't have time for a bath."

"You do now. I'll wash those clothes and dry them by the stove. I sure don't want you wearing them until they are laundered." She shivered at the sight of him. "I can't believe you would allow yourself to get this dirty."

Elise bustled to the stove and lifted the kettle. It felt half full. She began adding dipperfuls of water from a bucket into the cast-iron kettle.

"I'm leaving."

"Not until you've bathed."

"I'm leaving this place and I'm not coming back. I just wanted to say good-bye."

Realizing what he meant, Elise whirled to confront him, but before she could say anything, Blade and Penny entered the house. Spotting Adam, Penny gave a whoop of joy and flung her arms around him. Blade's gaze whipped up and down Adam's thin, scraggly frame. He glanced at Elise, and she saw his concern and knew that he'd heard Adam's announcement.

He removed his hat and hung it on a peg near the door. Raking his hand through his hair to lift it off his scalp, he nodded at Adam. "'Evening to you, Adam. Looks like you've been working hard in those clothes."

"He needs a bath," Elise acknowledged. "I'm heating water right now."

"Did I hear you say something about leaving for good?"

Adam sliced a glance at Elise, then at Blade. He jutted his pointed chin. "Yeah, that's right. And you can't stop me."

"I wasn't meaning to," Blade said with an easy smile. "I was just asking."

"Blade, we can't let him—" Elise snapped her mouth shut, numbed by Blade's look of censure. Was he going to let Adam leave? She couldn't believe he would allow such a thing.

"Where are you going, Adam?" Penny asked.

"I don't know. Away from here."

Penny's lips trembled. "Can I go, too? Can me and Elise and Blade go, too?"

"No. You stay here." Adam pushed Penny away. "Watch out. I'll get you dirty."

Elise stared at the platter of fried pies, her eyes filling with tears of helplessness and guilt. While she'd been reveling in her own happiness, her brother had become bitter, mistrustful.

Blade placed a hand over one of hers. His eyes shone with gentleness and understanding. "Elise, why don't you and Penny take some pies and go outside to eat them while Adam has his bath?"

She glanced at Adam before nodding. "Yes. That's a good idea." Turning her back to her brother, she mouthed to her husband, "Talk to him."

Blade chucked her under the chin. "Go on now. We men need our privacy."

Elise selected two pies. "Come along, Pen. We'll sit in the tree swing Blade made for us."

"Adam, you won't leave now, will you?" Penny asked.

Elise patted her sister's back in a comforting and shooing gesture. "He's not going anywhere but into the tub. Come along. We'll visit with him after his bath."

Penny let Elise take her by the hand and lead her outside.

Once they had gone, Blade moved to the stove and touched the pads of two fingers to the side of the teakettle. "Almost hot enough. You get those clothes off while I fill the tub."

Elise had filled three buckets earlier, probably thinking he or Penny might need a bath before bed. While Adam undressed, Blade pulled the shallow

tub into the middle of the floor to fill it. He added
a teakettle of the hot water and swished it around.
"All ready."

Blade gathered the discarded clothes and tossed
them outside. He figured they were only good for
burning. He sat at the table, his back to the tub.

"Soap, washcloth and towel are there on the
floor," he said, then helped himself to a pie. "Scrub
hard. You've got rows of dirt circling your neck
that I could plant potatoes in."

The water sloshed in the tub as Adam eased his
lanky body into it. Blade enjoyed the cocoa and
sugar pie while the boy bathed.

"You hungry?"

"Yeah. Kinda."

Blade pushed himself to his feet and went toward the stove. "We have some left-over ham here.
I'll heat up some of this hash for you." He set the
hash on the stove, then sliced off a generous wedge
of Elise's fresh bread for the boy. He arranged it
on the table along with a glass of apple juice.

"Where are my clothes?" Adam asked, the water
sloshing again as he stood in the tub.

Blade sat down again, his back to him. "If I know
your sister, they're burned or buried by now."

"Huh? What am I supposed to wear?"

"I can find something for you, I reckon. Wear a
towel for now and tuck yourself under this table."

Adam came into view, the towel wrapped
around his waist. "Don't bother. I got a change of
clothes in my bedroll," he grumbled. He afforded
Blade only a glance before attacking the plate of
food.

The gray tinge had been washed away, revealing
his pale skin and his tanned arms and face. Blade
noticed that he'd missed a few places and was

about to point them out when he realized they wouldn't wash off. A bolt of shock flashed through him. Bruises . . . around the boy's upper arms, throat, left shoulder, the right side of his ribs. Anger built in Blade, but he knew that venting it in front of Adam, who was already mad at the world, would do more harm than good.

"Where'd you get those bruises, little brother?"

Adam hiked up one shoulder. "Where do you think?" His blue eyes glinted with hatred. "But he doesn't hurt me. He tries to scare me. He cuffs me once in a while when I sass him."

"Maybe you should curb your tongue."

"Maybe you should try to live with him one day before you dole out advice," Adam snapped.

Blade tamped down his own temper. "I can see that you sorely tempt the back of a man's hand."

Adam glared at him, but said nothing.

"So you're heading out, are you?"

"That's right."

"You're a boy. How do you think you'll live, out on your own?"

"I can farm."

Blade chewed on his lower lip to keep from laughing. Adam hadn't even brought in a crop yet, but he considered himself worth wages. Well, he sure wasn't short on pride.

"Don't see how you'll be better off. Farming is hard work, no matter where you do it."

Adam ate heartily, abandoning talk until he was finished. He sat back with a sigh. His eyes glittered with something Blade didn't like.

"Will you take me in, Lonewolf?"

Blade's tongue felt like a flap of leather in his mouth. His mind whirled as he tried to find the right answer to the question, but the boy withdrew it before he could.

"Never mind. I want to get far away from here. Can I have more juice?"

Blade nodded toward the pitcher on the table. "Help yourself."

"I figure I can hop a train and get to another state," Adam said as he filled his glass again.

"You think the judge won't look for you?"

"I doubt it."

"He adopted you. He won't let you wander off without sending out a posse. Besides, your sisters would worry. You don't want to make them sad, do you?"

"I've got to look after myself!" Adam thumped a fist on the table.

"Stay put a few more weeks and I might see clear to having you stay here with your sisters."

An unpleasant smile drifted across Adam's face. "What difference will a few weeks make? Nothing's going to change." He touched the discolored skin on his neck. "The judge has *you* by the throat, not me."

Blade felt as if he'd been punched in the gut. He stared at the boy and saw not only disrespect but also a cockiness that made his blood boil.

"I know all about it," Adam said. "The judge told me. He says you won't be able to pay him back the money you borrowed and that he'll be plowing your fields next spring. I thought you were a smart fellow, but I guess I was wrong. Only a fool would be owing a snake like Mott."

A black film covered Blade's eyes and it was all he could do not to flip the table over and charge at the boy. Suddenly Elise strode into the cabin, the heels of her shoes ringing sharply as she marched over to her brother, her eyes spitting venom.

"How dare you sit at my table, eat my food and insult my husband!" Her voice rapped like a hammer against a nailhead. "You apologize to him this minute, Adam St. John." When Adam started to argue, Elise stopped him with a voice that shook with fury. *"This minute!"*

Adam stared hard at her, rebellion in the set of his jaw and the bunching of his fists, but then his eyes softened and he lowered his gaze. "I'm sorry."

Elise released her breath in a long hiss. "That's better." She looked at Blade and smiled. "Forgive him, Blade. Please, forgive him."

Blade would have forgiven the boy anything. Not for the boy, but for Elise. Running a hand over Adam's fiery hair, Elise pulled him against her. He pressed his face against her stomach.

"You're becoming a man, Adam."

"I know." His voice was muffled against her apron.

"But you still need guidance, and I hope you still need my love. Penny and I want you in our lives." She twisted to find Penny hovering in the doorway. "Come here and give your brother a kiss, Pen."

Penny came forward and bussed Adam's cheek. "You still leaving?"

Adam ran both hands through his wet hair. "I don't know." He glanced around. "I need to get dressed."

Elise looked sheepish. "I threw your clothes into the rag pile, Adam."

Adam looked at Blade and grinned.

"Told you," Blade said, then jerked a thumb to indicate the bedrooms. "You can dress in there. Either one."

"Thanks." Adam started to ease himself from the

chair, but Elise placed a hand on his shoulder.

"Are these bruises?" she asked in shock. "What has the brute been doing to you?"

"Nothing." Red stained Adam's face, almost obliterating his freckles.

"Nothing?" She tipped his head sideways while Adam squirmed. "What are these on your neck? He didn't—"

"He only cuffs me," Adam said, trying to duck away. "I never cry."

"Elise," Blade said, standing up and gently pulling her away from Adam, "let the boy get dressed."

"But he—"

"Let go of him." Blade pushed aside her hands, allowing Adam to escape into Penny's room, his bedroll under one arm. "You're embarrassing him. He doesn't want you worrying about him."

"But I *am* worried about him, Blade. If he leaves . . ."

"He won't. He's already having second thoughts about that. His belly is full, he's clean as a hound's tooth and he's feeling better about the world." Blade looked at Penny. "Go whistle up Bob for me, pretty Penny."

"You going somewhere?"

"I'm going to give Adam a ride home."

"Okay." Penny ran outside and began whistling and calling for the temperamental pinto.

Elise gripped Blade's shirtsleeve. Her eyes were dull, full of worry. "What if he—"

She didn't finish. Adam opened the door and joined them again. Blade could have sworn he'd grown three or four inches since he'd first seen him at the train station.

"Did your mare foal?" Adam asked.

Elise beamed. "She did. A filly that your little sister named Gwenie."

"Gwenie?" Adam's brow jumped. "After Mama?" He laughed when Elise nodded. "She would love it."

Elise sobered. "Adam, you aren't leaving, are you?"

He jutted his jaw, but shook his head. "Not tonight. Later."

Elise gathered him into her embrace. Blade cleared the table, giving them a minute of privacy.

"Adam, if you insist on wearing the same clothes over and over, it wouldn't hurt if you rinsed them out each night."

"I guess I could do that."

"See? You still need me to look after you."

"You know, Sis, I used to wish I had a big brother instead of a big sister, but I guess I got what I needed."

"Oh, Adam . . ."

Hearing the emotion clogging Elise's throat, Blade turned back to them. "Ready to ride, Adam?"

"Yes." Adam looked from Elise to Blade. "The old judge doesn't much like either of you. He says that you're hen-pecked and that Elise doesn't know her rightful place."

"My rightful place!" Elise set her fists at her waist in a defiant stance. "I've never been confused about that. My rightful place is with my family."

Adam kissed her cheek. "See you, Sis."

"Take care, Adam."

Blade felt Elise's worried gaze on them as he and Adam went outside. Penny had managed to summon Bob and had fetched his bridle, which she handed to Blade.

"Can you ride bareback, Adam?" Blade asked as he slipped the bit into Bob's mouth and fit the bridle over his ears.

"I guess."

Blade grinned. "Just hold onto me, little brother." He grabbed handfuls of mane and sprang up onto Bob's wide back. "Steady, son," he murmured to the horse, then reached out a hand to help Adam up to sit behind him.

" 'Bye, Adam!" Penny called before running up the porch steps to stand beside Elise, who was silhouetted in the doorway.

" 'Bye now." Adam gave a short wave, then grabbed Blade's shoulders to keep from sliding off Bob's back.

Blade reined the horse to a slow walk until Adam's grip lessened some on his shoulders.

"The judge is a harsh man, Adam. Running away from him will solve nothing. It will worry your sisters and you'll have the authorities after you." He glanced over his shoulder. Adam's face was in shadow, but he felt the boy's resistance. "If you run, run to me."

"Huh?" Adam whipped his gaze around to Blade's. "To you? But you're trying not to rile the judge so he'll let you keep your land."

"Some things are more important than land, my young friend. Promise me that you'll come to me if you find you can't stay at the judge's a day longer."

Adam didn't answer immediately. "If I stay at your place, he'll make big trouble for you. He'll take your land for sure."

"If I don't pay him back, he'll take it anyway." Blade hated to admit that, even to himself, but there it was. He hadn't enough money to repay his debt, and the judge was anything but charitable. Nothing was worth Elise being overcome with worry. "Promise me, Adam."

Adam's hands tightened on Blade's shoulders for an instant. "I promise . . . big brother."

Chapter 20

Airy Peppers lived in a one-room cabin in the middle of nowhere. Wild brush grew right up to her front door and the interior held only the necessities—a stove, a bed, a chair, a table and a chest of drawers.

Out back, a footpath ran through the brush and trees to a privy, then on through more brush and trees to a small clearing where Airy, Dixie and Blade had rebuilt the whiskey still. Afternoon sunlight slanted through the trees, flashing off the jugs and bottles Airy and Dixie filled with practiced efficiency.

"Almost done," Airy said, looking up at Blade and Elise, who stood off to one side with Penny. "I'll send a bottle of it home with you, Blade, if your better half don't mind."

"I don't like that smell," Penny complained. "When are we going home? I'm tired."

"In just a minute," Elise told her. "I wanted to see the still Blade helped build. Do you want a bottle of it?" she asked him, and was relieved when he shook his head.

"I've got a jug stashed somewhere for medicinal purposes." His eyes sparkled with mischief.

"Lordy, I've heard *that* a few times," Airy said with a laugh. "Medicinal purposes and for cooking; that's why folks buy this stuff. They never buy it to just drink."

"I'm all out of it," Dixie explained. "If I don't keep it stocked, my boarders get restless. We should have made a new batch last week, Airy."

"I know, but I didn't figure them cakes for the church bake sale would use up so much. Shoot, they soaked up the whiskey like sponges." Airy cackled and slapped the flat of her hand across her thigh. "Them cakes sold like ice in summer, just like I told you they would. All we had to do was stand back and watch the stampede."

Dixie laughed with her. "We are wicked. Truly wicked. Once we put that sign on them —" Dixie held a hand out in front of her as if she were reading a banner. "HIGH SPIRITS CAKE. Well, that's all we had to do. The men caught on real quick what was in them."

Elise joined in for a laugh, recalling how the men had smacked their lips and sniffed the cakes while their wives had stood back with pursed lips and censuring glares.

"It was for a good cause." Airy corked the last bottle and handed it to her cousin to add to the ones lying in a straw filled box. "The pastor didn't turn up his nose when we offered him the money we got for them."

"We made more money than anybody else there," Dixie noted with pride. "Our twenty whiskey cakes went in a flash."

"If we had brought regular fare, we wouldn't have sold a one," Airy surmised. "Them old buzzards, like Gladys Keizer and Sally Carpenter, had made up their minds they weren't going to buy nothing from the likes of us. But we showed 'em! Why, Samuel Keizer bought not one but two!"

"Personally, I think the idea was inspired," Elise said with a jaunty smile. "Crossroads is full of hypocrites, and it's our duty to point it out whenever possible."

Blade reached down and picked up Penny. He swung her high to sit on his shoulders, her legs dangling down his chest. "The people around here are getting better. They had trouble after the War Between the States. Slaves were used everywhere in and around Crossroads, and the landowners were slow to give up their old ways. They didn't want to pay the workers they had never paid before. Years and years went by before their pride finally crumbled and they hired workers or made deals with sharecroppers."

"Some still treat their workers like slaves," Elise grumbled. "And I don't like the way they treat you. You've done nothing to those people."

"They aren't all unfriendly," Blade pointed out. "Only a few won't speak to me, and that doesn't keep me awake at night."

Airy squatted by the wood box and hammered nails into the lid. "I know somebody who sure ain't happy that we're back to bottling whiskey."

"Judge Mott," Elise said with a nod.

"How's your brother doing over at his place?"

Elise shrugged. "Who could get along with that man? I think he spooked a mule one day so that it dragged Adam behind it just to teach him a lesson in paying attention."

"I had that same thing done to me once," Blade said. "It worked. I learned to keep my mind on my plowing and not to let the mules do all the thinking for me."

Elise tried hard to hold onto her temper, but it never failed to irritate her when Blade agreed with anything the judge did. "And did you enjoy the experience, Blade? Would you wish it on other boys?"

His eyes grew stormy. "I don't wish harm on anyone, but your brother does have a foolish tongue and often uses it when he shouldn't."

Elise bit on her lower lip and tried to remain calm in front of the others. "How can you take the judge's side when you know he's nothing but a bully? Sometimes, Blade Lonewolf, I'd like nothing better than to give you a good, swift kick!"

Dixie cleared her throat and voiced gaiety into the atmosphere, which had become tense. "All done here! Blade, will you carry this heavy old box to the buggy for me?"

"Be glad to." He swung Penny to the ground and lifted the box full of bottles and jugs without so much as a grunt. "Then we'll be getting on home."

Elise held Penny's hand and walked behind him—ten paces. She glared at his back, but common sense told her he wasn't too far from being right. Adam could sass with the best of them, but he didn't deserve to be struck for it! Of course, men tended to look at things differently. Brute force was something they lived with, even fostered and found pride in. To be fair, Blade wasn't a brute. What they needed was a good, long talk, Elise decided. A husband and wife shouldn't bottle up their problems like spirits and cork them with pride. Problems did not age well.

Rocking steadily, Elise practiced the crochet loops and half loops Dixie had taught her. Coming inside after his evening chores, Blade stood by the door and watched her.

He'd been proud of her at the bake sale. She'd charmed many of the doubters with her bright smile and friendly patter. The table she, Airy and Dixie manned had been the most popular, and Blade had noticed the many admiring glances his wife had received from the townsmen. Her beauty, her easy laughter and her good manners had won them over.

A couple of men had even winked slyly at him in jocular congratulations. Yes, he was a lucky man.

She didn't look up, but concentrated on the yarn and needlework. A few dark red strands of her hair had slipped from their anchors on top of her head and curled along her neck. He thought of plucking the pins from her hair and burying his face in the silky mass.

Staving off his desire for her, which never seemed to diminish, he crossed the room to the washbasin and began scrubbing his hands, arms, face and neck. Something was bothering her, he thought, noting her silence and the worry lines between her eyes. Probably Adam.

"You acted like you enjoyed the day in town."

She nodded. "I think it's good to get to know the townspeople better, and let them get to know us."

"Elise, if you want to speak to me about something, now is the time. If you're not pleased with something I've done, then you should talk to me about it. I suppose it's something to do with Adam."

She abandoned her crochet needle as her hands fell motionless in her lap. "He was in school only twice this week. I'm afraid he might run away, Blade."

"He might, but he promised me he'd come here first. I believe him."

She leaned her head against the back of the rocker. "I hope he honors that vow. I don't even recognize him sometimes, Blade. He's changed so much." She chewed fretfully on her lower lip. "I feel guility."

"Guilty about what?"

"It was wrong to ask him to remain somewhere that he hates." She twisted her hands in her lap. "I brought him food every day to school because he doesn't like what they feed him. He doesn't like anything about that place."

Blade sat at the kitchen table. "I should never have told the judge about the train."

"What?" She looked at him, and the glow of the lamp gave her face an ethereal quality.

"I told the judge about the orphan train. I never thought he'd ask for a child, too. He encouraged me to go ahead and adopt, said he'd loan me the money."

"All he wanted was your land, Blade, and to keep his foot on your neck. I know his kind. He's a lot like my grandparents. They must control. They must be obeyed. I think it bothers Judge Mott that you have land and that you married two white women."

Blade grinned. "He thinks I'm less than human and should be on a reservation."

"He won't rest until he has you on your knees."

"Never." Blade set his jaw. Did she think he would kneel before any man?

She stood up and moved like a sleepwalker to the door. Opening it, she gazed outside. A breeze scampered in, ruffling her skirt and hair.

"I was so happy today at the bake sale."

He studied her, unable to follow her quicksilver moods.

"The people were nice to me. They thought it was clever of us to spike the cakes with home brew. They called me Mrs. Lonewolf, and for a while I thought I could fit in here and make a happy life for myself."

"I saw the happiness in your face and I heard it in your laugh." He stood and moved close enough to drag a fingertip across the back yoke of her dress. "It gave me hope."

"But are we foolish to hope? I hate Julia for talking you into putting your family's land in jeopardy."

"It was my decision, too," he reminded her. "Julia never made me do anything I didn't want to do."

"So here we are, hanging on by a thread."

Her voice quivered and he realized she was close to tears. He curved a hand over the top of her shoulder, but she shrugged it off.

"I've grown accustomed to this place," she confessed, then tried to laugh, but couldn't quite do it. "Maybe I've always been a farm wife at heart. I'll miss it."

He bit back a curse. "What are you saying? I haven't lost this place!"

"But you will, don't you see?" She turned to face him and tears striped her cheeks. "Adam can't stay at the judge's. That's asking too much of a young boy. The judge has everyone jumping when he snaps his fingers, except for you. Once he has your land, he'll have you."

"I will burn this cabin to the ground and leave. He will never own me."

"Oh, Blade." She choked back a sob. "He already

does. He owns me, too, in a way. Neither one of us would be asking my brother to stay with him if that weren't true." Her eyes swam with tears. "I'm so ashamed. I should never have sent Adam back to that demon!"

Blade reached for her, but she sidestepped him. "Elise, please—"

"No, I can't. I feel terrible for being happy here while Adam is so miserable. I'm going to bed."

She went into the bedroom. Blade extinquished the lamps and followed her. Undressing by the window, she turned her back to him while removing her chemise. Moonlight painted her shoulders silver and brought out the fire in her hair. She reached for the nightgown she'd draped at the foot of the bed, but Blade snatched it out of her reach and held it away from her.

"Blade, please . . ." She covered her bare breasts with one arm and twisted around so that her lower body was curtained in shadow. "Not tonight. I have a headache and I'm not in the mood. I told you—"

He pitched the nightgown aside and took her in his arms. She was resistant at first, but gradually her lips relaxed beneath his and her hands moved gently over his shoulders. He looked into the deep blue pools of her eyes.

"Don't push me away, Elise. I have done nothing wrong."

"I know." She framed his face in her cool hands. "I should be eternally grateful to you, but I—"

"It isn't your gratitude I want," he interrupted. "I have never wanted that."

She lowered her lashes. "What will become of us, Blade? What will we do when we have to leave this place?"

"It might not come to that."

Her hands slipped down his face to rest on his shoulders. She delivered a glance that chided. "And how will you come up with the money in time? Will you borrow from Peter to pay Paul?"

"I will borrow no more. I've learned my lesson. Perhaps the judge will extend the time period."

"Ah, yes. And perhaps pigs will fly." She made a joshing sound and eased away from him to retrieve her nightgown. He frowned when she slipped it on before climbing into bed and burrowing under the top sheet.

"I haven't talked to the judge and neither have you. He might be willing." Even as Blade said it, he knew the improbability of such an act of generosity from the judge. He sat on the side of the bed to remove his boots and socks.

As Blade undressed, he pondered her question. What would happen to them? How could he make a living for a family without land to farm?

"We could go back to the reservation," he said, mostly to himself.

"Would that be a good life for Adam and Penny?"

He shook his head and lay down beside her, not touching her, feeling as if a mile separated them instead of inches. "They wouldn't like it there. You have no family to take you in while I look for other means to support us?"

"No." She turned onto her side, her back to him. "I won't go begging to my grandparents, if that's what you're suggesting."

He glared at the back of her head. "I wasn't," he assured her. "I'm only trying to answer your question about what will happen if I lose the land. Without it, I can't make a living. Not for a while, anyway. I'd have to find work somewhere—on a ranch or a farm. Even then I probably wouldn't make enough to support a family."

"I could find work, too."

He scowled into the darkness above him. "No."

"No?" She twisted around to face him. "And why not?"

"You're my wife. Your place is in the home."

"What home? If we lose this land, any work we find will be a blessing. What's important is keeping the family together." She didn't speak for a moment before adding, "That *is* important to you, isn't it, Blade?"

He frowned at her, resenting the question. "Yes, of course. I want to earn the living, though. I don't need a woman to work and pay my way."

She flopped onto her back. "I will work if that's what it takes to keep Penny and Adam with me. If I could have found a good job in the short amount of time they gave me back in Baltimore, I wouldn't be in this spot now. I would be working and making a living for them myself." Resentment colored her voice. "But the Society wouldn't give me time to find decent employment. I'm sure I could hire on somewhere as a cook or a nanny or even a sales clerk."

He told himself he shouldn't be so touchy, but her comments rankled. She talked as if Penny and Adam were her only family and he was nothing to her. She also sounded as if she had no faith in his finding work and providing for them. She stared at the ceiling, worry pinching lines along her brow and at the corners of her eyes and mouth.

"You forget that Penny is mine to provide for now. And Adam is the judge's."

She whipped her gaze to his. "But they're my flesh and blood!"

"You aren't my flesh and blood, but you're my wife. I am responsible for your welfare, too. You let me worry about providing a living—*if* this land is taken from me."

"Oh, Blade, don't wear a blindfold. You know the judge will take this land if you don't pay him."

"I know that only Usen can shape the future."

She looked at him. "Who?"

"Usen, the Giver of Life. The Apache's great spirit. Anything could happen in the next few weeks. The judge might fall ill by chance. Perhaps a snake or a coyote will cross his path and bring him bad luck."

"You don't really believe in that stuff, do you? Sounds like witchcraft to me."

He propped his head in one hand to face her. "Do you believe in people being turned into pillars of salt, in burning bushes that talk, in seas that divide so they may be crossed?"

She had the grace to blush. "Usen, you say?"

He smiled. "That's right. Anything could happen. The judge could even die."

Her eyes widened and she clutched his arm. "Blade, you wouldn't!"

"No, but it could happen," he insisted. "Only a fool plans each day before the dawn breaks."

"But we *must* plan, or we'll be forced out with nowhere to go."

"Maybe, or maybe we'll remain here." He trailed a finger down her cheek, which felt cool and satiny soft. "Who could have predicted that I would find a wife on that train? Who could have known, other than Usen or your God, that I would be lying next to her and wanting her so much that it takes all my strength not to force my will on her?" He captured one of her hands and guided it beneath the sheets to his straining, burning, rock-hard flesh. Her fingers shied away, then returned to close around him.

"Ah, yes!" he hissed between clenched teeth. He rocked his hips to create a delicious friction. He kissed her, his lips plucking at her, striving for an answering display of mindless desire.

Elise kissed him back, but her usual fire was lacking. Blade tried to stoke her banked embers by fondling her breasts, raining kisses over her face and lips, nuzzling the sensitive patch of skin behind her ear. She responded, but only that.

He pulled away, frustration writhing in his belly. For an instant their gazes met, and he saw acquiescence in hers. With a muttered oath, he moved on top of her and entered her. She opened her thighs, taking him in, and matched his rhythm, but she never shuddered beneath him, never sighed his name like a prayer. He released his seed into her, his own burst of pleasure too brief. He felt cheated and incomplete.

When it was over, he kissed her lips softly. "What can I do to make you happy, Elise?"

"Nothing." She shook her head and turned onto her side. "I'm tired, Blade. Good night."

He lay in the darkness, bereft, burdened. She shifted onto her stomach and rested her hand near his head. He glanced at her hand. It was bare, with no ring to show that she was married. Did she not feel married to him? Was she thinking of taking Adam and Penny and leaving him? Where would she go? Baltimore?

She said they had no relatives there who would help them, but he knew she had friends there. That woman she'd written to, he thought. Donetta? They seemed very close. Almost like sisters.

The thoughts bedeviled him, denying him peace or sleep. He couldn't let Elise go. Looking out the window, he stared at the spangled sky and knew he'd have to confront the judge again. He had nothing to bargain with—except for the boy.

The judge was having trouble with Adam. If Blade could strike a deal with him—more time in exchange for teaching Adam about farming, maybe even farming some of the judge's land with the boy—then that would serve them both well.

It was a long shot, but it was all he had. If he lost the land, he was afraid he might lose everything—namely, Elise. If tonight was a sign, she was already pulling away from him . . . and he knew that life without her would be no life at all. After Julia died, he had been lonely. He'd missed her company.

But Elise had shown him a life he'd only dreamed about. If the dream died, then he'd want to die with it.

He, Lonewolf, couldn't bear to be alone again.

Chapter 21

Blade hoed between the rows of his planted cotton, his mind worrying with his plan like a tongue worries with a painful tooth. He leaned on the hoe and uncorked his canteen. As he drank deeply, he thought of the boy.

Earlier, Elise had taken Penny to school, only to return with a frown marring her delicate features because Adam hadn't been there again. Blade mopped his face and neck with a handkerchief and stared at the horizon, picturing Adam toiling in the fields. If the boy was being mistreated, as Elise suspected, he'd have to take him from the judge. No compromise. No deals struck. Such an act would seal his fate—and everyone else's.

He dropped the hoe and walked to the road. He'd get no work done as long as this cloud hung over his head. Cupping his hands around his mouth, he whistled shrilly. Scanning the area, he listened, then whistled again. He felt the ground tremble beneath his feet and he turned in a circle until he saw Bob coming at him hard from the north. The thunder of Bob's hooves reached his ears. Probably been out by the stocked pond, he thought. Out there in the deep shade, just a step from a cool drink.

The pinto stopped a ways from him and reared, showing off. He pricked his ears forward, waiting for a word.

"Come here, son." Blade held out a hand. The stallion pawed the earth. "Now, don't go messing up my fields. Come here and behave yourself. I need a ride."

The horse high-stepped nearer, nostrils flared, tossing his head. Blade laughed as he grabbed a handful of the thick mane. He gave a hop and slid onto the horse's back. Bob pranced and snorted, waiting for Blade's next move after he'd gained a comfortable seat.

"Let's go." Blade tapped his heels against Bob's sides, and the pinto responded with a canter. Giving a tug on Bob's mane, Blade directed him toward Mott's land.

The sun was already hot, although it was only nine in the morning. Nearby, a mockingbird imitated a cardinal, a whippoorwill, a sparrow and a crow with rapid expertise. Blade looked at his land with eyes that paid close attention to detail. It was good bottom land, well known for its richness and deep top soil.

When he'd first seen it as a young boy, it was being farmed by his mother's uncle, who had been wounded in the war and was having a hard time making the farm pay for itself. Blade's father was dead and his mother was trying to find a place of her own again. She and Blade spent six months on the farm helping the uncle, who had shown Blade the satisfaction of field work. He and his mother had journeyed on, back to her parents' home, but Blade had never forgotten the farm.

He'd talked to his mother about the peace that had come over him when he'd worked under the sun and put things in the soil, joining partners with nature. She had understood and had drawn up a will, leaving the farm to him. When word had come of his uncle's illness, she'd sent Blade to stake his claim.

His uncle had detailed his planting schedule and had told Blade that Judge Lloyd Mott was interested in purchasing the whole farm outright, should Blade want to sell; then he'd left to live with a half sister in South Carolina. The judge had wasted no time in paying a call and offering to buy the land. Blade hadn't wanted to sell, and the judge had warned him that he wouldn't like farming, that he didn't belong and would have no more success than his uncle before him.

Over the years he and the judge had kept a wary distance from each other, even after he'd signed for the loan and put his land up as security. Blade knew the judge thought he had what he'd always wanted—more land and more power in the county. Blade had never seen it that way until lately. While Julia had been alive, Blade had thought that the judge would allow an extension. The man had a soft spot for Julia, and Blade figured he would extend the loan just to keep Julia around so he'd have someone to read poetry with and discuss what they called "the classics."

After Julia's death, Blade had known that nothing would keep the judge from snatching the land the moment it was available. He'd never liked Blade and would rejoice when Blade packed up and left. The old bastard.

Bob's warm hide slipped back and forth under Blade's rump. Bees buzzed and butterflies flitted among the wildflowers growing alongside the road. An aching started in Blade's heart and grew. He could lose it all. Then where would he go? Would Elise go with him?

His mother had decided to name him Blade at his birth, but by the time he was walking, his Apache grandfather, Graywolf, had decided he would be called Lonewolf because he rarely played with the other children, preferring his own company. It had been like that his whole life until he'd settled in this place and met Julia Lincoln. She had shown him that he wasn't meant to always be alone. He had liked her company, enjoyed hearing about her work at the school. Sometimes she read aloud to him from Dickens and Cooper. When she had died and her voice had been silenced forever, that was what he had grieved for the most—her stories. His mother had been quiet, speaking in muted, halting tones. Julia, being a schoolteacher and used to commanding a classroom of fidgeting children, had cultivated a voice full of drama and verve. She never failed to hold him enthralled, even if she was talking about something as mundane as the lesson she planned to teach the next day.

During his marriage to Julia, he'd discovered that he appreciated the company of a woman, and when she was gone, he'd thought he'd go mad from the loneliness.

Then a ray of sunshine had pierced his gray existence. Elise. Even her name sounded light and happy and beautiful, just like her. He must have been a blockhead at first not to see that she was a gift and not a curse. He had been blinded by his acute loneliness and had seen only the child as a cure for what ailed him. But resisting Elise was about as easy as resisting one's own natural urges.

If she left him now, it would be the same as if the sun set, never to rise again.

Approaching the judge's property, Blade felt a twinge of envy at the sight of numerous field hands dotting the land. The men and women working in the judge's fields were former slaves, now paid paltry wages and allowed to live in shacks on the outskirts of the property lines. He scanned the fields for Adam, but didn't see him. Since the boy wasn't in school, he must be working, Blade decided. Maybe he had chores inside the house.

He returned the waves of some of the field workers as he rode his flashy pinto toward the house. Sliding off the horse's hot hide, he tied Bob at the water trough. An old black woman sat on her knees by the front flower beds and pulled weeds from around rose bushes and irises. A wheelbarrow was behind her, nearly full of grass clippings, dandelions, chickweed and milkweed. Her white hair was covered with a yellow rag. She smiled at him, showing gray teeth.

"Good morning," Blade said, touching the brim of his hat as he passed by.

" 'Day, suh."

He took the steps two at a time and rang a brass bell bolted on the doorframe. Listening, he heard no footfalls or movement. He rang the bell again. This time he heard a soft rustling, and the doorknob rattled. Slowly, the door opened only far enough to frame Harriet's face. She looked pale and her eyes were big and watery. There was something different about her face, but it was shadowy inside the house and he couldn't see her clearly. She wore a pea-green dress, but she acted as if she weren't decent and couldn't invite him in.

"I've come to talk to the judge. Is he around?"

Harriet shook her head. The meager light played over her face, revealing to Blade the purple tinged skin around her left eye and the swelling of her lower lip. His stomach tightened and a blazing rage licked at his heart and scalded his throat.

"Do you need help?" he asked, lowering his voice to a whisper and stepping closer to the door. He removed his hat and angled toward her. She was shaking like a leaf in the wind. "Mrs. Mott, I'm looking for Adam. Is he inside with you? Are you two all right?"

"I'm fine," she said, her voice trembling and her words distorted by her swollen lip. "Go away. You'll only make things worse around here." She closed the door in his face.

He started to ring the bell again, but his better sense told him he shouldn't involve himself in what went on between the judge and Harriet. He'd come to talk to Adam and the judge, not to be a marriage go-between.

Standing on the porch, he put his hat back on and surveyed the flat fields. He saw no slight figure with red hair out there, nor did he catch sight of the judge, who usually sat in the shade in his fancy fold-up chair.

"Lots of yellin' this mornin'," the black woman said. She yanked at a dandelion and tossed it into the pile behind her. She didn't look at Blade, although her words were meant for him. "The judge be roarin' like a bull and seein' red everywheres."

Blade studied her shiny black face. Worry pinched the skin around her mouth and eyes. "You know where the judge is now? I need to talk to him."

"You be lookin' for the boy, too?"

"Yes, that's right. Adam . . . or Rusty. Do you know where he is?"

She raised her dirty, green-streaked hand and pointed to the back of the house. Blade bounded down the steps so that he could see where she pointed.

"The shed or the outhouse?" he asked.

"Them wouldn't be in the outhouse together, I doan reckon." She bent to the flower beds again. "During slave times that shed was used regular, but it don't get much use these days."

Blade gathered up the pile of weeds and dumped them into the wheelbarrow for her. He tried to remember what was in the shed—some tools, a few grain sacks. He'd seen inside it only a time or two.

"Better git," the old woman said in a singsong way. "Theys been in there a few minutes."

She wasn't suggesting, she was ordering him—warning him! A stone of panic tumbled through him, kicking up an avalanche. Something was wrong . . . this pretty day had a dark underbelly. His legs couldn't take him fast enough to the shed. The door was shut, but as he neared the structure he heard a crack and a moan. Rage exploded in him, pumping inhuman strength into his limbs as he grabbed the handle and nearly ripped the door off its hinges. The door popped open, slapped against the shed and slammed shut again. In that instant when the interior was visible to him, Blade saw Adam hanging by his wrists, his back striped red.

With a howl of rage, Blade grabbed a shovel leaning against the shed and threw open the door again. He charged inside and laid the flat of the shovel against the judge's back, knocking him sideways.

Adam strained to look over his shoulder, tears pooling in his eyes, and he sobbed with relief. "Blade, get me down from here," he begged.

"Relax, little brother." Blade stood over the judge, legs spread, feet planted, fists bunched at his sides. The judge stared up at him, still clutching the long leather strap he'd been using on Adam. "I ought to tear you from limb to limb, you old bastard," Blade growled.

Judge Mott narrowed his black eyes and scrunched up his face. "Don't hit an old man," he whined, lifting a hand to shield himself. "I was only disciplining the boy! He was being spiteful . . . he tried to run away."

"Who can blame him?" Blade confronted the cowering shell of humanity before him, and disgust blew out his blinding rage.

For years he'd put up with the judge's crude and rude remarks. He'd turned the other cheek when the old buzzard had treated him like dirt. He'd kept his mouth shut when he wanted to tell the sneaky old snake to keep off his land and away from Julia. Lately, he'd told himself that the judge wasn't really doing any harm to the boy by making him work hard and learn to keep a civil tongue in his head.

Blade had recalled the harsh lessons of his own youth when his Apache father had taken him out into the wilderness and left him to survive with only a hunting knife, a bow and a quiver of arrows. Unbeknownst to him, his father had kept an eye on him, but he'd been a terrified nine-year-old for the three days and two nights he was left alone. It had been a lesson in self-sufficiency, and not uncommon among his father's people. Blade had convinced himself it had been a good lesson, but now, as he stood over a white-livered coward, he knew the only lesson he'd learned during that ordeal was fear and abandonment. And he had never fully trusted his father again.

Elise was right. There were many other ways to teach than through fear, intimidation and pain.

"You're pathetic." Blade curled his upper lip and turned away from the lump of quivering flesh at his feet. He propped the shovel against the wall. "Hold still, Adam," he said, reaching to free the boy's hands from the leather cuffs biting into his wrists.

Six or seven angry welts crisscrossed Adam's back. Blade tried to be gentle. He circled the boy's waist with one arm, holding his weight while he freed one wrist and then started to work on the other.

"Filthy Indian." The words came from behind him in a voice full of hatred.

He heard movement, saw the fuzzy light shift, and then hot, blinding pain exploded in his head. Stunned, he acted instinctively, crouching on the balls of his feet and swiveling around to confront his attacker. The shovel came at him. He ducked and rolled, and the shovel whistled harmlessly through the air, throwing the judge off-balance. Blade surged up, grabbing the man around the middle and hurtling him off his feet. The two landed hard, the breath forced from their lungs, and scrambled for handholds. Blade ended up on top. The judge's nails scraped the skin on Blade's neck as he tried for a stranglehold. He was stronger than Blade had imagined, and his fingers felt like bands of steel. With a grunt, Mott bucked and unseated Blade. Before Blade could rise up off all fours, the judge laid the thick strap across his face.

The sting brought tears to his eyes and knocked him backward. The back of his head slammed against the wall. His ears rang and his vision blurred. He saw two judges advancing on him with straps in hand.

Blade shook his head, trying to get his bearings.

"You're a dead man," Mott said, and his voice sounded far away, as if he were down in a well.

Blade saw the shovel come up . . . slowly, slowly, as if time had spread like strings of molasses. Raising a hand, he told his body to move, to duck, to defend itself, but every effort was laborious. His head rang like a bell, and his lungs burned as he struggled for breath.

"No!" Another voice, shrill as a whistle, cut through.

In a haze, Blade saw Adam moving behind the judge. The boy still hung from one wrist, but he twisted his body and raised his knees. Stiffening his legs out in front of him, he kicked the judge in the shoulders and head, propelling him past Blade and into the wall.

Groaning, the judge slumped and sat down heavily, giving Blade precious seconds to draw oxygen into his lungs and clear his head. His eyes focused on the whipping strap and rage pumped energy into his body. Snatching the strap from the judge's hand, still feeling the sting of it across his cheek, he lashed out. The strap sang through the air and caught the judge across the chest. Mott squealed and scrambled to his feet, but not before Blade had struck again and the leather had snapped against Mott's neck and shoulder.

"How do you like the feel of that?" Blade asked, his breath coming sharp and harsh. He caught the man around the throat in one hand and threw aside the strap as he backed Mott up against the wall. The judge's eyes bulged from their sockets.

"Let go of me, you scalp-taking heathen!"

Blade buried a fist in Mott's midsection, doubling him over. A swift uppercut to the chin sent Mott jackknifing up and backward. He sprawled on the ground, his mouth and nose leaking blood.

"You'd better stay down unless you want your teeth hulled," Blade warned. "I'm taking this boy." He moved to Adam again, supporting him around the middle while he worked his other wrist free of the bondage. Adam wobbled, but stood on his own power.

"You got no right. He belongs to me." Judge Mott touched his beak gingerly and winced. "You've broken my nose!"

"And if you're lucky, I won't break your back." Blade looked around at the clutter before he spotted Adam's shirt. It had been torn in half. Ripped from his body, Blade guessed. "Adam, you go get what you want to take with you."

Adam glanced from Blade to the judge, then ran outside. Blade listened to his footfalls until they grew faint; then he reached down and grabbed a fistful of the judge's shirt and hauled him roughly to his feet.

"I'm taking the boy and I don't want to see you around. If you mess with my belongings or my family, I'll kill you."

"Your belongings, your family." The judge laughed, spitting blood that splattered Blade's shirt collar. "Start packing your things, Lonewolf, because I'll be taking over your place come the first of the month." He thrust his face closer. "You don't have the money to pay me. Julia told me before she died. She made me promise I'd give you more time to pay, but I'm not cutting you any slack. I was going to let you sharecrop it, but not after this."

Blade hated hearing him even mention Julia. He tightened his grip and shook Mott like a rag doll. "I'd never sharecrop my own land." Shoving the judge away, Blade released him.

"You can't just take the boy, you know. I'm his legal guardian."

"Take me to court." He jabbed a finger at the man's chest. "But stay off my land and keep away from my family." Finding his hat, he picked it up off the ground and whacked it against his pant leg, dislodging dust and dirt, before putting it back on.

"Your family. What a joke," the judge mocked as Blade walked away from him. "Think you can keep this wife happy? You sure made Julia's life a living hell."

Blade stood outside and took great gulps of the fresh air. Inside the shed it had been close and heavy with the stench of human sweat, blood and misery. Blade remembered now that it had been the whipping shed before the war, the judge's private torture chamber for his unfortunate slaves.

"Julia would have left you if it hadn't been for me."

Looking over his shoulder at the other man, Blade issued a short, harsh laugh. "And I'm supposed to believe you?"

"She told me how you were rough with her, and I showed her how a gentleman makes love to a lady. She couldn't get enough of me."

Blade whirled, ready to kill the man, but the childish smirk on the judge's bloody face took the urge to murder out of him. He swatted the air in a gesture of ridicule. "You're an old fool, long past your prime. You couldn't hump a knothole, so don't talk to me of Julia." He grinned when the judge seemed to age twenty years right before his eyes. Striding away from him, he felt better, but only marginally.

That Julia had discussed their most private issues with Judge Mott made him ill. Clammy sweat beaded on his brow and slicked his palms. He walked toward the house, his mind staggering and surging like a wounded animal. Had she allowed the judge to touch her . . . to be intimate with her? He clamped his eyes shut for a moment in concentrated denial.

"Hssst!"

His eyes flew open and he cast around wildly, expecting another charge from the judge. At first he saw no one. Harriet Mott emerged from behind a tree and beckoned him closer. She wore the shapeless green shift and her hair was haphazardly styled, half of it piled atop her head and the other half straggling down her neck and in her eyes. The bruises on her face had become purple and blue. When he got close enough, she grabbed his shirt-sleeve and yanked him toward her.

"You taking the boy?"

"Yes."

"Take me, too."

He retreated, shaking his head, but she held onto his sleeve and stumbled after him.

"I gotta get away from here."

"Ride one of the horses into town. Someone there will help you. The church pastor, or Dixie Shoemaker at the boarding—"

"No, you take me to your place. You protect me."

"I can't."

"I'll be good to you." She sidled up next to him,

rubbing her small breasts against his arm. "I'll take you in my mouth if'n you want. Bet your little wifey don't do that for you."

Repulsed by her crass offer, he yanked free of her. "No. I'm sorry for your trouble, Harriet, but I can't take you to my place. If you need money, I can give you a dollar or two."

Suddenly her eyes filled with tears and her lips trembled. She plucked a handkerchief from her pocket and dabbed at the moisture.

"You don't have to give me no money, but it's sweet of you to offer. I just..." She shook her head. "I ain't got the guts to leave him on my own." Taking a quick, deep breath, she looked fearfully toward the shed, but the judge wasn't in sight. "I heard him ... I heard what he said about him and Julia. Don't you go believing him." When she met Blade's eyes again, hers glittered with a hard brightness. "He got his pecker shot off during the war," she revealed in a vicious whisper.

Stupefied, Blade stared at her, not sure he'd heard her right.

"He don't want nobody to know it. He wants everybody to think he's a standing stud, but he's a gelding, I tell you. That's why he's a judge now. Some old pal of his—a colonel or something—felt so blamed sorry for him that he gave Lloyd that judge title. Why, he don't know nothing about the law! He got a title to take the place of his johnson, is all." Smiling wickedly, she winked with her good eye. "He couldn't do nothing with your wife, so don't you fret about that."

"I'm grateful to you for telling me."

Adam came around the side of the house. He had put on a shirt, but didn't seem to have packed anything. Leading Bob by the halter, he quickened his steps when he saw Blade.

Blade tipped his hat to Harriet. "Good luck to you, ma'am."

"Y'all go on." Harriet backed away, then turned and ran to the house.

"Let's go." Adam swung up onto Bob's back. "Blade? We're going, right?"

"Yes, so keep your britches on." He ran his gaze over Adam, then the pinto. "I thought you went to get your things."

"I don't have anything here I want. The judge burned everything I brought with me from Baltimore."

Blade heaved a sigh, distressed by the judge's deep-down depravity. He grabbed a handful of Bob's mane and hoisted himself up behind Adam. Taking the reins from the boy, he nudged Bob into a walk.

"Will he come for me?" Adam asked.

"I don't know. He might try something, but we'll be ready for him."

"Did Elise send you?"

"No, but she's worried about you."

"Let's not tell her about . . . about what was happening in the shed."

Blade angled his head sideways so that he could see Adam's profile. He saw pride and shame on the lad's face. "We're not going to lie to your sister, little brother. I'll tell her about how you and me beat the living daylights out of that old coon."

Adam's lips twitched into a lopsided grin. "Okay." Then his shoulders slumped as if he were suddenly bone tired.

Blade rested a hand lightly on Adam's shoulder and gave it a squeeze. "We'll be home soon. A good meal and a night's sleep will make the world look better to you."

"It looks better already," Adam said. He swallowed hard, and Blade saw the glimmer of tears in his eyes.

Halfway home, Adam's head dropped forward and he dozed. Blade wondered how long it had been since the boy had enjoyed a peaceful, fearless night's sleep.

Chapter 22

After making sure Adam was comfortable in her bed, Elise knelt beside him and kissed his forehead.

"I'm so glad you're here," she whispered, finding his hand and clutching it tightly between hers. "Are you sure you aren't hurting anywhere? How about those welts on your back? You want me to put more medicine on them?"

"No, Sis, they're fine." He smiled sleepily. "I'm worn out. Like Blade said, by morning I'll be full of spit and vinegar again." His fingers tightened around her hand. "He won't let the judge take me back there, will he?"

"No." She brushed his hair away from the tops of his ears with her free hand. "And neither will I. Now that we're back together, no one is ever going to separate us again."

He closed his eyes and wiggled into a more comfortable position, lying on his side. "Good night, 'Lise. I can hardly wait for breakfast."

Smiling, she let go of his hand and tucked the light cover around him. Her brother had eaten enough for two grown men tonight, and he was already dreaming of another meal. Her smile faded, chased by thoughts of what he must have suffered at Judge Mott's.

Rising, Elise crossed the room to check on Penny, who was sleeping, an angelic expression on her round face. She, too, was glad her big brother was home. When Elise and Penny had spied Blade riding toward the house with Adam slumped over the pinto's neck, Elise had screamed in sheer terror, thinking her brother had been killed. Her blood-curdling screech had awakened Adam and he'd sat bolt upright, his blue eyes blinking like an owl's. Elise had rushed forward, sobs of joy clogging her throat.

Elise stood by the bedroom window and looked at the quarter moon hanging in the sky. She felt as if she should pinch herself to make sure this wasn't a dream. She glanced over her shoulder to confirm that her sister *and* brother were, indeed, with her again. And she had Blade to thank for that.

Blade and Adam had forged a closer relationship. She'd noticed it at supper when Adam had looked to Blade for confirmation or a quick wink or smile. Their recitation of what had happened at the judge's had been sketchy, with Blade glossing over the violent parts. Elise could tell, however, that he had become Adam's hero.

Turning, she enjoyed the sight of the two lumps in the narrow beds. Smoothing her hands over her hair, then down the front of her peach-colored dress, she gathered her composure and left the dark bedroom. Blade sat on the porch steps, his back against a post. He looked up at her questioningly.

"Oh, Adam's fine," she answered, assuming he was wondering about their new boarder. "How are you?" She tucked her skirts around her legs and sat opposite him on the top step.

"I was just thinking that I feel damn good for a man who's lost his land."

"Oh, Blade." She reached out to take his hand. "I wish there were something I could do."

Sadness lurked in his eyes. "Ah, well. Only a fool fights fate."

"Maybe something will happen. There is still time."

"For a miracle? Do you think someone will show up at our door and offer me money? Or maybe we will print money ourselves." He pulled his hand from beneath hers and folded his arms against his chest. "No. It's better to prepare for one's fate."

"You don't mind if I remain optimistic? It won't dampen your pessimistic outlook?" She smiled, showing him that she was partly teasing. "I want to thank you for bringing Adam here, Blade. I know what you've sacrificed and I'll never be able to repay you."

"I seek no payment. Do you understand that I didn't know how bad things were for the boy?"

"Yes, I know. You thought the judge was toughening him up, making him sweat for a living."

"I couldn't believe my eyes!" He shook his head. "I know the judge used to beat his slaves, but to beat that boy! I'll never back down from him again. Today I saw a jackal in his soul and a weasel in his eyes."

Elise watched him uneasily, disturbed by his shuttered expression. He had made an enemy today, she thought. A dangerous enemy. She hoped he didn't take the judge too lightly. To Elise's way of thinking, Lloyd Mott was a hair away from being as crazy as a loon. There was no predicting how he might react, what he might do next.

Restless with a need to reach out to Blade, but not sure how to do it, Elise directed her gaze to the quarter moon. Blade sat, arms crossed, as remote as the stars in the sky.

"It's a pretty night, but a little warm," she noted.

"Ummm."

She didn't know what to gather from his grunt. "I couldn't help but notice how fond Adam has become of you. You've made an impression on all of us."

"Ummm."

Expelling a sigh of exasperation, she started to rise, thinking that he wanted to be alone. "You're tired, so I'll just go—"

His fingers gripped her wrist, keeping her seated. "No, don't go."

Elise met his level gaze. "What is it, Blade?"

"What will you do when the land is gone?"

She shook her head, baffled. "Wh-what will I do? Whatever I must, I suppose. But if there is any way to keep it, we should investigate. Maybe a bank will loan us the money."

He frowned. "Not to me."

"You don't know that."

"I have nothing to put up for the money."

"The land! The note can simply be transferred from Mott to the bank."

"Well, maybe. Mott is the biggest depositor at the bank, though, so I don't imagine they'll be too quick to go against him."

"Oh. Then we'll go to a bank in a different town."

"Deal with strangers, you mean?"

She was beginning to see that there was no way

out. Still, she hated facing defeat. "Perhaps I can sell my brooch—"

"No! You will sell nothing." His eyes flashed a warning. "That brooch means something to you. You will keep it and pass it on to your children."

Your children. She diverted her gaze, afraid he might see the disappointment in her eyes. Not *our* children. *Your* children. Was he planning to break free from the marriage if his land was lost?

"Blade . . . I must ask . . ." Her words died as his fingertips played lightly over her lips. She blinked, realizing that in the span of mere seconds he had gone from mild irritation to desperate desire. His quicksilver moods made her dizzy! Ah, but she liked him in this mood. She liked that his eyes blazed with banked desire and his chest rose and fell beneath his shirt as if he'd run a mile.

Longing blew through her like a hot wind. She swayed toward him, knowing full well that her expression gave her away, and not caring that it did.

"Oh, Blade . . . oh, how I want . . ."

He wrapped her in his arms and smothered her words with his warm lips and probing tongue. "I want you, too, but not like the last time. I took from you what you were not wanting to give."

"I was upset about Adam. I'm sorry . . . so sorry." She pressed kisses to his eyelids, his cheek-bones, the bruise along his jaw. "What you did to-day, what you've done for all of us . . ."

"I did it for me, too. I want to make you happy. I want Adam and Penny to be happy."

"We are." She smoothed a lock of hair off his forehead. "That's why it hurts so much to even think about losing this place. Penny and I have come to think of it as our home."

He smiled. "You've made it a good home for me

again." His dark gold eyes moved, taking in her features. "Let's not think about tomorrow. Tonight is ours."

Elise stood up and drew him up to stand beside her. In the next moment she was being carried to the bedroom, where she wanted to be with him. Her emotions overflowed as her mouth flowered over his. Once inside the room with the door closed behind them, Blade set her on her feet and began unbuttoning her dress.

"I need you tonight, my wife," he whispered, sliding his lips over her shoulder and into the valley between her breasts. "I don't want to think of tomorrow . . . only of tonight and what your body can do to mine."

"Oh, yes, that's what I want, too." Elise touched the welt on his cheek and kissed it gingerly while he undressed her. Then she undressed him, bestowing kisses down his bare chest and stomach. He'd taken a bath earlier and the scent of lye soap and rain water clung to his skin—rain water they'd caught in barrels while they had made love on the floor in front of the fireplace that first time.

The bed squeaked as they fell upon it in a jumble of tangled limbs. Feverish with need, Elise peppered Blade's shoulders and chest with kisses and ran her heels up and down his muscled calves. He buried his hands in the flow of her hair and held her head still so that he could properly ravage her mouth. Slipping his hands from her hair, he skimmed his palms down her sides and whispered to her of his needs, his burning flesh. She understood and urged him on with her hands and lips.

He tucked her smaller body more completely beneath his larger one. She parted her thighs, receiving him, growing moist to ease his gentle invasion.

"My body craves yours," Elise confessed. "I never thought it would be so . . . so . . ."

"So what?" His lips traveled between her breasts and flirted with her navel.

"So consuming. When I look at you, I can't help but think of this . . . of how you fit inside me and how perfect the world is when we're together like this."

His gaze licked up her body to her face, and his smile was carnal. "You like what I do to you?"

"Oh, yes," she said on a long sigh. "I can't imagine any woman *not* liking it."

He kissed his way below her navel and nuzzled her. Gasping at his audacity, she held her breath, not daring to move lest he think she was displeased. He probed with his tongue and breathed hotly against her.

"Blade . . . Blade . . ." She kept repeating his name as desire took her mind and surrendered her body to him.

His manipulations had her writhing and moaning, thrashing and gasping. When at last he positioned his body upon hers and entered her with a swift, hard thrust, she had to bite her lips to keep from screaming in ecstasy. Digging her fingers into his shoulders, she matched his rhythm, moving like a tide, in and out. Her release came shortly after his, and once again she marveled at their harmony and the sweet afterglow that flowed through her like honey.

She kissed him lightly on the cheek where he was bruised and battered, getting a smile from him before he rolled onto his back. Sprawled in all his male glory, he took up most of the bed, so she draped herself over him in utter contentment. Tracing one of the pale blue lines in the patterns on his chest, she glanced shyly at him through her lashes.

"Is that how the Apache do it?"

He caught her wandering hand. "I told you already. The tattoos didn't hurt. Took them most of a night and part of the next day, but I was besotted with—"

"That's not what I'm talking about," she interrupted.

He linked his fingers with hers. "What, then?"

"Is that how the Apache make love?"

A crooked grin quirked his lips. "That's how everybody makes love, as far as I know."

"With . . ." She swallowed and forced the words out. "With their mouths . . . down there?"

He laughed, the sound booming loudly in the stillness. Elise pressed a hand over his mouth. "Shhh! You'll wake up Penny and Adam! And what's so funny anyway?"

"You, my innocent. You are funny. You think the Apache are the first to make love with their mouths? I'm sure we would be glad to take the credit, but it would be a lie."

"I don't think my mother and father ever did it that way."

"Oh?" He touched the tip of his finger to her nose. "Then they are to be pitied, eh?"

His teasing made her laugh. She clamped a hand over her own mouth to keep from awakening the rest of the house. Chuckling, Blade wrapped his arms more tightly around her. She closed her eyes, loving the man and his moods. After a while, the troubles snaked into her mind again. She raised her head a little to find that Blade was frowning. She knew where his mind had wandered.

"You thinking about tomorrow?"

One corner of his mouth inched up. "Yes, but

don't worry. I was thinking that there are more important things than land. I was willing to sacrifice it for Julia so we could bring Penny here, and I am more than willing to sacrifice it to keep you and Penny and Adam together and happy—if it comes to that."

She closed her eyes, overcome by his generosity. "I don't think we're worth that sacrifice, Blade. This is your family legacy."

"But what is it without a family?"

Her tears tickled her cheeks and splashed onto his chest. Crooking a finger under her chin, he tilted her face up to his.

"Why are you crying?"

"Because I love you . . . I think." She held her breath in wary anticipation of his response. He smoothed the pad of his thumb down her cheek, following the track of a tear, and his expression was gentle but troubled.

"Do you think so?" he whispered.

"Yes."

His fingers threaded through the side of her hair and he coaxed her head back onto his shoulder.

Elise waited, and she knew it was in vain. It was a long time before his breathing deepened and lengthened into sleep. Staring into the darkness, she wondered if he had ever told Julia he loved her in this room and why he couldn't say it just once to her.

Airy Peppers threw a leg over her brown donkey and dropped to the ground. She reached for Penny, who had ridden behind her, and swung her off the animal. Airy's reddish-blond hair whirled around her face like a halo. After doffing her hat, she replaced it, wedging it down low on top of her ears.

"How-do to you, Mrs. Lonewolf. I'm delivering your kin from school just like I said I would."

Laughing, Elise dried her wet hands on her apron and moved away from the washtub, in which laundry was soaking. She hadn't seen much of Airy or Dixie since the church bake sale two weeks ago. Their whiskey business had kept them close to their new still.

"My, my, how formal! Thank you, Miss Peppers. You saved me a trip today."

"Weren't nothin'. Like I told you, I was going into town this afternoon anyways."

"Where's Adam?"

"He wanted to be let off back there. He spotted Blade out in the field and he was itching to tell him all about school and to see how many rows Blade weeded today. Seems like they're racing each other."

Elise gave Penny a kiss and pointed her toward the cabin. "Go change out of your school clothes, then start on your chores. Do you have homework?"

"Yes, ma'am."

"You can do that after supper. Go on now. Did you thank Miss Peppers for the ride home?"

"She sure did. That little gal's got manners." Airy winked at Penny. "Skedaddle, child."

Penny skipped up the steps and into the cabin. Elise grabbed the old mop handle she used to stir the laundry and poked at the clothes in the tub.

"These have some stubborn stains and need time to soak. Won't you join me in a glass of sarsaparilla, Airy?"

"Why, sure. That'd be nice." Airy sat on the top porch step. "I'll rest my bones here, if you don't mind. There's a nice breeze coming in from the south today."

"Make yourself comfortable. I'll be right back."

Elise fetched two cups of sarsaparilla and joined Airy on the top step.

"Blade's doing well with his planting. He'll be done by the end of the week." Airy tasted the beverage. "Did you make this?"

"Yes, I dug up the roots and brewed it myself. What do you think?"

"I think it's almost as good as my home brew." Airy took another swallow before shifting sideways to get a better look at Elise. "You wouldn't be pregnant now, would you?"

The question startled her so, she choked on the drink. Airy pounded her on the back until she was almost breathless. Waving off Airy's assistance, Elise gained her breath again and wiped tears from her watering eyes.

"Whyever would you ask that?" she croaked, her voice hoarse from coughing.

"Because you're looking so danged happy. Your eyes are brighter than new silver dollars."

"Well, I am happy, but I'm not pregnant. I don't think so." Everything went still inside Elise for a few moments as the possibility of motherhood bloomed in her mind. Could she be? Well, yes, she could . . . but was she? She counted backward rapidly. Too early for her cycle. But if she didn't begin in the next ten days . . . Well, of course anything was possible. Heavens, what would Blade say if she told him they were to be parents?

"Your thoughts are running away with you," Airy observed with a wry grin. "Guess I started you thinking about rocking babies and knitting booties."

Elise swept aside her woolgathering and laughed self-consciously. "I never thought about . . . that. Anyway!" She fluffed her apron and skirts. "The past two weeks have been the happiest I've had since my parents died. I think I can say the same for Penny and Adam."

"Heard anything from the judge?"

"No." Elise automatically looked toward the Mott landholdings. "Nothing. Thank God."

"I ain't seen him around much either. He's plotting something. I figure he might be firing off letters to those orphan train folks and maybe to some of his well-placed friends. Don't turn your back and don't get comfortable. He won't give up without a fight."

"I know." Elise sighed. "Actually, time is on his side. He doesn't have to do anything but wait. In another ten days, this place will be his."

Airy finished the brew and twirled the handle of the empty tin cup around her finger. "Ain't life a kick in the bee-hind sometimes?"

Penny bounded out of the cabin and scampered down the steps. "I'm going to see Gwenie and check on the kittens and baby chicks!" She ran toward the barn, pigtails flying.

"Them children think the sun rises and sets on Blade Lonewolf."

Elise wrapped her arms around her legs, drawing them up to her chest. "I know." She smiled, propping her chin on her knees. "We're all pretty impressed with him around here."

"Oh, you, too?"

"Me, too."

Airy leaned forward to see Elise's face better. "You in love with that half-breed stallion?"

Suddenly seized by modesty, Elise hid her face

against her arms and laughed. "Don't, Airy. You're embarrassing me."

Airy cackled like a setting hen and whacked her knee with the flat of her hand. "I knew it! I told Dixie Lynn it was only a matter of time afore you two were cooing like doves. Sometimes Dixie does darn fool things, but she was wise as Solomon when she stuck up for you at the train station that day."

Elise lifted her head, still laughing. "I'll always be in her debt for that. I'm not at all sure I could have forced Blade to go along with me if it hadn't been for your cousin. You know how bullheaded Blade can be."

Airy nodded, glancing around at the blooming flowers, tree swing, washtub and laundry dancing on the clotheslines. "I see he still has his skin lodge. Hope he's not sleeping in it."

"No," Elise said with a laugh. "But he and Adam go in there every so often. Adam is suddenly fascinated with Indians and Blade is teaching him about the Apache. They sit in there for hours and talk and talk. It's good for both of them, I think. And Penny and I sit and read books to each other. I'm teaching her how to sew and knit, too."

"Just like a normal family. Mama, Papa and their two sprouts."

Melancholy stole through Elise, tinging her smile with sorrow. "But we're not normal, are we?"

"Normal as you can get, I reckon. Don't be looking sorry-eyed, Elise. Someday you and Blade will have children of your own. Until then, you've got your brother and sister, and they need a heap of loving and caring."

"Yes, I know. I wasn't talking about that." Elise hugged her knees tightly. "He hasn't ever said he loves me, Airy. Do you think I'm being silly to worry about that?"

"I can see it worries you, so it don't make no difference what I think." Airy spun the cup handle around on her finger again.

"Let me get you more," Elise said, starting to spring up, but Airy placed a detaining hand on her shoulder and she settled back on the step.

"You told him?"

Elise nodded. "Once."

"And he didn't say nothing?"

"No."

"Did he act mad?"

"Mad? No."

"Did he laugh in your face and call you a fool?"

"No!"

"Well, then I reckon he's just reticent."

"Reticent?"

"Yeah, reticent. It means that he don't want to or don't know how to talk—"

"I know what it means; I just don't understand why he'd be that way. After all, what does he have to lose? I've already told him. If he loves me, why can't he just say so? But then, if he doesn't . . . if he's still carrying a torch for somebody else and can't blow that flame out—"

"A torch? For who?" Airy craned forward, squinting at Elise. "You're not talking about Julia, surely!"

"Why not? He married her. He went through a lot with her. He lost her. It's only natural—"

"Did he ever talk to you about her?"

"Yes."

"Then he told you about Julia's peculiar ways?"

Elise eyed Airy cautiously, unsure how to respond.

"Did he tell you that she didn't like being with a man?" Airy expounded.

Uncomfortable to be sharing such intimate tidbits with Airy, Elise shrugged. "Yes, but he loved her."

"I know, but it wasn't a complete marriage. Couldn't be, as long as Julia cringed every time Blade tried to do more than kiss her. Oh, I saw that look come over her face. Look of sheer panic, it was. And then Blade—poor son of a gun—would look like he'd lost his last and best friend. I tried to talk to her about it, but she got all uppity and flighty. Nervous, Julia was, so I hushed. That's why she and the judge got on so fine. They both loved to read about love, talk about it, spin poems about it, but neither one of them wanted to do it."

"The judge has the same—he doesn't like it either?" Elise asked, finding this difficult to believe. She remembered Mott's lewd comments and suggestive looks.

Airy leaned closer, raising a hand to her mouth in conspiracy. "Harriet told me once that the judge ain't never touched her in that way," she whispered. "And I believed her. She didn't have no reason to lie to me."

Elise considered this for a minute. "You know, Airy, sometimes I can't help but blame Julia for the mess we're in today. If she hadn't talked Blade into going to the judge for that loan . . ." She shook her head. "But that's all history. It's done and we have to live with it." Looking at the flowers nodding in the breeze, the old pump that she had learned to work with efficiency, the swing that Penny adored and the tepee that she herself had learned to accept, Elise ached deep in her soul to think that it might all belong to that terrible man in a few scant days.

The pain was so intense, it left her dry-eyed.

"I should be gettin' on." Airy stood and stretched. Joints popped and she yawned noisily, but cut it off in mid-groan. "Hey, you got more company coming, little missus."

Elise shaded her eyes with one hand. A buggy with a fringed top, pulled by a shiny black draft horse, rolled down the lane to the cabin. Standing, she ran a hand over her hair in a reflexive gesture.

"Wonder who that is," she murmured.

"Fancy outfit. Looks like a hired cab from the livery in town. Yep, that's the blacksmith's son driving it." Airy moved none too quickly to her donkey. "He's got one passenger. A man in a store-bought suit and city hat."

"I don't recognize him," Elise confessed, descending the porch steps.

The buggy stopped a little way from the porch. Dust rose up and drifted toward her fresh laundry on the clotheslines. The driver, a young man not much older than Adam, tipped his wide-brimmed hat.

"Howdy. You the half-breed's woman?"

Elise tipped up her chin in blazing affront. "I am Mrs. Lonewolf, young man," she said archly, and the driver inched back as if her voice were a whip aimed at him. "State your business, please."

From the corner of her eye she saw Airy grin and then climb aboard her sweet-tempered donkey.

"Yes'm." The driver glanced back at his passenger, then jerked a thumb in the man's direction. "I drove him out here to talk at you."

Elise peered under the fringed canopy. "Do I know you, sir?"

"No, Mrs. Lonewolf." The man sat forward into the sunlight, which sparkled in the lenses of his glasses. "I am Giles Lancaster. I'm a solicitor."

Elise regarded him warily. He spoke with an English accent and seemed completely out of place there. "I suppose Judge Mott sent you," she said, setting her jaw stubbornly. "He's a few days too early."

"No, I haven't been retained by any such person." He smiled benignly. "I've come from Baltimore."

"Baltimore!" Elise said, and heard Airy echo her.

"Yes. I represent Shelton and Katherine Wellby. Your grandparents, I believe?"

"Bless my britches," Airy whispered, turning her donkey around and giving him a kick to get him going.

Elise folded her arms and stared coldly at the man. "I have no grandparents, sir. They died the day I buried my father apart from my mother. Please be on your way. You aren't welcome here."

Chapter 23

Giles Lancaster patted the driver's shoulder. "You may park this vehicle in the shade while I conduct my business. I shan't be long."

"Yes, sir."

"I told you that I have nothing to say to you," Elise said, blocking the steps leading to the porch. "You might as well be on your way."

"I have something to say to you," Mr. Lancaster rejoined evenly, unruffled by her stern countenance. He alighted from the buggy with a leather satchel in hand. "I shouldn't be taking much of your time. I've brought a message from your grandparents."

"I told you, I no longer have any grandparents."

"Yes, madam, so you said. Very well, I have a message from the Wellbys." He pulled a silk handkerchief from his jacket pocket and mopped his brow and neck. His suit was shiny brown and he wore a wide green tie. "Would you be so kind as to fetch me a drink of water, madam? I'm quite parched."

Elise regarded him for a few moments, noting his friendly blue eyes and harmless smile. She shrugged. "You can come in, have your dipper of water, then be on your way."

"Yes, madam, and I'll deliver the message, too. That's what I'm being paid for."

"And handsomely, I'm sure." Elise pivoted, mounted the steps and marched into the cabin. She stalked to the water bucket and drew out a dipper of water, which she offered to the stranger. "Here you go." She knew he would prefer having his water in a cup or a glass, but she refused to treat him as a cherished guest.

While he sipped the water, she tapped her foot impatiently. Why had her grandparents sent him? Did they require her signature on some papers that would legally release them from any connection with her or her siblings? Well, she wouldn't sign!

He had removed his roll-brimmed hat upon entering the house, revealing that he was quite bald except for a fringe of brown hair running above his ears and at the back of his head. His mustache was thin, with a few white hairs appearing among the brown.

Giving the dipper back to her, he touched his handkerchief to the corners of his mouth. "Quite refreshing. Thank you very much." He adjusted his tie. "Mrs. Lonewolf—that is correct, isn't it? You've married?"

"That is correct." Elise folded her arms again and glared at him. "You may leave now, sir."

"Allow me to deliver my message, madam, won't you? What harm will come to you to hear me out?"

She supposed she shouldn't be taking out her hatred on this messenger. He was only doing her grandparents' dirty work. "All right. What is it?" she said in a rush. "Say it and then leave."

"Your grandparents would like to see you."

"Would they, now?" She laughed harshly. "They expect me to go back to Baltimore with you to sign some papers that will do me absolutely no good whatso—"

"Madam, they are here, not in Baltimore."

"H-here?" She looked past him as her blood ran cold. "Where?"

"In Crossroads, at the hotel. They would like to speak to you and your brother and sister. Today, if possible. Tomorrow at the latest. They have return tickets to Baltimore on the afternoon train."

"Good. The sooner they're gone, the better."

"You'll meet with them?"

"I have no desire to do so."

"Elise?" Penny hovered in the doorway. "Do we have company?"

"No, this man is leaving."

"Are you Penny?" Mr. Lancaster spun around to greet her. "Is Adam here as well?"

"He's out with Papa Blade, I think. But he'll be in soon. He's got to change out of his school clothes."

Papa Blade. The solicitor raised his brows at this, as did Elise. Of course, she should have been prepared, she told herself. She had heard Penny tell Blade that she was going to start calling him by that name, but it still sent a jolt through her. Penny must be calling him that to his face now, she thought. What would happen if he lost the land and couldn't make a living for them anymore? How would the children cope if they had to say farewell to yet another father figure?

"Penny, please go on about your chores," Elise said.

"Okay." Penny ducked outside and bounced off

the porch, a ball of energy with pigtails.

"She seems to have adapted quite well," the solicitor commented.

"And how would you know?" Elise challenged. "I don't remember seeing you before. My sister and brother have suffered greatly, thanks to the Wellbys. If they are adjusting, it's at a great cost, believe me. We have all fought hard to remain together."

"Yes, yes, of course." He arranged his handkerchief in the breast pocket of his suit coat. "I do believe that you should meet with the Wellbys, Mrs. Lonewolf. It will add a final chapter to this sordid story."

"The story's already over for me."

"Is it?" He gave her a skeptical look. "Isn't there anything you'd like to say to them? They have something to say to you. They have something to ask of you."

"What?"

"That is for them to say, not me." He smiled. "Please, may I tell them that you will come around? This evening, perhaps? Or in the morning?"

She caught a glimpse of a mule ridden by two. Blade and Adam had seen the buggy, she surmised, and had come to investigate. Feet landed on the porch and then Blade and Adam crowded through the doorway.

"Hello!" Mr. Lancaster greeted them with a broad smile and an extended hand. "Giles Lancaster. You must be Mr. Lonewolf." He shook Blade's hand, then offered to shake Adam's. "Adam, I take it?"

"Yes, sir." Adam wiped his hand on his pant leg before shaking Mr. Lancaster's. "Are you from England?"

"Yes, originally. But I make my home in Baltimore now."

"Baltimore?" Adam yanked his hand from Lancaster's and his gaze flew to Elise. "What's going on?"

"The Wellbys sent him. They want to talk to us," Elise explained. "They're staying in a hotel . . . in Crossroads."

"They're here!" Adam's eyes rounded with shock. "Why? What are they up to now?"

"I don't know and I don't care, as I have repeatedly told Mr. Lancaster here."

"Mr. Lancaster, won't you sit down?" Blade offered, pulling out one of the kitchen chairs.

"Blade!" Elise glared at him. "Mr. Lancaster is leaving!"

"Thank you, Mr. Lonewolf." The solicitor sat while the offer was still good. "I must be on my way, but I was trying to obtain from your wife an idea of when she might be paying a visit to the Wellbys. They have tickets on tomorrow afternoon's train bound for the East Coast, so if she could see them this evening or in the morning . . ."

"I don't want to see them at all. They're wasting their time."

"Why not see them?" Blade asked. "Maybe they've got good news for you. Maybe they want you to go back to Baltimore."

Elise stared at him. Was that what he wanted? Would he let her go, just like that? "I . . . I don't care what they want," she managed to say finally. "I am no longer interested in their wishes or desires."

"Me either," Adam chimed in. "And we don't need their permission to return to Baltimore anyway."

"That's right," Elise agreed. "They don't own Baltimore!"

"And they don't claim to," Mr. Lancaster noted with a shrewd smile. "But they would like to speak to you. Just a few minutes of your time, Mrs. Lonewolf. Is that too much to ask? As I said, it will be good for all parties to close this unfortunate business, face-to-face."

"I think he's right," Blade said. "One last visit to clear the air."

"I'm not going," Adam stated.

"Elise?" Blade nudged. "They came all the way here. You'll always wonder why, if you don't go see them."

Flapping her hands, Elise capitulated. "Oh, very well, but only me. I won't subject Adam or Penny to any more of their cruelty."

"That's fine, that's fine." Mr. Lancaster stood and tucked his leather satchel under his arm. "When may I tell them to expect you?"

"In the morning. I'll stop by after I drop off Penny and Adam at school. Around nine, I guess."

"Splendid. So nice to meet all of you." He put his hat back on and bowed. "Good day now."

Nobody made any attempt to see him out, so he left with another quick smile. Elise sat at the table, feeling as if she'd caved in.

"You would always wonder," Blade said. "You know you would."

"Yes, I suppose . . ." She looked from Adam to Blade. "But whatever could they want?"

"They probably want you to sign papers to officially disown us," Adam said.

"That's what I think," Elise concurred.

"Sign them," Adam urged her. "I don't want anything from those two."

"Don't you worry. I'll be glad to disown them as well."

Blade shook his head sadly. "You shouldn't be so quick to turn your back on opportunities."

"You expect me to be nice to them?"

"I expect you to think of your brother and sister as you have always done." He rested a hand on Adam's shoulder. "Why don't you change into some work clothes now, Adam, and give your sister and me a private minute or two?"

"Sure. Okay." Adam exchanged smiles with Elise before going into the room he shared with Penny and closing the door softly behind him.

Blade sat at the table and looked at her from beneath lowered brows.

"Are you all right? You were upset when I came in."

"I'm fine. I just wish they hadn't come here."

"They might have had a change of heart."

"Too late."

"Now, Elise . . ." He squared his shoulders and sat straighter. "It might be best. If they are willing to take you all back to Baltimore with them, it might be a good omen."

"How can you—?" She stared at him, her heart breaking. "You want us to go?"

"What I want isn't important. What *is* important is that I will probably lose this land in a few days and I won't be able to make a living for a family without it. You must think of what is best for you and Adam and Penny. That's what I'm thinking about. You could stay in Baltimore until I find some kind of work that will support—"

"No." She shook her head stubbornly. "You can't give up on this land, Blade. I won't let you."

"It's not in your hands."

"How can you talk like this? I know you can't bear to think of your land being farmed by Judge Mott!"

"You are the romantic, not me. I learned long ago to face what is real and deal with it. If your kin have come to make amends, you shouldn't allow your pride to cloud your good sense. When I lose this land, I'll have to start from scratch. I won't be able to provide for all of you."

"Then we will all find work. Maybe not Penny, she's too young, but Adam and I will find employment somewhere."

Blade removed his hat and mussed his hair with a rough hand. "Where? What will you do for money?"

"I can cook now. Adam can farm."

He shook his head, smiling faintly. "You refuse to hear me, so I might as well save my breath." Standing, he put his hat back on and headed for the door. "Adam, let's go to work!"

Adam emerged from his bedroom before Blade's last word had been spoken. He'd changed into overalls, a blue work shirt and a pair of moccasins Blade had given him.

"You're going to talk to them in the morning?" Adam asked Elise.

"Yes."

"I wish I could see them right now at the Crossroads Hotel." He grinned mischievously. "No servants, no inside privy. Can you imagine Grandmama trotting outside to the little house with the half moon on the door? Can you see her waiting in line to do her business?"

Elise laughed. "In her satin and pearls and lace?" She laughed harder when Adam did a pantomime of a prissy woman strolling across the room.

"Pardon me," he intoned in a high-pitched, nasal-induced voice. "But would you be so kind as to stand aside? I have most *urgent* business to attend to, don't you see? That's right." He flicked his fingers at imaginary people. "I am Katherine Hoffman Wellby, and I shall not wait in line for anything!"

Her eyes tearing, Elise laughed until her sides hurt. "Get out of here, you thespian!"

"Quite, quite." He took mincing steps out of the cabin.

Blade grinned and gave Elise a wink. "He's not the same boy who came here two weeks ago."

"No." She sobered quickly. "That's one of the reasons I don't want to leave."

Blade's smile was so sad it nearly broke her heart. "I don't want to leave either, but I don't think the judge will give us a choice."

Where had everyone gone? Elise wondered as she finished stacking the clean supper dishes on the shelf. Listening, she heard only frogs and crickets around the cabin. She crossed to the door and looked out. Light spilled from the barn. What were they doing?

She went to the bedroom she now shared with Blade and unpinned her hair, letting it fall to her shoulders. Drawing a brush through it, she closed her eyes and willed some of the tension from her body as she gave her auburn hair a thorough grooming.

An edginess rattled through her veins and she felt as if a weight sat in her chest. She dreaded tomorrow and her meeting with the Wellbys. Resentment toward them boiled within her, and her brush strokes became too rapid, too painful. She put the ivory-handled brush on top of the dresser and went outside, where a cool breeze stirred the tree branches and starlight showed her the way to the barn.

Happy laughter erupted from inside, enticing Elise. She crossed the threshold and stopped. Blade, Penny and Adam stood with their backs to her; the focus of their attention was Gwenie. The filly was putting on a show, prancing and kicking and tossing her short mane. Janie, the proud mother, extended her head and neck over the stable door and blew through her nostrils at her bouncing baby.

Intrigued, Elise ventured closer and saw the reason for Gwenie's acrobatics. She was wearing a halter. The filly leapt straight up and shook her head, trying to sling off the harmless rope halter. Penny and Adam doubled over with laughter again. Blade's low chuckle rumbled from his chest as he rested a hand on Penny's shoulder and winked at Adam.

"You'd think that halter rope was made of barbed wire, the way she's taking on," Blade said.

Adam struggled to control his guffaws. "What a spoiled baby you are, Gwenie! What will you do when a saddle is placed on your back?"

"Well, that won't be for a long spell," Blade said. "And she won't like that one bit either."

Seeing them enjoy one another, share a few minutes of fun and frolic, Elise swallowed the tightness in her throat. What would happen to little Gwenie, Janie and beautiful, spirited Bob? Would they be taken over by Judge Mott, too? She couldn't imagine anyone astride Bob other than Blade. Oh, she never tired of watching Blade ride bareback, looking every inch the Apache brave!

"Elise." Blade had spotted her and he beckoned with one hand. "We put a halter on Gwenie and she's throwing a fit."

"So I see." Elise stood on his other side and he slipped an arm around her waist. "You aren't going to leave that on her tonight, are you? She won't sleep a wink."

"No, I'll take it off in a minute. We'll get her used to it gradual-like."

Elise closed her eyes, unable to talk as if there were so many tomorrows here for all of them. Blade was right. Lloyd Mott would not give them more time. They had defied him by taking Adam. He had everything to gain and they had everything to lose. She opened her eyes and looked at Blade, who was smiling and chuckling at the bucking filly. How could he feel any joy when his land—his inheritance—would be stripped from him within a matter of days?

Unable to join in the laughter and on the brink of bitter tears, Elise wrenched away from Blade and started for the barn door.

"Elise, is something wrong?" Blade called after her.

"No," she said, but her voice was too high, too strained. She cleared her throat and tried to swallow the knot of misery in it. "Penny, Adam, you two need to come in soon and get ready for bed."

After reaching the cabin, she went directly to her bedroom and closed the door. Depression lowered itself over her like a gray mantle and she lay back on the bed with a broken sigh. After a while she heard the others come inside, but she didn't go out to them. She couldn't. The mantle was heavy and pinned her down. Noises drifted to her . . . shuffling, lowered voices, the other bedroom door closing. She dozed and awakened to a dark room. Someone had extinguished the lamp. A shadow loomed over her and a large, familiar hand stroked her cheek.

"Are you sick?" Blade asked in a whisper.

She shook her head against his hand.

"What is it? Are you upset about the meeting tomorrow? If you want, I can go with you. Adam can finish up weeding the rows tomorrow all by himself. He's handy to have around, that one."

Elise curled onto her side. "The fields. Why do you even bother? Are you trying to get everything ready for Judge Mott?"

"Ah, so we have switched places." He nudged her further onto her side of the bed and lay down with her.

"What's that supposed to mean?"

"You are now the pessimist and I am trying to believe in miracles."

"You shouldn't. No miracle will save us, Blade. What will happen to Gwenie and Janie, Bob, the mules, our chickens and ducks? The new kittens and the—"

"Shhh." He curved a hand around her shoulder and pulled her onto her back to look down into her face. "Let me worry about them. You have all you can do to think about your brother and sister."

"You'll let us go away? Just like that?"

"If there is no more home here, what do you expect us to do? There's a chance you might find a home again in Baltimore with your relatives."

"I doubt that. You don't know them like I do, Blade. They can't have a change of heart, because they have no hearts."

He smiled and kissed the tip of her nose. "Do you want me to go with you tomorrow?"

"No. Finish your work." She started to turn onto her side again, but he kept her anchored on her back, one hand at her shoulder and the other cupping the side of her face. "I should see to Penny," Elise said.

"She's in bed. I tucked her in." He kissed her lightly on her forehead and eyelids. "Let me erase these worry lines," he murmured, and his lips touched the corners of her eyes and mouth.

"Blade, what if Judge Mott—"

"Shhh." He hushed her again. "I've thought of nothing else all day. Give me something else to think about tonight, Elise. Please?"

Her depression lifted, replaced by an urgency to be swept into his arms and to drown in his kisses. She caught his hands and placed them on her breasts.

"Yes," she whispered. "I don't want to think, Blade. I just want to feel . . . to feel you."

He slipped a hand under her skirt and his palm skimmed along her calf, her knee, her thigh. Elise unbuttoned her cuffs and the front of her dress, eager to have his hands on her. They stared into each other's eyes as they busily removed their clothing, and seldom broke the connection until the tasks were completed.

The sight of Blade's nude body always heightened her longing for him. Solid, teak-colored, big and bold, he epitomized all she loved in the male form, with the exotic addition of those faint blue lines crisscrossing his chest and arms to form triangles and circles and rectangles. She licked one that ran from nipple to nipple.

"I love your body." She licked one of his tightening paps, then took it into her mouth. He cursed and groaned. She smiled and sucked harder.

"Sweet Giver of Life!" He grasped her head between his hands and brought her mouth to his.

She returned to his chest and her tongue painted over the lines. "These markings . . ." She followed another with her lips from his sternum to just above his navel. "They were part of a ritual that made you a brave man, a warrior?"

"That's right."

"The ritual worked." She looked up his body to find his dark, lustrous eyes. "You're the bravest man I've ever known. You are my warrior prince."

His eyes glittered like topaz jewels as he reached for her. Clamping his hands on her shoulders, he twisted her onto her back and unleashed a series of quick, tongue-teasing kisses that left her moaning for more.

She tried not to think that their nights of lovemaking might end, but the thought was there, in the corner of her mind, and it drove her to near desperation. He must have been fighting the same demon, for he loved her in a half-starved way. He opened his mouth wide over hers, and his tongue imitated the sex act so keenly that she felt an answering surge and retreat between her thighs. Cupping her breasts in his hands, he brought her nipples to his mouth, each in its turn, flicking them with his tongue and nipping lightly with his teeth until she could stand no more of the wicked pleasure.

"Now, Blade, now." Wrapping her legs around him, she reached down and caressed his long, hard length. She let the pad of her thumb tease the slippery tip, and he bucked and groaned.

Reaching up and back behind her, Elise grabbed the headboard and held on as he entered her, filled her, stretched her and created that divine friction that sent her up and out of herself. For those blessed minutes there were no Wellbys, no Mott, no lost farms. In those minutes, she could convince herself that Blade Lonewolf loved her and would never, ever let her go.

When his own pleasure had gripped and released him, he lay on his side, one leg and arm draped over her. He breathed deeply and his skin was shiny with sweat.

Elise ran a hand through his silky hair that had grown past his shoulders in back. She started to tell him that she'd trim his hair, but the uncertainty of tomorrow flooded through her, drenching her again in melancholy.

"How can you leave me, Blade Lonewolf?" she asked.

He lifted his head, and his face reflected a deep-down sadness. "It will be you who will leave."

"Okay. How can you send me away?"

"Because I want you to have a good life, and without this place I can't give you that."

"Maybe you can. Maybe we could have a good life just wandering from place to place. People do that all the time."

He kissed the side of her breast, nuzzling her intimately and pulling her closer to him. "I can't do that to Adam and Penny, and you can't either. If we had only ourselves to think of . . ."

"But we don't." She struggled to stave off another wash of tears and wished she could stop turning the problems over and over in her mind.

He kissed her pouting nipple and inched upward until his lips could pluck at hers. A simmering began in her and within minutes she was boiling again, clutching at him, writhing upon the bed while he moved down her body until he was between her thighs.

Ah, he was so very good at making her forget.

Chapter 24

Approaching the hotel room to which she'd been directed by the proprietor, Elise concentrated on breathing regularly while her heart somersaulted in her chest. She'd worn her best dress, the garnet one that had become her wedding gown, and the plucky black hat that had been her bridal veil on the fateful day she had married Blade Lonewolf. She touched her mother's brooch, pinned at her throat, for comfort and courage before knocking briskly below the painted number "3."

She heard movement on the other side, whispered voices, and then the door opened to reveal the smiling round face of Giles Lancaster.

"Mrs. Lonewolf! How good to see you again. Please, won't you come in? You look lovely this morning, if I may be so bold."

"Thank you." She swept inside, her finishing-school lessons holding her in good stead: head high, eyes flashing with confidence, spine erect, shoulders back, breeding apparent in her walk and demeanor.

The narrow entry opened into a small sitting room. A closed door to the left of the parlor gave access to the bedroom area, Elise supposed. Two chairs and a settee were arranged in front of a bank of windows. A tea and coffee service was spread on a low table before the settee. The service was porcelain, not silver, and Elise wondered with wry amusement how her grandparents were coping. Then she noticed the other person in the room.

"Hello, Nicole," she greeted the uniformed maid. "It's nice to see you again."

The middle-aged woman, who had served the Wellbys since she was a girl, curtsied. "'Lo, miss. Would you care for tea or coffee, miss?"

Elise removed her gloves and glanced at the tea tray again. "I'll have a cup of tea with cream, if you please. No sugar. Thank you, Nicole." She looked at the woman, noting the silver sprinkled through her dark hair and the crow's-feet at the corners of her eyes. "How have you been?"

Nicole glanced up nervously and shared a startled look with Giles Lancaster. "I . . . me, miss? I'm very good, miss."

Elise realized she had shocked the woman with her personal inquiry. Elise St. John would not have asked, but it was a natural gesture for Elise Lonewolf. Only one of the many differences that had taken place within her, Elise thought, pleased with the woman she had become, and proud that she no longer saw maids and butlers as things instead of as people who had lives outside their service.

"How do you like Crossroads, Nicole?"

Again Nicole glanced at Mr. Lancaster, as if seeking counsel on how to handle this uncommon exchange. "It seems a nice enough place, miss."

"Yes, it has its good points. Nicole, I've married since we saw each other last. I'm Mrs. Lonewolf now."

"Oh, yes, missus. Pardon me, missus."

Elise waved a hand and smiled. "No need to ask for a pardon from me, Nicole. I'm not the queen." She wrinkled her nose in a teasing fashion and saw the maid's own smile lose some of its nervousness. "You could call me Elise, but I know you wouldn't be comfortable with that."

"Won't you have a seat, Mrs. Lonewolf?" Mr. Lancaster said, motioning to one of the wing chairs facing the settee. Evidently the Wellbys would occupy that.

"Yes, thank you." Elise arranged herself in the chair, spreading her skirts just so and placing her reticule in her lap. She took the cup of tea Nicole had prepared for her. "And thank you, Nicole."

The maid bobbed like a cork. " 'Tis a pleasure, Mrs. Lonewolf."

Mr. Lancaster retrieved a cup of coffee that he must have been enjoying before Elise's arrival. He sat in the other chair beside hers.

"As you know, Mr. Lancaster, this isn't a social visit. Can we get down to business, please? I have chores at home I need to be tending to." She flashed a mischievous grin at Nicole. "Eggs to gather, butter to churn, bread to bake. Honest work."

Nicole covered her smiling mouth with one hand and retreated to a corner.

"The Wellbys will be out in a minute, I'm sure. They know you've arrived," the solicitor said.

Elise sipped her tea. "They may make their grand entrance any time," she said in a louder voice that would carry to the bedroom. "We're all in our appointed places, so let the performance begin!"

Mr. Lancaster hid his smile behind his coffee

cup. "You are a spirited young woman, Mrs. Lone-wolf."

"And a good thing that is," she responded tartly. "Otherwise I'd be working in a brothel somewhere, after what the Wellbys did to me and my siblings."

Mr. Lancaster frowned and eyed her dubiously. He opened his mouth to speak, but at that moment the bedroom door creaked open, and Katherine and Shelton Wellby entered as if they were in a processional. They walked straight to the settee, never once looking in Elise's direction, and Shelton held his wife's hand as she settled on one end of the furniture. Only then did he take up the other end. Katherine arched a brow and nodded to summon the maid, who came forward and poured tea, then retreated to her post in the corner once again.

Elise tilted her head and leaned forward. Neither Shelton nor Katherine had looked at her or acknowledged her in any way. Exasperated with their rude behavior, Elise waved a hand back and forth, testing for blindness.

"Hello? Have you two lost your senses since I've been away? Can you see me, hear me?"

Her grandmother puckered her lips in distaste and brought her gaze to bear on Elise. The old woman's hooded eyes reminded Elise of an eagle's.

"I see that your manners have not improved, Elise."

"Neither have yours," Elise rejoined, something she would never have done before. She had been taught to respect her grandparents. Although it had always been obvious that the Grandparents Wellby cared little, if anything, for them, Elise's mother and father had taught their children to show the proper respect for their elders. Considering how the Wellbys had treated Elise since her parents' death, she figured she was still treating them with the "proper respect."

Katherine looked like an icicle in her white gown and with her white hair piled high on her head. Beside her, Shelton was a peacock in a blue suit, shirt and red cravat. He had plastered his hair against his scalp with shoe-black, his vanity refusing him to be seen in public with white hair. He was four years younger than Katherine and had always thrown it up to her. Her family had left her a more sizable inheritance, and the Hoffmans were on a higher rung of society's ladder, but Shelton would always be younger and, he thought, better-looking.

"I will get straight to the point," Katherine said. "We have been inconvenienced and embarrassed by you."

"By me?" Elise spread a hand above her breasts. "How, pray tell, have I accomplished that?"

"By having lies printed about us in the Baltimore newspaper," Katherine replied archly. "And don't pretend that you aren't solidly behind the articles your friend's cousin has printed."

Donetta, Elise thought with a little thrill. What else had her friend been up to?

"I've been corresponding with Donetta Peterson," Elise admitted. "She's been concerned about my welfare."

"You don't seem any the worse for wear," Shelton observed, lounging back on the settee, legs crossed, teacup and saucer in hand. A gold-and-ruby ring sparkled on his left pinkie.

Elise said nothing, preferring to stare coldly at them while she waited for them to voice the reason for the meeting. Surely they hadn't come all this way to chastise her for contributing information, however indirectly, to the newspaper! No. Something else was on their narrow, little minds.

"We want these items in the newspaper stopped and we want a statement of retraction." Katherine Wellby set the teacup into the saucer firmly to emphasize her demand. "We will suffer no more embarrassment from you, Elise."

Elise arched a brow. "Is that so? I believe you've met with the wrong person, Katherine." She used her grandmother's first name on purpose and was glad for the shock it caused in the room. "You must approach the newspaper editor for a retraction. First, of course, you must be able to prove that what he has printed is incorrect. You may have a difficult time of that, I fear."

Katherine snapped her fingers. "Mr. Lancaster, show her the newspaper items."

"My pleasure." He opened his leather satchel and withdrew a few newspaper clippings, which he handed to Elise. "I've underlined the objectionable comments."

There were four clippings, each pointing out that the Wellbys' youngest grandchildren had been placed on an orphan train and adopted by strangers in Missouri, and that the eldest, Elise, had been forced into a marriage with a half-breed dirt farmer in order to stay near her siblings.

She passed them back to the solicitor. "All true."

Shelton Wellby stifled a yawn. "Offer her the settlement, Katherine, so we can be out of this hellhole."

Settlement? Elise looked from one to the other. Were they going to offer passage back to Baltimore and a house to live in as Blade had predicted?

"I want a peaceful and permanent separation,"

Katherine stated flatly. "Give her the terms, Mr. Lancaster."

Giles Lancaster cleared his throat and jerked at the knot of his black tie, loosening it. "The Wellbys are offering you a generous sum, Mrs. Lonewolf. You, your sister and brother will each receive an amount specified in this agreement." He removed a rolled parchment from his satchel. "In exchange for this, Mr. and Mrs. Wellby ask that you immediately cease any further exchanges to the newspaper or to your newspaper source and swear that you will not correspond with the Wellbys or any of their representatives. Also, the Wellbys ask that you write one final missive to the publication to clear up the misunderstandings you have propagated."

Elise received the document he had unrolled and read it. It seemed that everyone in the room dared not breathe while she considered the terms. The wording was legal, but not difficult to understand. She was being paid to lie.

"You want me to make up a story so you can save face?" she asked, letting go of one end of the document, which curled into a roll again. "You can take this officious paper and choke—"

"Mrs. Lonewolf, might I interrupt to expound on some points before us?" Mr. Lancaster asked, his tone and countenance unruffled. His and Nicole's were the only friendly faces in the room, but Elise reminded herself that these people were on the Wellbys' side, not on hers.

"Go ahead," she said, needing time to tamp down her temper.

"The monetary offer is quite generous, Mrs. Lonewolf. Isn't this a fair way to terminate an unfortunate, unfruitful relationship? Please remember that you are answering not only for yourself but also for your younger brother and sister. It is a serious decision, Mrs. Lonewolf, and I urge you to consider carefully before giving your final answer."

Questions dogged her and she found she couldn't keep them at bay. Facing the only people who could answer them, she struggled to keep her voice emotionless. "Tell me, did you ever care anything at all for your daughter's children or her husband?"

Katherine Wellby set her cup and saucer on the tray and waved off Nicole, who moved to pour again. "I loved my daughter, but I never made any pretense of hiding my great disappointment in her marriage."

"But you chose to support us financially."

"I would not have my only child live as the wife of a common cobbler," Katherine said, her upper lip curling. "Shelton and I agreed to maintain an acceptable style of living for Gwendolyn. We bought a house and let her reside in it and gave her an allowance that she spent as she saw fit. All we asked is that she insist that her husband stop practicing his trade in public."

Elise rolled her eyes, sickened by what these people felt was important, what mattered. Her father had made shoes and they found that occupation vile. A common laborer! Shudders!

"If you loved my mother so much, how could you both turn your backs on her children?"

"Anything that came of that union did not interest us," Katherine said starchly. "As I stated, we did not approve of or acknowledge *that man* as our son-in-law. Naturally, we were not interested in children he sired."

"We hoped that Gwendolyn would come to her senses and have the marriage annulled so that she could wed someone suitable," Shelton said, buffing his nails on his lapel.

"But each child was another heavy chain, keeping her shackled to that ne'er-do-well," Katherine added, her voice dripping with disdain.

Elise shook her head. "To punish innocent children—*your* grandchildren—it's despicable." She wanted badly to throw their offer back into their smug faces, to tell them that money would never buy her silence or make her lie for them, and that she hoped they suffered for their sins.

Mr. Lancaster, as if sensing her temptations, leaned forward, his expression partly pleading, partly encouraging. "Mrs. Lonewolf, will you walk away empty-handed, or with something in hand with which to build a better future for yourself and your brother and sister?"

"What sort of letter must I write to the newspaper?"

"I'll help you draft it if you wish," Mr. Lancaster offered. "The Wellbys feel you should discard any belief that you are destitute and grievously unhappy. They want it made clear that your removal from Baltimore was by choice and not by force. They wish you to convey that you and your siblings are living together in harmony."

She examined the two shallow people on the settee and knew that to ask for anything meaningful or emotional would be like asking the henchman for mercy.

"Since love is out of the question, I suppose that money will have to do," she said, then dismissed the Wellbys by turning sideways and addressing the solicitor. Solicitor! An idea rang in her head, clear as a bell. "Mr. Lancaster, I will accept these terms on one condition."

He glanced nervously at the Wellbys. "And what would that be, Mrs. Lonewolf?"

"Your services, paid by the Wellbys, to clear up a couple of legal matters for me."

"Do these matters concern the Wellbys or these issues we have addressed this morning?" Mr. Lancaster asked.

"No, and they can be handled quickly. You shouldn't be detained for more than another day here."

"Ah, then I see no problem." He looked at the two people on the settee and must have received an affirmative response, because he extended his hand to Elise. "It's a deal, Mrs. Lonewolf. I am at your service."

By the time Elise arrived home, she was bubbling with excitement and the world was bright and shiny to her eyes. She'd seen Blade in the fields as she'd driven the buggy along the road to their house, and she'd waved, signaling him to meet her at the cabin.

Now she paced restlessly on the porch, darting looks from time to time across the flatland in search of him. Where was he? Why didn't he hurry?

The sun was bright and fooled her eyes, but then she saw a dot, a moving shadow, and she ran off the porch and met Blade at the edge of the fields. Coiling her arms around his neck, she hugged him and kissed his warm lips with such enthusiasm that she knocked his hat askew.

He leaned back and his eyes held a hundred questions. Elise laughed joyously and straightened his hat.

"You're stuck with me, Blade Lonewolf. What do you have to say about that?"

"What happened in town?" he asked, not yet joining in her jubilation.

She released him, taking one of his hands in hers, and began strolling toward the cabin. "I saw them. They haven't changed. They're still cold and distant like the stars."

"Then why are you so happy?"

"Because they have given us our miracle, Blade." She smiled at him. "Oh, not by the goodness of their hearts, but through blackmail. But who cares? We're getting our miracle and they're getting what they want—for me and Adam and Penny to forget they exist."

"This makes you happy?"

"Yes, yes!" She danced ahead, then turned to face him while she walked backward. "Blade, they are giving us money to keep our mouths shut about their shabby treatment of us."

"Who have you been talking to about that?"

"Donetta, my friend. Remember I received a letter from her? Her cousin writes a column for the Baltimore newspaper and has printed what the Wellbys did to us—sending Adam and Penny away on the orphan train and all that." She pulled at his hands impatiently. "Come to the house and I'll explain it all to you."

She hurried him along, up the porch steps and inside the cabin. She whisked off his hat before he could and hung it on its peg by the door.

"Sit, sit," she ordered with a smile, and she sat in her usual chair to his left. "Remember how we prayed for a miracle last night?"

He nodded. "I remember."

"Our prayers have been answered," she announced, barely able to contain her joy. "Thanks to my stingy grandparents, we can keep this farm, Blade."

A guarded look came over his face. "What do you mean? How can we keep the farm?"

"By paying off the loan!" She giggled and clutched his hands, which were folded on the table. "They are giving me and Adam and Penny money in exchange for our never darkening their doorstep again or mentioning their names to anyone. My share of the money will pay off the loan, Blade. Their solicitor—the man who was here yesterday? Well, he's going to look over the original papers and make sure everything is legal and that we won't be bothered by Judge Mott ever again. And Mr. Lancaster is also going to help us rescind Adam's adoption. He is confident that with our testimonies of Adam's inhuman treatment, he can force the judge to relinquish Adam legally."

Blade bowed his head for a moment. When he lifted his face to hers again, Elise didn't like the stubborn glint in his eyes or the rock-hard set of his jaw. She knew the signs, but they were unexpected. She'd thought he would sweep her into his arms and that by now they would be in the midst of a loving, lustful celebration. But no. Elise sat back in her chair, dismayed. Not Blade Lonewolf, King of Pride.

"Blade, why are you looking at me like that? I thought you'd be thrilled!"

"You didn't accept their charity for me, did you?"

"I accepted for *us*, and it's not charity. They owe me, Adam and Penny for what they took from us. We have suffered because of them and they're getting off lightly, believe me."

"That's good for you and your brother and sister, but you won't use the money on this land."

"Not their money—*mine*," she corrected him. "My share will be enough to pay off the loan."

He smiled quickly, there and gone, and removed his hands from hers. "Much obliged, but I won't have you paying off my debts. They are *my* debts, Elise."

She pushed herself up from the chair in a surge of annoyance. "Will you swallow your blasted pride just this once? I did! Why can't you do it for me, and for Adam and Penny?"

"It's not a matter of pride—"

"Oh, yes, it is," she cut in, rounding on him, her hands clenched into fists and her voice cracking with strain. "It's all about pride with you. Don't you think it would have done my pride a heap of good to throw the Wellbys' offer back in their smug faces?" She bent at the waist, glaring at him. He sat in the chair and refused to meet her gaze. "Oh, how I would have delighted in that! And I almost caved in. I almost did it, but Mr. Lancaster reminded me that I shouldn't think only of myself and my own pride. I have others in my life, and so do you!"

"Elise, I appreciate what you are trying to do, but I can't have you paying my debts." He stood up and went to the bucket for a dipper of water.

Elise wished she could give his tight, well-defined butt a swift kick. "I accepted this trade, Blade, so we could have a future together. Can't you spend a little of your pride on a better life for all of us?"

He braced his hands on the edge of the counter. "I thought they'd offer to take you all back to Baltimore."

"They didn't. Are you disappointed?"

He turned, scowling. "Of course not! I don't want you to go."

"Then you'll accept the money?"

"No."

"Then you'll lose us. You'll lose me." She extended her hands to him, but he didn't take them. "Don't do this, Blade. Don't throw away what we have just because you're a stubborn jackass." She nodded at his look of surprise. "Yes, you called me that once, but the ears and tail belong on you now. We could have a good life here, but it's all in your hands. The money means nothing to me unless it can be used to save us."

He closed his eyes. "I don't know if I could live with myself."

"Of course you could!"

"Your father was used to his wife handing over money, so this is natural to you, but it's not natural to me, Elise. What kind of man would I be to spend my wife's inheritance?"

"It's not an inheritance, and you leave my mother and father out of this!" She wrestled for control of her mounting temper. "You might not think much of my father, but he wouldn't have stood by and let his family be torn asunder if there was something he could do to stop it!"

Blade grabbed his hat off the peg and strode out the door.

"Where are you going?"

"Back to work."

Elise stamped a foot in frustration. "Yes, you go on to your fields of futility," she shouted at his back. "Get the place in order so it will be nice and pretty for Judge Mott when he takes it over!" She stamped her foot again as he continued to walk away, never glancing back at her, never giving any indication that he had heard her. She slammed the door and flung herself into the nearest chair. "Stubborn jackass," she said, banging her fists on the tabletop. "Stubborn, prideful jackass! He's going to ruin us!"

Chapter 25

The letter was a challenge. It had taken Elise most of the day to put the words on paper. Well, at least writing had given her something to do, so that she wasn't pacing the floor and going crazy while waiting for Blade to return.

Where was he? She'd positioned the kitchen chair to give herself an unobstructed view out the window. She looked out now, but no one approached the cabin.

Picking up one of the balls of paper—her first attempts at writing the letter she'd promised which would remove her grandparents from the Baltimore rumor mill—she tossed it angrily at the stove, which she hadn't bothered to light today.

Last night she had tried to talk to Blade again after supper, but he'd given her nothing but stony silence. He'd gathered up his bedding, announced that he needed to be alone to think and headed outside for that blasted tepee of his! He'd stayed in there all night. Oooo, how she hated that thing!

When she'd arisen that morning and come into the main room to light the stove and prepare breakfast, Blade, already dressed, had been heading out the door.

"Just where do you think you're going?" she'd demanded.

"Out." His face set in stern lines, he'd aimed a warning finger at her. "You all stay put and wait for me. Don't take the children to school today. Stay here, and no back talk. I'm not in the mood for an argument." He had rammed his hat on his head and glared at her with bloodshot eyes. She had glared back, her eyes more bloodshot than his. "I mean it, Elise. You stay here and wait for me."

"Where are you going?"

But she'd gotten no more out of him, and she'd known better than to trot after him and beg for tidbits. When he had that look in his eyes, there was no reaching him.

Stubborn jackass.

Ah, but she loved him. And she would do anything for him. Anything. He had made great sacrifices for them, so why couldn't he relinquish an ounce of his blasted pride?

Where was he? What had he done today? How dare he stalk off and fiddle with their futures while leaving them all in the dark!

She caught a glimpse of Penny and Adam, who were playing a game of chase with Gwenie in the grassy paddock. Janie munched on grass nearby, keeping a motherly eye on the antics. Bob was off someplace. He preferred the outer pastures and his own company until it was time to mate, of course, and then he was more than happy to prance around the paddock with Janie. Just like a male!

She signed the letter, blotted her signature and folded the heavy paper into thirds. All done. Her part of the bargain was complete, but her hopes for a happy resolution hinged on Blade and what he'd decided to do.

Her greatest worry loomed in her mind again. Had he gone to the judge's to surrender his land? Had the prideful fool given in to Judge Mott when he could just as easily have paid off the old devil and been done with him?

"Blade, please, please," she murmured, begging a man who couldn't hear her and wouldn't listen even if he were standing before her right now. He'd made up his mind during the night and had set off with a purpose this morning. But what purpose?

Moving out to the porch, Elise glanced up at the sky. It was late afternoon—around five, she guessed by the position of the sun. Where was he?

Staring at the road, she felt her senses flutter when she saw a puff of dust rise in the distance. A buggy? A wagon? Her muscles tensing, she stood on tiptoe and gripped the porch support while she waited for what seemed like hours instead of minutes. The dust ball grew, coming closer. Yes, yes! A buggy and a horse and a rider.

She left the porch's shade and went to the end of the road to wait for them. The rider was Blade, but who was in the buggy? Propping one hand at her waist and shading her eyes with the other, she stood sentinel and prayed that Blade had done the right thing—the sensible thing. The day's travails burdened her, planting an ache in her temples and an uneasiness in her stomach.

The expression on Blade's face didn't allay her discomfort. The buggy was driven by the livery owner's son, and Giles Lancaster sat in the backseat. Elise looked from the solicitor to Blade. Neither man seemed the least bit pleased with the day's events.

"You did it, didn't you?" Elise accused Blade as

he dismounted and gave Bob a whack on the backside to send him trotting to the barn.

"Elise, let's go into the house. You need to sit down when you hear—"

"You did it!" Fury and despair collided within her and she struck like a copperhead, landing her fists on Blade's chest. He caught her wrists, and she twisted and fought to get free. "Blast your stubborn pride, Blade Lonewolf! You sacrificed our future because you couldn't take money from a woman—a woman who happens to be your wife and who loves you, you pigheaded fool!"

"Stop this and listen to me," Blade said, shaking her. "What's gotten into you?"

Sobbing, she finally wrenched out of his hold and spun away. She covered her face with her hands and let the tears come. "I hate you for this, Blade. I swear I do."

"Mrs. Lonewolf." It was Giles Lancaster. "Won't you come inside? We have sad news to tell."

"Elise, please . . ." Blade laid a hand on her shoulder, and she jerked away from him again.

"It's too late to comfort me now, Blade," she told him, wiping her tears with the heels of her hands. "Because of you, it's too late for everything."

"Mrs. Lonewolf," Mr. Lancaster said, his voice soft and soothing, "we've just come from the Mott farm."

Elise closed her eyes, preparing herself for the final blow.

"Judge Mott has been murdered."

"Mur—" Elise turned wide eyes on Blade, her heart heaving in her chest, her ears ringing with alarm. "Blade, you didn't!"

He shook his head and caught her around the waist as her knees turned to jelly. "No, I didn't.

Now, will you please come inside the house and sit down? We must talk, and Mr. Lancaster and I need a drink."

Elise let him guide her into the cabin, Mr. Lancaster bringing up the rear. She noticed the darker circles under Blade's eyes and the tight set of his mouth. He looked as if he'd been to hell and back. Maybe he had.

Penny and Adam came running, but Blade gestured for them to stay outside.

"We have grown-up things to talk about now," he told Adam. "You and Penny do your chores. I'll call you for supper in a while."

"Yes, sir." Adam took Penny by the hand and pulled her away from the house.

Elise sat at the table, where she'd been sitting all day, it seemed. She'd thought that Blade had wanted a drink of water, so she was surprised when he accepted a flask from Mr. Lancaster and poured whiskey into a cup. He handed the flask back to Mr. Lancaster.

"I need this." The solicitor glanced at Elise. "Would you care for a jot, Mrs. Lonewolf?"

She shook her head, and he tipped the silver container to his lips and took a swallow.

Blade sat at the table and drank his measure of whiskey quickly, tossing the liquid to the back of his throat and downing it in two gulps.

"Ah." He wiped his mouth on his cuff, and his shoulders slumped with sudden weariness. "Much obliged, Mr. Lancaster. Please sit down."

"Thank you. Excuse me for a moment." The solicitor stepped to the open door. "Young man, you may water the horse and yourself! I have business here; then I will require you to take me back to town," he shouted out to the buggy driver before he joined Elise and Blade at the kitchen table. "It's been quite a day. Full of nuts and jolts."

Blade laughed shortly. "That's for sure."

"Who murdered the judge?" Elise asked as she massaged her throbbing temples.

"Harriet."

"His wife?" Elise stared at Blade in shock. He nodded. "Did she confess? Is she in jail?"

"She's dead, too," Blade said in a flat, colorless voice. "It looks as if she shot herself after she shot the judge."

"My God!" Elise stared blankly out the window, shock stripping her senses.

"Mr. Lonewolf came into town this morning to fetch me," Mr. Lancaster related. "He was going to the judge's to settle the loan business and to discuss Adam."

Shimmering tears stung Elise's eyes. "Blade, you . . ." She gripped his forearm with both hands. Chains fell away from her heart and it floated free in her chest. "I was so afraid you were going to throw all of this away."

He glanced at Mr. Lancaster, and Elise sensed that he was uncomfortable discussing their private affairs in front of the solicitor. She stared into his eyes, wishing they could be alone so that she could throw her arms around him and smother him with kisses. Oh, how she loved him in that shining moment!

A hint of a smile poked at one corner of his mouth, and he rested a hand on top of hers in a gesture of comfort and understanding. Drawing in a shaky breath, she forced her mind away from her devotion to him and tried to concentrate on the horror he'd recently witnessed.

"How long have they been dead?"

Mr. Lancaster finished his spot of whiskey. "What would you say, sir? Hours? No more than a day."

"Probably happened yesterday," Blade said. "The blood had dried."

"Yes, that's true." The solicitor removed a handkerchief from his breast pocket and dabbed at his forehead. "Awful business, it was. And no one was around. The place was deserted."

"Really? Where were his workers?" Elise asked. "Every time I've been there, the place has been crawling with field hands."

"They lit out, I guess," Blade said. "When they found out what had happened in the house, they all left. Guess they were scared they might get into trouble somehow."

"And now that the wicked king is dead, they're free," Elise said with a grim smile. "I think Judge Mott kept those people there mainly out of fear. He had something on all of them or had threatened them. Poor Harriet. She had obviously reached the end of her rope, but who knew she was so desperate?"

"I didn't," Blade murmured, "but maybe I should have."

"What do you mean?"

"Last time I saw her—when I went and got Adam—she begged me to take her with us." He shook his head slowly, sadly. "I told her I couldn't, that I was married and it wouldn't be seemly. I said she should go into town and someone there would help her."

"Good advice, I'd say," Mr. Lancaster interjected.

"Was it?" Blade bowed his head. "I don't know. Maybe I should have done more for her."

"Blade, she wasn't your responsibility," Elise reminded him. "And you're right; she could have found help in town. Dixie would have taken her in. You couldn't have foreseen what she would do—that she could murder."

"He must have pushed her too far," Blade said. "She must have snapped like a twig underfoot."

"She was badly beaten," the solicitor said. "Black-and-blue marks were all over her body."

"How horrible!" Elise shuddered.

"The farm will no doubt be put up for sale. I hope you get better neighbors this time," Mr. Lancaster said.

"Maybe we can buy the land," Elise suggested, but Blade shook his head.

"That's too much to farm. We have all we need here."

She smiled, thinking that she couldn't agree more.

"It was carnage," Blade said, running a hand down his face as if trying in vain to erase an image. "They were upstairs in their bedroom. The judge was on the floor in a pool of blood, a big hole in his chest. Harriet was on the bed. She'd put a gun in her mouth and pulled the trigger."

"Oh, God, no." Elise shut her eyes and willed away the horror. "Why didn't someone go into town and report it? If the house servants saw them . . . ?"

"They were frightened, I suppose," Mr. Lancaster said, then slanted a look at Blade. "Mrs. Mott appeared to be a much younger woman."

"Younger than the judge, you mean," Blade said. "Yes, she was, and he treated her like dirt under his feet. Same as he treated everyone."

"That man was a monster," Elise declared, and

the two men nodded in ready agreement. "I'm so glad you got Adam away from him. No telling what would have happened to him if you hadn't." She squeezed Blade's arm and smiled into his eyes. "I'll always be grateful to you for that, Blade Lonewolf."

"So I'm back in your good graces? You won't fly at me with your fists any time soon?" he teased.

"I promise," she vowed solemnly. "I'm not usually so crazy-acting, Mr. Lancaster." She stood and went to the water bucket for a drink. "But I've been cooped up here all day, thinking that Blade might be forfeiting this farm instead of saving it for us."

"Your worries were unfounded," Mr. Lancaster said. "The farm is his—free and clear, I assume."

"You assume?" Elise turned to face them again. "I want more than an assumption!"

"Sometimes, depending on the provisions of the contract, survivors can collect on outstanding loans," he explained. "But the judge is thought to have no survivors, and the document he drew up, and which Mr. Lonewolf signed, provides for no transfer of papers and such. Therefore, in my legal opinion, the debt died with Judge Mott."

Rolling that information around in her head for a few moments, Elise grasped his meaning. "So the farm is Blade's again? Free and clear? No more debt?"

"That is what I just said," the solicitor agreed.

"And what about the adoption?"

"Well, now, that is a bit hazier. However, since you are Adam's sister and can provide for him now that you are married to Mr. Lonewolf, and since his grandparents have surrendered all rights to him as guardians, I see no reason why you shouldn't automatically become his legal guardian, Mrs. Lone-wolf."

Elise tried to follow his circuitous answer and looked at Blade for direction.

"No one's the wiser, so he's ours now," Blade confirmed.

"Thank heavens!" She glanced upward in gratitude. "It's over."

"Yes. The sheriff is at the Mott farm now. Terrible business, but it does clear up some legal obstacles. I've deposited the money in a bank account for you in town, Mrs. Lonewolf. I hope that meets with your approval."

"The money." She blinked away the fog that floated in her brain. "The money! Oh, yes. That's fine ... uh ... I have the letter." She removed it from her apron pocket and handed it to the solicitor. "Go ahead and read it. If you want me to change anything, I will."

"That's very agreeable of you, I'm sure." He smiled and unfolded the letter. "Now, let's see here ..." After fishing his glasses from his vest pocket, he slipped them on. He read, his eyes moving from side to side, he smiled and then he laughed. "How delightful! You're quite talented, young lady. Quite talented."

Blade peered at the letter. "What's so funny?"

Mr. Lancaster raised his brows above his spectacles. "May I?"

Elise nodded.

"Your wife is clever, Mr. Lonewolf. Very clever, as this letter proves." He cleared his throat importantly before he began reading Elise's carefully chosen words. "It reads: 'Dear Mr. Editor-in-Chief, this letter is meant to correct some unfortunate misunderstandings concerning my current status and that of my brother, Adam, and sister, Penny.

" 'We left Baltimore and struck out for Cross-roads, Missouri, where we are living exciting and fruitful lives. I have married a gentleman farmer by the exotic name of Blade Lonewolf.' " Mr. Lancaster paused to glance at Blade, who was beginning to smile.

Elise looked at Blade through her lowered lashes and was pleased to see that he was taking this well. She hadn't been sure that he'd find her version of events amusing.

" 'My husband inherited his land from his family. He can trace a branch of his family back to the landing of the *Mayflower*.' "

Blade let out a chuckle. "The *Mayflower*!"

"I have no doubt that your ancestors were on the shore to greet the *Mayflower* passengers," Elise said with an impish grin. "No doubt whatsoever."

"To continue," Mr. Lancaster said, letter still in hand. " 'We live on sixty acres of choice farm property near a small town called Crossroads. I live in a cozy house with my husband, my sister and my brother. We are a happy family, delighted with the open air, the beautiful countryside, our collection of animals, our wonderful friends and the many blessings that have been bestowed on us.' "

Mr. Lancaster paused, looking at Blade for a speaking moment before he went on. " 'I am blissfully happy to be married to a man of courage, honor and intelligence. I have made a match for myself here that would have been impossible in Baltimore, and for that I shall be eternally grateful. Missouri is the exquisite place where my lonely warrior prince awaited me. We have made this our kingdom on earth, and wish everyone could know the happiness we have found. Please sign me proudly and passionately, Mrs. Blade Lonewolf, formerly Miss Elise St. John.'" Mr. Lancaster folded the letter with a smile of satisfaction. "Quite well put, Mrs. Lonewolf. I shall deliver this in person to the editor of the newspaper."

Elise shared a long look with Blade. He smiled and his eyes shone with what she prayed was love.

The sound of thundering hooves broke the moment of sweet understanding. Blade pushed aside the fluttering curtain to peer outside.

"It's Airy and Dixie. Bet they heard about the judge."

"I bet everyone in town has heard by now," Elise predicted, rising to greet her unexpected guests, even though she desperately longed to be alone with her husband.

Airy strode in with Dixie on her heels. The women's faces said it all. They were both flushed and breathless, their eyes wide with excitement. Airy lifted a jug of her home brew high over her head.

"Get out your best glasses and let's pop this here cork," she stated with a grin. "The devil done collected Judge Mott and we got celebratin' to do!"

Hours later, Mr. Lancaster drank the last drops of the home brew.

Elise had insisted that everyone stay for supper. She and Airy had fired up the stove and thrown together a feast of fried chicken and all the fixings. They'd even invited the buggy driver inside to share the meal.

After supper, Elise had allowed Penny and Adam to stay up a while before insisting that they go to bed. Adam couldn't hide his relief when he'd learned of the judge's demise. Even Penny had let out a squeal of happiness, understanding that her brother would never have to go back to the judge's again. Elise had kissed them good night and joined the others, who had moved the celebration onto the porch, where a cool breeze blew in from the north.

Blade reached for her hand and pulled her down to sit beside him on the top porch step. She leaned against him and he draped his arm across the front of her, his fingers curving around her shoulder in an embrace that was nothing if not possessive.

She sensed the tension in him, which mirrored her own. Now that dinner was over and the brew had been finished off, she yearned to be behind closed doors with her husband. She had so much to tell him, so much to confess to him. She wanted him to understand how much he meant to her, how much she loved him. She shifted her hips against his fly. The hardness there was unmistakable. He wanted her, too. He tightened his embrace and she felt a sheen of perspiration form on his arms. Turning her head, she pressed her ear against his chest. His heart boomed rapidly. Oh, yes, he wanted her!

"I suppose I should be getting back to the hotel," Mr. Lancaster admitted. He covered a yawn with his hand. "I beg your pardon for staying so long, Mrs. Lonewolf."

Elise grabbed at the chance Mr. Lancaster offered. "We're glad to have you, but it is getting awfully late."

"The hotel?" Dixie Shoemaker said. She sat in the rocker Blade had brought out to the porch, and Airy and Mr. Lancaster sat in kitchen chairs. "Why are you staying there when I've got a vacant room at my boardinghouse? Don't you like home-cooked meals and soft feather beds and good company, Giles Lancaster?"

"I didn't know about your boardinghouse, Mrs. Shoemaker, but it sounds charming."

"Then you can just move yourself over to that empty room I've got," Dixie announced. "No use in you staying at the stuffy old hotel when you can rest easy in my establishment."

"That's kind of you, I'm sure," Mr. Lancaster said with obvious pleasure.

Elise suspected that he had drunk enough of the moonshine to agree to almost anything.

"Dixie, I was thinking," Airy pronounced. "We should pool what money we've got saved, sell that boardinghouse and buy back your house."

"What house?" Dixie asked.

"The old family place, of course," Airy explained, pointing in the direction of Judge Mott's farm. "It belongs in our family. That old goat bought it when our backs were turned."

"Yes, but Airy, running a farm is hard work. I'm not sure I want to pick cotton anymore."

Airy considered this response with a frown, then grinned. "Reckon you're right. We're too old to bust soil and pick weevils off cotton bolls. I was forgetting that we're not spring lambs anymore."

"Someone young will buy it," Dixie said. "I got all I can do to keep the boardinghouse going."

"Yeah, and I got my still to operate." Airy gave a sly wink. "That there is a sight more profitable than growing cotton!"

They all shared a laugh from the truth of that.

"Young, strong bodies are needed to farm," Dixie said. "If Judge Mott had relied on his own muscle, he would have grown dead sticks and stones."

"But this seems to be a good, clean life," Mr.

Lancaster noted. "It appears to be a plentiful, satisfying existence."

"Oh, it is," Elise agreed quickly. "I've found such peace here . . . and much more." She smiled when Blade's arm tightened around her. His breath warmed the side of her face as he bent closer to whisper right against her ear.

"If I don't have you soon, I'm going to bust."

She felt a tide of warmth infuse her cheeks and neck. A smile of satisfaction and pleasure curved her lips.

"I must say that this area is far prettier than I'd imagined it would be," Mr. Lancaster confessed. "I noticed that there is only one attorney in Crossroads."

"Yeah, and we could use another one," Airy said with a wink. "We need one with a funny accent. That's what we need."

Laughter floated across the porch. Blade's deep chuckle rumbled against Elise's back and she cuddled closer, pressing the base of her spine in the vee of his legs. She felt him stir and his heart kick in his chest. He blew hot breath on her nape. Elise shivered and closed her eyes as a weak, spiraling sensation erupted in her stomach.

Airy stood and stretched her arms above her head. "I should be taking this old body home, and that buggy driver probably would like to see *his* home before morning."

"True, true." Giles Lancaster sprang to his feet and straightened his vest and suit coat. "Driver, you've been inordinately kind and considerate. I shall pay you handsomely for it, too. I must be off. Mrs. Shoemaker, we shall follow you into town and I will transfer my belongings to your establishment."

"Good. That gladdens my heart." Dixie pushed herself up from the rocker and accepted Mr. Lancaster's helping hand to descend the porch steps. " 'Night, everyone! It was an evening to remember!"

Blade and Elise stood on the porch and waved good-bye to their guests. As the buggies rumbled down the road, Blade slipped an arm around Elise's waist. They watched until the night swallowed the vehicles; then Elise went inside while Blade carried in the rocker and chairs.

When he closed the door on the rest of the world, Elise was content to share a long, unguarded look with him. But that moment passed, and in the next she was in his arms. He molded his mouth to hers. She unbuttoned his shirt and sent her fingers sliding over his bare chest.

"Oh, Blade, I want you so much!"

"I know, I know," he almost panted, his fingers working feverishly with the buttons at the back of her dress. At last he freed the final one and pushed the material off her shoulders. He kissed her skin above the chemise, then slipped a hand beneath to fondle her breast.

Her knees turned to liquid, but he saved her from falling to a heap on the floor by catching her in his arms and striding to their bedroom. He closed the door behind them, but kept her cradled in his arms. His eyes bored into hers.

"You thought I had given up on us, didn't you?" he asked.

She shook her head. "Not so much on us as on this." She looked around at the bed, the room, their home. "I've been in a stew all day." Combing back his hair with her fingers, she kissed his wide forehead.

"I admit that accepting your money went against my grain." He laid her on the bed and slowly peeled off his shirt. His chest and arms bulged with muscle and sent longing curling through her again. "You're right. I'm a stubborn cuss, but I didn't want to lose you, Elise, so I decided to put aside my pride for you."

She smiled and trailed a fingertip down the center of his chest to his navel. "Then you were ready to do what my father did for my mother."

His head jerked up in surprise. He narrowed his eyes, not liking the comparison she'd made. "I wasn't going to let you make a living for me."

"No, but you were willing to compromise, to do something that you've just admitted rubbed you the wrong way." She unfastened his trousers and tugged on his waistband, trying to pull him into bed. He resisted.

"That's true, but your father—"

"My father was used to working for a living. He was a cobbler, a tradesman, and he fell in love with a woman who was used to a life he could never provide for her. But he loved her . . . loved her so much that he agreed to quit his job and live off the allowance her parents gave her." She raised herself up on one elbow, thrusting her face closer to his. "My father didn't like the arrangement, but he didn't want my mother to be without the things she'd become accustomed to, so he swallowed his pride. All for love."

Blade smoothed her hair, his gaze following the path of his hand. "But you became accustomed to that life, and you will never find it with me. No servants. No big house."

"Those things aren't important to me, Blade. This farm is what I want more than anything, because this farm is your home, your inheritance, your roots."

"Were your parents happy?"

"Yes. They loved each other, which made everything else bearable."

He smiled, then captured her hand and lifted it to his lips to kiss each knuckle. She shivered, watching his lips caress her fingers.

"I liked your letter."

She swallowed hard, desire clogging her throat. "Did you? It was all true."

"Remind me not to make you as mad again as you were today. You pack a punch, little lady." He grinned; then his brows shot up. "Oh, I bought something for you today. Used what little money I'd managed to save." He plunged a hand into his pant pocket.

"You didn't have to buy—" The words melted away as Elise stared at the gold band he held before her eyes.

Without another word, he slipped the wedding ring onto her finger, then kissed it.

"I figured it was time," he murmured.

Smiling through tears of joy, Elise knew she had never seen such a beautiful ring in her life. It was simple, gold, with no adornment, but it was hers, given to her by Blade, and it was priceless. She kissed him, her lips trembling.

"Blade, I'm going to make you happy. I'm going to make you a good wife."

His arms created a safe harbor around her. "You already are a good wife to me, Elise. My beautiful, spirited wife. My destiny. My woman."

Elise ran her fingertips over his high cheekbones, his lips, the fading bruises on his face. "You're my heart's secret wish, Blade."

"Secret?" One of his brows jumped up.

"Yes. Secret, because I didn't even know you were what my heart wanted until I saw you at the train station. I couldn't take my eyes off you!" She laughed and rested her forehead against his chin, remembering how he'd looked to her then and how she'd responded. "That was a terrible day, but I couldn't stop admiring you. So tall. So handsome. So different from everyone else. You were a peacock in a flock of prairie chickens."

He laughed and pulled her even closer to him. "I like that description. I remember you wore that red dress and that saucy little hat. To me you were a lady from a manor, fit for a king. I could tell that you were sad, but you were also full of fire and life."

"When our eyes met, I knew," she whispered, lost in the memories.

"Knew what?"

She lifted her gaze to his. "That I hadn't come to Crossroads just for Penny and Adam. I'd come for you, too, Blade. I'd come for you."

His mouth swooped to hers and a sound of joy escaped him. Joining her on the bed, he plucked pins from her hair, tossing them this way and that until her hair shimmered around her shoulders and pooled in his hands. "Sometimes I can hardly believe it," he whispered.

"I know," she said, understanding how being together sometimes seemed like a dream. She pushed his trousers down his hips. He kicked them the rest of the way off, then kissed her with devoted intensity.

"Elise, I love you with all that is holy and good inside me."

His words snapped her to trembling attention.

"Say that again, Blade! Oh, I've waited so long to hear you say that you love me!"

"Of course I love you." He slanted his mouth over hers first one way, then the other, until her lips throbbed and her lungs cried for air. He broke the kiss to remove her clothing, his hands gentle, arousing. "I love you, Elise Lonewolf, and I always will."

"Why didn't you tell me before?" she asked, pressing her breasts against the solid wall of his chest. It felt wonderful to be skin to skin with him again. One night away from him seemed like a thousand.

"I didn't want you to stay with me if you could have a better life somewhere else," he admitted. "And I thought that if I told you how much I loved you, you'd feel beholden to remain with me."

"Beholden?" she repeated in dismay. "Blessed, you mean. Any woman would be blessed to be loved by you."

He cupped her breasts and kissed her throat.

"Blade, do you know what I want on my gravestone?"

Frowning, he shook his head. "Don't talk of such things!"

"No, no. I want you to listen." She held his face between her hands and made him look at her. "When I die, years and years and years from now when I'm a very old woman, I want *my* gravestone to read, 'She loved Blade Lonewolf.' "

His eyes glimmered with emotion and she knew he'd made the connection with what was on Julia's headstone. "That's all?"

"That's enough."

"You want no children by me?"

"Of course, if it's God's will. But if not?" She

shrugged and kissed his full lips. "I have you and that's everything to me."

"Elise ... Elise. ..." He smiled, then pressed sweet, light kisses across her forehead, down the bridge of her nose. When he kissed her mouth, he became more insistent, drawing a response from her. She slipped her tongue between his lips and rubbed her tender breasts against his chest.

"I am so heavy and hard with need for you that I am miserable," he confessed.

She smiled, moving a hand down to feel for herself. "My, my! Well, what are you waiting for, Blade Lonewolf? We have love to make ..." She leaned upward to lightly nip his earlobe and to whisper, "And black-haired, brown-eyed babies to make!"

His grin broke on his face like a sunrise, bright and life-affirming. Wasting no time, he enfolded her in his embrace and warmed her with his love.

Avon Romantic Treasures

Unforgettable, enthralling love stories,
sparkling with passion and adventure
from Romance's bestselling authors

Avon Romances—
the best in exceptional authors and unforgettable novels!

Avon Regency Romance

SWEET FANCY
by Sally Martin   77398-8/$3.99 US/$4.99 Can

LUCKY IN LOVE
by Rebecca Robbins   77485-2/$3.99 US/$4.99 Can

A SCANDALOUS COURTSHIP
by Barbara Reeves   72151-1/$3.99 US/$4.99 Can

THE DUTIFUL DUKE
by Joan Overfield   77400-3/$3.99 US/$4.99 Can

TOURNAMENT OF HEARTS
by Cathleen Clare   77432-1/$3.99 US/$4.99 Can

DEIRDRE AND DON JUAN
by Jo Beverley   77281-7/$3.99 US/$4.99 Can

THE UNMATCHABLE MISS MIRABELLA
by Gillian Grey#   77399-6/$3.99 US/$4.99 Can

FAIR SCHEMER
by Sally Martin   77397-X/$3.99 US/$4.99 Can

THE MUCH MALIGNED LORD
by Barbara Reeves   77332-5/$3.99 US/$4.99 Can

THE MISCHIEVOUS MAID
by Rebecca Robbins   77336-8/$3.99 US/$4.99Can

If you enjoyed this book, take advantage of this special offer. Subscribe now and get a

FREE
Historical Romance

No Obligation (a $4.50 value)

Each month the editors of True Value select the four *very best* novels from America's leading publishers of romantic fiction. Preview them in your home *Free* for 10 days. With the first four books you receive, we'll send you a FREE book as our introductory gift. No Obligation!

If for any reason you decide not to keep them, just return them and owe nothing. If you like them as much as we think you will, you'll pay just $4.00 each and save at *least* $.50 each off the cover price. (Your savings are *guaranteed* to be at least $2.00 each month.) There is NO postage and handling – or other hidden charges. There are no minimum number of books to buy and you may cancel at any time.

Send in the Coupon Below

To get your FREE historical romance fill out the coupon below and mail it today. As soon as we receive it we'll send you your FREE Book along with your first month's selections.
